Front cover design by Simon Avery and Gillian Healey
Typesetting by Caroline Goldsmith

ISBN: 978-1-7395780-2-2

Also available as an eBook
ISBN: 978-1-7395780-3-9

ME TOO

Katharine Light

Praise for *Me Too*

'A rich tapestry of flawed characters rediscovering romance… A thoughtful and moving exploration of mature love.'
Julia Boggio, author of *Shooters*

'With a subtly satisfying ending, *Me Too* is deep, compelling and moving. We should look forward to more light from Katharine.'
Flora Dunn, author of *Summer At Tillingford Hall*

'…another brilliantly complex, multi-layered narrative which deals with mid-life relationships, stepfamilies, Me Too trauma, and desire, in a very readable and interesting way…

'…cleverly weaves the Jess and Sam story into this new one about Anna and Rob in ways I found compelling…'

'I am so adoring this series—readable, relatable, realistic! I blazed through *Me Too* and neglected all other duties. Cannot wait for book three!'

'It is wonderful. I was desperate, to the last page, for more…'

Readers who loved *Like Me*

'Life-affirming and witty, page-turning and poignant, *Like Me* celebrates the friends that walk with us along the rocky path from first love to second chances. Reading *Like Me* felt like a homecoming—a chance to hang out with old friends. Scenes from this novel have taken on the status of memories, as if I really knew these characters and was part of their lives. It was refreshing to read a novel so warm and humane.'

Emma Claire Sweeney, author of *Owl Song At Dawn*

'A heart-warming exploration of love across the decades. Katharine skillfully unravels her characters' past to help them forge meaningful relationships in the present.'

Rebekah Lattin-Rawstrone, author of *Home*

'I got completely involved in the story and the characters and found myself rooting for Jess and Sam...'

'...loved the relationship between Jess and Sam from the start...'

'I thoroughly enjoyed reading *Like Me*... I measured out my reading stints because I didn't want to finish it. It's great that it's the first of a series!'

For my sister Emma Light, the first reader of my stories,
and my brother Benedict Light.
Thank you for all the laughter, encouragement and enthusiasm.

The old school friends

Jess, 39 – full-time single mother of **Ben**, 7, and **Millie**, 5; ex-wife of **Tom**; lives in south London

Anna, 39 – women's fashion designer, long-term boyfriend **Jon**, 46; lives near Bath

Caroline, 39 – post-graduate student, married to **Philip**, 38, parents of two girls; living in Millingham, Manchester

Ruth, 39 – financier, married to **Andy**, 39, parents of small son; living in west London

Stella, 38 – jewellery designer, married to Doug, 40, three small children, living in north London

Sam, 39 – GP, single dad of **Kate**, 12, **Emma**, 10, **Josh**, 8; ex-husband of **Elizabeth**; living in Millingham, Manchester

Rob, 40 – successful broadsheet journalist; lives in London

James, 40 – former financier, newly elected Member of Parliament; married to **Fiona**, political PR executive; dividing time between London and constituency of Witney, Oxfordshire

Sebastian, 38 – media entrepreneur, married to **Tami**, 30; parents of newborn baby **Ava**

ANNA

On the pavement, about four doors away from Jess's house, Anna Makowski hesitated. It was that peculiar time between Christmas and New Year, when normal people sat around watching television, pretending to do jigsaws and eating too many chocolates. But it was stupid to be this close to one of her oldest friends, and not try the doorbell and say hello. *If* she was there.

Jess had spent Christmas in Brussels with her brother and family. Her small children—Ben, and Millie who was Anna's goddaughter—were with Tom, her ex-husband. Wasn't that what she'd said?

Anna shivered, although it wasn't really cold. A dank, dreary grey light tinged the south London street of terraced houses. Several houses squatted in the gloom, no lights on in the front rooms, and as she scanned, she could see that Jess's was shrouded in shadow.

Oh well. This was one way of filling the time, turning her attention from her endless emails and 'to do' lists. She'd ring the doorbell, retrace her steps to the tube and go back to her boyfriend Jon's flat in Kensington. Unsurprisingly he was working, although they'd arranged to meet for an early drink and a trip to the cinema later on.

The thought that they made such plans to fill the growing silence between them was not new. But that was almost incidental, compared to the vast unspoken lump of disappointment that filled her consciousness. The sense that this was not how her life was meant to be. At the age of thirty-nine, she had not expected to feel quite so alone, so trapped on the wrong path.

Weren't people meant to learn wisdom, to find a purpose, a direction, as they travelled through life? Her convictions about starting her women's clothing company had been so strong and for at least a dozen years she'd had that unsinkable drive.

Doing a Fine Art degree at the Slade, in London, she'd worked her way through painting—acrylics, gouache, oils—until she rediscovered pencil drawing. So freeing, so forgiving, so quick, so flexible. From there, via a brief passion for sculpture, she landed on shaping fabric, on moulding the structure of a garment, sculptural in its own way, in her quest for the perfect pair of black trousers, the superlative white shirt, the indispensable jacket. Her first collection contained very few pieces, each beautifully crafted, all deliberately made with a larger, curvier figure in mind. This was the era of the size 00 model, but Anna went the opposite way, hit a sweet spot with her quality, attention to detail, two luckily well-placed articles and one key influencer (long before they were called that). The collection sold out rapidly.

Anna now had a loyal clientele who'd continued to support her through the years. Sometimes she considered introducing brighter colours, more patterns, into her work, but mostly she stuck with what sold. Classics, in a limited and almost monochrome palette.

It had been so absorbingly creative and fulfilling, for more than a decade.

Until it was felled by the overarching need that had overtaken her conscious mind at the age of thirty-five. Nothing would quell it.

And nothing would make Jon acknowledge how all-encompassing it had become in Anna's mind. Somehow his promise to move out of London and into her lovely house in Purseton, a village outside Bath, was never mentioned. His work, and increasingly his life, remained in London. She was here for Christmas because that was what he had proposed. Nothing else.

She rubbed the back of the large diamond ring she wore on her left hand with her thumb.

Something had to give.

JESS

The doorbell rang far earlier than Jess expected, while she was still slumped on the sofa in the gloom, her bags dumped against the radiator.

She jumped up, shrugging off her coat, mopping her face with the back of her sleeve and trying to smooth away the mascara rivulets under her eyes. Endeavouring not to catch her pale reflection in the mirror over the mantlepiece.

Pulling open the front door, a smile pasted onto her face, she found not the children and her ex-husband Tom. Instead her old school friend Anna stood there, in a cream coat, a buttery cashmere scarf round her neck.

'Anna! How lovely!' She held her close in a quick hug, registering Anna's familiar scent, with its hints of jasmine and spice.

'Is everything OK? Sorry to pitch up unannounced,' said Anna.

'No, no, everything's fine. I thought it was a bit early for the children. Come in. Cup of tea? Or something else? What are you doing in this part of South London?' She took her coat, ushering Anna down the hall to the open plan kitchen at the back of the house.

'Tea would be lovely. What time do you expect them? How was Brussels?'

Jess glanced at her watch. 'Not for a couple of hours.' She flicked the kettle on, found a couple of mugs, sniffed the remains of the milk in the fridge.

'Did Patrick's wife have the baby?' said Anna.

Something about her tone of voice made Jess turn round. 'She did. A little boy. Santiago. How did you remember that?'

'You told me. All well?'

'Yes, all fine.' Jess turned her back to pour hot water over teabags. 'But I didn't go to Brussels.'

'No?'

'No. I…er… I was in Oxford.' She fiddled with the simple gold cross she wore. 'With Sam.'

'Sam Rushmore?'

'Yep.' She pulled her increasingly bobbly navy cardigan around her. Anna looked so sleek and chic in comparison. 'You didn't say why you're in the neighbourhood.'

'Why Oxford?'

Jess knew Anna would persist until she got an answer. In the old days—in their teens—she'd relished being pressed for information, but her delicate flame of a relationship with Sam was still too private to be scrutinised. She put a white bone china mug in front of Anna, grateful that, because she and the children had been away, the surface of the island unit in the middle of the kitchen was free of piles of stuff. The clutter was not quite as pervasive as usual. 'Sam was at his brother's house.'

'And his children?'

She gestured to the two stools on the other side of the island. 'Sit down. With his ex-wife.'

'And your two with Tom?' Anna sat down, unwound her scarf and folded it carefully on her lap.

Jess shrugged.

Anna eyed her over the rim of the mug. 'So, you've finally…after twenty years…'

Jess swallowed.

It had been a magical four days. After rashly abandoning her mother and stepfather at the Eurostar terminal at King's Cross St Pancras, she'd taken Sam up on his persistent offer to come to Oxford.

Her lost love. The never quite consummated passion of her teens, which had unexpectedly been reignited the previous summer, when she returned to Millingham, South Manchester, for a twenty year school reunion. It had indeed been consummated in Sam's brother Will's house in Oxford. She touched her fingers to her lips. She could still feel his hands, his weight on her, the exquisite sensations of skin on skin, his kisses, his taste, his—

'That good, then?' Anna grinned. 'Nothing wrong with sex.'

'Sorry.' Jess looked around the room. 'Mince pie? I've got some homemade brandy butter in my bag.'

'Jess.'

'Don't be nice. I'm on the edge.' Jess blinked rapidly. 'We need food.'

'It's OK. Really,' said Anna.

Was that true? Nothing wrong with sex? It was a question freighted with so much: guilt, pleasure, uncertainty, intense relief, doubt. Not about Sam and his sincerity. Of that she was certain. Did she need to re-think her stance on sex being a key aspect of marriage, a literal making of love? Were they making love, creating it between the two of them? Was that enough? How did that sit with her Christian belief, her relationship with God? Was a committed relationship—even one conducted at a two-hundred mile distance—good enough to assuage her conscience concerning sex outside marriage? Aware Anna was regarding her closely, she bolted back to the front room, scrabbled in her bag, grabbed a tupperware and returned peeling off the lid. 'You sure?'

Anna set down her mug. 'Go on then.'

'You didn't tell me why you're here.' On closer observation, although Anna looked as beautifully turned out as ever—a sharp taupe manicure, her blonde curls smooth and shiny, her cashmere sweater immaculate—her make-up looked heavier than usual. What was she disguising with the rose pink blusher, the white eye-liner along the lower lashes of her eyes?

'Came to see a new supplier. Beautiful leather bags.'

'That sounds good.' Jess busied herself with locating the biscuit tin of pies, plates, forks, a spoon for the brandy butter.

'Are you here for New Year?' said Anna.

'That's the big question. Here. Or Millingham.' The market town where they'd grown up was now a suburb of south Manchester, where Sam, a divorced GP, lived in his old family home.

'With Sam…'

'With *all* the children.'

Anna blinked; shook her head slightly. 'Ah.'

'What about you? Are you and Jon doing something fun?'

'We talked about going away. Paris or something. But neither of us got round to organising anything.'

Jess met her look. 'Everything OK?'

Anna frowned. 'I can't fault him. He's scrupulously considerate. But there's a part of me that thinks he'd rather be anywhere else—'

'Surely not. You have a history together. And a stonking ring.' Jess pointed to Anna's brilliant cut diamond ring.

When their little posse of friends from school—which

included Caroline, Ruth and Stella—had each got engaged, and then married, they'd all remarked on the beauty of Anna's ring, in comparison to their own. Although hers had yet to lead to a wedding. Anna lived in her beautiful house outside Bath, close to her design studio, but Jon remained in London. Their lack of children, too, was a subject that was never broached. Jess didn't know if it had been helpful or hurtful to ask Anna to be Millie's godmother.

Even with such a long friendship, there were still subjects that were taboo. She remembered the few days Anna had spent with her and the children in Devon the previous summer. A vivid picture of Anna nursing Millie's red gingham sunhat sprang to mind. Did they not talk about this because they'd been friends for so long? Was there a point when revealing hurt-filled intimacies became too difficult, stifled under the layers of a friendship that spanned almost thirty years?

When Jess's ex-husband Tom had left, there were times when she wished she'd never met him, but they were soon absorbed by the fierce maternal love she felt for her children. Had she been in Anna's position at this stage in life, without any children, how would she really feel? Did she even try to imagine? Perhaps she was projecting purely what she imagined she would feel, if the situation were reversed…

Anna took a sip of tea. 'I don't know. 2009 in four days' time. The year of turning forty. Who'd have thought?'

'It's shocking. Since having the—' She changed tack. 'Time has been accelerating the last few years.'

'Sometimes it's interminable. But you're right. At other times, whole years seem to have disappeared. What are you going to do about Sam?'

'He lives two hundred miles away.'

'That's just an excuse.'

'Maybe.' Was it?

'You don't want to pass up all that great sex.' Anna's smile didn't quite reach her eyes.

Jess spluttered over her hot mouthful of tea. '*What?*'

'It's the look on your face. You look considerably less tense than when I saw you in Devon.'

'Rubbish. I was perfectly relaxed. It was the summer holidays.'

'Rubbish. The sexual tension vibrated off you.'

Jess frowned. 'It did not.'

'Well, you look different now. What will you do about Tom?'

'What do you mean?'

'When you move to Millingham to be with Sam…'

Once Anna had left, Jess slumped back in her front room in the gathering gloom, knowing she should have taken the opportunity to shop for some food, but too tired to move. As a Christian, she believed that sex was for marriage. For her, at least. But there were always people about whom it was impossible to be sensible.

For her, it was Sam. It had always been Sam.

Now that she was away from him, she was striving, somewhat unsuccessfully, to keep the guilt at bay. Actually, it wasn't even the guilt that tipped the balance. She'd lived with it in her mind for the best part of six months. To have finally made love with Sam gave her more of a sense of relief than remorse. But she couldn't get over how shattered she felt, despite four child-free days.

Finally Tom's car pulled up.

The children leapt up the path, shouting about their presents, seven year-old Ben allowing himself to be hugged briefly before darting up to his room, while Millie, aged five, insisted on being carried by Jess.

'Everything all right?' she said, as Tom dumped the children's bags in the hall.

'Fine.' Tight-lipped, he surveyed her. 'You look… different.'

'When do you want to talk?' Jess knew there were things to say, however much she wanted to ignore Tom altogether. He was the father of their children, she should keep him informed. Although if she was going to tell him about her relationship status, she would have to work out what that was.

'I'll be in touch when I get back. After New Year.'

'Going somewhere nice?'

'None of your effing business.'

Jess swallowed and held on tight to Millie. 'How can I get in touch—?'

'Mobile.' He kissed Millie and was gone.

SAM

Sam was exhausted, after the busy drive back to Millingham from Oxford, and his immediate resumption of his role as father and host. His brother Will and family, who'd been holding the fort in his absence, were staying for another couple of nights. Sam's children—Kate age twelve, Emma ten, Josh seven—reappeared three hours after his return. He was of course delighted to see them, but unimpressed by how crotchety they were from their delayed flight home from Spain. They'd spent Christmas with their mother Elizabeth, at her partner Nigel's apartment in a golfing resort.

Typical of her to shove them into a taxi from the airport. He hadn't actually had more than two minutes' conversation with his ex-wife in as many months. The more information he prised from the children—well, from Emma, really, the other two were absolutely monosyllabic—the more he recognised Elizabeth's holiday mode, her head in a book, ignoring everyone around her with impressive concentration. His pangs of guilt as he listened to his middle child were subsumed quickly under visceral flashbacks to being in bed with Jess and the intense pleasure they had wreaked upon each other.

Diana, Sam's sister-in-law, had helpfully started supper, so they all ate before the children and their cousins dispersed to various screens throughout the house.

Only after cups of tea and Christmas cake did Sam check his phone. He and Jess had exchanged texts telling each other they'd arrived home, and he was very much hoping she'd drive to Millingham for New Year. But when he looked at the screen, the two missed calls and several texts were from his friend Rob. Rob Randall. Another old friend from school, in Millingham to visit his parents. A high-profile broadsheet journalist, his dark, glossy good looks continued to attract a certain degree of tabloid interest, well after the stormy end of his marriage to an American model.

Leaving Will and Diana in peace in the kitchen with the papers, he climbed the stairs to his study and dialled Rob's number.

'I can't believe you went away for Christmas, Sam.' Rob answered on the second ring. 'I was counting on you.'

'Happy Christmas to you too,' said Sam. 'I did warn you I was going to Oxford.'

'Which I don't get. If Will and crowd are here. What's that about?'

'They came to see Mum.'

'And?'

Sam contemplated ducking the question. But Rob, whose working incarnations had at times encompassed tenacious investigative reporter, would keep going. He'd end up telling him sooner or later. 'Jess met me in Oxford.'

'I thought you said she couldn't come.'

'She changed her mind.' Sam couldn't stop grinning. Thank God no one could see him. He hadn't felt like this in years.

Rob laughed. 'That good? I take it the performance prob—'

'Is no longer a problem.'

'Congratulations. I hope you'll be very happy.'

'Er. Thanks. What was so urgent?'

'Just looking for some light relief. Sometimes…'

'Yes?'

'Sometimes I can't remember what I have in common with my parents.'

This was a familiar theme in their conversations over the years. 'The cuckoo in the nest?'

'Yeah. Something like that.'

Sam leant back in his desk chair. 'How's your sister and family?'

'Sweltering in the heat. Mum and Dad are planning a trip to Sydney and the east coast, in the middle of next year.'

'What about you? Any yearnings to go to Australia?'

'Dunno. I ring Natalie for a chat now and then.'

'That's nice of you.'

'She's still my sister,' said Rob.

'Proves my point,' said Sam.

'What? Which point?'

'That you're a decent son. Beneath the act.'

'What act?'

'The playboy image.'

Rob laughed, although to Sam's ears, it didn't sound as natural as usual. 'Which sometimes works. Not everyone I interact with has known me since I was eleven.'

'So, where is the playboy spending New Year? I take it you're off, having done Christmas?'

'Uh. Well. There's a party in the Alps. Chamonix? Or something near Cannes?'

'See? I rest my case.'

'What about you?'

'Jess and the children are coming here. Hopefully.'

'With your lot? With Kate? You have my sympathies.

You won't get much sex while everyone is in the house together.'

'It's not just about sex,' said Sam. It really wasn't. But the relief of those blissful nights with Jess was still seeping through him. He was sure she'd come to Millingham. They'd trial all seven of them in the house.

'Sam? Reliving it all, are you?'

'You know you're welcome here anytime, if you decide to stay…'

'Thanks. See you next time?'

'Sure. Happy 2009.'

ROB

'Rob? Your mother's waiting to start the film.' His father Colin bellowed down the hall. The modern townhouse was not vast and the only reason to yell like that was surely because he couldn't hear properly. God forbid anyone—particularly Rob's mother Sue—suggesting he might have his hearing tested though.

'Two minutes, Dad.' Rob stubbed out his cigarette in the designated flowerpot outside the back door, waved the door about to dispel any lurking fumes, shut and locked it.

He picked up his glass of red wine from the counter and refilled it from the bottle of Claret he'd brought with him. His parents maintained they didn't really drink, and Rob knew to bring wine with him, if he wished to drink anything decent.

His father had been refilling his tumbler of whisky rather regularly the last couple of evenings. His mother tended to flit from seasonal tipples such as ginger wine and advocaat to 'a tiny glass of fizz, just this once' which Rob had ensured was crisp, dry Cava rather than sweet Asti Spumante. His parents' rather joyless experience of wine spilled over into many other aspects of their lives. Christmas in Millingham was never filled with abundant generosity. His mother's catering was rather precise, and he had almost caused an international incident when he'd wanted a third helping of roast potatoes to complement the turkey.

From them he'd learnt the value of being careful with

money. Despite all indications to the contrary, he'd set up pensions and health insurance as soon as he had a steady income. He'd almost paid off the mortgage on his flat in London.

He looked round his parents' practical kitchen. He rarely noticed that this was a house filled with very little beauty. Even the vase of flowers he had bought for his mother looked plonked rather than arranged, somehow. Not that this sort of thing ever bothered him. His flat was purely functional and he never thought of buying so much as a cushion to spruce it up. So why were these thoughts even occurring to him? He so rarely thought about another life. Was so appreciative of all the cautious guidance and support he'd received from his parents. They believed in justice and fairness and doing the right thing. Of course they loved both their children equally, and for that he was extremely grateful.

It was not a demonstrative sort of love, that was true. Sometimes it seemed more duty than delight. But he was well aware that his life could have been very different.

Maybe it was because it was Christmas, that it had seemed a rather dismal little gathering this year. Just the three of them, and The Queen on the TV. There should have been children there. Not that Natalie and her husband Scott, a solid Australian builder, and their two boisterous boys had ever contemplated Christmas in Manchester. Why would they, when they could spend it barbecuing and surfing in the summer heat? That imagined picture seemed suffused with warmth and plenty. Although it would be noisy. Those kids were so loud.

'Rob?' his father hollered.

'On my way,' he hollered back.

JESS

When Jess answered the phone, her old school friend Ruth said, 'Just wondering at what point I should take it personally, you not replying to any of my messages.'

'Sorry. I've only been back a few hours,' said Jess.

'And your mobile doesn't work in Europe? Have you thought of doing something about that?'

'My mobile does work. I was in Oxford. I just haven't had a chance to text back.'

'I thought you were going to see Patrick?'

'Long story.'

'The short version?'

'I was with Sam.'

'Thank God for that. Are you going to be in Millingham for New Year?'

'That's the plan.'

'We're at my parents. Let's go to the pub.'

'Um, we'll have five children to look after between us.'

'We'll come to you. Make sure your phone's on. I'll text you.'

'Ow, Mummy, he hit me,' Millie wailed, from the seat behind Jess.

'I want to go home,' said Ben.

'Darling, we're going to stay with Josh and all his Lego. Then tomorrow night it's New Year's Eve and you can all stay up late.'

'Are they going to make us eat vegetables? I'm not

eating vegetables,' he said.

'There'll be sweetcorn and broccoli. You like those,' said Jess, trying to remember if they'd passed Junction 18.

'He doesn't like broccoli,' Millie piped up. 'I like broccoli. I'll eat it.'

Jess flipped the mirror down to see her daughter's beaming 'butter-wouldn't-melt' face.

'Do they have pasta?' said Ben.

'Of course they do.'

'Where do I have to sleep?' he said.

'I'm sure Sam will put you somewhere very nice. Would you like to sleep in Josh's room?'

'I want to sleep in Emma's room,' said Millie.

'We'll have to see. We'll all have to be very nice and kind. And say lots of pleases and thank yous. OK, Ben?'

'You said that already.'

'Ow,' Millie yelped. 'He hit me again.'

'Millie,' screeched her brother as her fist connected with his shoulder. 'You're not allowed to hit me.'

'Please, I don't think I can bear any more of this. I'm going to put the music on.' Why did she think driving to Manchester was a good idea?

'Heads, shoulders, knees and toes,' Millie shrieked.

'No. My music.' She put on Lou Reed and hoped they couldn't understand the lyrics.

Jess felt an involuntary jolt of lust when she finally pulled into Sam's drive and saw him strolling down the front steps. All she wanted to do was throw herself into his arms. As it was, she bit her lip very hard and concentrated on extricating the kids from the car. The back seat was littered with the detritus of uncapped felt-tips, raisins, discarded wrappers, crushed crisps and bits of bread stick.

Sam pulled Jess into a hug. 'Boy am I glad to see you. Thought you might be here a bit earlier.'

'Terrible traffic and two loo stops.' French kissing him in front of the children would be bad. She opened the boot and he reached for the bags.

'Let's find the others; I think they're watching television,' Sam said to the children.

Jess followed them into the house and stuck her head round the sitting room door, where Emma, Josh, and now Ben and Millie were engrossed in *Star Wars*.

Sam deposited the bags at the bottom of the stairs. 'Tea?'

Jess met his eyes briefly. 'Where's Kate?'

'Refused to spend New Year in the bosom of her family unless she could have moral support. So her friend Alice —sorry, Ali—is staying tonight and tomorrow night.'

'Ali from church?' Jess's heart sank. She remembered well the oppressive presence of the two eleven-year-olds last July.

'The one and only. Come on. Tea.'

Emma and Josh were perfectly fine towards Jess during their supper. But Kate wouldn't even look at her. What had felt like relatively predictable antisocial pre-teen behaviour in the summer had taken on the sinister importance of a deliberate and vindictive feud against a potential stepmother, and Jess could see how little Kate welcomed the idea. She had managed a monosyllabic hello to Jess only when pressed by her father, and then with very bad grace.

Jess knew the wisest thing would be to do nothing at all, however much she was provoked. Being given a large glass of Chardonnay made it easier. She tried not to make eyes at Sam.

Both children were going to sleep on the top floor, and Jess's bag was already in the spare room. At the opposite end of the house to Sam, with his elder daughter between them. She walked carefully along the landing trying to gauge the creaky floorboards, until Kate and Ali thundered up the stairs, staring at her malevolently. They're eleven years old, she kept telling herself. Eleven.

'Everything all right?' Sam came into the kitchen and grabbed the bottle of wine out of the fridge.

'The young ones seem fine. Not sure they'll get much sleep, I'm afraid, but—'

'Never mind.' He topped up both their glasses. 'Sorry about my appalling daughter.'

Jess's eyes widened. Since when had Sam become a mind-reader? That was the very word she'd landed on. Appalling, appalling, appalling, while her inner voice countered, with, *Like me, like me, like me…* One of the surprising aspects of adulthood—of being nearly forty, for God's sake—was how much more together she had expected to feel, and how very adolescent and at the mercy of her needy emotions she still felt. Held hostage by a child. Deep supportive breath. 'She's not appalling. She's trying to work out what's going on—'

Sam kissed her. 'Sorry. You were saying.'

'No idea. Things like that short-circuit my brain.' Which, when she was in a spiral of negative thoughts, could only be a good thing.

'Don't look like that. Talk to me while I cook.'

'That is one of your best lines. Impossible to resist a man who cooks.'

'Yeah, yeah, yeah. Just make sure you don't hang around anyone else who says it. Or drives. Or does anything sexy with their hands. In London. While I'm in Manchester.'

Jess squirmed, remembering her admission that Sam's driving was very attractive. 'Promise.'

Sam slung packets of chicken breasts, salad and potatoes out of the fridge on to the work surface. 'You've got that counting look.'

Jess shook herself mentally. *All shall be well. All manner of thing shall be well.* 'Ruth and Andy are at her parents with their son Jack. They want to vet you.'

'That's all? When?'

'They're going to the pub tomorrow evening. Wanted us to join them. Now want to drop in afterwards.'

'I did wonder if we should dilute the situation anyway. With other people.'

'Who did you have in mind?'

'My colleague Matt and his wife Jane. He was at school with your brother, wasn't he?'

'Good idea. How about the children eat together, except Kate and Ali, and then the six of us eat later?'

'How about the four of us eat in the dining room and the two girls have their own private party in the kitchen?'

Jess met his eyes. 'You think that would be better?'

'I don't want Kate to make you unhappy. I saw what she was like, despite a serious talking to before you got here. She's got no right, but she's so angry about everything at the moment.'

'She has every right. I'm a threat. I understand that.' Perhaps if she kept repeating those words, she'd start living them. At the moment there was a strong urge to slap something—or someone—which she firmly sat on. These heightened emotions made her feel daring, ashamed, and alive, all at once.

'But you are nothing to do with why her mother and I split up.'

'Doesn't matter. My mother was nothing to do with why my stepfather and his first wife split up. Didn't stop all sorts of people rewriting history as if it was her fault.' Jess understood that, however much she might strive to be liked, there were sometimes people who couldn't be won over.

She needed to focus on caring about the people and things that were important.

The other stuff, she had to let go....

SAM

Kate is so lucky it's you, Sam thought, as he walked Jess to her room. It had not been the most relaxing evening. Once the younger children were in bed, they'd had several visits, particularly from Ben, not to mention the brooding presence of Kate and Ali watching television in the front room. He shuddered to think how the couple of women he'd met in the past year or two would cope with a stepdaughter like Kate, but he had real hopes for the power of Jessica's compassion as far as his elder daughter was concerned.

He put his arms around Jess and kissed her outside her door. He kissed her again, slow and deep. The third time he kissed her they heard a thud from Kate's room.

'This should be getting easier.' He dropped his arms as Jess slipped into her room.

He knocked on Kate's door. 'It's gone eleven, girls. Way past time to turn the light out.'

'Dad.' Kate stopped when she saw his face.

'I'm expecting everyone to be sunny and polite tomorrow. And for that we all need a good night's sleep.'

'All of us, including you,' said Kate.

'All of us. No more noise, now. Night, Ali.'

He closed the door and waited until the light was turned off. Then he washed his face and brushed his teeth. On the way to his room he met Jess coming down the stairs from the top floor.

'They're all fast asleep,' she said.

He grabbed her hand and pulled her into his room. 'Wish you could sleep in here.'

'Likewise. Not sure being walked in on by any of our children is such an appealing thought, though.' She turned away and he reached for her, pulling her backwards on to the bed on top of him.

'Sam—' but his hands were in her hair, his mouth firm and insistent beneath hers, kissing her thoroughly, pressing her body to his, ensuring she knew exactly how aroused he was, so relieved that she was kissing him back, hands round his neck.

'OK,' he said at last, pushing her up, sitting up, automatically running his fingers through his hair.

'Now you're happy, are you? Leaving me in this state?'

'Just wanted to remind you what you were missing.'

'Very helpful.' She walked to the door. 'I hope you sleep as badly as I do.'

ANNA

New Year's Eve. One of her least favourite days of the year. Jess was right; time did accelerate as they grew older, but for Anna it passed in big fat dollops.

Her year was dictated by two main collections. The winter collection launched in September and the spring collection at the beginning of February. From October she would concentrate on the spring designs, and from May it switched to winter, so her head was always filled with the fabrics, patterns and prints for the wrong time of year. If she went to trade shows to promote her next collection, she'd find herself at the height of summer, modelling wools and heavy cottons, or in the depth of winter, floaty silks and feather-light chiffons. This lent a jarring aspect to her existence. Never quite in her own life. Never quite in sync with the world around her.

The dollops of time also produced—particularly when she was tired—peculiar time warps; endless Novembers skidded into Christmas Eve. Interminable Aprils ploughed straight into August.

And now it was New Year's Eve. It should have been a relaxing day, but the plan for the evening pervaded her consciousness from the moment she woke up. Jon's bed was big. They could comfortably lie in it, and sit to drink tea first thing in the morning, with quite an expanse of duvet between them.

Anna had a bath, something she rarely indulged in. Did she really not have time? In the water, she felt cocooned and safe. Her pale skin took on a bluish tinge in the bright white of the bathroom, her stomach soft and yielding under her fingers.

Jon suggested they go out for lunch, so they walked to a local French restaurant. The buzz of chat from other tables wafted around them while they read various of the weekend papers between courses. She flicked through the life-style and culture pages. She didn't stop to read Rob Randall's latest celebrity interview or take any particular interest in a photo of him, an attractive young model on his arm, at a Bond Street jewellery store Christmas party. Not that Jon was paying attention. He was gutting the business sections, the pages firmly grasped between his long hands.

They retraced their steps through a thin drizzle and sharpening wind. Anna held her scarf to her throat, relieved to reach the flat and curl up on the sofa. Resisting the temptation to fire up her laptop—it was New Year's Eve!—she let an undemanding Christmas-themed film wash over her for a couple of hours, while Jon 'checked his emails' in his study.

The looming dinner with Jon's business partner Charles occupied too much space in her mind. She'd known Charles and his wife Arabella for several years. They were loud and laughed at everything. She felt lacklustre in comparison, although that never mattered. There were no awkward silences with Charles and Arabella.

Charles had definitely overstepped the mark when she'd visited Jon's office in the autumn. He'd greeted her with relish, by giving her a full-bodied hug, including putting his hands on her bottom, effectively trapping her in his arms. She'd exclaimed and stepped back swiftly. She hated to be enclosed like that. He'd let go, laughed and winked.

When she mentioned it to Jon, saying 'Charles touched me inappropriately,' he deflected her by saying, 'Yeah, he's touched me inappropriately too. Don't take it personally.' Which had shocked her into silence. They hadn't referred to it again.

Anna couldn't reconcile the episode with the rest of Charles's behaviour. He had always been tactile with her, but it was only that last encounter that had cast a sordid shadow. She shuddered. Had he been gauging her reaction to see whether she might actually like it?

She spent a long time getting ready to go out, eventually choosing a pair of black silk satin trousers from her own collection. Beautifully cut, even if she did say so herself. She'd known from the moment Margaret, her skilled and very experienced pattern cutter, had produced a toile version, that the flat front, slightly high waist, wide trousers were going to work well in any colour. Over recent collections they'd produced them in midnight blue, dark purple and charcoal grey, and clients kept coming back for more.

She procrastinated about which top to wear. In the end, she chose a mandarin collar raw silk blouse in deep plum. It was a top she loved, but she needed heightened make up and strong lip colour to stop from looking washed-out and every year of her age. High heels, a fine cashmere wrap in ice blue, and a maroon velvet clutch bag completed the outfit. She scrutinised herself in the full length bedroom mirror. The dark colours were definitely slimming, and the high neck would stop any over-appreciative leers from Charles. Finally, after various tries, she gathered her hair into a loose top-knot. She turned away before she fiddled any more.

Jon looked smart in a floral shirt and dark trousers. He eyed her briefly. 'Very glam.'

What did that mean? When had he morphed from boyfriend—life partner even—to polite flatmate? He gave so little of himself away. In the beginning, his inscrutability had intrigued her, but increasingly she suspected it didn't hide a rich inner life. His interests were prosaic in her mind. Sport. Tech. Computer games. Electronic music. What had, once upon a time, seemed new and exciting, now struck her as increasingly alien and incomprehensible.

The first noise that greeted them when the door to the smart terraced house in Fulham was opened, was a female shriek. Anna's heart sank. Saskia, Jon's assistant. She hailed from Woking, where her Chinese parents ran a popular restaurant and catering business.

'Charles! Hands off.' The sound of a slap.

'Darlings, at last.' Arabella ushered them into the elegant beige and pale grey hallway. The narrow console table displayed willow baskets filled with white hyacinths. 'Oh fuck,' she said, as a heel caught on the coir flooring. 'Why do I even try to wear heels, but Charlie insisted.'

'Arabella,' said Jon, kissing her on both cheeks.

'Coats, coats. Charlie!' Arabella yelled.

'Ooh, hello gorgeous.' Charles appeared, his grin wolfish. 'Anna. What a vision.'

She put out her hands to prevent a hug, submitting to boisterous cheek kissing instead.

'Come and meet Raymond. Sass says they're brother and sister, but technically they're cousins. Keep it in the family, what hey?' Charles nudged her playfully, before giving Jon a back-slapping hug. 'Three sheets to the wind already. We started on the champers several hours ago.'

And so the evening wore on. Arabella produced symmetrical, shop-bought smoked salmon hors d'oeuvres, followed by a beef in madeira casserole which should have been tender and tasty and was not quite either. Charles got louder and louder.

Did no one else notice how he progressively slurred his words? His pale pink shirt strained over his belly. A heart attack waiting to happen.

The thought made her feel sick. She tried not to think about the functions of bodies very much. She studied the form, the shapes, angles and proportions, but as long as her own body transported her safely from one place to another, she had no wish to think about health, digestion, fluids or odours. And she certainly did not want to dwell on how her own body had failed her and how fast the clock was ticking down. Her hand crept to cover her stomach.

No. Not tonight.

She glanced up and met Raymond's eyes. He held up a water jug and she picked up her glass for a refill. His look was tranquil and calm. He did not wink.

'Oh, Anna!' Arabella shrieked. 'Small world. James Gorton. He married Fiona, my best friend from school. You're one of the Millingham crowd, but we didn't see you at the wedding?'

James Gorton. There was a blast from the past. Anna was aware that he'd recently become an MP, and that Jess and Sam had been to his wedding in Oxford. They'd met up with others too—Sebastian? And Rob Randall? She'd skipped over his interview earlier but she knew he wrote well. His byline photo looked the same, but more so. He had always been rather too much for Anna in their teens. Too loud, too wild, too dangerous. In a pedestrian, 1980s, middle-class sort of way.

'We haven't really kept in touch,' she said.

'Oh, you'll want to re-establish contact,' said Arabella. 'Fiona's very excited. He's already made quite the impression at The Treasury.'

'Goin' places, don't-cha know,' slurred Charles.

Anna almost laughed out loud at their transparent desire to call James Gorton a friend, but she had no desire to reconnect.

She knew things about James. Things she'd rather not know.

Giggling from the other end of the table drew her attention. Saskia, her hand draped over Jon's forearm, her dark nails reflecting the candlelight, gazed up at him. He wore his inscrutable look, but he also managed to appear more alert and animated than Anna had seen him throughout the Christmas period.

She made this observation with detachment. If she and Jon were secure and comfortable in the longevity of their relationship, then a besotted young thing was not a threat… unless what it revealed was that neither of them cared enough about each other for it to matter. She couldn't quite decide. If they were in a rut, would it pass? Perhaps her first New Year's Resolution should be a quest for more courage.

'Poo? Mo—poo?' Charles slurred. The volume of his voice had increased in proportion to the alcohol consumed.

'Oh, Charlie, no. It's champagne, not shampoo!' Arabella fell about.

Raymond gave Anna a small smile.

She discreetly looked at her watch as Charles paraded around the table refilling glasses. Quarter past ten. As she feared, it was going to be a very long night.

ROB

He was glad he'd hired a car at Geneva airport. Despite knowing people on his flight who would have given him a lift to the house party in Chamonix, he'd gone with his gut and collected a powerful Mercedes.

He'd wanted to come here. Had enjoyed skiing on the bright, sunlit slopes above the low-lying cloud. Once the apres-ski alcohol and drug-taking took over, and he was the only person still conscious enough to hold a conversation, he'd given up and gone to bed.

He might have slept in, but another text from his friend Pete, a fellow journalist turned radio producer, had him rise early and drive to Mougins, just north of Cannes in the south of France. With little traffic and clear motorways, he arrived in the middle of the day.

Sitting on the terrace with beers in hand, Pete filled him in on his Christmas in Leeds, with his mother and sister, as well as extracting the necessary information on who was pairing off together in Chamonix. He was, if anything, even more commitment resistant than Rob. A blond, curly-haired serial monogamist who was practised at withdrawing from a relationship just before anyone got too serious, or hurt. That was his strategy.

'You are an incorrigible gossip,' said Rob.

'Journalism, dear boy. What shall we do tonight?'

Rob groaned. 'Can't we stay put? I've driven all this way.'

'Don't be a wimp. We'll go into Antibes.'

'Do we have to?'

'It's New Year's Eve. Much as I like your company, I'd prefer to spend the night with a woman.'

Rob swatted him with his free hand. 'You are a walking cliché.'

'They're cliches for a reason, dear—'

'Stop. You go. I'll soak up the sunset.'

'You protest too much. It'll be fun.'

Pete was right. It was fun. Well, more fun than Chamonix. They sauntered past the marina, along the sea walls, through the old town with its narrow, hilly streets, down towards the covered market, and found a bar. They ordered a bottle of red wine, which came with generous bowls of salty bar snacks: cashew nuts, olives, and slices of toasted baguette slathered with tapenade.

They got chatting to a charming couple at the next table. He was French, and by Rob's estimate, in his sixties. She looked younger: long dark hair, a cinched-in velvet jacket over a brightly patterned dress. She spoke impeccable French, but hailed from Edinburgh.

'Why do you look familiar?' she asked Rob, just as three teenage girls approached, nudging each other.

Rob had clocked them from the corner of his eye, turned his shoulder away to deter them, but they edged towards him.

'Adela King?' the pretty blonde one asked, in her charming French accent.

Rob met Pete's eyes and shook his head fractionally. Pete carried on his conversation with the man, while Rob shrugged an apology to the woman.

'Pas ici, pas avec moi.' Rob lifted his empty hands, palms up.

'Non? Où est-elle?'

'Je sais pas. A Londres, peut-être?

'Ouf.'

'Vraiment?'

'Vous pouvez donner un message?' The three of them spoke over one another.

'Oui, si vous voulez.' He glanced apologetically at his companion. She watched the proceedings with interest.

Once they'd tried to scrawl something on a paper napkin, he took pity on them and offered a couple of squared paper pages from the notebook he kept in the inside pocket of his jacket.

After a lot of lively chatter, the note was finished: 'Adela King, we love you, bons baisers, Beatrice, Juliette et Marine. Come and visit us in Antibes.' There were then a lot of details—addresses, mobiles, landlines—and many kisses.

'Merci monsieur.'

'Vous êtes très gentil.'

'N'oubliez pas. Merci.' The girls waved and blew kisses as they moved on.

The woman said, 'I wish I understood what that was all about. Adela King?'

Rob gave her a wry smile. 'The next big thing in pop music. Phenomenal voice.'

'Are you in music?'

He laughed. 'I wish. No. Journalism.'

'What did you say your name was?'

'I didn't.' He grinned and held out his hand. 'Rob Randall.'

Her hand was small and warm. 'Lisette. That is Gregoire.'

'Lisette. I thought you said you were Scottish.'

'Half. My mother was French.' She tilted her head, running one finger along his forearm. 'Would you like to come back to our house? With Gregoire?'

He waited for a moment, wanting to confirm what was or wasn't on offer. 'But not Pete?'

Her hand lightly encircled his wrist. 'Perhaps you are gay? You are a couple? No. You are both interested in women.'

Rob sat back and she released his wrist. Her direct, assessing attitude was disarming. 'This is true. I'm staying with my friend. Thank you for the offer, though.'

Lisette lifted her eyebrows. 'What a shame, Rob. You will discover that we all have less time than we think.'

Rob picked up his glass. 'So, let's have a drink.'

JESS

By early evening, Jess was seriously wondering whether packing up her children and driving back to London wouldn't be a better option than trying to get the three of them, the four Rushmores, plus guests, to have a civilised New Year's Eve together. The thought of having to keep her eyes open past midnight was exhausting.

The afternoon had deteriorated quickly, with *The Sound of Music*. There was plenty of stuff to be getting on with in the kitchen, but the lure of Julie Andrews had hooked her. She'd forgotten what a long film it was. The boys soon got bored and decided that playing football in the hall would be a great idea until Sam removed them to the garden. By the time she started on supper for Josh, Ben, Emma and Millie, everyone was snappy.

'I'm so hungry,' Millie whined again, while Jess waited for the kettle to boil. In the unfamiliar kitchen, everything took longer than usual. Not that she could complain to Sam. He'd left them to the film after the nuns started singing and sat in the kitchen and peeled all the vegetables listening to Radio 5 Live. He was now laying the table and trying to disguise the less attractive aspects of the dining room, which had not been decorated or updated in many years. In her mind he won a massive number of points, whatever he managed. Tom had become practised at sloping off to do something incredibly important just as any chores became urgent, long before he'd actually left the marital home.

'I'm doing pasta. It won't be long now,' Jess said.

'I'm *too* hungry,' Millie wheedled.

'Millie, I swear, if you say that even one more time—' Jess saw Kate and Ali exchanging rather triumphant '*I told you she was the Wicked Witch of the West*' looks in the doorway. She bent down and picked up Millie. 'Would you help me measure out the pasta, darling?' She could tell the older girls had gone by the slamming of the door.

'Here we go.' She balanced Millie on her hip, one hand holding the large pan she'd found, her free arm pouring the freshly boiled water into it. Millie squirmed and Jess's hand slipped as she steadied herself, sending scalding water over her thumb. The hot water bounced and fizzed on the Aga hot plate. 'Shit,' Jess swore, dumping Millie on the floor, shoving her thumb under the cold tap, spraying water everywhere as she turned it on too hard.

'Mummy, you said "shit",' said Millie, an admiring look on her face.

Jess grimaced, her shoulders hunched. *Stupid, stupid.*

The door opened and Jess swung round to face down any clever comments from two resentful eleven-year-olds.

Instead Sam came towards her, holding his hands up as he saw the look on her face. 'Wasn't me, honest.'

'Mummy said "shit",' said Millie.

'Amelia, I am warning you.' Her thumb throbbed. Unhelpful.

'What did you do?' said Sam, taking in the kettle, pan, hand under the tap. 'Let me look.'

'It's nothing.' Jess turned towards the sink. 'My hand slipped.'

'Where?' said Sam, neatly taking her wrist and turning her hand under the water, causing her to twist towards him.

'Thumb.'

'Jess, you poor thing.'

'Bloody idiot,' she said under her breath.

'I take it you're referring to yourself,' he said, so close she could feel his breath on her cheek. He bent and kissed her ear. 'You'd better be nice to me, I'm a doctor.'

The slightest whiff of that alluring aftershave. 'Idiot.'

'Mummy, you said—' Millie started.

'Millie, love, go and ask Emma for my bag, would you?'

Millie beamed at Sam and trotted off.

'Keep it under the water.'

'*I know*. I'm not a complete idiot.'

'Don't think I mentioned that word at all. What are we doing here?' He gestured at the pan. 'Pasta for four?'

She nodded and watched him re-boil the kettle, set the pan of water on the hot plate and measure out the pasta. He had such competent, manly, sexy hands. The remains of last summer's tan, those strong fingers, sent her hurtling back to those few days in Oxford. He looked up, raised an eyebrow, and winked. So much for being mysterious; he knew exactly what effect he had on her.

Millie brought back the bag and Sam lifted her up to sit on the table. 'Millie, this is my doctor's bag and I have some special cream in it that's going to make Mummy's thumb better. Will you help me?'

'Yes,' breathed Millie. 'Can I be the nurse?'

'Absolutely. There are two important things to remember. One is that we only ever use this bag when I'm there. That's why I keep it high up in the hall cupboard. Do you understand?'

'Yes.' Millie stared at him with solemn eyes.

'The other thing is that you must be very gentle with

your patient. So, we're going to ask Mummy to bring us her sore thumb to dry very carefully. OK?' He smiled and Millie beamed back.

God, he really was good at everything. The thought depressed Jess. She couldn't get Kate to look at her. A state of affairs that seemed to deteriorate each time they were in the same room together. She tried to remember herself at that age, but Kate conducted herself so differently, with very little of the common people-pleasing oldest child syndrome in evidence.

Sam talked Millie through the task of drying the thumb and then put the cream on Jess's finger. 'It's the stuff they put on burns in A & E,' he explained. 'It should stop the throbbing. Now, Millie, you help me with the bandage.' Together they bandaged the thumb and put everything back in the bag. 'I know just whose help to ask for, next time there's an accident, Millie. Now, do you want to call the others to come and have some food?'

'You're so good with her.' Jess watched her go. Such a good man, such a caring father, such irresistible and capable arms, and hands that could drive her to the heights of passion. Was this a bubble of idealistic dreams that could never be sustained? A shortlived honeymoon that would burst at the beginning of January?

'Well, she's a delight. And your children are that much younger, which makes it easier.'

Afterwards, Jess realised that had been the oasis of calm in an evening of strife, familial and otherwise. Emma and Millie both turned their noses up at the bowls of pasta with slivers of chicken, pesto and parmesan.

'Can't we have something different?' said Emma, while Sam was taking candles to the dining room. 'You're having a big roast. Kate and Ali are having crispy duck. It's not fair.'

'I'm sorry if you think it's a bit boring,' said Jess. 'But I'm sure there'll be some meat left over from tonight. And there's Christmas pudding for afterwards.'

'That's boring,' Josh joined in. 'We've had Christmas pudding every day.'

'Can we have some chocolate?' said Ben.

'Yes. We'll need to divide it up so that everyone gets some,' said Jess.

'That's not fair. It's my chocolate,' Ben said.

'Well, either you and Millie share it or nobody's having any,' she snapped.

Emma's eyes widened.

Jess felt like having a tantrum. In the privacy of her own room. Not Emma as well. She'd always struck Jess as a potential ally. How were she and Sam going to manage if at least one, and quite possibly two of his children were doing their best to make her feel as unwelcome as possible?

'I don't want this chicken,' said Ben. 'It's disgusting.'

'Benedict,' said Jess, as Sam reappeared.

'How's it going?'

Jess turned away to cut up some fruit for the children. She felt pathetically close to tears. Throwing herself into his arms would only confirm her enemy status to his children.

'Cup of tea?' he said. 'Or something stronger?'

'If I have something stronger, I'll never last until midnight,' she said, not meeting his eyes.

He put his hand on her shoulder, which she quickly shrugged off.

'Why don't you go and have a bath?'

'I'm fine. I still have to do the pudding. The others will be here in less than an hour.'

'I can do it.'

'And get the children organised.'

'They can wait.'

'Dad.' Kate opened the door from the hall.

'Hang on a second,' he said, over his shoulder. 'Jess. Go on, have a break.'

'No. Find out what Kate wants. I'll do the rest of tea.'

Jess concentrated on cutting up apples and bananas without using her left thumb.

Sam went into the hall and closed the door behind him.

'I can't eat any more,' said Millie.

Jess glanced at her laden bowl. 'Millie, have you eaten anything at all?'

'Yes. I can't eat any more.'

'Well, you're just going to have to try harder. There'll be no chocolate for people who don't eat their main course.' She spotted an exchanged look between Emma and Joshua, took a deep breath and didn't scream.

Eventually, after a lot of persuasion, Millie ate most of her pasta and chicken and the other three finished theirs. They ate their fruit with bad grace, and Ben started wailing when Jess suggested sharing out some of the inordinate amount of chocolate her children had acquired over the holiday period.

Sam opened the door. 'Is a doctor required?' he asked, winking at Millie.

'We're just having a disagreement about chocolate,' said Jess, thinking that if she committed GBH on her son, at least there'd be a doctor present.

Sam walked over and bent close. 'Go and have a bath. I'll deal with this.'

'But it's my son—'

'You know as well as I do that sometimes it's easier for someone else to diffuse the situation.'

Jess took her cup of tea into the hall, as Ben stopped wailing to listen to what Sam was saying. Bugger, she thought. He's bloody perfect. Then she caught Kate's eye as she pounded down the stairs and flounced into the sitting room. Apart from the fruits of his loins, that is.

Her bandaged thumb reminded her how quickly she could usually wash, dry and dress herself. Pulling her long skirt and boots on took minutes, but she had a feeling it was going to be cold in the dining room. The only room that seemed to be really warm was the kitchen. Right beside the Aga. When she tried to imagine a future —a blended family of seven!—it was this house she saw. There was never a credible version set in her small London terrace. But how would she navigate this space, that had been Sam's domain for the majority of his life? She couldn't envisage it ever feeling like their house. Only ever his…

She zipped down the stairs to finish off the pavlova before Matt and Jane descended on them.

Ah. Her favourite people. Kate and Ali.

'Everything all right?' she said, crossing the kitchen to take the cream out of the fridge. Ridiculous to feel nervous of them. And yet she felt the hostility radiating in her direction. No. She was tired and stressed. She was imagining—

'We were just—' Ali started.

'Let's go.' Kate stared Ali down until she put the foil tray containing all the bits and pieces for crispy duck on the table.

'Shall I put it on for you?' said Jess. 'How long does it take?'

'Forty-five minutes,' said Ali, turning back from the door, despite Kate's signalling.

'I could put it in the top oven now,' said Jess. 'I'll need to crisp up the potatoes in there, but not for an hour or so.'

'As long as we're out of your way before then.' Kate snapped.

'It's not that. I'm just trying to work out how we can all live together.' The slip of the tongue was out there before she could stop it.

'We're not living together,' Kate spat.

'I mean get on together.' *Shit*. Deep breath. 'If I put this on for you now, you can both come and have a drink when the others arrive, then eat about eight o'clock.'

'OK,' said Ali.

Kate said nothing.

Jess knew that now would be absolutely the worst time to blow up at her, particularly as it was so patently what Kate wanted. *Lord, give me strength*, she muttered.

'Fine,' said Jess, blinking hard, pulling the lid off the double cream, finding a bowl, wondering what sort of equipment Sam had for whipping cream; absolutely certain she was not going to ask his elder daughter. She heard them go out and then she leant over, forehead on her forearms, on the work surface. She was not going to cry. She was not. *Just because I can't bear people not to like me. Like me, like me.*

The doorbell rang. Shit.

'I'll get it,' shouted Sam. She heard the door open, murmured hellos, footsteps.

Concentrate. Whipped cream. She found an electric

hand whisk in one of the drawers and plugged it in. Apron. Would be better than splattered cream everywhere.

'Jess?' Sam appeared in the doorway, followed by Matt. She blinked several times and sniffed in an effort to pull herself together, before she turned round with a smile plastered onto her face.

'Jess. You look just the same.' Matt was grey-haired, shorter than Sam, no trace of a Northern accent. He kissed her cheek.

'As do you,' said Jess.

Matt winked. 'There are many women, my wife included, who think grey hair is very distinguished.'

'As do I,' said Jess, smiling at the woman coming into the kitchen. She had dark, curly hair piled up on top of her head and was wearing a deep red velvet shirt.

'And you believed me?' Jane laughed.

'Drinks,' said Sam, putting his hand on Jess's back for a moment. A small gesture. But so very much appreciated.

SAM

Sam watched Jess's shoulders descend, in tiny increments, from somewhere up by her ears until—by the end of the delicious pavlova—she looked relatively normal, and her breathing had deepened again. Better. But he could see he was going to have an uphill battle to persuade her to come and stay again if all the children were going to be here. His mind flickered over what to do about Kate, but he had no idea how to improve things without losing his temper. Having a reasonable, mature discussion had done no good at all. He refocused on Jess, who was fielding increasingly personal questions from Matt. All proportionate to the amount of wine that had been consumed.

'Well, he's a different man since he met you again, that's all I'm saying,' said Matt.

'In what way?' She caught Sam's eye, shrugged an apology.

'More laid back,' said Matt.

'But he's practically horizontal. I just can't imagine him being even the slightest bit uptight,' said Jess.

'You haven't seen him being fawned over at work,' said Matt.

Jane laughed. 'You do just fine too.'

'He does. But it's true that you get into fewer tricky situations when you're married or in a relationship.' Sam gazed at Jess, feeling the heat rise quickly.

'Anything else?' she said.

'More confident,' Matt said.

'*More?* This is one of the most certain men I've ever met.'

'Yeah. Around you.'

'I don't believe it. He knows what he wants. It's *very* attractive.'

Sam caught her eye. Good thing he was sitting down. Good thing the house was full of people, or he'd have his way with her right here on the dining table.

'What I'm trying to say,' said Matt, 'Is that he's happier. Which can only be a good thing. All you need to work out now is the logistics.'

Sam couldn't tear his eyes away from Jess.

'It's not always that simple,' Jane murmured.

'Coffee? Tea? Anyone?' Jess jumped up, clattering plates together.

'I'll do it,' said Sam. In a minute. When he could stand up.

It was twenty to midnight when they left the table and proceeded to the sitting room. The children had worked their way through an array of films. Millie was practically comatose, but she wouldn't be carried up to bed, too scared of missing something good.

'I'll grab the champagne and we can watch Big Ben,' said Sam.

'Dad, we can light the candles in here.' Emma indicated the candelabra on the round table by the window.

'We could. Jess, would you help me with glasses?' He chose to ignore the look on his elder daughter's face.

He followed Jess down the hall, closed the door behind them and kissed her, his hands on the small of her back, spreading his fingers around her waist.

Jess kissed him back, her arms round his neck.

'Champagne,' he said.

'Glasses,' she countered, as the doorbell rang.

Emma greeted the visitors on the step.

'Oh, God,' said Jess.

Sam shouldered open the door into a hall full of people.

'Where's the champagne, Sam? The pub's heaving with undesirables,' James' voice boomed. He draped his arm around his wife Fiona, resplendent in a turquoise coat. They looked every inch the successful couple; he a rising MP, she a political PR consultant.

Ruth shoved past them and proffered her cheek for a kiss. 'What can I say? We tried to lose him.'

'Ha ha,' Sam said, kissing her, shaking hands with her husband Andy, and with James. He kissed Fiona on the cheek.

'It was too crowded for words,' said Fiona. 'We simply couldn't have stayed a moment longer.'

'Come into the sitting room. James, do you remember Matt? A friend of Jess's brother Patrick? And this is his wife Jane…' Sam watched as James's frozen expression was quickly replaced by broad smiles and the shaking of hands.

'Where's Jess?' said Ruth.

'Here,' Jess said, a tight smile on her face.

'My God, what have you done to her, Sam? She looks positively wiped out,' said Ruth.

'Happy New Year to you too,' said Jess.

'No, really.' Ruth kissed her, lowering her voice to a theatrical whisper. 'I hope, if you're not sleeping, it's for an exciting reason.'

Sam noticed that although they kissed on both cheeks, Jess and James didn't utter a word to each other. He grabbed her hand and towed her along the hall to the kitchen.

'Everything all right?' he said, as he picked up the tray of glasses.

'Yes,' said Jess.

He surveyed her pinched face. 'Sure? Nothing to do with—?'

'Nothing to do with. Go on.' She held the door for him.

Sam edged into the front room.

'We need some matches,' said Emma.

'I've got some in my pocket,' said Sam.

Emma started feeling for them.

'No. Wait. I'll get them,' he said, frantically scanning for somewhere to put the tray. He handed it to Jess, but it was too late.

Emma had pulled a small, square foil package with an unmistakable circular outline out of his left pocket. 'What's this—?'

He took it back and produced the matches from his right pocket, but not before most of the adults had seen what it was. Not before Kate and Ali had seen what it was.

Emma opened her mouth, but closed it when she saw her father's face.

'Matches,' he warned.

'Well, well, well,' said James.

'Better to be safe than sorry,' said Matt.

'Shhh,' nudged his wife.

Sam cleared a space on the table and watched Jess put the tray down, hiding her burning face. He tried to catch her eye, but she didn't look at him. Despite the awkward situation he felt on the brink of desperate guffaws and wondered if she felt the same. Maybe that was why she was putting her face through a bizarre muscular work-out.

'What do you—?' Kate began, but he swung round and cut across her.

'Not now,' he said, stepping forward, suddenly thankful that he was not above using the full height of his physical presence to persuade his daughter into silence.

'Millie, darling, let me take you up to bed,' said Jess, scooping her daughter into her arms.

'Don't go, just when things were getting interesting,' Ruth said.

Sam bit his lip hard, concentrating on the cold, heavy champagne bottle.

'No, Mummy,' said Millie.

He realised she'd felt the atmosphere in the room change and was now wide awake. 'Here we go,' he said, easing the bottle and cork apart, pouring champagne into the tall glasses. They'd brought liqueur glasses for Kate and Ali. Ali took hers eagerly, and after a mental battle played out on his daughter's face, Kate took hers.

'Well, it's great to see you again, Jess,' said Matt. 'Thank you very much for having us.'

Sam caught Jess dropping her face on to her daughter's neck. Weeping or laughing?

'Yes.' Jane smiled. 'Lovely to meet you, Jess.'

Kate made a tutting noise and her eyes flew to her father's. Her look of shock told him she'd meant it to be quieter. He let it pass.

Jess swallowed and raised her head from her daughter's hair. 'It's good to be here.'

Sam caught her eye and exhaled slowly. She was trying not to laugh. She'd caught Ruth's eye and the giggles were bursting out, no matter how hard she tried to clamp down on them.

'So lovely…to be made…so welcome,' Jess said, the

giggles escaping in little snorts. 'Sorry. Must pull myself together.'

'You must come up again soon,' said Jane.

Kate and Ali stood there open-mouthed, watching the adults.

'Why the hell leave?' Jess sobbed with laughter. 'Why not just stay?'

'Why not indeed?' said James, his eyes on her.

She turned firmly towards Sam, rubbing the back of her hand over her face. 'Sorry, Sam. What time is it?'

'Where is that?' said Josh. He and Ben watched the television screen.

'It's nearly time. Here comes Big Ben,' said Sam.

'Happy New Year,' said Matt.

Sam kissed Emma and Josh and then Kate, who let him, with a brittle flinch, as he put his hand on her shoulder. Then he went over to Jess and Millie and hugged them. 'Happy New Year.'

'Happy New Year, Sam.' She stepped back from his arms and turned towards Ben. 'Hope it's a good year for you, darling.'

'Me too.' He wriggled away towards Joshua.

Jess nodded at Millie, who curled her arms tighter round her mother's neck. 'Now it really is time for bed.'

JESS

Jess leaned on the edge of the crowded wooden table. Sam's kitchen bore the detritus of a three-course meal, with crockery, glasses, ripped Christmas crackers and torn napkins on every surface. Deep breaths. New Year's Eve always felt like a long night, but this one had no end.

Water. Would be good. Rehydration after all the wine. She extracted a tall glass from the cupboard and paced to the sink to run the cold tap. She drank a long draught, then rocked the side of the glass across her forehead in the quiet. Eventually the visitors would leave and the braying laughter would cease.

Images sliced across her consciousness. Her ex-husband Tom's face twisted in vitriol. Silence blanketing the room when he flicked off her choice of music. Raising her arm to wipe the spittle from her cheek with her sleeve. A supper hosting neighbours at home in London, and Tom saying, 'Jess's taste in music is abysmal.' Her friend Lucy speaking into the silence, attempting a light laugh, trying not to flinch when he cut across her.

Jess put the glass on the draining board, her hands either side of the sink. She pulled her shoulders down and tipped her head forward to stretch the back of her neck. The slightest flicker of a shadow caught the corner of her eye.

She swung round but James was close behind her. She sucked in a breath, jerked back to the sink, her arms braced, not meeting his eyes reflected in the window above.

He stood, too close behind her, hands in his pockets,

radiating body heat.

As long as he didn't touch her.

The space of twenty years telescoped into nothing. She was back in a badly lit downstairs loo. Drunk on red wine and no food, flailing for breath as James gripped the back of her neck, forced his tongue into her mouth…his weight pinning her against the wall…panic rising as she tried to wrench away from his firm grip…

Not now. He was not doing this to her again.

Jess felt the flood of saliva, clenched her jaw, steadied herself with her hands. Despite the cool white porcelain of Sam's kitchen sink, her hands were sticky, her armpits already cold with the rush of sweat. She began to shake her head.

Elbows sharp, she side-stepped towards the fridge. It would be unbearable for Sam to find them, to sense the atmosphere, to ask what was going on.

James hardly seemed to have moved, and yet he was standing far too close. Not quite touching her. She could feel his fixed stare.

'Just making sure we understand each other,' he said.

She met his eyes for the first time. 'Worried people are going to discover the real you?'

He laughed, turning to face the table, not the door. 'You've got nothing of interest to say. Sam wouldn't understand, and you don't want to lose him. Twice.'

She stared at him. He looked big and confident. Swaggering, almost. But then she saw that arrested, frozen look again. That fraction of a doubt.

That millisecond of hesitation had saved her once. The sexual assault had not become a rape.

She was not a naive teenager any more. 'Get away from me.'

SAM

When Sam realised he hadn't seen Jess for a while, he extricated himself from Fiona and Ruth and wandered down the hall to the kitchen. Jess was putting cups on a tray already set with a jug of coffee, milk, teaspoons. James leant against the table and watched her.

'What's going on?' He meant to be light-hearted, despite his tightening chest.

'A private chat.' James smoothed his hands down his white shirt into his trouser pockets.

'Nothing,' said Jess. 'He was just taking the coffee through.'

James' eyes flickered from the back of Jess's head to Sam, with the slightest shrug of his shoulders. He picked up the tray. 'I'll leave you to it.'

Sam shut the door behind James. 'Are you all right?'

'Fine.'

'Come and have some coffee. Then we can politely throw them out,' he said. He waited for her to turn around. When she didn't, he went over to her, but before he got to the sink, she turned and hugged him hard, her head on his chest. 'What is it? Is it James—?'

'Nothing.' She pulled away, pushing her hair off her cheeks with her palms.

'What were you thinking?' Jess asked, as they stacked the dishwasher after Matt and Jane had gone home, and—after several more cognacs—the others had left.

'About what?' Sooner or later Sam was going to have to ask Jess about James, but he was not at all sure he wanted to hear what she would say.

'What were you thinking?' she said, pulling the condom from his pocket.

'Give me a break. I know I'm meant to behave like a responsible father of three, but I feel as if I've discovered sex again. You have no idea. The relief, the…there you were, walking around, looking all sexy… I thought… better safe than sorry.' He shrugged. Now that James was out of the house, Jess had started smiling, and her breathing had deepened.

She closed the machine. 'When were you thinking you'd have a chance—?'

'I hadn't really thought that far. Anywhere. Any chance.' He stacked the last of the plates, leant back against the sink.

'You are not serious.'

'Of course not. In my grown-up moments. But when I become my adolescent self, then there's no stopping me.'

She eyed the condom. 'You know, it really is a shame we're both so very responsible and sensible.'

'I couldn't agree with you more. Any spontaneity I ever had has been squashed out of me.' He lunged and grabbed her, faster than he'd moved in a long time. 'Give us a kiss then.'

'You do realise Kate hates me now more than ever, don't you? And I don't think the laughing helped.'

'I did wonder whether you were crying to begin with.'

'It is no laughing matter.'

'Come to bed.' He had a vision of Kate bursting in. That would be bad. Much worse than the condom incident.

'Come to my bed.'

JESS

By mid-afternoon on New Year's Day, Jess was stupid with fatigue. The children, exhausted and unfit for anything other than lying on the sofa while something familiar flickered at them from the television screen, had nevertheless been dragged on to the common for an hour. The worst thing was the way Kate physically recoiled from Jess whenever she was within three metres of her.

Sam had sent Ali home, hoping things might improve without a partner in crime, but Kate had merely gone to ground in her room.

Jess felt her patience snap, deep inside her. She put her mug of tea down and walked out of the kitchen, ignoring Sam's questioning look, straight up the stairs to Kate's room. She knocked and opened the door before sense took hold of her.

'Kate,' she said, her hands clammy, her mouth dry. 'I'd like to talk to you.'

Kate sat on her bed, hunched into a huge sweater, her knees pulled up to her chin. She didn't look up. 'I don't want to talk to you.'

'That's fine.' Jess raised her voice to fake courage. Her legs were about to give way. She pushed the door to, and sat on Kate's chair. 'You don't have to say anything.'

'I don't want you—'

'I don't need you to like me, Kate. I'm not doing this for me. But I am doing it for your dad. He deserves more than this.' She waited for a moment; Kate was perfectly still. 'I know the thought of your parents having relationships is disgusting to you. I thought that too. My parents split up when I was in my teens, so contrary to what you believe, I've got a pretty good idea of what you might be thinking and feeling. What I really want you to remember is that your dad is human. Although to you he is first and foremost your dad, he's a divorced man, and when we were both feeling lonely and sad, we met again. We're trying to work out how to be together. How it might work. And it's difficult because there are so many people to think about. And the first person your dad thinks about is you, Kate. You are his eldest child and you are totally special to him. He's not going to do things to make you miserable. But think about how your behaviour affects him. Because it does. A lot.' Her voice sounded peculiar and gasping by the end because she was too nervous to stop and take a proper breath.

She tried to breathe normally, but it sounded inordinately loud and animal to her ears in the quiet room. Kate could have turned into a statue she was so still.

'OK. Well. Thank you for listening.'

Jess nearly fell over Sam, sitting on the stairs outside. *Oh shit.*

She stepped past him and didn't stop until she got to the kitchen. 'Sorry. Patience has never been one of my virtues.'

'Don't be sorry. Maybe it'll work.'

'I wouldn't hold your breath.'

He wrapped his arms around her. 'Thank you,' he said, into her neck. They stood like that for a long time, listening to each other's heartbeat, to their synchronising breathing.

It didn't work. They all ate leftovers together. Kate did deign to join them, but she wouldn't look at Jess, barely looked at her father, and was even more monosyllabic than usual. Jess did wonder if this was a good sign. Maybe some of what she'd said had got through and Kate was embarrassed. But then again, maybe she was so livid she couldn't utter a word.

The children went to bed without a fight, exhausted from the night before. Sam and Jess ended up watching *Sleepless In Seattle,* parts of which felt uncomfortably reminiscent of Jess's speech to Kate.

Because, of course, she really wanted the Hollywood Ending. She wanted Kate to come downstairs and throw her arms round her father and agree to try again with Jess, so that they could all live Happily Ever After. Just like the movies.

Sam must have picked up on her mood, because he just sat on the sofa beside her while they watched.

She kept stamping on the idea that she really would have to tell him about James. That long ago event was now so tiny and far away, clamped into the locked box at the furthest reach of her mind, that it seemed unnecessary, or too much effort to bring it out into the light. She was petrified that what she knew about herself would somehow shatter, if she told him. The rational part of her brain reminded her she was very unlikely to bump into James on a regular basis. He'd made it clear he had as little wish as she did to make any of it more widely known.

But another part nagged her about her rules on honesty. She'd been hard on Sam when she thought he wasn't being honest with her.

Why shouldn't the same rules apply to her?

SAM

When the film ended, Sam turned off the screen and switched on the side lamp. He stood in front of her until she looked up.

'Is there something I should know about James? Something about the past?'

Jess pressed her hand to her chest.

He sat beside her. 'It's OK. You can tell me anything.'

'It's not even significant. It happened such a long time ago.'

He waited. *Keep calm and focus.*

'I can't destroy your faith in your oldest friend. Your lives have been intertwined since you were at school together.'

'There's no rush.' He picked up her hand and held it in his larger, warmer one, concentrating on the feel of her skin, detracting his mind from the dread settling in the pit of his stomach.

'Do you remember, right after our A Levels, Tim and Susannah had a *Brideshead Revisited* party? You came to it, but you were going on somewhere else. I remember you were driving.'

'Vaguely. I remember people complaining of major hangovers afterwards.'

'It was the first time I got properly drunk. I started drinking red wine and missed the food. It was stupid.' She put her free hand over her mouth. 'I went to the loo. I could hardly stand, and even sober I couldn't walk in my heels. I forgot to lock the door.'

He watched her head dip as she swallowed.

'James followed me into the downstairs loo and tried to have sex with me.'

He tried to make the words fit into some sort of meaningful order, only conscious of the tight grip he had on her hand when Jess flexed her fingers and he eased the pressure. 'You mean he raped you?'

'No. He never…his belt got stuck on the back of my dress and tore the fabric. Took some explaining to my mother. It was her dress.'

He searched her face in an attempt to understand what she was saying. 'How had he…? How had he got that far?'

Jess shrugged. 'He was much bigger and stronger than me. When I tried to escape his grip, he pushed me, face down, against the washing machine. I couldn't shift his weight. I tried to get away, but the noise of the party was too loud, he'd locked the door, his hand was on my neck. I tried to breathe, but then he couldn't get my dress up. I remember thinking that a thin dress and knickers wasn't much of a barrier but I was grateful they were still between me and him.'

'Oh God, Jess. What happened?' He felt as if his heart would accelerate out of his chest. How could she not hear it?

'He got his belt caught and in trying to free it, he let go of my neck and ripped the dress. I managed to turn round and throw up on him. Then he was gone.'

'But then what? Who did you tell?'

'No one.'

'No one at all?'

'Not for a long time.'

'What about your mum?'

'She had other things on her mind. Besides, I was too ashamed, too embarrassed.'

'But what he did was outrageous.'

'And I was stupid and drunk. If I'd locked the—'

'He forced himself on you. What he did was inexcusable!'

'But he stopped. He didn't rape me. He tried to pretend it hadn't happened, afterwards. That I was overreacting.' She clenched her fist against her mouth. 'After a while you begin to think they might have a point.'

'And you told no one?'

'I told Caroline a few years ago.'

Sam raised an eyebrow. 'No one else? Not Tom?'

'No. It was a long time ago. And people view things like that very differently now.'

'So, last night, when I came into the kitchen—'

'Was the first time he made any allusion to it in twenty years. And he didn't even say anything. Just stood behind me, trying to frighten me.'

'He wouldn't dare—'

'But he wants to guarantee, if he's launching a high-flying political career, that any skeletons are staying firmly in closets.'

'That's why you like to see my face. I'm so sorry you didn't feel able to tell me before now. That I made you go to his wedding, for Christ's sake.'

'It happened a long time ago, Sam.' She put her hand on his cheek.

He held it against his face with his other hand. Breathing. Trying to calm his racing pulse, his heart thudding alarmingly against his ribs. 'Thank you. For telling me.'

'I know he's an important friend of yours. Good people sometimes do bad things and bad people sometimes do good things. When it came to it, he stepped back from the brink. And I've no reason to think he's done anything like that since.' She dismissed an overheard conversation in Oxford before the wedding. Adventurous sex could mean a lot of things.

'But hold on, he would have carried on if…?'

'He stopped though.' Her words sounded constricted.

'Because you threw up on him?' It was crucial he understood what she was saying.

She blinked. 'I don't trust my memories any more. I don't know.'

'You think he would have raped you. If it hadn't been for the…vomiting…'

She shivered. 'Possibly.'

'God, Jess.' He squeezed her hand. 'I'm so sorry.'

A heavy silence hung between them. The house was quiet and still.

'I'm not paying attention. Are you cold?' He glanced at his watch. 'The heating went off a while ago.'

'It's late. I should go to bed. To sleep this time.'

He eyed her. 'Understood. Is there anything I can do?'

Jess met his gaze. 'It happened a long time ago, Sam. I'm not expecting… It doesn't define me…. It's important to move on.'

'Do you want a hot drink or anything?'

'No thank you. I'll grab some water.'

He escorted her to the kitchen, ran the tap for her. Kissed her cheek outside her room. 'Shout if you need anything'

'I will Sam. Sleep well.'

He slept fitfully, awaking with a jolt from another of those dreams spent pursuing James down darkened corridors.

How could he make sense of what Jess had told him? He'd badly wanted to unburden himself about James's brother Stuart's fall, but he didn't want to get it wrong. The incidents were completely separate, even if they both involved James.

In the cold light of day, over a drawn out breakfast with all the children wandering in and out of the kitchen, he appreciated that trying to have a proper conversation was going to be a challenge, but he had to try. Honesty. That's what Jess had rated above everything else. It was imperative to tell her before she and the children drove south.

Jess was clearing the table. He took a breath. 'Please stop for a moment.'

She turned and surveyed him. 'Sounds serious.'

He clasped both her hands.

'There's something I've been wanting to tell you.'

'Go on.'

He took a long breath. 'Did you ever hear about James and me climbing the tree in their back garden, and Stuart following us and falling?'

Jess examined his face, and he withstood her unblinking gaze. 'He was knocked out and ended up in hospital?'

'He fell out of the tree. That much is true. But what actually happened is much worse.' He squeezed her hands and she clasped his more firmly. 'James was furious with Stuart, who was being annoying as only younger brothers can be.' He took a breath, searched Jess's eyes. 'So much so that James stamped on his fingers. He lost his grip. That's what made him fall.'

Jess sat back in the wooden kitchen chair, took away a hand to slowly tuck her hair behind her ear. 'I don't remember hearing that.'

He cleared his throat. 'No. You wouldn't. James insisted it was an accident. But I knew it wasn't.'

'And no one found out?'

'No. Their parents were in enough of a state with Stuart's injuries. He was concussed and vomiting by the time they got home. They couldn't wait to get rid of me, and I couldn't wait to leave. None of us said anything to anyone.'

Jess pulled away her other hand, and Sam let it go. 'Then it was much worse than anyone thought?'

'Yes. I'd helped Stuart up to the lowest branch, not for a second imagining he'd manage to follow us so far up the tree. I couldn't forgive myself. For not standing up to James. For allowing it to happen. For letting him get away with it.'

'How old were you?'

'Stuart was nine, so that means I was twelve. Old enough to know better. When his mum's house was sold, James got me round there in the garden under the tree, with his phone camera.'

'Why?'

'Same reason he stood behind you in the kitchen, I imagine. Wanted to make sure the story would never come out. He's ruthless. Particularly when it comes to his political career.'

Jess rubbed her forehead. 'I can't take it in. Why he would do such a thing.'

'We were kids. He was angry and probably scared that Stuart had climbed up so far. I can't explain why he lashed out at him, because he must have realised it could have dire consequences—'

'Do they think the head injury had a lasting effect?'

'I don't suppose we'll ever know. I don't think Stuart's ever reached his potential. Cleverer than any of us. The whole thing is surreal now. Was surreal at the time. I've never understood why I didn't challenge James's account of events.'

'It was a long time ago, Sam. Time to let it go.'

'For you too, Jess. Time to forgive yourself. You know it was not your fault. What he did to you was far worse than—'

'Yes, but you've been carrying this for a long time, too.'

'I still can't make sense of it. Why didn't I stand up to James?'

'Because you were a child and he's always been a forceful personality.'

He searched her face, but she kept her eyes averted, her hands tucked under her arms.

She looked closed off in a way that reminded him of a dreadful conversation in her kitchen, the previous autumn, when he couldn't reach her. He wanted to touch her, but he also wanted to give her time to assimilate this information.

'James doesn't think like other people,' he said.

'He doesn't behave like other people,' she said.

'I wanted to be completely honest with you. I wanted you to know the truth.'

Jess finally met his eyes. 'Yes. Me too.'

JESS

After she'd trawled the house for forgotten belongings, they had another conversation of sorts, fragmented by the children's various interruptions.

'Let's all move. To Birmingham,' Sam said.

'Too close to my in-laws. Ex-in-laws.'

Once the children were in the car, Sam gave her a hug and said he'd call her. But she saw something like defeat in his eyes. He knew she wasn't coming back. That the only time they'd be able to meet would be when they could offload their offspring. And yet this visit had pulled into sharp focus Sam the father. Yes, he could inhabit all sorts of other roles—doctor, lover, friend—but she was not seeing the whole person if she only saw him without his children.

How long could they keep going with such odds stacked against them? Geography. Children. Hostility. The hurdles seemed insurmountable. And now they had a whole subject area to avoid. She steered her mind away, whenever it veered, even minutely, towards James, or anything remotely connected with him.

It wasn't that she now saw him in a different light, knowing more about Stuart's accident. Children did stupid things, for which they must be forgiven. She kept imagining that scene, and how James must have dominated it, forcing Sam to go along with his version of events, through sheer force of personality. How could a twelve-year-old boy resist that?

And yet, if Stuart was really changed by the accident, by his head injury, no wonder Sam felt responsible. Bound by the past. The possibility of a different trajectory for Stuart's life.

Focusing on what Sam had told her helped keep her mind off what she had shared with him. Disconcertingly, it had begun to feel outrageously, weirdly normal to be in the same space, breathing the same air as James, on the occasions they'd met over the last few months. Even that peculiar encounter in the kitchen two nights ago had seemed normal on some level—he had imbued it with an almost prosaic sense of ordinariness—except it absolutely wasn't.

It had been about power and fear and she wanted nothing to do with it.

She replayed Sam's words over in her head. 'You know it was not your fault.' It had taken her a long time to believe those words. Maybe understanding how James had behaved towards Sam, towards his brother Stuart for God's sake, would help her remember that.

There was another nagging, growing thought.

If she stayed away from Sam, she'd have no need to normalise her body's reaction to the presence of James Gorton. She'd never have to share the same air with him ever again.

SAM

Sam scanned the further reaches of the echoing café until he spotted James at a corner table.

'What was so important it couldn't wait?' He looked red-faced and cross. 'I haven't got long. I'm meeting Fiona in twenty minutes.'

Sam sat opposite him, raised his hand to order a flat white. 'I spoke to Jess.'

'OK.' James laid the biro in his hand on top of his notebook, finished his espresso.

'Not OK. What was wrong with you that summer? Why would you think that was acceptable behaviour?'

'What are you talking about?' James leaned back in his chair, legs spread, his hands expansive on the table.

'The night you tried to rape her.'

'What the hell?'

'How would you describe it, James? You trapped her in a downstairs loo, and you held her down to have sex with her against her will. That's the definition of rape.'

James sat forwards and held up his hands. 'You'll find Jess is mistaken. Nothing happened.'

Sam leaned towards him, palms flat on the surface between them. 'We both know that's not true. Something happened.'

Elbows on the table, James steepled his hands. 'I had no idea you were so gullible. I'm not going to pay any attention to such utter fabrication.'

'She was only eighteen. Her father had just buggered

off. You crushed whatever self-esteem she had left, and it took her years to recover. In fact I don't think she did, she met that shit of a husband and—'

'Sam. Stop. For God's sake. Her disastrous marriage was not caused by anything in her past.'

'It didn't help.'

'You need to stop making completely unfounded allegations.'

'Unfounded allegations? Seriously?' Sam stopped as his coffee arrived, a beautiful thing in a grey and sage coordinating cup and saucer, to match the knocked back painted wooden furniture and powdery plastered walls of this stylish Millingham cafe. Not the café Stuart worked in.

James lowered his voice. 'You need to get this through your head. Whatever she's brain-washing you with, it didn't happen.'

'Why was that, James? Weren't you stopped by your stupid belt? By Jess throwing up on you? Or are you saying you'd have stopped?'

'I have no idea what you're talking about. I can't even have this conversation. Not at this stage in my career.'

'You are unbelievable. Deluded, if you think what you did had no consequences. You let her believe that's how men behave. That it was somehow her fault. Did you even talk to her about it afterwards? Did you ever say sorry?'

'Listen to what I'm saying, Sam. Nothing happened. There was nothing to say sorry for.'

'Can you hear yourself, James?' Sam rubbed a hand through his hair.

'Look. Stop playing the avenging male. She's perfectly able to take care of herself without you charging about on her behalf.'

'I know that. I'm telling you that it's time to make amends. Do the right thing.'

'Which is changing the subject.' James fiddled with the ball-point pen, clicking the point in, out, in, out.

'She didn't want to talk about it. Not for a long time. But she told me.' Sam paused, drank his coffee. 'Secrets are not good—'

'Oh, Christ. What did you do?'

Sam stared him down. 'Good. Start reacting. I told her about Stuart's fall. This is a relationship that deserves honesty.'

James put his head in his hands. 'Fuck. Another person who you think you can persuade to believe your version of events. What the hell were you thinking?'

'What are you so afraid of, James? You've surrounded yourself with ambitious aides, not friends and you think journalists have power. That they could build you up and then crucify you, whenever they like. But only if they've got an incriminating story and a credible source.' Sam stared at the top of James's head, which he'd never noticed from this angle. His hair was receding, and noticeably thinning. 'There's no story, James. There's no source. And if you think either Jess or I would ever talk about you to the press, then you really don't know me, and I don't know what we've been doing for twenty years. Twenty-five years. Most of our lives.'

James lifted his head out of his hands and met Sam's eyes. 'I do know that. Most of the time.'

'Apologise to Jess. Then we'll talk.'

ANNA

'Do you *really* not dwell on the past at all?' Jess asked.

Anna had rung her on the off-chance she'd be free to chat. It was after 8.30pm and they were both curled up on sofas, a glass of wine in hand. 'Uh. When did I say that?'

'Last summer. I was impressed. I turn it over in my mind the whole time,' said Jess.

'The whole time? You couldn't function if you did that. What are you thinking about? Specifically?' She knew she was great at dishing out advice on how *not* to over-generalise, disappear down self-imposed thought spirals, or flail at the mercy of her critical internal voice. Maybe if she said it out loud enough, she'd be able to put it into practise.

'Do you remember Tim and Susie's *Brideshead Revisited* party?'

Anna cast her mind back to being eighteen again. To the constant challenge of disguising her increasingly curvy figure. By then she felt her breasts were huge, accentuated by a slim waist and only somewhat balanced by wide hips. She'd chosen voluminous, bottom-covering tops (it was the 1980s, so the silhouette was fairly baggy anyway, enhanced by shoulder pads and big hair). 'I do remember dressing up in 1920s costume. I found a vintage black dress gran had squirreled away.'

It had been heavy silk satin, with black lace inserts across the bodice and upper sleeves, beautifully crafted with handkerchief hems, if a bit tight across the bust.

They obviously didn't have bosoms in the 1920s, she'd thought.

'Do you remember those black and white photos we took? I've got a couple in frames,' said Jess.

'Who's in the photos?'

'You and me, Caroline and Susie…and Tim…and… another boy, I think? I realise I haven't looked at them properly for years.'

'Well, who else was there that night? Sam?'

'It's not him,' said Jess. 'He was off somewhere else…'

'Sebastian? Or James?'

'No. Definitely not James. I think it was a friend of Tim's from school—Matthew?'

'That sounds about right.' There was something in Jess's uncompromising tone of voice Anna couldn't decipher. 'I do remember it was a gorgeous long summer's evening. Oh. You disappeared, didn't you? You did something to your ankle.'

'Did I? It was such a long time ago. Are you coming to London anytime soon?'

'I don't have any plans at the moment. Finalising the Spring Collection.'

'Oh of course. Here's me wittering. How's it going?'

'It's fine.' It was fine. Not exciting. Ten years ago, she would not have accepted the compromises she now settled for.

'What's your favourite piece?' Jess asked.

Anna reflected on the collection as a whole. Mostly her signature monochrome, although this end of the year the colour palette was paler, with accents of cream, navy, taupe and gold. But she'd chosen an Indian fine cotton lining in a delicious paisley pattern, with marmalade, citrus and chocolate accents. 'There's a cream fitted jacket with a round neck, with a lining in hot, spicy colours.'

'Ooh, you do like a colourful lining, Anna. Is it reversible? What if you like to wear your patterns on the outside?'

'Oh no,' said Anna. 'It's the lining.'

'Have you ever thought of making something reversible?'

'Not really…' When had she started shying away from bright colours, she wondered. In her teens, she'd hit the 1980s neon fashion, the bright tartans and busy hair accessories. There'd been a major black period, which coincided with finals and lasted for at least a year. Her inspiration had been heavy Victorian mourning. She'd gone through a period of reading Gothic horror, which developed into modern horror films. The thrill of being so frightened. Now she avoided wearing black anywhere near her face, and she'd gone right off horror in any medium.

Not that she'd embraced colour. Resurfacing from the phase of black, black and more black, she'd embraced neutrals, and she'd never quite thrown them over for anything else.

The house was different though. She'd allowed her love of colour free rein, particularly here in the Chinese red sitting room. Cushions covered in bright sari fabrics were placed along the cream sofas. In fact, that paisley pattern would look fantastic in here…

Perhaps a reversible jacket was a thought. Already she could see flashes of emerald, coral and kingfisher beneath lapels, in pockets, along waistbands—maybe even as a blouse? One statement piece pulling the whole collection together. It would have to be just the right pattern… available in quantity at this very late stage.

'Anna? Have you disappeared?'

'Just having an idea.'

'Good. Bit of colour, great for cheering you up.'

'What do you mean?' What had Jess sensed?

'Just that this January is very grey. And endless.'

Anna's heart steadied. Maybe that was all this was. Seasonal Affective Disorder. She could buy one of those special lights. Much better than her designer Olga's careless comment about early menopause, when Anna said she was exhausted and not sleeping well. Olga had no filters and said exactly what she thought. But she'd caught sight of Anna's face. 'I'm sorry Anna. That was thoughtless.'

'No matter,' Anna had replied.

But it did matter. It couldn't possibly be early menopause. She hadn't had the chance to have a baby.

She had to have that chance.

Which meant doing something different.

'Oh Lord, the patter of tiny feet. Only not so tiny,' said Jess, to a soundtrack of stomping. 'Sorry love, I'm going to have to go. Someone has escaped. Benedict, back to bed.'

Anna visualised Jess's seven-year-old son, with his blond hair and dark brown eyes, smiling disarmingly at his mother. 'But you haven't told me the latest with Sam.'

'I mean it. Thirty seconds. I'm counting.' Jess raised her voice. 'Sorry Anna. Not much to tell. Sam's there. I'm here.'

'So, do something different,' said Anna.

Maybe that could be her 2009 resolution. She was not having much success on the courage front…

ROB

Rob stretched out on the sofa and prised his shoes off with his toes, one heel at a time. He and Pete had spent a relaxing few days pottering in and around Mougins after their enjoyable evening in Antibes. The rest of the time they'd whiled away on backgammon, single malt whisky, and politics, accompanied by an all-encompassing eighties soundtrack. Everything from The Clash to Sade, by way of Bowie, Madness, The The and Duran Duran.

Coming back to London had been fine. He was his own master. He could choose to do whatever he wanted, which was why he now found himself lounging on the sofa, a beer in one hand, his phone in the other. As he tipped the bottle to his lips, the phone rang.

Rob answered and Sam said. 'How was France? Skiing or sunbathing?'

'A bit of skiing; not much sunbathing. It wasn't that warm.'

'And Happy New Year to you too. What's up?'

Rob took a breath. 'Not a thing. How were your celebrations?'

'Ah,' said Sam. 'Stressful.'

'The social experiment wasn't a success?'

'Not exactly. Kate as key manipulator. Unhelpful.'

'Just when you've finally laid a ghost.'

'Very witty.' Sam laughed.

'Not exactly a ghost, then?'

'Flesh and blood. Ahem.'

'That's my boy.'

'Anyway.' Sam sounded as if he was trying to pull himself together. 'What are you doing answering a message on your phone in the middle of the evening? Don't you have places to go, people to see?'

'Where do you get your information? I don't party *every* night.'

'No one you're keen to see?'

'Sam. You're reminding me of my mother. Stop fishing.'

'What happened with that girl from work? You never did tell me her name. Did you decide she was too young?'

Rob's mind slid over Hannah. Shiny, smooth, moulded, firm. A bronzed body that was almost entirely devoid of hair. Too perfect. And definitely too young. She'd been an infant in the 1980s and missed his most treasured cultural references.

'Rob?'

'Yeah. Verging on cradle-snatching.' He knew he could start it up with Hannah again. Knew that's what she wanted. Which made him feel guilty. Wielding too much power. It would be too easy to treat her badly, to remind himself of a side of his character he didn't like, a ruthless streak he was almost scared of. Which was why he kept away.

'Finally! Find yourself someone closer to our age. You might like the company. And you won't be alone on a Friday night.'

'I'm fine. I like my life.'

'Yeah, right. Say it often enough you might even sound like you're telling the truth.'

When they ended the phone call, Rob let something loud and action-packed wash over him on the TV. It was when he finally pulled himself off the sofa to brush his teeth and go to bed—rather than wake up stiff and dry-mouthed hours later—he noticed the loud silence of his flat. He barely admitted to himself that it had felt good to share a living space with Pete for four days. He'd liked hearing him padding about the bedroom opposite, making coffee in the morning, opening the big doors onto the terrace to admire the view towards the Mediterranean.

The quiet sang in his ears as he watched his reflection in the bathroom mirror. He rarely paid more attention to what he looked like than checking he'd shaved adequately and didn't have anything stuck in his teeth, but now he met his dark eyes, noticing the fine lines that bled into his top lip. Smoking. He really should kick that filthy habit.

'You look disappointed,' he said to himself, to hear what it sounded like. Slowly, he shook his head. 'No. Sad.'

He grimaced, held the pose, let his face relax. 'No you don't. It's just January. Get some sleep.'

JESS

When Jess answered the landline with a breezy, 'Hello?' she'd expected it to be Sam, or possibly her mother. But the voice at the end of the line was much more business-like.

'Jessica? James here.'

She recognised his voice immediately, her mouth dry, the hand clutching the phone slick with sweat. 'Er… James.'

'Thank you for hosting us on New Year's Eve. Fiona enjoyed getting to know Millingham. She was very interested to see where I grew up.'

'You're—you're welcome.' Her voice caught in her throat. 'It was Sam, of course.'

'I'm sure you had a substantial hand in the hospitality plans. Either way, it rounded off our night perfectly.'

Jess rubbed her forehead. 'Well, that's good.'

'So, how was the rest of your stay? Not too busy?'

Jess shook her head. Could she and James just pick up again, with niceties and polite conversation? There was a sense of unreality, as if they were reading out lines from a script.

'It was fine. It's always busy, but that's fine too.'

'I can imagine. I'm sure it's a wonderful thing to have children. But the noise…'

'Maybe that's why most people do it earlier in life, while they're young enough to withstand it.'

'I'm sure you're right. So. Jessica. I don't want to keep you. Just wanted to say thank you. For not dwelling on the past. Life is very different now. Of course, none of us would say or do things which, at the time…were quite normal. Well, at the time were socially acceptable. We all drank rather a lot, didn't we?'

'I'm not sure that's changed very much,' said Jess.

'No. I'm sure you're right. And I'm very much hoping you'll support me. It got to the point that… Well. I've been very fortunate in my career. I thought it was time to give something back. Do the right thing. For the greater good of society. You understand that don't you, Jess?'

God, she hated it when he called her Jess. 'I will be pleasantly surprised if your government are planning reforms for the greater good of society. The whole of society, rather than purely your voters.'

'Yes. Well. We all want what's best. For everyone, don't we?'

'That's a nice thought, although I'm not sure we're talking about the same thing,' said Jess. How to end this conversation? Where were the kids when she needed them?

James laughed. 'We can but hope, Jessica. All the best for the new year. Fiona's looking forward to seeing you and Sam again.'

'That would be nice,' Jess said. Really, the platitudes, just to get him off the phone.

But much later on that night, lying on her back in the middle of the double bed, trying to still her racing mind, and fall asleep, she realised something continued to unsettle her. Even via a phone call, James had the effect of making her feel tainted and vulnerable. It had done the opposite of what he hoped it would achieve, she suspected. There were good politicians who did essential work and spoke the truth.

So, why didn't she believe a single word he said?

Would this be the unreconcilable wedge between her and Sam? In so many ways it felt like a more sinister issue than how to make friends with Kate.

She stretched her limbs out into the colder parts of the bed and then rolled onto her left side, tucking the duvet behind her, and hoped to breathe towards sleep.

SAM

'You'll never guess who called,' said Jess, when Sam answered his mobile.

Sam closed the front door and switched on the lamp on the hall table to dispel the gathering darkness. 'Don't tell me. James.'

'How did you know?'

'Lucky guess. What did he say?'

'Well, to begin with, he did his politician's dance. Glad mouthing everyone, you and me included. But eventually he got to the point.'

'Which was?' He was not expecting to hear that there had been an apology.

'He didn't get too specific. And he didn't say sorry, but he did say there were things he regretted saying and doing. That things were very different twenty years ago. He said he was pleased we'd made contact again, and Fiona in particular hoped to see both of us soon. I'm afraid I was non-committal about that.'

Sam sat down at the bottom of the stairs, on the edge of the pool of light. 'Good. You are not obliged to be in the same room with him if you don't want to be. You were very brave to come with me to his wedding.'

'Ah yes. Spending a few days in your company was absolutely not the incentive. It was all James.'

'I'd be happier if he actually admitted his guilt and apologised.'

'Let's not hold our breath. You know, it's strange. I

thought I'd dealt with all of this, that I didn't need to hear him say any of it, but... He took the time to phone... You know that sensation of slipping off your shoes at the end of a hectic day, not realising how restrictive they've been...the sheer bliss of spreading your toes...'

He pressed his fingers into the inner corners of his eyes. 'We don't have to see him.'

'Did you ask him about Stuart?'

'Didn't get very far. Not sure anyone will shake his confidence in his version of events.'

'If we don't see him, then we don't need to think about him either.'

'If that's what you want, you've got it.' He had no wish to seek James out. There had always been something dark about him, that seemed to draw him to the edge of decent, acceptable behaviour, and Jess's revelation had confirmed this half-conscious understanding. He owed him no loyalty, felt no particular pang at the idea of not seeing him. Jess, and her wishes were so much more important.

When Sam put the phone down, he continued to sit at the bottom of the stairs, the house settled and quiet for once.

Whatever Jess wanted, it was fine with him. He imagined for a long moment coming home to her night after night, batting away the hurdles, the problems, the issues that would have to be solved to make that possible.

Prayer. That would help. Prayer for an everyday miracle that would bring them together under one roof. Permanently.

ROB

Walking down St James' Street from Piccadilly, Rob questioned himself again. Why had he agreed to meet Pete tonight at this private members' club, after a hectic day of interviewing, drafting, editing and scheduling when there was football on the TV, beer in the fridge? Plus, the wind was bitter. He pulled his scarf tighter around his neck.

Pete was waiting just inside the two sets of massive doors, complete with sound-muffling dark velvet curtains. Well, not exactly waiting for Rob. He was chatting up the slim, attractive young women on reception. They wore fitted jackets, pencil skirts and vertiginous heels, as it became apparent did the other female staff, when they were escorted up two flights of stairs, past the first floor bar and smaller dining areas, to the main dining room. It was seven o'clock and already half full and buzzing.

They were shown to a table along one wall, opposite another impressive bar—all bottles, mirrors, and glass—with alcove tables at either end of the room.

Pete sat down and surveyed the scene. 'It hasn't opened officially yet. The launch is next week. This is practise.'

Rob took in the various occupied tables. It was one of those places—one of those evenings—where everyone looked slightly familiar. 'Who are all these people, then?'

'Reviewers like me. I bet you'll have an invitation buried in the depths of your inbox somewhere. People of influence.' Pete grinned. 'On second thoughts, maybe you're not on the list... Restaurant and wine critics. They reputedly have an amazing wine cellar, and they'll store your own wine for you, too.'

'Speaking of which...' Rob picked up the menu and wine list.

'How about a selection of starters and mains? Gives me a range to review.'

'Sure.'

'And let's start with—a Martini?'

'Works for me.'

'Followed by their recommended house white and red. Let's see what they've gone for. What is it?'

Rob was watching the arrival of six men who were ushered to an alcove table at the far end of the room. 'There's James Gorton. And Patrick Hampson-Smith. Who are they with?'

Pete turned and studied the group. 'The Chancellor of the Exchequer? I'd say the others were political aides.'

Besides the two politicians, the other four were younger, leaner, and dapper in their dark suits.

'Civil service? Pay must have gone up. They're wearing designer suits...'

Pete raised an eyebrow. 'You're not wrong.'

Rob shrugged. 'You know what they say about public school. You went there.'

'So did you. Manchester Grammar.'

'But not boarding...'

'Oh I see,' said Pete. 'What you've seen is a procession of rent boys because boarding school was all about shagging and sodomy.'

'Er. I'm not sure I'd have put it like that.'

'Your problem, Rob, is that you have an overactive

imagination. It was not great being cooped up with testorerone-filled boys for all those years. Why do you think I'm so appreciative of women? But in my experience, there was not that much sex happening…'

'You order the drinks.' Rob pushed his chair back. 'I'm going to say hi.'

'Anyway, James was at school with you, not Patrick Hampson-Smith. What if he doesn't want to say hello?'

'Then he shouldn't have come here. Tonight.' As he walked towards James's table, he tried to quieten his mind. He wanted his full attention on James's reaction. Wanted a steer on whether his senses had picked something up or not.

He walked slowly but deliberately, giving James plenty of time to recognise him. Both he and Patrick Hampson-Smith were sitting, somewhat in shadow, with their backs to the wall, facing into the room.

He saw James's eyes widen, the edges of his mouth tighten, but then he broke into a wide smile, stood to shake hands, introduced Patrick Hampson-Smith, and then the pretty boys: Oscar, Bruno, Giovanni, and Rufus. 'Tell this man nothing,' he said. 'He's a journalist. So, Rob, what are you doing here?'

'I'm here with Pete Fletcher.'

'He's still knocking around? I heard he'd been reprimanded for allowing that on-air display of bad language.'

'Ooh, that was him?' said one of the pretty boys, twisting round in his seat.

Rob shrugged. 'You brief a guest. He knows the rules. If he chose to flout them on live radio, there are two choices about how you deal with it.'

'As the producer, he should have stopped it sooner.'

'Or perhaps it gave listeners more of an idea of what that person is really like.'

'Who was it?' one of the other boys said

'The Party chairman,' said James.

'Well, enjoy your evening,' said Rob. 'I hear the wine list is fantastic.'

'You too, Rob.'

'Give my love to Fiona.'

'Of course.'

He turned around, not before he'd seen exchanged looks from the young men. Patrick Hampson-Smith had worn a practised look of polite interest the whole time.

By the time he reached his table, the Martinis had arrived.

'Interesting?' said Pete.

'Very.' One of the young waitresses sashayed past. Rob watched Pete study her. 'Appreciative of women. That's what you said?'

Pete glanced at Rob as he took another sip of his drink. 'Your point?'

Rob shook his head, watching as she made her way towards the alcove tables. There were no appreciative looks from the two married men facing her.

JESS

Not having had awkward silences in the past few months, Jess and Sam seemed suddenly tongue-tied on the phone. Sometimes she wanted an absolute reassurance from him that he'd severed links with James, but at other times this seemed too much to expect, despite his behaviour in the past. Did she forgive James? Assume he'd learnt and moved on? If so, why did she want some sort of validation from Sam? And did he avoid any mention of James because he didn't want to upset her? This was the problem with long distance phone calls. Everything felt loaded in a way that would not apply if they were spending time in each other's company and speaking face to face.

Jess wanted to ask about Kate, whether anything had changed, but she couldn't bear to hear that everything was the same, or worse. So, that was two subjects they were avoiding. Three, if they included marriage. Jess shut down any attempts to move the conversation in that direction. It was simpler that way.

She was also trying, with varying degrees of success, to suppress thoughts of sex. Any images of Sam's hands, or mouth, or body, she quickly stamped out, but sometimes the clarity with which she saw his fingers on her thigh as she got dressed—or worse still, undressed—was disorientating.

Her prayer life had also been seriously derailed by her trip to Oxford. She could manage very little more than the shortest of prayers, although they were certainly heartfelt. But what used to feel like a conversation now sometimes felt like a futile appeal to an angry red wall in her mind. She knew that was her own guilt, that she believed in the power of redemption, of forgiveness, of complete acceptance, of a loving and merciful God. But at this point, she knew it all more as intellectual belief, than heartfelt conviction.

'Please, it's time to be in bed with the lights off.' She heaved herself off Ben's bedroom floor.

'Mum,' he said. 'I'm still doing Lego.'

'It's late.' Hopefully Millie—already read to, tucked in, light off—was almost asleep in her room. When had he stopped calling her Mummy, incidentally? He was only seven. 'I need to go downstairs and tidy up after the chaos of giving you and Millie a very late supper.' She bit back her frustration at Tom dumping the children home, exhausted, hungry and confused. He was the adult and it was his fault, and she should know better than taking it out on the kids.

Why was Tom insisting on meeting her for lunch in a public place tomorrow?

Something in what she said must have reached Ben, because he brought his Lego creations and positioned them on the bedside cabinet.

'Thank you, darling.' Jess tucked him into bed and turned the light off. 'Sleep well.'

'Night, Mummy,' he mumbled beneath the covers, making her heart sing.

Jess ran downstairs, shoved dirty plates into the dishwasher, skimmed a damp cloth over the table, flicked the kettle on, and watched it begin to bubble. Tom wanting to meet meant he had news, opening up an array of possibilities, none good.

It was now clear that the moment he left he had shut her out of everything. Her ex-husband—her husband of nearly ten years—was a stranger to her. Not only his clothes, but his style of dressing. Sloppy cords and pale jumpers had morphed into sharp black jeans and slim-fit maroon merino sweaters.

Tonight's change of plan—again—made her wonder why she clung so hard to the notion that it was not possible to move to Manchester to be with Sam. Yes, Tom would have to work hard to see the children on a regular basis, but he was present in their lives very much on his own terms, and never around to scoop them up on the rare occasion when her childcare arrangements fell apart. She would not be depriving them of seeing more of their father.

So why was she using Tom as an excuse not to try to make this relationship with Sam work? Was it cowardice that wouldn't allow her to contemplate the possibility of moving back to Millingham? She couldn't work out if in the depths of her mind returning to where she grew up, to be with the person for whom her affection had been largely unrequited throughout her teens, would somehow seem like a retreat. She and the children could live unchallenged in the London house until Millie turned eighteen. However disconcertingly Tom might have behaved, he had more sense than to stop mortgage payments, or insist that they leave the family home.

Would moving the three of them to live with Sam and his children prove too much of a loss of independence? Was that what she wanted?

She arrived early at the sleek, echoey restaurant Tom had chosen to meet for lunch. He was already there, wearing a dark suit, his palms flat on the table, as if willing himself not to fiddle. She smoothed her hands down her dress, the umpteenth outfit she'd tried on, shutting out the thought of the chaos of clothes strewn over her bed.

'Drink?' he said, as she sat down.

'Um, water?' She noticed his glass of red wine. He'd never been much of a drinker during the day. But she didn't know that about him any more. She hadn't known anything about him for the last three years.

He caught her eye.

'Dutch courage?' she asked, her mouth dry.

'No, nothing—everything's fine.'

'So what is it?'

'I apologise for losing it on the phone.'

Bloody hell, you must have terrible news to break to me. 'Accepted. Why don't you just tell me?'

'What are you going to have?'

She sighed inwardly. He was making sure they did things on his terms. The more she pushed him, the longer he'd take, so she might as well sit back and enjoy the meal. Or manage to eat something, if her churning stomach would let her. Maybe he was finally going to tell her what was going on in his life.

They ordered and Jess tried to concentrate on swallowing each mouthful, half listening to Tom talking about the political situation, the shocking state of the country and the top ten most idiotic things taxpayers' money was currently being spent on. Eventually, at the coffee stage, he sat back and scratched his scalp through his undeniably thinning hair. *Have the guts to cut it aggressively short*, she thought.

'Jess,' he said, and the dull dread at the pit of her stomach coagulated into something more. He never called her Jess. Ever. 'I've been promoted.'

'Congratulations.' She matched his flat tone of voice. There was more to come.

'Global marketing director.' He took a measured sip of his coffee.

'Are you pleased?'

A look of annoyance crossed Tom's face.

She swallowed and gripped her cup. Jumping up and down yelling, 'Tell me, you bastard,' was not going to get her anywhere.

'Based in New York.'

'What?' Surely she'd mis-heard him?

'New York. I should be there already, but I've managed to put them off until next week.'

Jess blinked, desperately trying to assimilate this information. Something at the back of her mind demanded her attention, but she needed to focus on the task in hand: not screaming at Tom.

'I don't—' She stopped and took a deep breath. 'Is this full-time?'

'Of course,' he snapped. 'You can't be global marketing director on a part-time basis.'

He sounded like a petulant child and she had the dreadful feeling she was going to laugh. 'I mean full-time in New York.'

'Full-time, based in New York.'

'What does 'based in New York' mean? How often will you be in London? How are the children going to see you?' She clamped her lips together.

'There are loads of flights every day. It's just a few hours.'

'You are joking. How often are you going to see them?'

'Don't be so melodramatic. There will be hardly any difference in the amount of time I see them.'

'But you're going to live in New York..' Really, she should try hard to keep her voice down. A shock of something that might even have been joy passed through her. If Tom wasn't living in London, then she really didn't have to either.

'It's not the other side of the world.'

'It's the other side of the Atlantic,' she spat. 'They're your children, Tom. How can you not want to see them?'

'For God's sake.' Tom glanced around the restaurant.

Yeah, that's right, not in a public place. He was far more concerned about the prospect of a public scene than about her being upset.

'I'll see them every couple of months. And holidays and all the usual stuff. That's way more than my parents saw me.'

'Don't you dare bring your emotionally stunted upbringing into this. I would no sooner send my children to boarding school at the age of eight than I would throw myself out of a plane without a parachute. *With* a parachute, come to think of it.'

'Stop crying,' he hissed.

'Yeah, you'd like that, wouldn't you? No public displays of emotion. No public displays of affection—'

'Can't you be happy for me? For my job?'

She sat back and mopped her cheeks with her napkin. 'You are unbelievable. You know, I thought you were going to tell me you'd met someone.' She saw something flit over Tom's face. 'Or tell me something about your life. I don't even know if Kurt still cuts your hair.'

'Don't change the subject.'

'I'm not changing the subject. I'm trying to understand you. I'm not sure I ever did.'

'I'm not sure you ever tried.'

She bit down hard on her bottom lip to stop crying.

Blinking, staring at her hands, trying to remember how to count to ten. Wanting to be at home. Not having to get up, out of this restaurant and fight her way onto the tube.

'I apologise. I know you tried. For several years.'

'Just not hard enough for you,' she whispered.

Somehow Jess got home. Quarter to three. Twenty minutes to pull herself together before she had to pick up the children. She washed her face and lay down on her bed for five minutes. At five to three the doorbell rang.

'Are you walking to pick up the children?' Her great friend Lucy, a mum from school with children of a similar age to Ben and Millie, stood on the doorstep.

Jess held the door open for her and tried to talk normally. 'Come in for a minute.'

'What is it? Has something happened?' Lucy searched her face.

'Tom's got a job in New York. Starting next Monday.'

'What?'

Lucy's look of outrage almost made Jess laugh. Or cry. 'Everything's arranged.' She sat down hard at the bottom of the stairs.

'So what are you going to do?'

'There's nothing I *can* do. It's already—' Jess stopped, open-mouthed.

'What? What is it?'

'Already.' She put her head in her hands. 'When I was trying to get hold of Tom before Christmas, I rang his office. Someone said his assistant Denise was already in New York. Already. They're together.'

'He's always denied it, hasn't he?'

'That's where he was last week. He wouldn't tell me where he'd gone.'

'Jess, you might be right, but you might not be. You—'

'No, I'm sure. There was a funny silence on the phone when the girl asked who I was. I knew there was something going on, but I couldn't work out what. And then it was Christmas—'

'A funny silence doesn't necessarily mean—'

'I know, but there was something today as well. When he told me about the job I said I thought he might be going to tell me he'd met someone. I couldn't work out what it was at the time, but there was a look of panic in his eyes. Barely definable, but that's what it was.'

On Wednesday morning, Jess stopped at the Stratford Services on the M40 and rang St Michael's Medical Practice. She asked when morning surgery finished, and if it was possible to speak to Dr Matt Bayliss.

'He's with a patient,' said the receptionist. 'Can I take a message?'

'Yes, please. Could you say Jessica Lamb called?' She left her mobile number and her phone rang twenty minutes up the motorway.

'Jess. Everything OK?'

'Yep. Fine. Thanks for calling back. Hoping to see Sam at lunchtime. Will he be there for a while after surgery?'

'Don't know. Want me to hold on to him for you?'

'Yes, please.'

'No problem. What sort of time?'

'Before one o'clock, if the traffic carries on like this.'

It had been a frantic twenty-four hours. By the time Lucy came back from school with the children, Jess had wrung from Tom the admission that he was seeing Denise, that the longest he would admit to being with her was six months. *How convenient*. She'd also arranged for Tom to have the children for two nights, with a possible extension over the weekend, depending on how her trip to Millingham went. When he resisted the arrangement, she reminded him that she'd hardly be able to ask him to do any spontaneous childcare once he got to New York, and at that he shut up.

She even managed to pray that night. God's presence was no longer a fierce red wall, but a place of grace, acceptance and love.

SAM

Sam had a typically busy January morning surgery. Then he had four visits to dying and elderly patients before he could go home and clear some of his paperwork. At least this afternoon he'd have time for some jobs. Book the car in for a service. He planned to drive to London and back this weekend, and the brakes needed checking. Try and get hold of the decorators Jane had recommended. Perhaps he could entice Jess to come back if he got rid of the tired Laura Ashley wallpaper in the spare room. Not to mention an overhaul of most of the other rooms in the house. He gathered what he needed for his visits and reached to switch the computer off. There was a rap on his door.

'Yes?' He could do without any delays.

'How's it going?' Matt lounged in the doorway.

'What are you looking so cheerful about?' The more he stared, the more Matt grinned.

'Nothing. Got many visits?'

'Of course. Are you on something?'

Matt shut the door and sat down. 'The usual. Wine. Food. Sex.'

'Did you want something specific, or are you just being annoying?' Sam picked up his bag.

'I did want to ask you something.' Matt glanced at his watch.

Sam could do without this. But Matt was a good friend. He sighed and put his bag back down. 'What is it?'

'Well,' said Matt.

'You don't look like someone with an embarrassing medical problem.'

'Neither do you.'

'I'm not.'

'Ah, the lovely Jess. How is she?'

'What?' Unusually, Jess had not returned his call last night. Maybe she'd been out and got in too late to ring back. *Where?*

'When are you seeing her next?'

'Look. Matt. Much as I'd love to carry on in this vein, is there something you wanted to ask? I've got loads of—' The phone rang on his desk.

'Sam? Visitor for you,' said June the receptionist.

'Who is it?'

Matt leapt out of the chair with alacrity and opened the door.

'Come on, Sam.'

'Could you come out here?' said June.

'For fuck's sake,' said Sam under his breath. He immediately regretted that word. There was nothing like it for escalating minor annoyance into full scale fury. He grabbed his bag and pounded down the corridor after Matt, swung around the corner into reception and stopped dead. Jess and Matt stood in front of the wide desk, June and Marjorie behind it.

They waited for him to say something.

'Jess. What are you doing here?' He felt caught off-balance. Thrilled. Unprepared. Nervous.

'I was just passing?' she said.

'June, Marjorie, this is my friend Jessica,' he said.

'Pleased to meet you,' they said.

'Shall we?' Sam said to her, indicating the door.

'Take it easy.' Matt kissed Jess on the cheek. 'See you

later,' he said to Sam, his eyes gleaming.

'Behave,' Sam replied. He ushered Jess through front door of the surgery towards the carpark.

The glowering clouds frowned down on them. 'Let's go and drop your car off.'

They drove in convoy the short journey to Sam's house and left Jess's car in the driveway. He would need to do his visits, but they could all wait an hour or two. 'Get in.'

'Where are we going?'

'I'm working on it. Still, it gives me an opportunity to drive you somewhere. Hello, by the way.' He kissed her. Her lips were cold but her mouth was warm, firing the blood in his veins. He reversed the car out of the driveway.

'Sorry to turn up unannounced.'

'Not a problem. What exactly did you say to Matt?'

'Just asked him to stall you. Didn't want to miss you.'

'It was rather odd. I started thinking he really did have some embarrassing medical problem. Good job you arrived when you did.'

He parked the car in the lane outside Rossington church, where they'd met in September. 'Will you be warm enough?'

'Yes.'

They walked through the lych-gate and round the side of the church to the silvered wooden bench with the view over the mere. The clouds were still lowering.

They sat for a long time, looking out over the Cheshire plain, watching the dark, bare trees being ruffled by the breeze. A lone bird wheeled over the mere on taut wings.

'Thank you for being here,' Sam said eventually.

She took a deep breath. 'You know that question you wanted to ask?'

He turned his head to look at her. 'I do.'

'I think I might—'

He closed the gap between them, kissing her cold lips. Then he pulled back and held her hands. 'Marry me?'

'Are you sure?'

'I'm sure.'

'Yes?' A smile spread across her face.

'Really?' He gave her plenty of warning, not breaking eye contact, before he kissed her again. She met his look, her smile wide, deepening the kiss, bringing back all sorts of memories of Oxford, lost in her arms, her silken soft skin, the scent of her filling his senses. Now he hugged her tighter, pulling her closer when they came up for air. 'Stay. Don't go back to London. Ever.'

She laughed. 'Ever?'

'Well, just once or twice. For very short visits.'

'Sorry to turn up at the surgery like that. I didn't mean for it to be an embarrassing public meeting.'

'Not a problem. What changed?'

'Tom's going to New York. On Monday.'

'For how long? To live?'

'Promotion. And I decided to take control. Actually, I'd already come to that conclusion.'

'How does it feel?'

'Good. Scary.'

'Wow. Look.' Sam gazed beyond her, over the mere, where the sun spilled out of the clouds on to the water. They blinked in the sunshine.

'Do you think it's a sign? Despite all the insurmountable problems?' said Jess.

'What insurmountable problems?' He pulled her closer, his arms around her waist, and kissed her, feeling light-headed.

'There's a lot to sort out.'

'Yeah, yeah, yeah. Later. Let's go home to bed.'

'Ah, that's another thing. I've been able to pray again. No sex till we're married.'

'You are not serious.'

'I am afraid so.'

'But that could take months. Unless we got married in a register office.' His heart sank as he looked at her face. 'You don't want to get married in a register office.'

'Not really. Will your vicar marry us? Slightly bizarre getting married in the church where we were both married to other people, but a certain symmetry to it.'

'That could take weeks.'

'Easter, if we get our act together, or just after. What do you think? An April wedding?'

'But what am I going to do till then?'

Jess disengaged herself from him, grinning. 'You're just going to have to exercise a little self-control.'

'But we can do what we did before?'

'No. I think the rule says something about not touching anything you don't both have.'

'What rule?' He thought rapidly. 'Well, we've both got nipples. And bottoms. Men have breasts too.'

She started walking away from him. 'I'm not sure that's what it means. I'm expecting you to be on your best behaviour.'

'For three months?' he said, appalled.

'Engagements always go very quickly. There'll be such a lot to organise—'

'And lips, and mouths, and necks, and skin, and elbows and backs of knees, and toes—'

'Shut up.'

'And ears, and calves, and eyelids, and foreheads—'

'Sam.' She swung round to face him.

'You'll have to kiss me to shut me up,' he said.

So she did.

ANNA

Anna jumped at the shrill of the telephone behind her. Not because she was absorbed in the mind-improving book group novel she held in one hand, her other arm tucked across her stomach. In truth, she'd been paying less attention to the words on the page, and more to the nagging voice in her head, urging her back onto her laptop for more final checks of the imminent spring collection. She let the book fall from her fingers and slither off her lap, unconcerned for her place in the pages, turned around and stretched for the phone. 'Hello?'

'Anna, I'm so glad you're there, I have news,' said a familiar voice.

'Jess? Is that— What's the—?'

Jess interrupted her disjointed utterings. 'We're getting married.'

'Wha—what?' Anna blinked, gripping the phone so hard her teeth ached. She opened her mouth and the grinding sound stopped. Grinding her teeth while conscious. Not good.

'I know. Crazy, crazy. I don't know what I'm doing, but it feels so right,' said Jess.

Anna sat down hard, luckily onto her comfortable sofa. 'I take it— I assume we're talking about Sam?'

'Of course Sam!'

'I thought you said spending New Year together had been a bit of a…a disaster?' She leaned back, her forearm against her forehead, the phone cradled between head and shoulder.

'Yup. His eldest, Kate, can be an absolute madam. But, somehow we'll manage, I know we will. And of course we had our four heavenly days in Oxford together at Christmas without the children,' said Jess.

'I don't think I'd— realised it was this serious.' She reached for the throw neatly draped over the back of the sofa. It was chilly on this January night, even with the heating on. Did it all feel too neat and symmetrical, a completion of a love story, a 'Happy ever after', and was that why she felt a rising pressure in her chest? It was a shaming feeling she didn't want to investigate. Not jealousy, she insisted to herself.

'Well, New Year was fraught, but despite that…I decided to go and see him. Just got in the car and drove… We're getting married—in Barton church, of course—the weekend after Easter,' said Jess.

'Knock me down with a feather.' Anna closed her eyes. She made a conscious effort to unclench her jaw again. 'I'm sorry. Congrat— congratulations, I hope you'll be very happy together.' She was pleased for Jess. Since Tom had left Jess and the children, life had been really tough. Even without her own children, Anna knew enough of her friend's life to empathise about Jess's total lack of a break, and how lacking Tom was in his role of father. Hopefully now she could relax.

'I know. It's so quick. Still, I suppose at our age…'

Anna winced. Nobody could ever accuse Jon of being quick. She twisted her platinum and diamond ring. Ten years it had been there, unencumbered by another band. 'So…you're getting married in the same church?'

'Yup. There's some weird symmetry to it. It's where Sam got married, too.'

Anna could hear the smile in Jess's voice. 'Oh, for God's sake.'

'I know,' Jess said again.

'And what's he like? Still— as gorgeous as he was last year?' Anna tried to visualise the teenager they'd all had various degrees of longing for, not least Jessica. She must have met him at various weddings, but she recalled more about his wife, an imposing hospital doctor with long dark hair and sharp dress sense. Somehow the image of Sam, the self-contained man beside her, hadn't changed very much over the past ten or fifteen years. And her designer's mind always paid more attention to his wife's clothes rather than his dark suit.

'Oh yes, he's attractive. All his own hair, but grey now. Think a mature Clark Kent.'

'And…he has how many kids?' A dull ache settled under Anna's ribs.

'Three.'

'Bloody hell.'

'I know.'

'When— when did he ask you?'

'When I drove up after New Year. I hadn't been able to work out how we could be together, what with Tom based in London. Not that he saw an enormous amount of the children…'

'But…something changed?'

'Tom's gone to work in New York.'

'Wow.' Anna leaned back into the cushions. 'I knew you liked Sam, from the way you talked about him—or didn't talk about him—but I didn't know he was the one.' But even as she said it, she felt stupid. Of course she knew. Jess had, in her own way, been indicating that he was the one since they were fourteen years old. So. Two marriages, two divorces and five kids later, they'd finally got their act together.

'Well, it's different this time. Anyway, less of that. How are you?'

'Fine, fine. So…you've set a date? Where are you going to live?'

'The Saturday after Easter. Barton Church and then at Sam's house on Woodham Road.'

'You mean you— your house too,' said Anna.

'I suppose I do,' said Jess.

'What about your house…in London?'

'Oh, my sister's going to move in here and pay the mortgage. The children will transfer to school up there for the summer term.'

'Wow. How do you feel?'

'Nervous. Excited. Snowed under with trying to organise everything.'

'I bet.'

'How's business? And Jon?'

'Fine. All fine.'

There was muffled shouting from Jess's end of the phone. 'Sorry, Anna, hang on a sec. Will you two stop it, I can't hear myself think. Back in your own beds, I'll be up in thirty seconds,' she bellowed. 'I swear they save their arguments up to have while I'm on the phone. You know what they're like.'

'Absolutely.' Despite holding them when they were tiny infants and trying to vist fairly regularly, she floundered to talk to Ben and Millie. Which made her feel guilty. She was the adult, she should know how to engage them.

'I'm afraid I'm going to have to go. I really, really hope you'll come to the wedding?'

'Of course I will.'

The phone line went dead. Anna leaned around to set

the receiver back on its cradle. One of the disadvantages of living in a village like Purseton, was that—depending on what sort of mood it was in—her mobile signal could be very erratic. Hence the landline, although few people called her on it; her father very occasionally from Poland, her mother even more infrequently from Geneva.

She thought of Jess, stepping into the unknown, her voice full of colour and hope, which made a change from when Anna had seen her last summer. Pale, hunched in on herself somehow, although even then there had been the promise of Sam, hovering between them those few sunlit days. She'd looked more on top of things in December, if a bit tear stained.

The five friends—Ruth, Stella, Caroline as well—had tried to meet for lunch before Christmas, but family and other commitments had prevented it, and they hadn't all been together since the school reunion the previous July.

She couldn't already be into the phase of her life when everyone only got together at weddings and funerals. She was only thirty-nine. This couldn't be it.

With a sigh, she fished for the dropped book. It had seemed a good idea, to join the local book group, an assortment of women of the village, led by Jenny, the vicar's wife. She had started out with good intentions, making sure to pick up the latest book at one of the terrific independent bookshops in Bath. But she hadn't loved many of them so far. She found her mood would be strongly affected by the subject matter. A Martin Amis quote came back to her: something about what you read being a constituent of how you feel...

The phone rang again, after Anna had, finally, hauled herself up from the depths of the sofa and made herself eat something. At least, in the comfort of her own house, she could be quiet and peaceful. Ten-thirty. She contemplated leaving it for the answerphone, but it could only be Jon, and then she'd have to go to the effort of ringing him back in case he wondered where she was. Not that he would. She doubted that he'd notice. No, that was not fair. Of course he'd notice.

She levered herself up from the softly worn wooden table in the middle of the large kitchen, and picked up the phone.

'Hi,' said Jon. 'What are you doing?'

'Not much,' said Anna.

He sighed. 'What is it?'

'Nothing… I'm tired.' Lonely. Alone. And sick of it. She'd bought this beautifully light, square, early Victorian house ten years ago, with the proceeds of the sale of her grandparents' house in Millingham. Jon's promise to transfer whatever he did in the city (something to do with reinsurance), to be with her had never materialised, and the seasonal demands of work meant she had not been to London since the beginning of the year.

'Bad day? Tell me about it,' said Jon.

'Go on then…' said Anna.

'What?'

'T— tell me about your bad day,' she said.

'It wasn't a bad day,' he said.

'But…you just said, "tell me about it,"'.

'I meant it literally,' he said, enunciating each word. 'Tell me about your day.'

She glanced towards the door into the hall. She wanted to climb into the bath. She wanted Jon to be here to give her a massage. Actually, it didn't even have to be him. A trained masseur would be even better. She took a deep breath, and told him about her day.

After a quick bath, she lay in bed, watching the shadows play across the ceiling. A slight breeze ruffled the leaves outside her window. She didn't begrudge Jess her happiness. Life had been grim for her after she separated from Tom, and Sam—what she'd heard of him—sounded great.

The idea of rekindling a lost love, returning to her roots, setting up home with someone from her youth, sounded reassuringly romantic. A happy ending that book-ended and made sense of her intervening life, seemed so satisfying. It was a universal, appealing love story. *Persuasion* had long been her favourite Austen, the eight years of misery between Anne Elliot's refusal of Captain Wentworth and final acceptance of his hand in marriage made worthwhile by the happy ending.

Although that was fiction.

She clenched her teeth. She was an emancipated feminist, despite the hindrance of having been brought up by her old-fashioned grandparents. She did not need to be defined by a man. Marriage was not the answer to her dilemma.

To Anna, an enduring marriage seemed more a matter of luck than judgement. So many of them seemed to continue long after the happy ending, disintegrating into disillusionment the longer they endured. She fervently wished Jess and Sam all the very best, despite the ex-spouses and several children they would have to build their blended family around.

The idea exhausted Anna. She knew she was in a rut and needed to make changes or she was going to desiccate, emotionally and creatively. She thought of her increasingly fraternal relationship with Jon, and the kind concern of her design team at work. Olga and Stefan kept encouraging her to innovate and take bold steps with the next clothing collection, while she hesitated, undecided, wanting to stay safely with what worked, what sold.

Even her life in Purseton seemed entirely pedestrian, compared to bustling Millingham. She had her lovely neighbours, Elena and Hein, South Africans who were always keen to see her when they returned from various grandparenting duties. And Jenny and Dave the vicar. Being childless, they badgered her to accompany them into Bath to see a film now and then.

The temptation to lay low, to refuse to go to the wedding, was very powerful, but not as overwhelming as the fear of missing out, and the compulsion to see Sam and everyone again.

It was the comparisons that were hardest. Because she'd grown up with that cohort, it was impossible not to look at their lives—their children, their families—without a sense of emptiness.

She'd realised her need for a child much later than all her peers. So much later that it was now too late?

ROB

Rob grabbed the pile of post, dropped it onto the coffee table, and dialled Sam's number. He listened to it ring several times before it was answered.

'Hi, Rob. You got my message?'

'I did. This is not good, Sam. James last year, you this. I can't have all my old school friends sucked into marital bliss.'

'You know, maybe you should try it. Well, try it again. With someone closer to your own age this time.'

'I have neither the time nor the staying power.'

'Quitter. What's not to like? Trust me, I'm a doctor. Married people—especially men—live longer, happier, more fulfilled lives. Companionship. Regular sex. Someone to talk to, someone to care about you and give you a hug whenever you need it.'

'Not to mention the domestic drudgery of their grey knickers hanging on the drying thing, and whining children, and being nagged to empty the bins, and them wanting to watch romantic films and—'

'What are you talking about? I thought you were all over girls' knickers?' Sam stopped. 'That didn't come out quite how I meant it. I'm sure you're a sucker for lingerie.' He said the last word in a French accent.

'Lingerie,' said Rob, imitating the accent, 'I'm completely into. The idea of silk and lace and suspenders and all that, bring it on. But then they stop wearing it, and it's knickers that have been washed a thousand times, hanging on the—'

'If that's what stops you getting married, buy her some new ones every couple of months, and chuck the others in the bin. It's not like you couldn't afford it.'

'I will bear that in mind should I ever find myself in danger of straying too close to the idea of matrimony.' Rob sank back into the sofa. It had always been uncomfortable, but he'd never had a strong enough urge to change it. 'Anyway. Congratulations. I hope you'll be very happy.'

'Thank you. That means a lot coming from you.'

'Really. I hope it turns out for the best. How's Kate taking it?'

Sam sighed. 'Not so well. My first-born is proving a trial. She's barely twelve and sometimes I wish she was… closer to eighteen.'

'And how's Jess?'

Sam laughed. 'Great. Throwing herself into organizing the wedding. Please tell me you can make the date.'

'Yep. I'm in the US for various things in March, but I'll be back by then. I'll probably be around the week before, as I'm planning to spend Easter with Mum and Dad.'

'Oh good and dutiful son. How are they? I haven't seen them for a while.'

'Obsessed with plans to go to Sydney to see Natalie and the grandchildren.'

'Ah.'

'What does that mean?' Rob demanded.

'Nothing. Just goes back to what I was saying earlier.'

'No it doesn't. You were talking about marriage, not procreation.'

'Which often goes hand in hand. You should think about it.'

'No. I want a wife and child like I want a hole in the head. Anyway, this flat isn't big enough. The lift's not that reliable. Carting a buggy up four floors would be a deal-breaker. Not to mention breathing in polluted Earl's Court air and—'

'I am fascinated that you've thought so long and hard about this.'

Rob paused, reflecting on what he'd just said.

'I think you're so set on saying no to this, you no longer entertain the possibility of another sort of life.'

'No, Sam.' That was his reflex answer, and he was sticking to it. He had no wish to change his life, and relished the idea that he could dash off to Reykjavik or Istanbul or Bangkok at a moment's notice. Could. If he wanted to. 'So, the wedding. Is James going to be your Best Man again?'

'Uh, no. I've asked Will this time.'

'Why?' Rob sat up, elbows on his knees.

'I wanted my brother. Should have asked him last time.'

'What about James? Is this because he didn't ask you to be *his* Best Man?'

'No. I just wanted Will. No other reason.'

Rob waited. What was he missing? What Sam was telling him didn't make much sense. James was his oldest and best friend. Wasn't he?

'Really. There's no angle here, Rob.'

'If you say so.'

He reached for his notebook and made a couple of notes after he put the phone down. Maybe he'd ring James. Just to get his side of the story.

EIGHTEEN YEARS PREVIOUSLY

It had been in her final year at university. A night when a friend had appealed to her, having missed the last train.

'Fine,' she'd said. 'But I'm only offering you the floor.'

They'd had a few lagers in the clubhouse of the hall of residence over the course of the evening. She'd had halves to his pints, but even so, she didn't consider either of them drunk. He'd behaved gallantly, retreating to the communal bathroom on her corridor while she got ready for bed. Once the light was off, they had chatted a bit, him lying in her camping sleeping bag on the rug on the floor, one of her two pillows tucked under his head.

It had taken her a while to get to sleep in her single bed, the unfamiliar sound of his breathing, his faint male smell heightening her own awareness. He'd even suggested a cuddle, low laughter hitting her solar plexus when she demurred.

The next thing she knew, was the weight of him on top of her, pushing himself into her, his thighs rough and hairy against her nakedness, pressing her legs apart. Dry skin. Endless friction. In out, in out. Pain that radiated through her core, a terrible feeling of revulsion, of 'Get out!' His head beside hers as he manoeuvred.

Scalp-crawling horror overtook her. A feeling of inexplicable incomprehension. The sense of hurtling into the epicentre of an experience with no understanding of what had happened. How was she lying here pinioned by his weight? How was he doing this?

She didn't cry out, couldn't open her parched mouth. She kept silent, eyes shut, arms on the bed. Skin on skin friction continued as he grunted, breathed harder. Harder. Until he slumped, his full weight on top of her. He was very heavy, her breasts squashed.

He lay, his penis shrinking, the hot pain dulling, until she feared he'd gone to sleep, but then he levered himself up, pushed off the bed.

She turned on her side facing the wall, dragging the duvet over her nakedness, pulling her t-shirt down over her raw, exposed breasts. There was light beyond the curtains, shafting through the cracks at either side, but it was the orange hue of electric streetlights, not natural sunshine. She kept her eyes shut. She had no sense of what time it was.

She heard him stretch out into the sleeping bag. Quickly his breathing deepened and he began to snore. She didn't dare turn round and feel for her watch. Instead, she lay there with her tears seeping into her pillow, feeling her nostrils become clogged with snot. No tissues. No handkerchief. None for her nose. None for the cold trickle between her legs.

She folded her arms over her chest, pressed her face into the pillow. Eventually he would leave, and she would open the window, strip the bed, wash the sheets, get rid of her pyjamas.

He did finally get dressed and leave, her shoulder resolutely turned away from the room, her hands clamped under her armpits, feet tucked under her bottom. She sensed rather than heard him turn to look at her, before he opened the door.

She willed him not to say anything.

She counted to ten after he left.

Then she took two steps to the door, turned the lock, two steps back, wrapped herself in her duvet and eased her mouth open, trying to unclench the muscles in her jaw.

When she'd stopped shaking, when she heard her next door neighbour Liv moving about, she'd tied her dressing gown over her t-shirt and retrieved her pyjama bottoms from the floor. Every movement was an effort, as if she'd forgotten how to co-ordinate her limbs. She made her way gingerly to the communal bathroom.

There she ran a bath, had the hottest shower she could stand. Cupped herself between her legs where she could still feel a terrible friction, and eased herself into the bath when it was decently full. Slowly, she lathered under her arms, across her bruised and tender breasts, over her stomach, her thighs, anywhere she'd had to endure his skin on hers.

Then, she put her palm once again on her pubic bone, fingers between her legs, feeling the bruised, stretched flesh, so hot and sore to the touch.

It seemed inconceivable that she regained consciousness so late, once he had pulled off her pyjama bottoms, pushed up her t-shirt, was already on top of her, thrusting into her. How could that be? How could she tell anyone what had happened? Who would believe that she had not consented? She hadn't even said no.

She hadn't had the guts to say a single word.

She vowed she would never be alone with him ever again.

JESS

Wrapped in a white towel, Jess stared out of the bedroom window to the wide lawn below. She was in her mother's great friend Mary's house, getting ready for the wedding. Odd really, to be here again so many years later; a marquee had been pitched on that lawn to celebrate Jess's first marriage to Tom, many years before.

So much had happened since then. Now she had a seven-year-old son and a five-year-old daughter. She and Tom had been divorced for nearly three years, separated for longer, and the trajectory of her painfully empty life had been switched onto a very different path by encountering Sam Rushmore again the previous summer.

Returning to Millingham for the twenty year school reunion last summer had broken the seal on the past. Teenage parties. Pop songs. Sunday morning church. Sunday night YF (Youth Fellowship, a youth club connected to the church more by geography than faith). Girl Guides. Riding her bike. Her sloping roofed room at the top of the house, where she had lain in her single bed and fantasized about Sam Rushmore.

That childhood bedroom had been her world for so many years. She remembered revising for her A Levels at the same time as her father was in the throes of leaving her mother, and the intensity of that period of study. European history: the Renaissance in Italy, the Reformation in Germany. British history: the Tudor dynasty, Henry VIII, Elizabeth I. In literature it was *Macbeth*, *Coriolanus*, Milton's

Lycidas, the novels *Middlemarch* and *Emma*. Still she could quote them. Usually the bleak, depressing passages: *Bitter constraint and sad occasion dear/Compels me to disturb your season due;/For Lycidas is dead, dead ere his prime,/Young Lycidas, and hath not left his peer.*

When she met Sam again, in some way it felt as if their interrupted story was picking up where it left off. Each with a failed marriage behind them and a handful of children, even the most casual of meetings—a cup of tea, a phone call, a meal—felt imbued with significance. She had to keep telling herself to stay in the moment, although the compelling urge to veer off in other directions, as her mind landed on this scenario or that circumstance, this look or that touch, was almost impossible to resist.

When she spent time with Sam, that first week the previous July, she had felt as if her mind was screaming at him. That she couldn't possibly be acting normally. That he must have been able to hear the shouting in her head.

It helped that he had been so calm, so kind. He had left space for the voices to dwindle to a whisper. In the end she could hear what he was saying, rather than continuing to exist in her own impermeable bubble, batted about in a loud, rough world. The bubble itself dissolved away when she sat in his garden, their hands almost touching, nothing between them but air.

With her living in London, the days they spent together last autumn became intense passages of time, culminating in her running away from Christmas in Brussels with her brother and family, to meet Sam at his brother's house in Oxford. All the children with their other parent. Alone at last.

She had a visceral, physical memory of Sam's weight, moving between her thighs, of his hands on her breasts, of the cool, sweet taste of his kiss.

A technicolour promise of sex, after three long months of chaste engagement. Which had seemed a romantic idea at first…

Sometimes standing too close to him, her senses assaulted by the tang of citrus, her stomach would somersault, her palms itching, her mouth drying on the instant.

She shook herself, glancing at the cream satin dress that hung on the wardrobe door. She had to get a move on. They'd got this far, in the face of some interesting curve balls, such as Kate agreeing to be part of the wedding party ('Don't mention the word bridesmaid!'), as long as she could wear black. Eventually a maroon dress had been agreed upon. It really suited her, complementing Kate's dark colouring, and long dark hair—in many ways so like her father—and Jess had felt momentarily magnanimous as they bought it, suppressing her own opinion. Maroon was one of her least favourite colours.

Emma and her own daughter Millie, had been very happy with similar dresses in a deep pink, and the flowers had been chosen accordingly. There Jess's pleasure was undiluted. Downstairs, in buckets, stood a large hand-tied bunch, and three posies, of mainly white and pale green flowers, with a few pink roses, and a dark velvety red one. Maybe no one but Jess and her parents would remember the significance of that rose. Her father Nathaniel had sent his elder daughter a dozen red roses on the morning of her first A Level exam, having left the family home to live with his secretary barely a fortnight earlier. He had walked her down the aisle once before. Their wobbly détente had extended to asking him to do the honours once again; he had accepted with alacrity.

Jess twisted the sapphire engagement ring on her left

hand. The pleasing weight of it. The way it had woken her up. This marriage was going to be very different. She and Sam knew each other so much better than she'd ever known Tom. That quick engagement and marriage had caused her close friends—and her mother—to question the need for such haste. The overnight change in her ex-husband's behaviour when they returned from honeymoon had been a dreadful shock, for which she'd somehow felt culpable. She should have *known* he was a control freak, but she'd been so overwhelmed by Tom that she'd refused to contemplate anything that didn't fit her fairytale.

But that wasn't Sam. He was a solid, dependable presence; a true partner. He didn't strive to change her.

Somehow they would combine their families into a smoothly working unit. And she wasn't doing any of this alone. It was an exciting project.

Yes, she was exhausted, but Sam was wonderfully unlike Tom. He allowed her to be the person she was, rather than performing a part and falling short. With Tom, there had always been an underlying agenda, for which she'd had no brief.

She had a second chance at contentment, and if she was feeling nervous, that was only to be expected. Engagements were always a strain, weren't they? Not to mention the "no sex" rule. Yet again, she questioned the wisdom of imposing such a constraint on herself and Sam.

It had been an aspiration, a pure, pleasing, honouring goal, which had begun to feel like yet another heavy burden to shoulder. She shivered and pulled the towel tighter around her. It really was time to put on her wedding dress.

Things wouldn't go wrong this time. They simply couldn't.

SAM

Eventually, Sam managed to disappear upstairs for a shower. His brother Will and wife Diana had hit the ground running when they arrived earlier in the week. Producing regular meals, taking their girls, and whichever of his own children could be persuaded, to run off excess energy on Barton Common, and generally keep control.

He had finished his last GP surgery on Friday afternoon, and now had a week off work. During this three month engagement, which seemed to have simultaneously lasted for ever and to have become a bullet train hurtling to its destination, he and Jess had enjoyed many speculative conversations about where they could go on honeymoon. A European city break. Something closer to home: York, Glasgow, Edinburgh, Bath. An adventure in the Mediterranean, or further afield. Finally Sam had asked Jess if she'd really like a busy, activity-filled week, or if she'd prefer quiet: a peaceful room with a comfortable bed, meals on hand, fresh air and big skies. They'd chosen the Lake District. He'd booked two nights in a special hotel overlooking Windermere, the remainder of the week in a cottage towards Coniston.

And now here he was, hurrying into his best dark suit, on his wedding day. He thought back briefly to his previous wedding—getting ready in the same house, being married in the same church—and yet so much had changed. Then, James, his best friend from school, had been his Best Man. This time it would be his brother Will. James, now that he was an MP and a rising star in the government, had found himself with some essential constituency business to attend to this weekend. Not that Rob needed to know any more than he already did.

When Sam had met Jess again the previous summer, he realised he didn't spend a huge amount of time dwelling on the past. Not in the way Jess did. One of the things that training to be a doctor had taught him was the importance of being present in the room. He shuddered to remember his first rotation in Accident and Emergency, one of the most stressful periods of his working life. He could tell that his body was on high alert—in the throes of that 'fight or flight' stimulation—forever expecting the vast double doors to the ambulance bay to crash open and some indescribable human calamity to flood into A & E. At a time when any of the doctors who actually knew what they were doing had faded away for a coffee or a kip.

All junior doctors had tales of dreadful mistakes, the jeopardized patient, the fatal decisions, but what Sam learned in those early years, was to stay in the room. Daydreaming, imagining, remembering, these were all dangerous luxuries. A good doctor focused on the patient. Looked, listened, touched, intuited. There was no substitute for acute observation and attention to detail.

Being a GP now, he didn't need the heightened levels of awareness he learned in the hospital A & E departments and wards, but it was useful.

It had been really useful when he met Jess again. They had crossed paths infrequently over the years, although he didn't think either of them had been paying much attention. But there was something about her, when she and her children pitched up on his doorstep. Three waifs and strays, a palpable air of sadness hanging over them, which certainly brought out the doctor's instincts in him.

He soon noticed that the calmer he could be, the more Jess matched him. He deliberately left pauses, not just so he could hear what she would say, but to slow the pace of communication. She often had that look on her face, the one where he could tell she was listening to a compelling inner voice. Her breathing quickened, shallowed, her movements jerky, flighty, her attention elsewhere. Her hands would twist together, fiddling with her rings, her earrings, tucking her hair continually behind her ears.

There were things he hadn't noticed when they were growing up. Then, she was surrounded by bigger characters, girls who attracted the gaze of the boys, while Jessica, slightly behind them, quieter, hesitant, haunted the shadows.

The night she came into focus—*that* New Year's Eve, the last year of sixth form—she was soft and sweet and sexy in a completely unexpected way. He didn't know why he reached for her that evening, nor why he didn't reach for her again, but that one night was perfect. She had felt so right in his arms, the weight of her, the smooth pallor of her skin—her cheek, her hands, the soft touch of her lips, the warmth of her mouth. Holding hands with her as they walked to Lake Court and back in the snow, felt natural and right. She was the right height, her arm was the right length, her strides mirrored his. They could easily have won a three-legged race because they were two matched halves of the same whole.

Sam extracted the silk tie Jess had given to him to coordinate with the white, pink and green theme, and stood in front of the full length mirror on the front of the mahogany wardrobe. He had played hide and seek many times as a child, trying to unlock the door without a sound, squeezing into the space between his parents' evening clothes, clutching the door closed, holding his breath for a sound. It had been his preferred hiding place, and it had taken a while for him to work out why his brother was so successful at finding him. He focused on his reflection, pleased that Jess had advised him to have his hair cut three weeks ago. It was the right length now, not too long on top, still short and smart around the back and sides, as he tied his tie. White shirt. Handkerchief. Rings.

The promise of sex, after three long months.

'What are you grinning at?' Will appeared at the door. 'How're you doing for time?'

'Fine. Do you want these, in your capacity as Best Man?' Sam handed him the rings.

'Thanks.' Will stood behind Sam in his dark suit, fractionally taller, wearing glasses. They were unmistakably brothers. 'Shall I drive you to the church?'

Sam turned away from the mirror. 'No. I want to walk.'

'Nervous? Want me to get you out of being the groom?'

'Absolutely not.'

'Good, we like her.'

Sam turned away from his brother. His pulse picked up when he thought about Jess. Three months was too long. There had been a couple of heated moments when he wanted nothing more than to make love to her, but they'd agreed to wait. He relived moments from their four days in Oxford at Christmas—the taste of her, the feel of her arms and legs wrapped around him, the sense of coming home. The need to hear her sharp intake of breath, the flush of heat on her skin, her eyes half closed as his fingertips traced across her collarbone, stroking down to her breast, heavy in his hand.

'You're getting married,' he told himself. 'In church.'

Will clapped him on the back. 'That's my boy. Just keep telling yourself, and you'll be fine.'

ANNA

Caroline crossed the road to kiss Anna. 'Hello, love, how are you?'

'Fine— thank you. Déjà-vu— or what?' said Anna, hanging onto her hat. It was that sort of wedding.

Caroline, in an elegant lavender dress and coat, was wearing a pale pink hat on top of her curly dark hair, which she gripped as she bent her head carefully to be kissed on both cheeks.

Anna was in one of her own creations. A stone-coloured linen sleeveless dress, coat and chiffon scarf, her blond curls trapped under a cream hat. The dress was flattering, skimming in all the right places, and the floaty scarf gave her a cloud of gauzy camouflage to hide behind. Which suited both the subdued palette of her clothes and her mood. She had no wish to draw attention to herself in any way.

'Isn't it just?' said Caroline. 'I didn't go to Sam's wedding but we were all here for Jess's, weren't we?'

Anna's eyes flickered towards Caroline's husband Philip, who was walking at a slower pace with their daughters, Rebecca and Catriona. She put her hand to her chest, glancing round for Jon. How long did it take to park a car? She'd be glad to have him beside her. She had of course known Philip would be here, had thought it would be *fine*, but somehow she felt caught. Jittery.

'Where's Jon?' asked Caroline.

'Par— parking the car. Nearer to the...house.' Anna

cleared her throat firmly. *I am a grown up who can speak in complete sentences.* She turned away abruptly, jolted by an unexpected sense of guilt and betrayal. Caroline was the last person from whom she wanted sympathetic looks.

'Thankfully everything's close,' said Caroline. 'We can roll down the hill from the reception. Oh, there's Stella.'

Their old school friend, two small children in tow and a fourteen-month-old in her arms, reached the low wall of the churchyard and waved.

'And— there's Ruth,' said Anna. All together again. Families. Apart from her and Jon. For so long, her child-free life had been just what she wanted. Unencumbered. Flexible. Selfish.

Suddenly it wasn't enough.

'I've just seen Rob Randall,' said Stella, as she met them, a willowy vision in an art deco patterned dress and vast wrap. Douglas, Stella's tall, good-looking husband caught up with his wife, grabbing their two sons before they scattered.

Stella looked radiant, fecund, sexy.

'You're so slim,' said Anna. *Tummy in, shoulders back, head up, lose that double chin.*

'Rob's exactly the same. So good-looking. Can't believe all those drugs and debauched living have left no mark on him whatsoever.' Stella kissed them both.

Anna had found herself wondering if Rob would come to the wedding and concluded that he probably wouldn't. She envisioned a complicated choreography throughout the reception, avoiding Philip *and* Rob. His stupidly alliterative name set her teeth on edge.

Jon's absence was beginning to annoy her. She had had serious misgivings about coming to this wedding, and it would have been a hundred times worse, if she'd had to navigate it alone. But increasingly, even when Jon was right there, she felt alone. Somehow last year, around the twenty year school reunion, it had been so much more manageable. Then, it had just been the girls. Then, she'd been able to tease single Jess about finding and using a man for sex. Now, with the situation so very different, she felt at a disadvantage. All her own values and choices no longer seemed so strong, so right, so firmly planted.

'Haven't we been here before?' said Ruth, husband Andy and two-year-old Jack beside her. She squinted up at the square sandstone church tower from which the bells rang out.

'At least it's dry and sunny,' said Caroline.

'Do you remember Friday evenings in the graveyard when we used to stand round those vast tombs and try to summon spirits?' said Stella.

'You sound like Jess,' said Ruth.

'Speaking of whom,' said Jon, wandering up at last. He looked unmistakably English, in a slim-fitting, buttoned-up dark suit.

His nonchalance grated on Anna. Despite the breeze, she felt hot and cross.

Jess's brother drove up to the church gate in a dark Volvo.

'They're walking home to the reception, so they decided against a special wedding car,' said Caroline.

'Ooh,' said Stella. 'We'd better find a seat.'

Jess, a vision in deep cream bias-cut satin and light wrap, emerged from the car, her father beside her. Anna nodded. The simplicity of the elegant dress suited Jess's slim figure perfectly.

Contrary to the usual feeling she had when she visited places from her past, Anna was surprised by how big the church was. She'd forgotten its vast presence on the brow of the hill, overlooking the Cheshire plain. Brought up by her grandparents on the other side of Millingham, she had not frequented the church as often as her contemporaries who lived much closer. Stella had been in the church choir, along with Sam, Sebastian and James. Curiously, it had been one of the things Anna had liked about Rob—that he *wasn't* in the choir.

She and Jon found a pew with Ruth and Andy.

She looked around, spotting Jess's mother, stepfather and sister in the front left-hand pew, and two heads, one greyer than the other, on the right-hand-side, presumably Sam and his Best Man. As if on cue Caroline turned from the pew in front and whispered, 'His brother Will's Best Man, remember him?'

The sounding of the organ drew their attention and they all stood up. Anna looked from Sam beaming up the aisle, to Jess, her brown hair shining, her face creased into a smile, on her father's arm. Nathaniel Lamb was as dashing as ever, and Anna smiled. She'd always had a soft spot for him—a nightmare as a parent no doubt—but a delight to flirt with at drinks parties. 'No, no, call me Nathaniel,' he would say, keeping his eyes firmly on her face. It was a slightly hysterical, intense gaze she soon learnt to recognize when she went to university. The polite 'I'm treating you as an intelligent human being, even though I'm dying to stare at your breasts,' look that produced a fine sheen of sweat on men's upper lips. Or temples, in Nathaniel Grove's case, she recalled. Nowadays she took pity on men and most of the time wore all-covering shifts, never anything tight. Definitely no cleavage. She glanced down. This dress was the most fitted garment she'd worn in ages, but luckily the long coat and scarf disguised the lumps and bumps to a degree.

She watched Jess reach Sam, his grin wide, and then felt her stomach fall away as she saw Will Rushmore. He'd always been Sam's unobtainable older brother. He was wearing exceptionally well: no excess weight, just the odd grey hair.

Anna turned her head and caught Ruth's eye. So many people she used to know really well. Sometimes, even with the girls, they were more like familiar strangers. Maybe this was what happened when lives moved in different directions. There were fewer and fewer shared life experiences to keep them together.

The service was short, and for Anna the most moving moment was when Jess and Sam turned to face each other for the vows. Their voices were full of certainty, as they committed themselves to this marriage. Anna herself had never felt that pull. Commitment didn't need a certificate of authentication. Was that why she'd never brought up actual marriage with Jon, once she'd accepted his ring? She couldn't even remember. He hadn't mentioned it for years. But maybe it felt different if children were involved. Maybe that was why Jess had been so keen. Twice. That, or God. Anna couldn't quite understand the difference between sex in a committed relationship or in a marriage, but Jess did.

The watery sunshine outside made them blink as they followed the bridal party out of the south door into the graveyard for photos.

There was a lot of kissing of cheeks and repeating exclamations, 'You look exactly the same,' and 'I can't believe it's been nearly twenty years…' Babies and children were cooed over and Anna breathed a sigh of relief for Jon's detachment. Whatever he might think about things privately—and less and less did she seem to know his mind—he could just switch off and chat and deflect unwanted questions and be. Just be. His self-containment had always been attractive, had been something to learn, to aspire to. So her growing irritation made no sense. She wanted that self-possession, that assured confidence, didn't she?

'Gorgeous, isn't he?' Stella said into her ear.

Anna jumped, aware she'd been staring vacantly into space. Or, as it turned out, not quite space, but the broad torso of a man in a light linen suit, tie already loosened, top button of his shirt undone. She lifted her gaze to the brown flashing eyes of Rob Randall. Instantly recognizable, not just because he still looked remarkably familiar and youthful, but also from his by-line photo. He raised an eyebrow and grinned at her.

What an idiot she was. She turned to Stella. 'Uh… Who?'

'You know who. He's just been in the States for three weeks. Reported on the Oscars among other things. Obviously got some sun while he was there.'

Anna turned her back on Rob. He had that appraising look she'd seen before on journalists' faces. The one she didn't trust. Standing talking to Andy, and Stella's husband Doug, Jon's precise attire made a marked contrast to Rob's open-neck relaxation.

After photos, they walked down Woodham Road to the house in which the Rushmore boys had grown up, and where Sam, and now Jess and the children would live. It all felt too neat, too 'Happy Families' to Anna, but maybe that was because she was jealous. If that was what she was. Extremely young looking waitresses (apparently sixth formers at the girls' grammar school) took their coats—Anna elected to keep hers on—and handed them glasses of champagne. She drank hers too quickly, and found herself planning all movements deliberately, so as not to give herself away, self-conscious when she least wanted to be. Idiot. On an empty stomach too.

She chatted with Ruth about her high-powered job in the city and the impossibility of being a working mother, with Caroline about her part-time Psychology MSc and her daughters, with Stella about her children and the jewellery business. She talked to Jess and Sam, who both looked heart-breakingly happy. He made an endearing speech about how the timing had never been right until they met again last summer, that their story had not been complete until they reached their happy ending. Will's speech about the sheer relief he'd felt on hearing that Sam had got together with Jess made them all laugh, and reminded Anna of the teenage crush she and the girls had had on him. His wife Diana looked as calm and beautiful as ever. And slim. Anna sucked in her tummy, trying not to stick her chest out at the same time. She felt like a tube of toothpaste, and about as attractive. Squeezing one part of her only made it all bulge out elsewhere. Maybe there was no other alternative. Getting drunk was the only way to survive.

'Ooh, Rob.' Stella grabbed his arm as he wandered past and drew him into their circle. 'You look so great.'

Anna's gaze flicked towards Doug, who rolled his eyes and carried on his conversation with Jon about house prices. She turned back towards Stella and Rob, who met her gaze.

'Thank you,' he said.

He looked good for forty, with his luxurious dark hair, his smooth brown skin.

'How've you been?' said Stella. 'How was LA?'

'Fine. Busy. LA was great.' He turned his head to look at Stella, but Anna had the sense he hadn't finished with her yet.

'That's the most phenomenal cake,' said Ruth.

Anna caught her eye in mutual understanding: look, don't touch.

'It's vast. What are they going to do with all those layers?' said Caroline.

'That's easy,' said Stella. 'The top layer's a Christening cake of course.'

Anna winced. So delightful to be surrounded by the perpetually fecund. A quick glance told her Jon had chosen to ignore the remark. A physical ache started in her chest and to her horror she felt tears hot and threatening in her eyes. She had to get some fresh air. She focused on her champagne glass, which had been topped up several times already. How disappointingly predictable. Silly cow that she was.

'You're not serious,' said Ruth.

'Don't be so sure,' said Stella. 'They're besotted with each other, of course they want a baby together.'

Anna swallowed, blinked, caught Rob's eye opposite her across the group. She looked away, took a step backwards, willing the conversation not to stop, put down her glass, made for the French windows. The garden was closer than the loo. She stepped outside, shivering at the cool air after the warmth of the crowded house.

Some of the children were playing with a ball at the end of the lawn.

Anna blinked and imagined for a second that one of

those soft cheeked, smooth-skinned faces was hers to kiss and comfort. One small fantasy before she stamped on it again.

'Adorable, aren't they?' said a deep voice beside her. A brown hand held out a glass of water. She assumed it was water.

'Water?' she said, not looking up.

'Would you prefer vodka? Or gin? It can be arranged.' Rob's elbow nudged hers through the thin linen sleeve. Their fingers touched briefly as she gripped the glass.

'Cigarette?' he said.

'I don't.'

'I shouldn't.'

The act of smoking had lost none of its sexy charm since last she looked. Disgusting habit that it was. She blinked rapidly, focusing on the small, sturdy figures at the end of the garden.

Rob stood there, taking the occasional drag. Quiet. Calm.

He felt substantial beside her. Tall. Over six feet and broad with it. No paunch to be seen. All over tan, perhaps?

Millie started wailing. 'Ow, it hit me,' she gulped, pointing to a silver football. She ran towards them.

Anna bent down to the little girl. 'Where? There?' She rubbed Millie's shin. 'How's that?'

'Better,' said Millie and put her arms round Anna in a hug.

Afterwards Anna wondered if she might have papered over the cracks, without that hug.

'Millie. Honey. Could you take this glass back into the house for Anna? There's a love,' Rob said. He disengaged the small arms and transferred the water glass from

Anna's hands to Millie's, who trotted towards the kitchen.

'Why don't we take a walk?' said Rob, taking Anna's hand and pulling her up.

'Uh… Where?' she said, taking back her hand.

He shrugged. 'Tennis courts?' He nodded towards the gate at the end of the garden.

Anna was too tired to raise objections. And she wanted some privacy. One pair of prying eyes was better than fifty or more.

'After you,' he said.

So she walked down the path with the tears washing down her face, silent still, but knowing the snivelling, snotty, nose-dripping stuff was welling. She had a handkerchief in her bag. But that was inside the house. Strange how one's brain could settle on the most mundane, practical problem in a crisis.

She stopped at the gate and Rob leaned round her and opened it. There was a knack with the catch. The tennis court closest to them was empty.

'The common?' he said, pointing to the right.

She turned, blind and blocked up from the tears, in the direction he pointed, stopping to let him open the second gate onto the wide expanse of green dipping away from them, oaks and beech trees in bud in the distance. It was quiet apart from a couple of dogs and their owners.

Rob walked beside her, a clean, folded, white handkerchief held out in his hand.

She raised her eyes for a split second in acknowledgement, grabbed it and blew. Perhaps he wouldn't notice if she just covered her face and never resurfaced. She mopped her eyes. Piggy and red, they'd be. Clogged with mascara. Really attractive.

There was the remembered hot flush of teenage

embarrassment when she'd been caught gazing inadvertently at Rob's midriff less than two hours ago. The heat of her back plastering her linen dress to her skin, the pooled moisture in her armpits, under the soles of her feet.

Stella's twittering comments about how good-looking Rob was had made her feel uncomfortable. Physical beauty—why did it matter? So much had changed over time. Twenty years in the past, she'd worked in places where misogyny and derogatory comments were the norm—and laughed off as jokes—whenever a brave female took exception to something.

Her professional life had focused on appearance, and—like it or not—there was no getting away from the inevitable judgement on what a person looked like. So what if his smooth brown skin gleamed, his dark, dark hair shone, his deep brown eyes sparkled so appealingly? He was just a man. Shouldn't his actions count more than his ease upon the eye?

In his teens he'd been an enthusiastic, bouncing bundle of slightly unpredictable energy. Well-meaning, but not entirely safe. Now, his colourful media profile, his loud opinions, his bad boy reputation, produced a prickly awareness that crept across her skin, as if she'd ignite if he touched her.

She blew her nose again and folded the handkerchief. 'I think…I think I'll have to send it to you.'

'Keep it,' he said. 'What about your shoes?'

'You want them too?' She stared at her cream, heeled sling-backs.

'They are pretty gorgeous.'

'The only bit of me that never puts on weight.' She slapped hand to forehead. 'Sorry. Sorry.'

'Can you walk in them?' he said, indicating the path.

'I think I'll manage.'

'As long as you're not going to give me grief about your feet hurting.'

'Hurting?'

'They're heels. They might rub. You could get sore feet,' he said; slowly, clearly.

'I get the idea,' she repeated; slowly, clearly. 'There's a distinct possibility I've worn heels before.'

'Just checking you're not a whiner,' Rob said.

'You can always go back,' she said.

'When I'm having this much fun?'

They walked across the common and Anna was grateful for the silence. Maybe the hoards were too much for her. Perhaps she spent too much time on her own.

'Lake Court?' said Rob, when they arrived at the trees on the other side.

'Is— is it still there?' Anna said.

'Far as I know.'

They walked through the old stone gateway and round the small lake. It was more of a large pond really.

'Shame it's too cold to sit down,' she said.

'Are you cold?' he said.

'Cold?' she replied. *Why am I unable to answer a question?* She hadn't thought about it, but perhaps she was cold.

He picked up her hand. 'Cold.'

She pulled away. 'I'm fine.'

'Yeah.' He eyed her. 'You look fine.'

She swallowed and averted her face as they walked up the path past the old house, onto the abundant grass that, twenty years ago, had been two well-kept tennis courts.

'I will be fine.' She spoke more loudly than she meant to.

'Good. Want to tell me about it?'

'No.'

'Fair enough.' He surveyed her.

She scanned the green landscape. 'Do you…have kids?'

'Not as far as I know.' He blinked. 'No. I don't. What have you heard?'

'Nothing. Except your— your reputation precedes you.'

'My what?' He swung round to face her, pulling her around by her arm.

She shrugged. 'There are things I know about you.'

'No. There are things you've read about me.'

'You deny it all?'

A twitch of the lips. 'Well. That depends.'

His smile—'his dazzling smile' was actually an apt description—distracted her for an instant.

'On what? On how you like to portray yourself?'

'Don't forget, you knew me long before all the fame stuff.'

'So, you haven't changed?'

'Do people change? Don't we fundamentally stay the same?'

'That's depressing,' she said.

'Or comforting. To have friends around you who've known you for so much of your life.'

'Do you see much of Sam?'

'Yup, we stay in touch. Like you and Jess and the others…'

'Mm.'

'You like the consistency of old friends who know you well, I'm sure.'

'So, this wedding—old friends reunited after so many years—has a pleasing symmetry to you, does it?' Why was this conversation so annoying? It was as if they'd swapped roles. He wasn't saying anything she disagreed with, but from his well-formed, generous lips, his deep, modulated voice, the prickly discomfort she felt only increased.

'A pleasing symmetry,' he repeated slowly. 'I like that.'

She blinked. It didn't matter what innocent words he uttered, his intentions seemed quite blatant. 'Uh, no, that's not going to work.'

'I wonder why not.'

'For a start, I'm not half your age.'

'But you are younger than me…well over a year if I remember correctly. Isn't your birthday in March?'

'Not exactly.' This was not the time or place. 'Wrong generation.'

'Wrong generation? I'll say it again, slowly. Don't believe everything you read.'

She folded her arms, pulling the fabric a bit too tight over her chest. 'So, how does that work then? Those journalists over there are unscrupulous, or sloppy, or lying. But you and your pals over here? Well, you deal with the high profile, you have to do a better job.'

'Maybe.'

That appraising, confident look.

'You were married,' she said.

'I was.'

'What happened?'

He shrugged; grinned. 'Didn't you read about it? I was no good for her. I hadn't realised she was a mentally unstable narcissist.'

'Not incredible though. A model who's a narcissist.'

'No. But not a given.'

'So, lots of others happy to hang off your arm?' And other things, no doubt. Why did she sound as if this meant something to her? It was none of her business.

'It tends to be of mutual benefit. They get to wear a pretty frock and be photographed.'

'And you? Do you like being photographed and recognized?'

'Not really. It happens much less than you think. At the wedding, I'm just Rob.'

'I doubt it. Not with your LA tan.' She clamped her lips together.

'Not interesting. What about you? Business good?'

'That's interesting?' She moved away.

Rob followed in long, easy strides. 'Sure it is. I have a colleague who is the very proud owner of one of your black jackets. She says it's one of the best investments she's ever made.'

'Don't joke.'

'Scout's honour.'

'You were never a scout. Or a choir boy.'

'That's true.' His elbow nudged hers, through two layers of fabric. 'So, what was that about? Earlier? Your secret's safe with me.'

'Yeah, right.'

'I am other things than a journalist.'

'Such as?'

'I can be whatever you want me to be.'

Anna let out a laugh which turned into a snort. 'This actually works, does it? As…as a line?'

'You're here, with me, aren't you?' He unleashed his dazzling smile again.

'For a start, I'm not *with* you…'

He spread his hands. 'I'm being nice. You could give me less of a hard time.'

'You think I'm giving you a hard time?' She blinked at him. 'And you, a hard-bitten journalist?'

'Boy, do you have an attitude problem,' he said, but then he stopped, turned towards her and smiled, hands in his pockets.

She shook her head. 'No smiling.'

'No smiling? Are you serious?'

'Anyway, wouldn't Sam's daughter be more your age range?' Anna said.

Rob took out another cigarette and lit it. 'I'll think twice about offering a woman a handkerchief next time.'

'Nobody asked you.' Anna felt painted into the role of petulant adolescent.

'No. Nobody asked me. But I didn't see lover boy rushing to your aid.'

'Lover boy?' It was so incongruous. She laughed, in spite of herself.

'Jonathan? Jon? Whatever.' He turned away to look across the gardens. 'So, what's that about?'

'No, really. Don't feel you need to spare my feelings by not asking me any personal questions.'

'It's what I do.' He took a long drag on his cigarette. 'Ask questions.'

'I have to keep walking.' She folded her arms around herself.

'Fair enough.' He fell into step beside her as they walked past the ornate Victorian building. 'Did you know Winston Churchill stayed here in 1905? He was Liberal MP for Oldham, and then North West Manchester. Before he switched to Conservative. Guess where he went next?'

'Where? How do you know this stuff?'

He grinned. 'It's only fun if you guess.'

She pursed her lips. 'Kent? Essex?'

'He ended up in Essex, but before that he represented Dundee.'

'Scotland?'

'Yup.' He stubbed out his cigarette in the bin as they

passed under the roofed gateway to Lake Avenue.

'What?' she said, feeling his eyes on her as they quickened their pace.

He shrugged and took off his jacket.

'What are you doing?' she said, as he draped it round her shoulders.

'Don't fret. It's only a jacket, not a commitment,' he said.

'You don't have to.'

'I know that.'

If all she ever knew about someone, was what she'd read in the press, would that give her any sort of rounded picture of what they were like as a person? Couldn't she remember Rob as a lanky, likeable teenager, before he filled out so impressively? Did that mean he could only be defined by his one-dimensional media reputation now?

Would there ever be a point at which his observable behaviour—what he actually did— could oust the tabloid persona? She felt as if she needed time to think about this. 'I'm seeing a whole other side of you.'

'I'm sure my secret's safe with you,' he said.

She hugged his jacket to her. 'Are you cold?'

'Nah. How are your feet?'

She looked down at them. 'Numb. I think.'

'You want to get in touch with your feelings, you do,' he said, his cream shirt solid in the gathering dusk.

She stopped to face him. 'You know, you don't look stupid.'

He stopped and stared back at her. 'Neither do you.'

'I'm not justifying myself to you.'

'Fine.' He stepped forward and lowered his voice. 'You know, you don't look like a coward.'

She stared up at him as he moved closer. Even with her heels he was still several inches taller. 'Uh…'

'They come in all sorts of shapes and sizes.' He reached for his jacket, which was no movement at all he was so close, hand to her waist and kissed her. His lips were cool upon hers. Unexpected, and everything changed with that touch of lips against lips, a gathering pressure. Her brain took ages 'to get with the program', by which point he'd pulled her against him, an arm round her waist, and he was warm and hard to the touch, bending her backwards until she lost her balance.

He felt so unfamiliar, so unlike Jon, that she had trouble reacting. A part of her wanted to swing at him with all her strength. Strange lips, strange taste, so much bigger and bulkier than Jon. No one had ever kissed her like this—with such overwhelming presence and certainty. No seeking permission. Just swooping in. Hands in her hair, cradling the back of her head, the tip of his tongue against her bottom lip.

She resisted the urge to stay put and see what happened next. 'Watch it.'

'Sorry,' he said, not taking his arms away but pulling her back against him instead.

It was warm there, in his arms. 'Get off me.'

'Why?'

'You can't just kiss me.'

'Except I just did,' he said.

'Well you can't. Get off.'

'Are you serious?' he said for the second time.

She pulled away, immediately colder, and wondered if her feet were sore. Difficult to tell. She touched her fingers to her lips and started to laugh.

'What?' he said, reaching for his jacket again.

She batted his arm away. 'I think I can feel a tingling in my toes,' she said, approximating Tony Curtis's impersonation of Cary Grant.

'*Some Like It Hot*? And I was going for my cigarettes, not for you,' he said.

'You can have them when I give you back your jacket,' she said.

'You're beginning to seriously piss me off,' he said.

'No I'm not. You were pissed off already.'

He grinned. 'Not that pissed off. I've changed my mind. Give me my jacket.'

'No.' She turned away and walked off.

ROB

By the time they arrived back at the front door of Sam's house—Sam and Jess's house, Rob supposed—dusk was falling and he was beginning to feel the cold. He rang the bell, hoping someone would hear over the hubbub of a well-watered wedding crowd.

'Thank you for the jacket,' Anna said, shrugging it off her shoulders.

'My pleasure,' he said, meeting her eyes. 'Um...' He leant forward and indicated her face.

'What?'

'You're looking a touch ravaged.' He licked the pad of his thumb and smoothed it across the mascara mark under her left eye. 'Hang on a minute.' He did it again. 'Better.' She was very close. Fluttering under his gaze.

'Thank you,' she said, stepping back, folding her arms across her body, turning away from him. Pity. He could easily have kissed her again. Surprised for the second time by the fear in her eyes, the soft, cool mouth. Just as well. Two kisses and she'd start thinking they had some kind of relationship. Nightmare time. The thought struck him. Maybe that was where he was going wrong, kissing people a second time. Maybe he was a one kiss kind of guy.

Kate, Sam's sullen twelve-year-old, a beauty in the making, with a petulant temper to match, opened the door.

'Hi, babe,' said Rob. 'Don't you look lovely?' He saw

Anna narrow her eyes. *Serves you right, talk about high maintenance*. But that thought was followed by something less familiar.

She passed him his jacket, gave him a blank look and stalked off.

Stroppy, he thought, watching her. Great legs.

'Oh, Rob,' said Kate, twining her arm through his.

'Don't "Oh Rob" me. Jess is not a wicked stepmother. Get over it.'

'But she is. She hates me,' said Kate.

'She doesn't. She wants to get to know you. You think about how hard this is. To take you lot on, as well as her two. Give her a break.'

'I can't believe you, I thought you'd understand,' Kate said.

'I do understand.'

'Yeah, right.' She stalked off too.

Rob sighed and reached for his cigarettes, until he remembered his doctor host really wouldn't appreciate him lighting up in the house. It was almost dark now, and he was cold from the walk. He wandered down the hall into the large back room, where his old school friend Sebastian stopped him.

'Where've you been?' he said. 'You've got some catching up to do.' He signalled for a glass of wine from one of the waitresses.

'What the hell,' said Rob, scanning for Anna. Just for information. He was staying with his parents tonight. Down the hill into Millingham. Walking distance. He took a swig of wine. She was talking to Caroline. Where was Jonathan?

'Who are you looking for?' said Sebastian.

'No one. Where's your wife?'

'Settling Ava, with any luck. Otherwise it could be a long evening.'

Rob sensed rather than saw Anna turn in his direction. Still stroppy. He smiled.

'What?' said Sebastian.

'What?' said Rob.

'You're grinning.'

'It's a wedding.'

'That's not why you're grinning,' said Sebastian. He followed Rob's eyes to the group of women on the other side of the room. 'Stella still looks really good.'

'Yep,' said Rob. He watched Anna's face as she listened to Ruth. Too far away to hear what was being said.

'Great tits,' said Sebastian.

'Yup.' Rob stopped and turned to face Sebastian. 'What did you say?'

'I said "Great tits",' he said.

'Stella?'

'No. The pair you can't take your eyes off.'

'What are you talking about? I think you'll find you're making unwarranted and unwelcome sexist comments,' said Rob.

Sebastian sighed. 'Yeah, right. Anna and that fitted dress.'

The heat of the room, after the cold of outside, had had its effect on Anna. Her coat was draped over a chair, her cheeks flushed.

'I didn't notice.' Rob knocked back the last of his wine and looked for some more.

'Sure you didn't,' said Sebastian.

ANNA

Thank God Ruth was mid-anecdote and chose not to stop the conversation and ask where she'd been. Only Caroline caught Anna's eye and raised an enquiring eyebrow. Jon was nowhere to be seen. When Ruth paused for a second, Caroline said, 'The boys have gone outside for a breath of fresh air.'

'Disgusting habit,' said Anna, reminded continually by the unfamiliar taste in her mouth that she'd been kissed by a smoker. It was playing havoc with her senses. Everything felt heightened. Her feet were now killing her, the wine tasted like the most Chardonnay-est Chardonnay she'd ever tasted, she could detect both Ruth's Opium and Caroline's Ysatis without any leaning in at all, and even kidded herself she could sense Rob's aftershave from a distance of three metres. She could certainly still feel his arms around her, as did all the parts of her he had touched.

'Absolutely.' Caroline gazed steadily at Anna.

She turned aside and let her gaze flicker over Sebastian and Rob; boy would she like to be a fly on that wall.

'Hello, flower.' Ruth's husband Andy appeared and kissed Anna's cheek. 'All OK?'

'Fine,' said Anna, pleased he'd noticed her absence; resigned to the fact Jon probably wouldn't allude to it now or later. He followed behind Andy, focusing on what Doug was saying. It was easier to ignore the crevices which made truthful communication with Jon more and more unlikely. Trying to bridge them would take too much effort.

'Where've you been?' Caroline whispered, under the cover of general conversation.

Anna glanced at Jon, who ignored her. 'For a walk. Lake Court.'

'With somebody? Or would another noticeable absence just be a coincidence?'

'Just coincidence, I'd say,' said Anna. 'How noticeable?'

'Only to people who were looking, I'd say.' Caroline glanced across the group to Jon. 'What's going on?'

'No idea,' said Anna, following her eyes. Jon hadn't looked in her direction even once. 'But it doesn't look good, does it?'

Caroline had already turned her attention towards the other side of the room. 'Oh, I think Rob looks really good.'

ROB

The sensible thing to do would to be to stop downing the Chardonnay like it was going out of fashion (surely it had already gone out of fashion?) and eat some food, but Rob knew he wasn't in a rational frame of mind. Instead he walked out of the kitchen and along the hall to the downstairs loo. As he turned the corner, Anna, mobile in hand, and paying more attention to that than where she was going, walked straight into his chest.

'Whoops, sorry,' she said.

'No worries. Happens to me all the time,' he said, his hands on her shoulders to steady her. Warm bare flesh. Smooth and silky to the touch.

She took a step back, forcing him to let go. 'Yeah. Right.'

He tried to remember what he'd said to make her look at him with such aggression. Catch her off-balance in mind as well as body, that was the trick. Do something unexpected.

'So, give me your number.' He reached into his breast pocket for his phone. Since he'd put his jacket back on, he'd found himself reluctant to remove it, even if he was a tad warm.

'Like you want my number.' Her eyes flashed.

'Sure I want your number,' he said. What was he doing? It would just cause resentment and embarrassment that he hadn't called her, next time they met.

'No. Really. Such a kind thought. But you don't have to.' She enunciated clearly. Slid sideways to pass him.

He put his hand on the wall to block her path. 'No.

Really. Your number.'

'Like you're going to ring for a chat? Cup of tea when you're passing? I don't think so.'

'For God's sake. Give it to me.' She was exasperating.

'Give me a good reason.' She folded her arms and he willed himself not to look down to all that stretched fabric.

'Maybe I do want to ring for a chat. Maybe I will be passing.' Dear God. Was this really the best he could come up with?

'No, not convincing. Let it go and let me pass.'

'I can easily get it from someone else,' he said, not moving his arm, despite her shoulder now being shoved against it. Warm too.

She laughed, but not so it reached her eyes. 'Sure. Fine. Whatever. Now move.'

'Hey, stop with the whatevers. It doesn't suit you.'

'Which bit of our previous conversation did you not understand?' Her eyes flashed. 'You don't get to tell me what to do. What to think. I'm not interested in your opinion.'

'Sure you are.' He grinned, leaning towards her. God, she was kissable. *No.* Not kissable. Mildly diverting to look at when she was cross. And he'd only just decided he was a one kiss guy. Hadn't he?

She scowled at him. 'Give it a rest. You forget. It doesn't work on me.'

'You say the words. But you don't mean them. There was that kiss.' Oh hell. Why did he feel the need to mention that?

'Yes. Thank you for that. The nicotine taste is so much appreciated.'

'Well, at least you can't forget me.' He watched her eyes widen.

'It's my addictive personality. I can't give up.'

She snorted in disgust. 'Move. Now.'

He dropped his arm and held up his mobile in his other hand. 'Any chance—'

She stepped past him. 'No. None at all.'

SAM

He looked at his watch. Half past eleven. Time to depart.

'Boring you, are we?' said Sebastian.

'Not at all. Where's Jess?'

'Lost her already?' Rob grinned.

'Over there.' Sebastian pointed over Sam's shoulder. 'Girl talk.'

He turned to see Jess engrossed with Caroline, Anna and Lucy, who had come up from London.

'What happened to James, by the way? What was his excuse for not being here?' said Rob.

'Constituency business,' said Sam.

'Over a weekend? This time of year? I don't think so,' said Rob. 'Anything to do with Jess?'

'Of course not. What do you mean?' said Sam. Sometimes Rob was too perceptive for his own good. What inkling had he winkled out?

'Just thinking about that extraordinary evening last autumn.'

'What evening?' said Sebastian.

'Nothing,' said Sam. 'Look, I'll see you later.'

Sebastian switched his attention to Rob.

'We met at James and Fiona's London flat, and Jess didn't even last to the end of the meal before storming off into the night,' said Rob.

'Interesting,' said Sebastian. 'What was that about?'

'Really,' said Sam. 'It's been a long day. Time to take my wife away from all this.' Somehow he didn't think his wedding night was going to turn into the night of his dreams. The night he'd been anticipating for three months. He squared his shoulders and made for the four women.

'Darling, I think it's time we left.' He addressed Jess, who almost met his eyes.

'Yes, of course,' Jess said, not moving.

'I'll start saying our goodbyes,' he said.

'Lovely,' she said.

'Lucy, so good of you to come up for this.' He kissed her cheek.

'Wouldn't have missed it,' Lucy said. 'Come and stay sometime.'

'Love to.' He kissed Caroline, and then Anna, who turned her head at the last moment, so he almost missed her cheek.

'What a lovely day,' she said, looking pinker than usual. She met Sam's eyes only fleetingly.

His focus moved to Jess. His wife. 'Shall we?' He held out his hand.

'Yes, yes, in a minute, I'll catch you up. Anna, carry on.' She put her hand to the back of her hair, where it had begun to fall down from its up-do. A white star-shaped flower dipped low on its hair grip.

Sam dropped his hand. 'Two minutes, then.'

He turned to find Jess's father Nathaniel smiling at him.

'Extricating the Lamb women from a social function takes a while,' he said.

'I'm beginning to understand that.' It was difficult not to be charmed by his father-in-law, whose enthusiasm for life drew everyone in. Even Felicity, his mother-in-law, and Martin, her husband of many years, appeared more fond of him than anything else. Which, considering the acrimonious breakdown of Jess's parents' marriage, due mainly to Nathaniel's affair with his secretary, was remarkable.

'Great to see all these girls again. Anna looks well.'

Sam followed his line of sight to where Anna looked more flushed and animated than she had done earlier.

'Where's Ruth? I was always fond of her.'

'Excuse me, I'm going to find our coats and things,' Sam said.

'Ah, there she is.' Nathaniel set off for Ruth, currently attended by Andy and Doug.

Sam watched as she drew Nathaniel into the group.

After twenty minutes he'd located Jess's voluminous cashmere wrap, ballet pumps and clutch bag. Their overnight cases were in the hall. He'd made his goodbyes. His children Emma and Josh had been persuaded to go to bed, along with their cousins Freya and Natasha, under the kind, firm supervision of Will and Diana, who were staying in the house for the week he and Jess were away in the Lake District. Kate absolutely refused to go to bed until her father left.

Jess kept getting stuck hugging friends and family members. Thank the Lord for his new mother-in-law.

'Jessica, darling,' Felicity said, extricating her daughter from another tearful embrace with Caroline. 'It really is time to go.'

Kate threw herself into her father's arms. 'Dad.'

'Have a lovely week, darling.' He squeezed her tight. 'See you next weekend, OK?'

Kate disappeared behind Rob as Jess approached.

Sam held his wife's gaze. 'Shall we?'

Sam took hold of Jess's hands once they were alone in their room. 'I know you must be tired, but did something happen that I should know about?'

'No, Sam, I'm fine. Tired as you say. What about a cup of tea?'

'Are you sure? Not a glass of champagne?' He indicated a bottle in an ice bucket.

Jess bit her lip. 'What do you think?'

'Whatever you like, darling. And then we can just sleep if you want. No pressure.'

She flicked her eyes towards his for a split second. 'But I've deprived you of sex since New Year. And it's our wedding night.'

'But that doesn't mean I have to persuade you when you're shattered.'

'No.' She pleated her hands together.

'We don't need to go anywhere until tomorrow afternoon. We have plenty of peace and quiet to become acquainted again.'

'Mm.' She slipped off her shoes, opened the door to the bathroom, put her handbag on the bedside table.

'Come and sit down for a minute,' said Sam, indicating the wide sofa beside the window.

She fiddled with her bag and smeared some lip balm across her lips.

'Jessie. Please.'

Once he had his arm around her, he tried again. 'Are you sure there isn't anything? Not having cold feet already?'

'Of course not.' She turned in the circle of his arm and met his gaze for the first time since they'd arrived at the hotel.

He squeezed her waist. 'That's good. I did wonder if anyone had said something to upset you?'

She put her head on his shoulder and he couldn't quite see her expression.

'Sam,' she said eventually, lacing her hand through his, balanced on his knee.

'Jess.'

'Did you think—were you thinking—did you imagine…'

He squeezed her hand gently. 'Give me a clue.'

'Why did we have a three tier wedding cake?'

He pulled back, not expecting that. 'What? You chose the cake. You wanted the flowers like that, and it looked stunning. Did you try some?'

'Only a tiny bit when we cut the cake.'

'My piece was delicious.' He waited.

'So you weren't thinking of anything in particular when we decided to have three tiers?'

'I think you decided, my love,' he said. 'What happened?'

'I heard Ruth say something.'

He rolled his eyes. 'Go on.'

'Something about the top tier being a Christening cake.'

'Oh Lord. Is that all? I thought you were worried about something serious.' He laughed. 'No, I do not have designs on you. No, I did not marry you to have another baby. Look at me, Jess.'

He pulled back so that they faced each other. 'I'm not in this marriage for another baby. I'm in it for you. You want another baby, let's talk about it. But that's not why we got married, is it?'

'I'm just not sure I could manage a new baby,' she said. 'I can't even see how I'm going to handle five children as it is.'

Sam stood up and reached for the bottle of champagne. 'No harm in having a glass—I don't think you had more than a few sips all evening. It would be a shame not to have any at all, don't you think?'

JESS

Jess watched her husband of ten hours discard his jacket, loosen his tie and undo his top button. The smooth cotton of his white shirt contrasted with the dark hair at his neckline. She liked his shorter haircut. It emphasized how thick his hair was, and showed off the elegant shape of his head.

He eased the cork from the bottle, poured two flutes, and crossed to the sofa. 'To us.'

'To us,' she repeated, gripping the proffered glass.

'So good to see you, Jessica.' He sat beside her.

'Likewise.' The champagne was cold and delicious.

'Jess, the thing about marriage is that you do it to tackle life together, to not be alone. We'll take it one step at a time.'

'I know. It's just that sometimes it's overwhelming.'

'You just need to take your mind off it. Drink up.' He grinned and took another sip of his drink.

'This was a good idea.' She felt alert as she hadn't been all day. She wanted to feel his heartbeat beneath his shirt, the pulse in his neck, his breath on her cheek, his arms around her, the weight of his torso on hers.

'We have all the time in the world.' He held her gaze. 'And if you want to go straight to sleep, that's fine.'

The bias cut silk satin dress had a clever layer underneath that covered a multitude of sins: no visible panty line to spoil the effect. She'd managed to lose most of her tummy. Yes, exercise had helped, but the stress of organising a wedding long distance, as well as move her life in London for the best part of twenty years, back to Manchester—with all that entailed when there were two children and an absent ex-husband—meant that her body was for once, pleasingly, almost the shape she would wish it to be.

Sam slid his hand along her bare arm, as the delicious, chilled champagne slipped over her tongue. Ah. Skin on skin. Her skin, his skin. The faintest hint of his Italian aftershave. Four weeks previously, in Peter Jones, Sloane Square, she'd searched out the bottle, sniffed, felt her stomach fall away as she remembered the touch of him, those four days in Oxford.

She took another sip. It was good stuff. But the all-encompassing, holding-everything-in dress was fatiguing. She wanted to be free of it. She wanted to be unencumbered by anything between her body and his. Her fingers traced the skin at her cleavage. The new white lace bra and knickers suddenly itchy; biting into her skin. He held her look as she stood up, kicked off her cream shoes, put her glass on the bedside table.

The room was not that warm, but Sam's gaze made her feel hot and brave enough to unpin the flowers in her hair and unhook her bracelet. He was too far away still, but she could see the look in his eyes. He was as alert as she was, poised to spring into action at a moment's notice.

She reached for another sip of champagne, never breaking the look between them, and when she put the glass down, he unfurled from the sofa in one fluid move, reaching her and pulling her against the hard length of him, his arms around her, his hands at her waist, not a chink of light between their pressed together hips. She ran her hands up his back to mold the contours of his corded muscles against her palms, impatient for the warmth of his smooth skin. Her fingers traced around the buttons of his shirt, freeing the sight of his dark chest hair, feeling her face flush as she released his shirt from the waistband of his trousers.

He ran his hand up the side of her dress. 'What's this fabric? It feels fantastic.'

'Satin.'

'I like it. Wear more of it.' He located the concealed back zip under a swathe of silk chiffon and undid it one-handed, his other arm still around her waist. 'As I said,' he murmured against her lips. 'Just say the word and we can stop and go to sleep.' He kissed down the side of her neck, easing the chiffon aside to find her leaping pulse, above the contours of her collarbone. His hand whispered across the beginning of the fine swell of her breast, the top of the lace bra.

'It unthreads.' She raised her arms to undo the chiffon scarf around the top of the dress, letting him pull it free from her shoulders.

'Oh, Jess, you are absolutely beautiful.' A little shower of rice confetti dropped to the carpet, released from the confines of her dress as it slithered to her waist.

'Rice,' she said.

Caroline, Anna, Ruth and Stella had showered them with handfuls of rice as they left the house, and rice fell from their hair, from Sam's lapels, from the creases of her dress, in a little cascade of confetti over the back of the car as they were driven to the nearby hotel. Now the beads of rice lodged in the cream carpet. Sam stroked the side of her waist, finally skin to skin, her breasts firmly pressed against him through the white lace.

She shuddered beneath his touch. It had been too long

since she'd felt his hands on her, and the worries of today, of the past week, of the last three months, fell away. She'd felt so guilty after Oxford, after such fantastic sex. Unhelpful phrases, 'out of wedlock', 'sinful', 'ungodly', had crowded into her mind.

Was it, she now wondered? Between two people who loved each other? Who wanted to express that love for each other? She placed her palms over his to feel the pressure, wanting the warm weight of him all over her body.

'God, Jess, you're— Don't move.' His fingers found the dress's zip again, released it further, so that the silk glided down her thighs and heaped in a creamy pool at their feet. His look was intent. 'I don't think I can take much more of this. You're too dazzling.'

'Oh, no you don't.' She laughed. 'Keep breathing.'

He pulled back the sheets, picked her up and laid her on the bed, hands stroking her arms, her shoulders.

She found his belt, and he shrugged off his shirt, kicked off his trousers, nudging a knee between hers.

At last, his weight on her, skin to skin, arms around his neck, tipping his face to hers, and he kissed her, his tongue hard in her mouth. An intensely erotic shudder rippled through her whole body.

He eased aside the lace cup of her bra, her nipple connecting with his palm, hooking her feet behind his ankles, impatient to feel the whole length of his naked body along hers. With quick, deft fingers, he pushed away her lace knickers, the smooth silk of her tights, and then his boxers, so that only skin connected them. So smooth, warm, firm.

Hands on her hips as he kissed her deeply.

'I want you now,' she whispered against his mouth.

'Thank God,' he said. 'Hold that thought.'

He rolled off the bed, found the inside pocket of his jacket for a condom, then the weight of him between her legs, hips against hips.

'My, Jess, you're so…'

'And you.' She held his gaze as he slipped, exquisitely slowly, into the depth of her wet warmth.

'Home. At last.' He raised himself up on his arms, to focus on her. 'You have no idea—

'I do.' She held his upper arms, locked her ankles behind his knees, met his kiss, the slow pulse of him moving inside her echoed by his mouth, his tongue. The taste of him was simultaneously familiar and strange, fuelling a primitive need deep within her. She felt the sort of warm completion that banished any recollection of cold from her mind.

The heat rushed through her, all the way to the tips of her fingers, the ends of her toes, as they rocked together, breathing in rhythm.

'Look at me,' he said.

She returned his look, seeing that heat in his dark eyes.

'I love you. I'll never stop loving you, Jess.'

'I love you.' She shuddered against him, pulling him even tighter, and he wrapped his arms around her, stretching against her, such pressure she could feel him everywhere, as they surged higher and higher against each other, reaching ever closer to the cliff edge. Dizzy with itch and sensation, breaking, gasping for breath, as their heart rates began to slow down.

'That was a good idea,' she whispered in his ear, when she could speak again. 'I was so tired, but you woke me right up.'

'My pleasure,' he said. 'My absolute pleasure, my darling.'

'Sam?'

'Yes?' He propped himself on one elbow.

'You are delicious. And very heavy.'

'Ah, yes, sorry.' He pulled away, found the covers, brought them over them both.

She wriggled. 'There's quite a lot of rice in this bed.'

'Who cares?' He reached for their glasses.

The champagne was still gloriously cool on her tongue.

He took a sip, then bent his head to kiss her breast. 'Drinking champagne with no clothes on is a very good idea.'

She laughed, her fingers in his hair.

'I'm so glad you weren't interested in hours of foreplay. That could have been extremely taxing. You have no idea the anticipation of making love to you, after more than three months.'

'I do actually. I've been dreaming of the weight of you, woken and had to bear you not being there…'

He rolled on top of her again, still holding his glass upright. 'This weight?'

'This is fine,' she said, looking up at him. 'It's when you're slumped and sated that you're too heavy.'

He set down his glass, put hers beside it. 'Well, now that I'm here…'

'Believe me, you are irresistible. It's just that—'

'I know. It's been a long day.' He manoeuvred onto his side, kissed her, their limbs entwined, his hands at her waist, on her ribs, warm under her breasts. She eased onto her side and he curled himself around her, his hand moving up to stroke her breast. She pushed back against him and he reciprocated with an answering pressure, fingers gliding around her nipples, circling the swell of her breasts.

They lay together, warm skin against warm skin, until her body began to twitch as she fell towards sleep. 'Sam. I need to get up and brush my teeth.'

'Mmm.' His lips nuzzled her neck.

'Really.' She sat up, loving the slide of her body against his.

'Come back.'

'I will.' She found a robe in the bathroom, and her sponge bag, toothbrush, cleanser.

Sam opened his eyes as she returned. 'My turn.' He swung out of bed and held the covers for her, completely at ease in his own skin.

'Wow,' said Jess. 'I see what you mean about the rice.'

ANNA

Anna sat in the open plan office, rubbing her wrists in the slant of late afternoon sun.

'So, what are you up to this week?' said Jade, her eyes on her computer screen.

'This and that.' Anna read the most recent message on her mobile and shook her head. She had to admire his persistence.

'Meaning?' said Jade.

Anna looked up and met her dark haired assistant's eyes. Ten to five, with a long, empty week stretching ahead of her. There were of course lots of things she *should* be doing. Plenty of gardening to be done now the evenings were long and light. Finish that book group novel. Numerous things she'd recorded and not quite got round to watching. Emails that needed a response. Phone calls to return. Admin. Filing. And all of that if she made herself put actual work aside. Over the years she'd realised the wisdom of taking breaks from it all on weekends and holidays, but running her own business was all-consuming, and she had to consciously make herself stop. She put her head down on the desk and groaned.

'That good?' said Jade.

'Jon's got tickets to a film premiere on Thursday night, but I just can't face it.'

'Sure you can. Leicester Square?'

'Yes.'

'So. Stay for the weekend.'

'Jon's off surfing. Cornwall.'

'Even better. Live it up in London for the weekend. We can cope without you on Friday. Go and have some fun.'

'When did I turn into a completely boring old cow? Fat, boring old cow?' said Anna.

'You didn't. You just need a change. And you're not fat.'

'But I'm not thin.'

'Curvy. Voluptuous. If you ever let anyone past the layers. Isn't Jon a breasts man?'

'I don't think Jon's a much of anything man.'

Jade raised her eyebrows.

'Sorry. I'm just fed up.'

'Well that's progress,' Jade said. 'You've worked out that much. Go to London. Go and see your friends from school, what are their names?'

'Stella. Or Ruth.'

'So, ring them. What's the film?'

'What? Oh. New Tom Cruise, I think.'

'How come Jon's got tickets?'

'Some client do or other. It's the red carpet, champagne reception, full works…'

'Sounds great. I was going to suggest a pizza in Bath, but this sounds so much more fun. What are you going to wear?'

Anna gave up and smiled. 'I haven't said I'm going yet.'

Jade shrugged. 'But you will. And I forbid you to wear a black trouser suit. In fact black anything.'

'I'm not going in a frock, if that's what you're thinking,' Anna snorted.

'Go on. Ring the girls, see who's around over the weekend. Then tell Jon the good news.'

Anna pursed her lips together.

'You know you want to.'

'We're not talking about a second dessert here,' said Anna. She felt fluttery for the first time since— No. Never mind. Still. Maybe she would ring the girls. See who was there.

Stella's home answerphone was on and Anna left a brief message saying she might be around at the weekend. Then she rang Ruth at work, thinking she might just catch her.

'Ruth? Anna… I'm possibly coming up this weekend and wondered if you and Jack are going to be at home on Friday during the day?'

'Afraid not. I've got a meeting so I'm taking Thursday off instead. When are you coming up?'

'Um. Well. I've got to be in town for Thursday evening.'

'So come for lunch. Or tea. On your way through.'

It made sense. Ruth's house was in Chiswick, Jon's flat in Kensington. 'Let me see what I can organise. I'll call you tomorrow, OK?'

'Now Jon?' said Jade, when Anna had put the phone down.

'Later. Maybe.'

'Whatever.'

'Don't say that. I got told off for saying that.'

'Why? Who by?'

'No one. Really.'

Jade raised an eyebrow again. 'Are you sure nothing happened at that wedding?'

'What? No. Of course not. Like what?'

'I don't know. You still jump every time your phone goes, and it was a fortnight ago.'

Anna instinctively looked at the display panel on her

mobile. Another message received. 'No. Really. Nothing happened.'

'But you wanted something to happen?'

'What? No. What are we talking about?' said Anna.

'I don't know. I guess we're not talking about Jon.'

Anna met Jade's eyes fleetingly. 'Really. Nothing to report.' She felt foolish. It wasn't that Jade would judge her. She was one of the least judgmental people on the planet, but Anna did not feel good about having kissed Rob back, even if it was only for an instant. She was not the cheating sort.

But her unruly mind would not be governed. At lunchtime she'd walked past a smoker and her stomach had flipped at the smell, and the visceral memory. The reason she jumped every time her phone beeped was because Rob had sent her several texts since the wedding. 'Is there anybody there?' —she assumed it was rhetorical—through to 'I'm passing your way next weekend and am thinking of stopping off for a coffee.' Succinct reply in the negative.

And, as for her dreams… Well, traitorous, eminently unfeminist, of the fainting heroine swooning into strong manly arms, her lips bruised by his harsh mouth, her—etc, etc. Every night. She thought of herself as a good sleeper. Tidy. Neat. But of late she'd entwined herself in the duvet, woken up hot and sticky. Had she been a man, she'd definitely have had an erection. Maybe there were advantages to Jon spending ninety per cent of his time a hundred miles away.

Anna sighed, lifted her eyes and met Jade's gaze. How long exactly had she been lost in thought? 'OK. I'll ring Jon.'

He picked up on the third ring. 'Anna.'

'Hi. I thought I would come on Thursday, if that's still OK.'

'Sure it is. Can you get to Kettners for champagne? Six thirty-ish? It starts seven-thirty.'

'What's the dress code?'

'Smart. A dark suit and heels will be fine.'

'Oh.' Suddenly a dark suit didn't sound so interesting. 'Very dressy?'

'Sure. Saskia's got some amazing ball gown.'

Anna's heart sank. Of course Saskia would be there, it was a work do. She'd look fantastic even if she wore a bin bag, with her petite frame, her long dark hair and eyes.

'Can I call you later? I've got someone here,' Jon said.

'Fine. You should have said,' she said into the void. He'd already disconnected. She shrugged her shoulders at Jade. 'A dark suit and heels will be fine.'

'Not fine. And no linen. Something really dressy. Go into Bath and treat yourself.'

That was easier said than done. She did have a meeting on Wednesday morning and spent lunchtime in the centre of Bath, doing the shops, but nothing that caught her eye fitted properly. In some labels she was a size 14, in others a 16 would barely touch her, which added to her depression. So she packed her favourite navy wool crepe suit from last year's collection, a violet sequinned top and high mules.

Unexciting. Safe.

Well cut. Classic. *Boring. Staid.*

The top was pretty and showed a little cleavage, but it would be hidden under the jacket anyway. She sighed for the nth time that day. Is this it? *Thirty-nine and when I try to buy a proper dress, a frock even, I fall at the first attempt.*

When she told Ruth about her shopping trip—knowing

she'd understand precisely, being a solid size 16 herself—Ruth's eyes gleamed.

They were sitting in garden chairs on the patio of the house in Chiswick, while two-year-old Jack tore around the garden, splashing in and out of the paddling pool.

'I have exactly the thing. I bought it for the work ball last year. Try it on,' said Ruth.

'Oh no, it's fine,' said Anna. 'I've brought my suit—'

'How are you going to feel in that suit when the vamp swans up in a ballgown? Go and try it on. It's in my wardrobe, on the left-hand side, in a long dry-cleaning bag. Off white. And silver. The most fantastic back.'

'No. Really.' The very thought made Anna nervous. 'I haven't put any fake tan on. I haven't got the right sort of bra—'

'No bra,' said Ruth. 'This is not a dress that needs a bra.'

'No bra? You're joking. My boobs don't go braless. Not a good—'

'Anna. Go and try it on. You may well look fabulous in it. You've got much more of a waist than me. It's a curvy dress.'

Ten minutes later, Anna had shed her clothes, and just in her knickers, contertina-ed herself into the dress. Ruth was right. It was a Ginger Rogers of a dress. Generous, floaty, full-length skirt, and a beaded, fitted top, with several cross-over straps across the back, each with a bit of give in them. Which made the fit quite remarkable. Snug around her waist, straining across the bust. But not bad. Good in fact.

Surprisingly comfortable.

Amazingly unfamiliar. She couldn't get used to her reflection at all. She hadn't shown this much cleavage since... She'd never shown this much cleavage. And despite it being a dress you couldn't possibly wear a bra with, her bosoms didn't come down to her knees. She stared at her chest. The fabric was facing considerable strain, but it seemed to be rising to the challenge (ho, ho), so far.

'Any good?' Ruth called up the stairs.

She took a deep breath and stopped when she realised it caused everything to shift slightly. Pause. It was only Ruth. Showing Ruth didn't commit her to wearing it. 'You were right, it fits.' She opened the bedroom door, trying simultaneously not to round her shoulders, nor to stick her chest out any more that it did already.

'Wow. You look fantastic. I knew it'd suit you. What about your hair?'

'My hair?' She'd blow-dried her fringe that morning, but the rest of it was screwed up in a sloppy knot. 'Oh. No. It's a stunning dress. But I couldn't possibly. I don't think I've ever shown this much flesh.'

'Of course you can. It'd be such a waste not to wear it. You need some fancy clip or something. Keep your hair up, but softer. And lots of pink lipstick. Very sexy.'

'Very sexy.' Jack repeated, hugging his mother's leg, at the bottom of the stairs.

'Seal of approval,' laughed Ruth. 'How can you refuse, now?'

Less than two hours later, Anna left Ruth's house in the dress, full make-up, her hair in an artfully tousled up do, and the lilac mules, bag and wrap that she would have worn with her suit.

Ruth had fortified her with a great deal of flattery, and at the last minute, just before she left—sensing the fear behind Anna's eyes—a tiny sherry. 'Good for the nerves,' she'd said.

Anna drove her car to Jon's flat in Kensington and dumped her bag. Funny how, even when they were planning the move to Bath together, moving out of two separate flats and buying this flat, it had never been anything other than his flat, somehow. The house was never anything but her house. Separate lives. The idea frightened her. The energy for new experiences, new people, had melted away but she'd spent so much time on her own, rattling around in her spacious house, that she knew she no longer wanted a life alone.

Her mobile buzzed in the hushed cool flat and she jumped. It was a message from Ruth. 'No second thoughts. Get a cab and go for it.'

Back on the street, walking down to the Cromwell Road, her wrap seemed woefully inadequate as any sort of cover-up. The skirts of the dress frothed around her ankles. She stood on the pavement to hail a cab, hoping she didn't look like the high class call girl she felt she resembled. Surely no one would actually think that?

A cab pulled up. 'Where to?' he said, showing very little interest in the dress. She'd pulled the wrap across her folded arms. So there wasn't that much to see. 'Soho please. Kettner's in Romilly Street.'

The cab sailed through Knightsbridge and up Piccadilly. As they drew up she saw the back of Jon's head, taller than the rest of the group, going into Kettner's.

'Wow, you look amazing, Anna,' said Saskia.

Anna wished her tone of voice was not quite so surprised.

'So do you,' she replied, concentrating on Saskia's

midnight blue satin sheath of a dress. *Definitely magic knickers,* she thought, holding in her stomach, trying to stand up straight.

'Anna.' Jon's eyes widened. 'Don't you look lovely.' He kissed her cheek.

She resisted the urge to flinch. Not the remotest glimmer of interest. Did Jon not possess that gene? Or was it only Anna he blanked? And at what point was she going to have the courage to stop flogging this dead horse?

I don't want to be alone. But you are alone. But I don't want to be. What had been the purpose of wearing this dress, if not to impress Jon?

'Champagne?' said Saskia, holding out a glass.

'Thank you.' Anna turned away from Jon. She was livid. With herself for being talked into the dress. Furious that she barely had the guts to wear it. Beside herself that Jon's lack of reaction should hurt her so much. Well, sod him. A client do, huh? She felt like running screaming from the building, getting the hell away from there. From him.

She took a gulp of champagne. She was being introduced to various of Jon's clients. Advertising director of some telecoms company; brand director of a cognac; someone or other from a big insurance company. As she shook hands with the three men, someone-or-other grinned at her. She smiled in reflex. Another gulp of champagne. Jon was talking to the telecoms guy.

'Come here often?' said someone-or-other.

Anna realised she had no idea of any of their names.

'Never. You?'

'All the time.'

She took another swig and tried not to register his glazed look as his eyes fell to her cleavage. Poor man, there was such an expanse of it, he could hardly avoid it. While he was distracted she saw that he was young and good-looking. She smiled again, and it felt less plastic than the previous attempt.

'Quite a dress.' His eyes glinted at her.

'Thank you. It's borrowed.'

'Good fit.'

There was no reply to that. She found herself staring at the bottom of her empty glass. *Where did it all go,* she wondered.

'Another?' he said.

Alcohol would annihilate the self-consciousness. And submerge her need for Jon's approval. 'What the hell,' she said, their fingers meeting as he handed her a glass.

A lot of the rest of the evening passed in a blur. She got quite drunk pretty quickly. Oh dear. At what point did these episodes become less of a pattern and more of a serious problem? She tottered to the limousine for the short journey to Leicester Square. And tottered onto the red carpet at the other end. There were various greeters who did that almost recognition thing—the beginnings of a smile as they saw Anna's face—followed by a swift frown as they took in the rest of her. So good for the ego.

Someone-or-other, whose name turned out to be Greg, steered her by the elbow, past the ranks of flash photographers, into the cinema. Huddles of people eyed each other up, wondering if they were in the presence of anyone famous. And suddenly they were. Diminutive Tom Cruise was in their midst, smiling that white, white smile, and shaking hands, surrounded by assistants and admirers. Anna was shocked by his magnetism. Whatever charisma consisted of, he had it in spades.

The film passed her by in a maelstrom of colour, noise

and movement. There was a lot of graphic action which made her feel sick, but took her mind off being desperate for the loo. As soon as the applause at the end showed signs of dying down, she attempted a discreet and dainty exit. Sadly she tripped over her skirts at the end of the row and only a firm, brown hand catching her arm saved her from collapsing in an ignominious heap on the floor. The vast room seemed to tilt as she righted herself and suddenly the person she least and most wanted to see in the whole of London was standing in front of her.

'Escaping?' he said, looking down the row behind her.

'The loo,' she said, and he dropped his grasp. She watched the skin on her arm where he'd caught her until her bladder could take it no longer and gave her an urgent warning. 'Excuse me.' She fled.

Her reflection in the mirror over the basins looked remarkably calm, even when Kylie Minogue dashed into the cubicle behind her. Rob Randall. What the hell was he doing here? *Don't be stupid, he goes to this sort of thing all the time*. Probably research for an imminent in-depth interview with Tom Cruise himself.

She flicked the water off her hands and stuck them under the dryer, licking her dry lips. She grabbed her bag, dropped everything, scrabbled for her lipstick. *Keep calm. He's just someone you used to know. He means nothing*. Her stomach heaved.

Outside the loos the hoards were pouring down the corridors to the exits. Several household names and familiar faces whizzed past, but no sign of Jon or Saskia. Or Greg. Or Rob.

They were going on to some post-party at BAFTA on Piccadilly. She was relying on an arm to grab while she negotiated the pavements in her high mules. Bloody hell.

It was true what they said about pelvic floor exercises. Babies or no babies, you had to do those exercises.

She joined the throng and found Jon and the others outside the cinema. 'Come on.' As soon as he saw her he started heading west.

'All right?' said Greg.

'Fine thanks,' she said.

He had his hands in his pockets. The DJ definitely suited him. He gestured with his elbow.

'Thank you,' she said, and took his arm.

ROB

Rob didn't usually go to film premieres. There were the odd invites, and he could have wangled it most of the time, but they were tedious. Had he not been about to interview the star for one of the Sunday broadsheets he would not have been there. It had been a bind, rushing back to his flat in Earls Court to throw on his dinner suit, dashing back to Leicester Square. The film was loud and absorbing. Standing ovation at the end, and then this woman lacing her way to the aisle, virtually flinging herself at his feet in her hurry. Apologetic as she stumbled and he gathered her. Anna. Pink lips, a white, jewelled dress, pale flesh, curves and cleavage.

He couldn't remember what he'd asked her, but she'd prised his hand from her arm and fled.

Later, at the BAFTA party, he watched her back. The dress was long and clinging, catching the light, her hair curled and pinned. The straps crossed her back diagonally from shoulder to hip, exposing diamonds of pale skin. She didn't talk to her boyfriend Jon, who paid more attention to a girl in a long dark dress.

His fingers itched, but of course this was another place you could no longer smoke. Really, he should give up. But there was too much he liked about it. Even with another friend diagnosed with cancer, losing her hair, diminished by the brutalities of chemotherapy. He resisted the temptation to go outside for a cigarette.

When she slipped away the second time, Rob followed

Anna and waited. The low bodice at the front of her dress was festooned with minute silver beads. He didn't say anything.

She opened her eyes wide, lips parted, as he stepped closer. At the last moment her eyes closed, a gleam of feathered light on her cheekbone. She tasted of champagne.

'We should go away,' he said, taking his phone out of his inside pocket.

She put a hand to the wall to steady herself. 'What?'

'Unfinished business. You know I always liked you, but you were more interested in Ian Guthrie.'

'Who?'

'I remember everything,' he said.

'I sincerely hope you don't,' she said.

'I was thinking of Bishopstrow. That's down your way, isn't it? Or would you prefer the sea?'

'How do you—?'

He grinned. 'I *know* everything, too.'

She folded her arms and looked over his shoulder, towards the crowds.

'OK, Sam told me where you live,' he said. 'You know. Sam, the groom.'

'Sam,' she said.

'When are you free?' he said. 'Quick, before Jon comes looking for you.'

Her eyes flickered. 'Neither of us thinks that's very likely.'

ANNA

'You do know there's a terribly callous, not to say calculated, reason I've agreed to come away with you.' Anna studied the refracted candlelight through her champagne.

Rob smiled and sat back in his chair to admire the view of Anna, centre stage in the shadowed dining room, against a backdrop of floor to ceiling French windows opening onto the garden.

'You're the perfect candidate really, a commitment-phobe who wants to keep things simple and unemotional,' she said.

'Really,' he said.

'Stella told me about the divorce. And the girl in every city. What bothers me most is why you'd want to spend the night with me. I'm twenty years too old for you.' She put down her glass. 'Or is it because of what you said before: you think of me as the one who got away?'

'Possibly. But you're not twenty years older than them.'

'OK, then, twenty pounds heavier.'

Rob raised his eyebrows. 'Suffice to say I wouldn't have suggested this unless I thought there were certain benefits for me too.'

'I believe you,' she said.

'It's true. Are you going to tell me your reason?'

'Why here? Why the Isle of Wight?' They'd spent the afternoon walking the sandy length of Compton Beach. Under a vast dome of sky, they were buffeted by the fresh, salty air, dancing waves lapping at their bare feet.

'I told you. Uni friend who lent me the house with the view.'

'Been here before?'

'Yes. With him and his family. I don't make a habit of doing this.'

She could not control her mind. She had wanted this. Had thought about it so much. And yet, now she wanted it to stop.

Somehow Rob had manoeuvred them from the table to the sofa, sinking into the cushions, Anna beneath him, kissing her, paying close attention to her mouth. He held her in his arms, one hand flat at the small of her back, heating the skin beneath her t-shirt, easing the cotton aside to connect palm with skin. He had seemed unhurried and relaxed, one movement flowing into another, until she found him firmly between her legs, hips to hips, feeling the hard pulse of him pressed against her abdomen.

A cold clamminess hit the backs of her knees, the crooks of her arms, the nape of her neck. Rob was bulkier, more substantial than Jon, and it had been a long time since she'd been in this position, the full weight of a big man on top of her.

That was when her body stopped answering his.

Her mouth dried on the instant, her desire desiccated into detachment. She felt nothing, only saw herself underneath Rob as he moved. There had been a rhythm of sorts, punctuated by the panicked phrases of her conscious thought, but now she couldn't move.

He pushed himself up on one elbow to look into her eyes. 'What is it?'

She turned her head away. Raised a hand to screen her eyes, careful not to come into contact with him. Touched the tip of her tongue to her dry lips.

'Anna?'

'Sorry.' She took a breath, hunched her shoulders and rolled away from him with enough impetus that he pulled back to free her.

She fled up the stairs with her bag, stumbling into a room with a single bed and adjoining loo. She shrugged off her pumps, dragged the chair in front of the door and lay down, pulling the covers right up over her shoulders, braced for sounds of footsteps on the stairs, but all was quiet.

ROB

He stretched to turn off the one side lamp beside the sofa and lay, feeling winded, until the fading twilight had completely dissolved into night. The only light in the room came from the flickering wicks of white wax on the table. Anna had found two stubs of candle in a kitchen drawer and wedged them into the brass candlesticks she'd noticed on the mantlepiece.

What had felt like sudden revulsion had certainly dampened his ardour. He'd intended to climb the stairs behind her, to have it out, to find out why, with such a promise of sex, she'd stopped and escaped. His journalist's mind considered option after option. Was it just cold feet about having sex with him when she was in a relationship with another man?

She hadn't looked at him, had seemed unable to meet his eyes. Was it shame? Or was it something else?

He let the candles gutter in their sticks. Even then, the room was not dark. The late spring night was illuminated by strong moonlight. He could see the contours of plants beyond the French windows, dark outlines of trees, the gleam of the calm sea down the hill, reflecting the moon itself.

Eventually he gathered the plates and glasses and took them to the kitchen. Then he found his bag and climbed the stairs. Beside the closed door, another stood ajar. He pushed it open, into a spacious room with a white double bed, and a view out to sea. He stood at the window gazing at the moonlit seascape for a long time, the house completely silent behind him.

ANNA

She leaned against the open window and stared out to sea, alert and listening for any sound of Rob. The water was becalmed, grey, a shade darker than the pale sky it met at the horizon. Not a vessel broke the straight line from east to west.

Behind her, the room was white and bare, the sort of room she hankered for when she pored over interiors magazines. Completely de-cluttered. Probably had never been cluttered in the first place. She liked the air here. The space. The fresh white sheets, the white painted chair, the slim table by the bed.

She had left the curtains open, not expecting to sleep, and spent a long time lying on her back, trying to quieten her mind through the repeated tensing and relaxing of various muscles in her arms and legs. Concentrating on measured breathing in, breathing out; counting; catching her thoughts. Telling herself over and over again that she was safe.

When, eventually, she heard the steady tread of Rob's feet as he ascended the stairs, she'd turned her head towards the door. She reached out and pulled her mobile phone under the covers, tight in her grasp. Gauging his direction as he reached the landing, the clicks of the handles and locks as he opened and closed a different door, his fading footsteps. She craned to hear a single sound above the palpitations of her heart.

Slept finally, still dressed, curled into a ball on her side, facing the door. Awoke too soon, early light seeping across the ceiling.

Now the rising sun was already strong as she gazed out to sea.

A movement on the patio below the window caught the corner of her eye and she jerked backwards into the room.

ROB

Bloody typical. Bloody fucking typical. Scooping the kettle off the Aga hob, he splashed boiling water onto the coffee grains and retrieved the lone carton of milk from the vast fridge. He reached instinctively for his cigarettes from the pocket of his shirt, but of course it was empty. For a second, he imagined dashing the mug with a satisfying smash onto the flagstones. Instead he picked it up, took it outside and slouched onto the bench, ignoring the flutter of white at the upstairs window, and scalded the roof of his mouth as he gulped the bitter coffee.

Rob yearned for a cigarette, imagining the smooth weight—so light, and yet full of substance—between the first two fingers of his left hand. The nicotine stains were still there. They would take longer than six days to fade. That was six lots of twenty-four hours. One hundred and forty-four hours. Almost to the hour.

He was right-handed. But he'd always smoked with his left. Perhaps he knew when he started that it would be useful to be able to take notes and smoke at the same time.

The gum was upstairs, in a heap of his things—his watch, today a Simon Carter, pale, open-faced on a classic brown leather strap; his slim silver phone; his black notebook, a Moleskine, the sort now found in every Waterstones, which he'd been using for years and years—among the debris of change and the screwed up, mascara-stained white cotton handkerchief. Why spoil something with a pattern, when plain would do?

The gum made him feel nauseous even before he put it in his mouth now. The patches itched like hell. Not helped by the untypical baking hot weather. He squinted at the fast ascending sun. The car cowered by the gate, its sleek black exterior already dank from the heat. So much of him wanted to grab his bag, shove his stuff into it, and leave without ever having to see her again. But he knew he wouldn't do this. Not just because she was a friend of Jess and Sam's. Bloody weddings. Bloody fucking weddings.

He made himself fill and boil the kettle, find another mug. Tea or coffee? Maybe, after last night, there was only one answer. Knocked before he shouldered the door open.

'Here. I could only find instant.' He crossed to the window and handed her the mug.

'Thank you.' She didn't look at him. 'How did you sleep?'

'Fine. You?'

She put the mug down on the windowsill and reached for her watch on the narrow table. 'It's nearly eight. What time do you want to leave?'

'There's no hurry, is there?'

'I'll have a shower.'

He left her to it, gathered his paraphernalia, remade the bed and took his bag downstairs.

He had not slept well.

He was well practised at sleeping in a different bed, blocking out peripheral noise, finding comfort in strange bedclothes, greeting swings of temperature and bizarre smells with equanimity.

But here, with the gentlest of sea breezes, lying under soft, freshly laundered cotton, the quiet and stillness had left him so much space to think about Anna sleeping in the room next door. Had she left her door open even an inch he would have been tempted to nudge it open, but she wasn't in any of the other bedrooms on the first floor, and the door was firmly closed. Not that it had stopped him in the past. There had been weeks of shouting and slammed doors as his brief marriage imploded—more than six years ago now—and he'd given as good as he got.

Something held him back, and kept him here, despite the strong temptation to drive off and leave her to it. It wasn't just that he didn't want it to get back to his mother that he'd done such a thing. Was it?

He had even contemplated texting her, but he didn't know what to say.

ANNA

She scrunched across the wet sand in her flip-flops, and crouched onto a rock, glad she'd put her swimming costume on under her jeans. She ignored Rob, no longer bothered if he was behind her or not. It was still early. The little cove felt as if it was waking up. A couple of families with toddlers picked their way onto the sand, laden with brightly coloured bags and plastic toys. She stared at the unengaged, sighing parents and wanted to shake them. Didn't they understand the gift they'd been given? Couldn't they imagine the physical pain of not having a child?

'Anna,' said Rob.

She glanced around. He looked as if he'd been trying to attract her attention for a while.

'I'm going to the café.' He indicated a hut with a low roof and wide veranda at the end of the cove. 'Do you want something?'

'What are you having?'

He shrugged, his hair ruffling in the wind. 'Dunno. Coffee?'

'Espresso?'

'I'll see if they do that. It's just a beach café, you know.'

He walked away, long, loose limbs in khaki shorts and a blue short-sleeved shirt. A little girl, already stripped to pink flowery swimming costume, collided with him. He put out his hands to steady her, but she turned away, searching for an adult she recognized.

Anna shaded her eyes and gazed at the horizon. Three or four large container ships were anchored to the east, at the entrance to the Solent, waiting to dock at Southampton. Away to the west, yachts with pale sails proliferated effortlessly. A noisy speedboat glided past on the glassy sea.

She took her cardigan off and tied it round her waist. Then she shoved the short sleeves of her t-shirt onto her shoulders, grabbed her sun cream from her bag and applied it to her arms, neck and décolleté. She hurried, not wanting to be doing this with Rob looking on. Her fingers were cold, slippy, despite the warmth of the sun. She fished for her cap, shoved her hair through the hole in the back, and pulled it down, over her forehead.

Rob was too observant. There was no point in trying to talk to him sensibly about Jon, or about what had her coming to the Isle of Wight. The iceberg of her overwhelming desire blanketed everything else. It was the prism through which she calibrated her existence and she was well aware that it would not be possible to have a rational conversation without Rob perceiving the cracks in her performance.

It was better not to engage at all.

ROB

While he waited to be served, Rob scanned the accumulating people. Banker, banker, accountant, IT specialist. Yummy mummy, shop girl, teacher, fitness freak. Journalism had a lot to answer for. Living in his head would be a lot more restful if he didn't think like this. Constantly.

I don't even like her, he thought, as he agonized over the flapjack. Would she want one? Would she be disgusted if he bought her one? If he didn't?

He knew the answer to, 'Does my bum look big in this?' Of course he did. Every man did. But he didn't know how she felt about her weight. Except, no doubt, she wanted to be thinner. She'd be less alive if she were thinner. He had a theory about everyone having their own optimum weight. Some people were meant to be thin. Some people weren't. If Anna lost weight, she'd lack lustre. Her skin would lose its luminosity. Her lips would narrow, her dimple would diminish. Her figure would comply but the curves of joy would have sunk, faded, eroded. He nearly bought a second flapjack. But the guilt of her teary blue eyes, the little pools of mascara, stopped him.

He picked up the two mugs of coffee in one hand, the flapjack in the other, and retraced his steps. The beach had filled up. The sand dried, as the tide receded, and rugs and towels littered the widening expanse in neat rectangles. Anna, her knees drawn up, sat on her rock watching the waves.

'Careful, it's hot,' he said.

She regarded him properly for the first time since the previous night.

He felt hot under her gaze. Eventually it dawned on him that she didn't want him, she wanted the flapjack. 'Oh, for God's sake,' he said, breaking what was left in half.

'Don't force yourself, Rob,' she said.

Rob. She said his name. He turned his back and looked up the hill, at the stone cottages and wooden houses perched above them, at the pathways, and the hard at the top of the beach. 'Why are those people milling about in posh outfits on a day like this?'

Anna swung round. 'Party? At least they're not venturing onto the sand in their stilettos.'

'Thank God for shorts,' he said. 'What possessed you to wear jeans?'

She grimaced. 'I didn't have time to pack for all eventualities. It's May. I wasn't expecting this sort of weather on the Isle of Wight. Anyway, I've got my costume on underneath.'

He swapped his coffee from one hand to the other, as they both gazed out to sea. From the corner of his eye, he watched an escaped curl flutter in the breeze by her ear. Her tone of voice triggered all sorts of angry retorts, but he swallowed, regretting the vehemence of his words.

Something had happened which meant her responses were not normal.

He could choose to exude calm and peace. However much he might feel like hitting something.

ANNA

'What's that?' she pointed out to sea, to the mouth of the cove.

'Where?' said Rob. 'Just a rowing boat.'

'No it's not,' she said. 'It's a wedding. The boat's full of bridesmaids.'

Rob slumped down on the next rock. 'They're going to get extremely wet coming ashore.'

She glanced past him, up the beach. 'No, they're not.'

They watched as several hefty lads in dinner suits, barefoot, their black trousers rolled to the knees, waded ankle deep into the gentle surf, and fished the bridesmaids into their arms, one by one. They were clad in gauzy aqua dresses, mermaids from the sea.

'How romantic,' she couldn't stop herself murmuring.

'For crying out loud,' Rob muttered under his breath.

She glanced sideways at him. He looked calm, but his words belied him, and he had yet to discover how acute her hearing was.

'Oh my, another boat. It's the bride. Doesn't she look exquisite?' She couldn't help sighing, as the bride was gathered into the arms of handsome princes and carried across the sand.

'I'm going to get another cup of coffee.'

Anna made no reaction. Spending less time in his company, with fewer opportunities to let something slip, suited her. Oh, how she'd like to be home alone, distanced from this farce of a weekend, from this blip that could have yanked the clear trajectory of her life off course.

Anna gave the old man in the jaunty sailor's cap two pounds for the deck chairs, and was trying to remove her jeans decorously, her towel wrapped around her, when Rob reappeared with two mugs. Despite her inner conflict, the weather was fabulous, the bright blue sky stretching clear and wide above the sunbaked beach.

'You're not going to swim, are you?' he said. 'The breeze is getting up.'

She stared at him. 'It's boiling hot and getting hotter. Hold my towel, will you, so I can strip off with some degree of decency?'

'Can't you manage?'

'I've got the message,' she said. 'You're hating every minute and can't wait to get back to London. Well, neither can I. But as this is the best weather I've had on an English beach for at least a decade, I'm not having you ruin it, however hard you try. Hold the towel.'

'Don't start,' he said, but he took the edges of towel.

Carefully avoiding her fingers, she couldn't help feeling. Well, that suited her. This—this…assignation…or whatever it was, had never been going to work.

'I'm not starting. You can grit your teeth long enough to hold my towel and then you can fall into that deckchair. No eye contact necessary. Just shut up and hold the towel.'

'I didn't say a word.'

'Very wise.'

ROB

Once the wedding party moved further up the beach, Anna pitched forward into the water. She was swimming now. Breaststroke. Not too far out, head above the water.

She was right. It was hotter than ever. He concentrated on the heat on his back, his shoulders, his head, to distract himself from the constant, underlying craving for nicotine. He yanked his shirt over his head and dropped it on the sand. At the water's edge a father and his small daughter crouched. He looked put-upon and bored. Actuary. Or possibly tax inspector.

It felt safer to ignore Anna as she walked out of the water. Nothing like Ursula Andress.

When she remarked about the loveliness of the water, he kept his line of sight firmly on the boats beyond the cove.

She punched his upper arm as she fell into the deckchair beside him.

He couldn't think of a response. What was wrong with him? He was usually the first one in the water, a keen sea swimmer whenever he had the chance. But there was a degree of risk to occupying the same space as Anna. He might reach for her. She might wrench herself away again.

The skin where she'd made contact tingled until he heaved himself out of the deckchair. 'I'm going to get—'

'Yeah. I know. Another cup of coffee.'

ANNA

Anna towel-dried her hair and put on her t-shirt, which clung to her damp swimming costume in a revealing way. Why did the sex part always get in the way? She'd been so prepared to go to bed with Rob, so convinced it was what she needed to jolt herself out of her rut of depression. So horrified when she was catapulted back in time and couldn't go through with it.

Rob didn't need to hear her issues. He had every reason to be furious with her. She'd made a promise. She'd betrayed it. He could have carried on. But he didn't. Didn't pursue her up the stairs, or even knock on the bedroom door.

It had not been her intention to take him up on his offer. It had been a war of attrition. Bombard her with texts, with offers, with suggestions, until she had eventually said yes to this weekend.

But there was an embryonic idea forming in the back of her mind.

Maybe he would do.

Maybe he would do it.

She had thought they knew each other better than they did. Friends of friends. Not really old friends. With whom she imagined she still had things in common. And yet that had been blotted out in an instant, on that sofa last night.

It had taken a long time to settle her fear, to calm her mind, to convince her body she was not in danger.

This morning, although she couldn't quite meet his perceptive gaze, there had been moments of kindness. The cup of coffee. Even if it did have milk in it. The attempt to change their ferry crossing to an earlier time (not possible on a busy May weekend). The proposal that they would drive to the Botanic Gardens and walk down to Steephill Cove in an attempt to fill the six hours.

'I think you'd like it,' he'd said.

She felt worse than ever, in the face of his reasonable behaviour. No awkward questions. Yet. But she knew he was biding his time, that at some point she'd be asked for an explanation. She didn't know what to say. Even the truth sounded pathetic in her mind.

It was lucky she'd bagged these deckchairs when she did, the beach was heaving. She scrabbled around in the bottom of her bag for her watch. Nearly twelve o'clock. Another two hours before they needed to leave for the ferry.

Rob loomed above her, two paper bags in his hands. 'Crab or prawn? I didn't know what you'd like.'

She studied the sand. Stopped herself from saying, 'I never eat bread.' Instead she held out her hand. 'Would prawn be OK? I'm not so keen on crab.'

'Fine.'

She felt as if she was with someone who was forcing himself to pick up spiders. With her as the spider.

He inhaled the sandwich, it was gone so quick. He reached for his breast pocket, then glanced at Anna.

She met his eye for the second time that day.

He shrugged, hands out, palms up-turned, looking so young, transporting her back to his charming, feckless youth. In the intervening years, the things she'd gleaned from the media, from their mutual friends, suggested that he hadn't changed very much. And yet, his rather flat persona was not the whole person. She could almost perceive a more solid, subtler identity at the edge of her conscious thought. Her fatigue somehow brought this knowledge into focus.

'Did you know Charles Dickens wrote *David Copperfield* near here?' he said.

'Funnily enough, I didn't.' Her tone was dry. 'How do you retain all this…information?'

'Bravo for omitting the word "useless",' he said.

ROB

The warm heat of the car, as they sat in the long queue to the motorway, sent Anna to sleep and when they reached the M27 he turned the car west, towards her house near Bath, not east towards London.

It was the decision of a moment. He didn't know why.

It was true that he was a creature of habit. It was true he'd smoked for twenty-three years. But he hadn't had a cigarette for one hundred and fifty-four hours, and however bad the craving and the headache and the shitty mood, occasionally he thought it was not quite as bad as it had been sixty minutes before.

It was overwhelming though. Had taken up so much of his conscious mind that he had not made the effort to swim. Had paddled, feeling somehow emasculated. Hadn't succeeded in seducing Anna. Couldn't even manage a dirty weekend.

Was that it then? He didn't usually chase. Hadn't had to make that much effort, if truth be told. Transforming his text monologues into conversations had been a challenge he'd enjoyed. Anna was different because she saw through him, and he was convinced she didn't like what she saw. Somehow they'd found themselves in an unfamiliar situation. He knew he'd had too much sex with too many women who were in relationships with other men, but he was convinced she'd never done anything like this. It was conscience that had got to her, last night. But that wasn't the whole story. There was something more. Something had been triggered in her as they rolled around on the sofa. Something that had her fleeing. Not that he was likely to find out what, because he didn't think they could mend what had been broken when she wrenched herself out of his arms.

They hadn't touched since then. Had her fingers shrunk from his touch every time he'd handed her a mug of coffee? The closest he'd been to her was when he'd held her towel, had caught the slightest scent of her hair.

Beside him in the car, she was quite still, her hands in her lap, and as he glanced at her, he knew the back of her hand would feel warm and soft to the touch.

ANNA

She woke with a jolt, a strangled scream in her throat as she hurtled towards the back of a silver car, her hands pressed against the dashboard, her right foot slammed into the floor.

'It's all right,' said Rob. 'You were asleep.'

'I realise that,' she snapped. 'Can't you slow down?'

'I always drive fast. It keeps me alert.'

'I've never heard anything so stupid in my life.'

'Are you always this grumpy when you wake up?' His grin was even more infuriating than his words.

'Where are we? This isn't the A3.'

'I'm taking you home. There didn't seem much point in driving you back to London. You'd only have had to get on a train back to Bath.'

'How do you know I didn't drive to London? That my car isn't trapped in some extortionately expensive carpark, charging me more and more, the longer it's left there? How do you know I haven't lined up some crucial meetings in London tomorrow?'

'I don't,' he said. 'Do you want me to turn round?'

She crossed her arms, staring out of the side window. 'Are you always this high-handed?'

He shrugged. 'Always.'

She pressed her lips together. She would not give him the satisfaction of laughing.

'You'll have to give me directions at some point.'

'Just as long as you're not expecting me to invite you

in.' The words were out before she could stop them.

'The thought had never crossed my mind.'

ROB

She'd been quiet now for at least the last forty miles. Her breathing was slow and measured. A bit too slow and measured to convince him she was really asleep. Even if she was, he'd have to wake her soon. He knew her address, but not the exact location of the house in the village. He was still driving west towards the setting sun, watching time slip behind the horizon.

Automatically, yet again, he reached towards his breast pocket, but as he stretched his fingers he stopped, his hand still mid-air.

Anna turned her head towards the movement. 'Bravo.'

These questions were still rattling round his mind when he surfaced from a heavy sleep the following morning. A familiar feeling. Coffee, toast and three paracetamol was what he craved. A loading dose, Sam the GP would call it. Two never quite hit the spot.

He skirted round the lurking presence of Anna in his imagination. She had been a total pain, he justified to himself, but somehow his argument was wearing thin. He strongly suspected there had been tears in the car on the way back, but she'd discreetly gazed out of the window, a swift flick of a finger under an eye, when he should have been focusing entirely on the road. In the confines—the intimacy—of his car, he'd veered from trying to make her laugh, to being annoyed to the point of callousness, unable to get rid of her quick enough. Reversing his car out of her driveway the second she closed the door. But now he felt a lack of congruence, a leaden dread in his stomach at the state he'd left her in.

When all was said and done, she was an old friend. He'd known her since he was fifteen. There had been an intense period of a few years—before they all escaped to university—when they had spent hours of every weekend in each other's company. She'd never quite taken him up on his offer. But given it had been an offer extended to practically all the girls in the group, he understood that now. The pleasure he'd gained from their friendship, he realised, had been from making her laugh. Helplessly, her eyes disappearing into crescents, tears running over her cheeks, descending into snorts of laughter. Which had only made them all laugh harder. Kissing her in Lake Court after Sam's wedding had been the first time. Teenage spin the bottle didn't count.

However he thought about it, she deserved better.

He shoved his arms into yesterday's t-shirt and sweater, pulled on the jeans heaped over the armchair in front of the window.

Coffee. Toast. Paracetamol.

His mobile lay, still and blank, on the bedside drawers. The sleek contours of the device drew attention to the cabinet itself: old and scuffed, like most things in his flat. He didn't spend much time here, but his lack of care for the environment he'd lived in on and off for the best part of ten years, depressed him. He'd bet a large sum of money that Anna's house was infinitely preferable.

It wasn't Rob who was rocking the boat. Anna had texted to invite him to the Summer Exhibition at the Royal Academy. She had made the proposition. Not him.

He recognised his own baser, male instincts when his instinctive response had been yes. It had been a long time since a woman with her natural curves and attributes had wanted to press herself against him. They would of course have to talk about what happened—or didn't happen—on the Isle of Wight. Or maybe they could just get past it. He could slow down. Pay her the attention she deserved.

He liked the thought that he would be doing her a service. Just fulfilling a particular need. One that Jon seemed not to be able to fulfil.

She wore pale trousers and a light cardigan over a chiffon blouse, her hair loose, curling around her softly flushed face. Looking at the art with her and noticing what caught her attention, was already an erotic experience before she said, 'I've had this realization.'

She was absorbed by an oil painting of a naked woman in an airy, high-ceilinged room.

He focused on Anna. 'Yes?'

'My arms are empty.'

'You—'

'I couldn't work it out at first. It's a physical feeling, almost. My arms are empty.' She cradled an imaginary baby. 'See?'

He put his arms round her and pulled her into a hug. 'Not necessarily.'

'Rob. Please.' She drew back, her eyes flicking towards his, then back to the painting.

He dropped his arms and waited.

'Your arms are empty.'

'I'm thirty-nine. A woman's fertility drops off a cliff after thirty-five.'

'Anna.' He held her upper arm, gently propelled her to face him. 'What are you saying?'

Her face twisted towards the painting, eyes on the naked woman. 'Nothing.'

'What do you mean?'

She walked away from him, wrapping both arms around herself.

He found her, still in that self-hug, in the middle of the large room towards the end of the exhibition where vast, dark canvases rose above bright ceramics and small mixed media sculptures. The air was cooler, the crowds thinning. He shrugged off his linen jacket and draped it around her shoulders.

She grasped its edges in her hands. A brief glance.

'Come on,' said Rob. 'I'll buy you a coffee. Or whatever you want.'

She showed her card and they queued for coffee in the Friends Room.

'They say there are plenty of secret passages throughout these buildings,' he said.

Anna folded her arms. 'And you know this, how?'

'Something I read? What did you think of the art?'

'I liked all the colour,' she said. 'Was it Picasso who said something about good taste being the enemy of creativity? I find I'm only drawn to the stuff I like, the pictures I could imagine on my wall. I can appreciate the other stuff, but it doesn't move me. I think that shows my lack of imagination.'

'Or your good taste,' he said.

Another brief look. 'Or fear. Or complacency. Or cowardice. Or inability to change.'

He leaned towards her. 'So, does needing a baby force you to do something different?'

She stepped back. 'We were talking about art.'

'Why don't you say what you want to say? What's the worst that could happen?'

Her eyes finally connected with his. 'That you run screaming from the room?'

He laughed. 'That's easy. I've never run screaming from the room.'

He bought her a cappuccino and they found a table for two at the lighter end of the room, towards the big window onto the courtyard. He watched her sipping her coffee until she put her cup down.

'I read an article by a journalist who was talking about her sadness at not being a grandmother. She'd pursued her career and not missed having children, but was now bereft at not having grandchildren. She described physical, humiliating feelings of jealousy towards her friends with grandchildren.'

Rob leaned across the table and took her hand. 'Anna. She was describing a particular feeling unique to her. If you don't have children, you may be entirely relieved not to have snivelling, self-centred grandchildren dumped on you.'

He could see the tension in her lips, clamped over her teeth. 'What are you proposing?'

She flinched.

'OK. Suggesting.'

'I want a baby.' She turned her face up to the ceiling, blinking rapidly. 'I thought you might be the person to help.'

'Not…?'

Jon's name hovered between them.

'I feel as if I'm running out of time. I need to do something different.'

He rolled his shoulders and breathed. Not only had art galleries become erotically compelling, but he could feel parts of his insides breaking away from each other as she talked. It was as if unseen internal muscles roped together by stress hitherto unknown were relaxing and realigning. A feeling at once alarming and disarming.

When she told him about the abortion, his insides melted and he clamped hold of her hand as if it was the only thing he could grasp.

'It was stupid. So stupid,' she said.

He waited, watching the taut muscles around her eyes and mouth, catching her trembling fingers.

'I really liked him. Really liked him. Fell hard and fast. Quickly went on the pill, but didn't give it enough time. Got pregnant.' She took a juddering breath. 'I panicked. Didn't even tell him...'

Rob held her gaze when she looked up from the table. 'When was this?'

'Thirteen years ago. If it had gone to term, I'd have a twelve-year-old by now.' She blinked, pulled her hand out of his, pressed her palms together.

'Anna.' He didn't know what to say. 'What a thing to go through.'

'Yeah. Well. Whatever.'

He let it pass. 'Did you tell people?'

'Not at the time. Jess was the only person who knew, for a long while.'

'She would have been sympathetic—'

'Yes, she was very supportive.'

'So how do you feel now?'

Anna sighed, propped her head on her hand. 'Better, and worse. The guilt has faded. But that was when I was young and naïve. I didn't think it would be my only chance. I didn't think I'd be childless at the age of thirty-nine.'

'It's not over till the fat lady sings.'

She smiled a small smile for the first time since they'd sat down. 'What does that even mean? I get it's an opera reference, but—'

'Thirty-nine is not too old—'

'I know. Not impossible. Just less and less likely. I realise I have filters up for this stuff, but anything you read, watch or listen to and plummeting fertility rates are all you hear.'

He watched her scoop the last of the froth from her coffee with the teaspoon. 'So you're serious. This is what you want.'

She raised her eyes to his. 'Yes. Anyway. Where are you off to? You said you had to meet someone?'

He glanced at his watch. 'In an hour or so. Actually, it's Sam.'

'Really? Give him my love.' She paused, regarding him. 'Or not. If that would be too weird.'

'No, no. I'll pass that on. Thank you for the invitation.'

Her eyes connected with his.

'To see the art. I haven't done this in a long time, and I really enjoyed it.'

'You're welcome,' she said, staring at the empty cups between them.

ANNA

Rob had got up and gone to the loo, and she'd assumed when he came back, that he'd pick up his jacket and leave. Now that she'd lost her sanity and blurted out her desperate desire. Instead he said he needed something more to eat and drink. So she switched to tea, he ordered another espresso, and persuaded her to nibble a corner of his croissant. Carbs.

He'd obviously been gearing up for more conversation. 'Just so I get this straight, no involvement at all?'

'None. You'd be under no obligation. You wouldn't be required to do…to be…' Her voice petered out.

'So, how would it work then? What would you tell your parents, for instance?'

"I don't know, Rob. I haven't thought it all through.' Why the hell hadn't she kept her mouth shut? She wasn't really going to blame it on the disarming beauty of the art, was she? The more they spoke, the more lunatic the scheme sounded. 'All I'm trying to say is I wouldn't expect anything from you.'

'Apart from the baby.'

Anna examined his face as he contemplated the pastry crumbs on the plate between them. 'I thought this would be helpful. I thought it would be what you want. I'm not looking for more from you…'

He pushed himself back from the table, looked out into the courtyard, and rubbed his jaw. 'What if we'd had none of these conversations, Anna? What if you and I had just fallen into bed together because we were so…because we got on so well together? And what if, after that, you got pregnant by accident? Would we really be having this conversation? Wouldn't you expect—quite legitimately—a great deal more from me? Support: financial, emotional, something?'

Anna closed her eyes. 'We're not in that situation though. We're trying to make a rational agreement about something I long for, and with which I would need your help.'

'Have you considered a donor?'

'OK. Fine. Let's forget the whole thing.' She felt so foolish, so vulnerable. Was it purely the beautiful, illuminating art that had brought on all this heartfelt exposure? She gathered her bag from her feet and turned to unhook her cardigan from the back of the chair.

'Look… Just… Sorry. Please don't go. I didn't mean it like that.'

'No. You're right. A donor would be the way to go.'

'But you asked me.' His tone was flat.

After a moment she slumped back in her chair. 'Don't be angry. I shouldn't have asked you.' She knew it was an unreasonable request. One she hadn't intended to articulate.

'Why don't you want me to be involved? Would you tell people it's Jon's baby?'

'No. I just don't want to make any demands… I wouldn't expect anything else from you.'

'But this rational agreement doesn't take into consideration that we're talking about a baby. A baby that would benefit from having two parents.'

'Rob.' The obsession over having a baby blanketed everything else. She'd barely considered the father having a relationship with her or the baby.

'Don't you think I'm up to it? Too flaky, too much of a commitment-phobe to do that? Do you really think so little of me?'

She watched his fingers rake through his hair. It was springy and abundant. Would he think her pathetic if she leant across and touched it? 'I think you are capable of many things, and one day, if parenthood is what you want, you'd be a brilliant dad. All I'm saying is that I would not expect you to be fully involved.'

'Unless I want to be?' He looked at her without blinking.

'Well.' Her heart thudded. 'That would…we could… work out how—'

'You do not sound convinced.'

'I'm taken aback. You've caught me—'

'You really do think so little of me.'

'Please, Rob. Let's not fight. I didn't think—'

'That I'm capable of looking beyond sex?'

'I thought I was being helpful. Clear about my expectations. Not because… I'm not making judgements about your lifestyle.'

'My *lifestyle*?' Rob exploded.

'Oh God.' Anna put her head in her hands. *Don't cry. Do not cry.*

'Anna.' He reached out and took her hand. 'I understand your need. Your want. The whole idea of your arms being empty. There are aspects of this that are very attractive.' He closed his eyes. 'Sometimes I want nothing more than to fall into bed with you—the Isle of Wight notwithstanding—to make love to you... But.'

She looked up at him. 'I get it. It's OK.'

He rubbed his thumb over the back of her hand. 'I'm not saying no, I'm saying this is more of a commitment than just leaping into bed. If you get what you want, then there's another human being involved. One we've created. There are consequences to our pleasure. I need to think.'

Anna blinked. All she could feel was the gentle smoothing of her skin by the warm pressure of his thumb. Making love. Consequences to our pleasure.

ROB

Sam grinned. 'You're late.'

Rob turned his wrist over, remembering the sweet pressure of her hand in his. 'By three minutes.'

'Still. That means you think your time's more important than my time.'

'Well it is. Nice to see you too.' Rob hugged his friend. 'What's up? Jess?'

'Jess is lovely. Forbearing. My elder daughter, not so much.'

'Oh, Katie's a pussycat. She just needs to be reminded who's boss.'

'You're not helping,' said Sam. 'And you sound like an American sit-com.'

'Are we going in?' said Rob. He gestured to the stairs into the National Gallery from Trafalgar Square. 'I'm sure we could find a quiet spot. Or a coffee. Or a drink?'

'Or we could walk down to the Summer Exhibition.'

'Ah. I've seen it,' said Rob.

'Really. A work assignment? You're not usually this cultured.'

'How do you know? I'm here, aren't I? Let's go and see Hendrijke.' He took the stairs two at a time.

'Who?' Sam bounded after him.

'Rembrandt. His housekeeper, who became his mistress. He married her after his first wife died.'

'OK, Rain Man. How do you know this stuff?'

Rob grinned. 'Someone told me.' He marched into the first gallery.

'Oh yeah? Who?'

Rob ignored him. 'So, Katie. What's the strategy?'

Sam's shoulders slumped. 'I have no idea. Jess is really patient. But the way Kate speaks to her—*when* she speaks to her—feels more and more provocative.'

Rob raised an eyebrow. 'So? Call her out. Defend the woman you love.'

'What's got into you?' Sam lengthened his stride as Rob powered through the rooms.

At the other side of the building, in one of the smaller rooms, Rob stopped in front of a painting of a woman with dark, sad eyes, wearing a pale fur, against a sombre background. He shrugged on the linen jacket he'd hooked over his shoulder, the one he'd draped around Anna in the end rooms at the Summer Exhibition, and her scent settled over him as the fabric fell into place. *Boy, am I in trouble.*

Eventually he registered that Sam was studying him rather than the painting. He glanced up. 'What?'

'You tell me,' said Sam, the ever patient doctor.

'Don't you like her?' Rob gestured to the painting.

'Illuminating,' said Sam, still staring at him. 'You know, Sebastian said there was a point at the wedding reception when you disappeared. For at least an hour. Apparently Anna was gone for the same length of time.'

Rob shrugged, trying hard not to smile at the sound of her name. Anna. 'What's that got to do with the price of fish?'

'You tell me.'

'We were talking about your domestic arrangements. Not mine.'

'Just as long as you're not including Anna in any domestic plans of your own. She's been with Jon for a long time, and it's obviously a situation that works for them both.'

Is it? Is it really? Rob pressed his lips together. 'Drink?'

They stood for a few more moments looking at the portrait.

'She's lovely,' said Sam.

'I know,' Rob replied.

They walked down to the café that overlooked Trafalgar Square. At the tail end of the afternoon, visiting matriarchs from the country were about to be replaced by gasping office workers. They bought a couple of beers and found a small table.

'So, how's it going? Married life with five children?' Rob swigged his beer, which was satisfyingly chilled.

'Matrimony I can recommend. Jess is very kind—even to Kate—and she's great company. Coming home to adult conversation and shared responsibility, after years of juggling alone, is wonderful.'

'How does Elizabeth feel about all this?'

'My ex-wife is a calculating machine. It suits her that I have the kids most of the time. She can concentrate on work.' Sam picked at the foil around the neck of his beer bottle.

'And what does she think of Jess?'

Sam looked directly at Rob. 'Let's not ask stupid questions. They've hardly had to meet, and I plan to keep it that way.'

Rob raised his eyebrows.

'And Kate's learnt how to be a master manipulator. Playing three of us off against each other could give her too much scope, so in theory having all the kids at ours the majority of the time should be easier.'

'Doesn't give you much of a break, though.' He set his beer down. At this rate he'd finish it in less than a minute.

'We were never going to get much of a break with kids this age—however few. Or many. Anyway. What's going on with you?' Sam took a sip of his beer, now that the top had been stripped of foil.

'So, what's Kate's plan? Make Jess's life hell?'

'Something like that. Wearing.'

Rob shrugged. 'Marriage. Commitment. Children.'

Sam stared at him. 'You say them like they're dirty words. Why?'

'Once bitten.'

'Don't give me that. You knew your ex-wife was unhinged and you thought you could change her.'

'Did I? I'm convinced now that people don't change.'

'No. Intrinsically nice people we've known most of our lives tend to stay nice.'

'You've lost me.'

'Faithful. Committed. Don't threaten the status quo.'

Rob drained his beer. 'OK, Sam. You've stated your position.'

Rob realised he was moving at a fast pace when he found himself almost at Victoria, having missed St James's station entirely. He wheeled round, then stopped. Victoria would do just as well. He made a conscious effort to breathe.

It was not as if he'd made any commitment to Anna. All he'd said was he needed time and space to think. But the more he thought, the less he could see. His conversation with Sam really hadn't helped.

His imagination, in glorious technicolour, kept suggesting brightly coloured close-ups of him in bed with

Anna, the soft heaviness of her breasts pressed against him, which left him dizzy and light-headed. But sex was not the problem.

His mind misted over when he thought about a baby, a child—*his* child—in the world, without him there to guide and protect it. All the paternalistic, possessive feelings he'd resisted for over twenty years reared their heads to wind him.

He moved out of the path of three teenage girls: tight trousers, long flicking hair.

He needed a drink.

No. He did not need a drink.

'Let me get this straight,' said Sam. 'Anna propositioned you because she wants a baby?'

Rob cradled the mobile between ear and shoulder, grabbed a bottle of beer out of his virtually empty fridge and shoved the door shut with his elbow. He paced the four steps from his tiny kitchen to his small lounge, fell onto the scuffed leather sofa and kicked off his trainers. 'Yup.'

'What about Jon?'

'He doesn't seem to feature.'

'Have they finished? They must have been together for the best part of a dozen years.'

'I don't know.' Rob swigged his beer.

'Maybe you should grab her and marry her. Have all the sex you want,' said Sam.

'Who says I want to have all the sex?'

'Rob. Please. It's Anna we're talking about.'

'I know it's Anna. I've been trying to get my head around this for days.'

'So what's the problem? She's a sweetheart who wants

a baby. And of all the people she could have asked, she asked you.'

'It's complicated.'

'Well, uncomplicate it. Stop with the philandering and settle down. Properly.'

'You forget I tried that. It didn't work out. And divorce is one of the most painful things possible.'

'Agreed. But it was never going to end well. You were landed with a mentally unstable wife who had no ability to communicate. Who behaved very badly.'

'If you knew all that, why didn't you stop me?' said Rob.

'Had I met the bride before the wedding, it might have been possible to assess the situation and warn you. In the state you were in on the day, not so easy.'

'The state you were in.'

'You were always a bad influence,' said Sam.

'Yeah. Thanks. You're not helping.'

'Can't you imagine what going home to Anna at night would be like? And you get to have all that procreative sex. You're actually trying to make her pregnant.'

'Speaks the man whose first three children were accidents, Dr Rushmore.'

'Give me a break. Emma was planned. Kate was unexpectedly early, that's true. Josh was an attempt at reconciliation.'

'I know this part.'

'How have you left it with Anna?'

'I told her I needed time to think.'

'When was this?'

'Saturday.' Friday.

'But you've been in contact since then?'

'I'm thinking.'

'Rob! It's Tuesday!'

'I'm still thinking.'

'Poor woman. She showed her ultimate vulnerability and let you into her most intimate secret, and you fuck off?'

Rob held the phone away from his ear. 'Warn me if you're going to yell.'

'Get your act together. Get over there. Tell her, of course you'll give her what she wants.'

'Yeah, but what do I get out of it? She doesn't even want me involved.'

'She said that categorically?'

'She said she had no expectations.'

'You know that's not the same thing. I thought you were renowned for your insightful interviews. Why are you being so dense?'

Rob drained the last of his beer and put it on the sludge-coloured carpet. He'd done virtually nothing to the flat in the years since he'd bought it, and boy did it show. 'She was quite clear that she had no—'

'That she was not going to freak you out with her hopes and dreams. Look. She's trusted you with something immensely private and personal. Saying she had no expectations of your involvement doesn't mean she wouldn't want it. Doesn't long for it.'

Rob leaned back into the sofa. 'I don't think I'm prepared for there to be a child of mine in the world who doesn't know his father.'

'Is this the adoption thing?'

'Don't psychoanalyse me… I just don't want that…'

'Have you told Anna?'

'No. And I'm not planning to bring it up.'

'But you are at least planning to talk to her?'

'When I've worked out what I'm going to say.'

'So. Ring her. Now. By the way, we're all fine here. Even Kate.'

The phone went dead. Rob stared at it, switched it to silent, laid it beside him on the sofa and closed his eyes.

He rarely thought of his birth mother, and hadn't felt the need to investigate his background. His parents had never kept the information of his adoption from him, and Natalie had always just been his sister. It hadn't even been weird that only he was adopted—that she'd come along naturally within a year of his arrival in the family.

All he knew was that he'd been born in Liverpool, to a nurse. Nothing about the father. No indication of her situation, whether she'd wanted to get rid of him. She had named him Robert, and his parents had respected that choice. That felt like a big, generous gesture on their part. Somehow Robert didn't seem like a name his parents would have chosen. His middle name, Alexander, fitted better with Natalie, somehow. His mother had never allowed any shortenings like Robbie or Bob, but when he went to secondary school, he became Rob and never looked back. Rob Randall was who he was, and he felt comfortable with that.

There were times when he went back home—such as Christmas—when he truly felt like the cuckoo in the nest, and the horizons of his parents seemed so very different to his own. But maybe his sister had felt stifled too, which was why she'd found herself establishing her own family on the opposite side of the world. Occasionally he felt nostalgic for a different family history. When he looked at how Sam and his older brother Will supported each other—had such a strong friendship as well as sibling relationship—he felt pangs for what might have been, but most of the time he shut down such thoughts. When he'd gone to Uni, urged by his father to do a science degree that hadn't suited him, he'd felt loneliness more intense than at any time of his life. For a while drink and drugs had filled a void. It was the discovery that he could write, the post-degree journalism MA, the beckoning vista of political stories and then wider interviews, that had quietened any internal questions.

Was this why he'd never been interested in having children? Did it open up horizons he'd never contemplated? Would his own parenting ability be horribly hampered by being given away by his birth mother?

These were questions he'd never really allowed himself to consider properly. But now, they wouldn't leave him alone. Turning forty certainly focused the mind. He could remain an island, without children and family, or he could jump into another life.

If he did, there would questions he needed answering. He would have to take that step to discover more about his birth parents, to finally overturn all the reasons not to find out more.

ANNA

Wednesday evening, Anna was lying on her sofa, trying to gather the energy to switch on the TV. The self-improving novel had still not been opened.

The fourth time Rob rang, Anna picked up, more because the persistence of his calls was grating on her nerves, than that she wanted to talk to him.

'Anna. I'm sorry.'

She waited. Nothing. 'That's it? I'd appreciate it if this would go no further, I feel stupid enough as it is.'

'No. I mean I'm sorry I haven't called. I've been thinking.'

'Well.' She couldn't think of anything else to say.

'I'd like to— Could we meet? Are you at home?'

'Really Rob, there's no need.'

'Yes, there is. Please. We— There are things to discuss—'

'I think I'd rather not, if it's all the same to you,' she said. 'It's totally fine that you'd rather not—'

'That's not what I'm—'

'Really.' She swallowed hard, suddenly on the brink of tears. 'Goodbye.'

Why did she have to play out so many different scenarios in her head? The vast majority of which found herself with a baby in her arms, and Rob in her peripheral vision? She felt out of control. He had rapidly filled her consciousness, eclipsing Jon so completely. She knew it was dangerous to cast him in the role of her saviour when nothing was certain. It was exhausting being this untethered, this dislocated from her safe, established life.

SAM

He found Jess in the inordinately tidy kitchen, folding clean underwear into piles.

'What a day,' said Sam, kissing his wife. 'How was yours?'

'Busy. I've been to look at paint colours, and the children have some very strong ideas about their bedrooms. Oh, and I did a shop, and I may have found a—'

'Cup of tea?' He flicked on the kettle.

'Yes, please.' She tucked her hair behind her ears. 'Um, I may have found a job.'

Sam blinked. 'A job?'

'They're looking for someone to run the community hall bookings. It's not much, but I could do it from home. All I need is an email address and a—'

'Are you sure about this? Do you want to start something so soon? There's absolutely no pressure to—'

'I know. I do. But I want to contribute. I don't want to be a kept woman.'

Sam slid his arms around Jess and held her tight. 'I've always rather liked the idea of a kept woman.'

She cuffed his shoulder. 'Be serious for once.'

'Let's have that cup of tea.' Every surface was shining, including the old oak table, polished as it had never been. A glance down the garden took in several loads of washing, methodically folded over the washing line, to minimize the ironing. As Jess had explained, when she shook and re-hung a lot of the washing he'd slung over the drying rack. Occasionally he had to remind himself of the many advantages of being married to Jess, when her need to keep on top of running the house took over from spending time together. But it was crucial they could both relax, too.

He thought back to their honeymoon. Two nights in the country house hotel overlooking Windermere, followed by several days staying in a cottage belonging to Matt and Jane, in Satterthwaite, a village between Windermere and Coniston Water. Cold and blue-tinged when they first arrived, it soon warmed up, and the rest of the week had rushed by.

Inside the cottage, it was absolutely quiet. Just the two of them, reading in the front room, armchairs opposite each other, either side of the fire. Jess had brought her sketchbook and made small pen drawings of the views from the windows.

They'd avoided the busier towns, the shops and the hubbub. Preferred the open spaces, including a soggy morning in the Grizedale forest, where the views were breathtaking.

He put tea bags in cups, found milk from the fridge. 'Why don't you sit down?'

'I was just going to iron a few things.'

He'd heard all about Jess's theory about ironing piles: don't have one. Just move the essentials that had to be ironed, from the line or rack straight to the ironing board and then, folded, upstairs to the airing cupboard. Watching her could be exhausting. He'd tried to be helpful, but he wasn't familiar with all the unspoken rules about how cotton boxers could be hung with minimum creases, or socks smoothed into the optimum shape for folding once they were dry…

'Darling. We haven't seen each other all day. Sit down.'

'Oh. OK,' said Jess.

He stretched across the table and took her hands in his. 'You're doing a terrific job. Looking after us wonderfully. But it's good to stop and rest.'

'I just want everything to run smoothly.'

'I know. Something smells delicious.'

'I've done a chicken casserole in the slow cooker. Will your three eat that?'

'I'm sure they will.'

'I just want it all—'

'I know, darling. Everyone will settle down. We've got to get used to each other.'

'It's just that…now Emma…'

'She's at that age when having her older sister's approval is very important to her.'

Jess pulled her hands away. 'What time is it? I should put the rice on.'

'I can do that. In a minute. You drink your tea.'

'Things were fine with Emma, and she's so good with both Ben and Millie. It's as if, now she's turned ten, she doesn't want to spend time with us. Well, with me.'

'I'll talk to her,' said Sam.

'No. Really. Don't. I'll work it out.'

'You don't have to. I expect all three of my children to behave well towards you, darling.'

'But you can't force them. They'll hate me more than ever.'

'They don't hate you. They're trying to get used to a new reality. Aren't they? We all are.'

'I know. When I'm feeling rational it makes perfect sense. It's only sometimes it feels overwhelming.'

'Which is completely understandable. You're entitled to give yourself a break.'

Sam put the rice on, topped and tailed the green beans, warmed the plates and set the table. He kept Jess amused with tales from the receptionists at the surgery, including the latest random phone calls from patients.

When the children came downstairs to eat, he observed Emma closely. She deferred to Kate and looked to her for approval, he could see that, but she also paid attention to Jess and watched for her reactions, particularly in reference to Kate's behaviour. Must be exhausting, being caught between the two of them, he thought.

Despite Jess's plea not to talk to Em, he did think it would be worth doing, given her level of emotional intelligence. But he'd need to find the right moment, and he had no idea when that might be.

JESS

There were many things Jess liked about the house. There was a lot more space than her terraced house in London. It wasn't overlooked by houses at the back, and the spacious garden and vista across the tennis courts, towards Barton Common, the large oak and beech trees, and Lake Court beyond, gave her a sense of space and fresh air that she rarely felt in the capital. Downside? Much more to keep clean and tidy.

She had all sorts of ideas about what they might do to spruce things up. Her immediate dream would be to paint the kitchen, including the dark wood cupboards and units. It was all solid and well made, but a part of her longed for a pale, restful palette of dove grey or a knocked-back slate green, the surfaces streamlined, everything having its place. She was very conscious that she and Ben and Millie were entering into an established family home with decades of history—Sam had grown up here—in which each member had their own ideas about how things should be.

In her more optimistic moments, she did think that she might find an unexpected ally in Kate, who had definite ideas about how she liked her own bedroom to be, and might well be someone to appeal to as and when—*not if*—relations mellowed between them.

So, Jess cleaned and tidied—nothing too radical to begin with—and focused on providing tasty home-cooked meals for Sam and the children. Not all her efforts were successful. The roast chicken was fine, although they preferred roast potatoes to rice, and leeks were not acceptable. The moussaka even less so. As Josh, newly turned eight, told her in no uncertain terms, aubergines were just wrong. A view that was echoed loudly by seven-year-old Ben.

Tonight, the satisfaction of seven almost completely clean plates after the chicken casserole and rice, was somewhat spoiled by Kate's silent departure from the table. She had looked wan, chilly even in the warm, late spring dusk. Now, Jess observed Emma, who avoided her eye, but unusually did not disappear after the table had been cleared.

'Everything OK?' said Jess. 'I'm going to bring the washing in.' When Emma followed her down the garden to the washing line, Jess waited to see what she would say, a technique she'd learnt from her wise husband. The silence made her palms itch, but Emma eventually filled it.

'Do you only do the washing on certain days?'

Not what Jess had been expecting. 'Um. Well. Not really. Mainly when I can't get the lid to stay on the laundry basket. What makes you ask?'

Emma screwed her eyes shut. 'Nothing.'

'I suppose I try not to spend the whole weekend washing. It's nice to have a rest, especially on Sundays.'

'Oh.' Emma fiddled with the edge of her t-shirt. 'Mum only does it at weekends.'

Jess kept unhooking the washing from the line, folding it and dropping it into the capacious basket. 'Well, that makes sense. She has a busy job, your mum, during the week.'

'Yeah. If you forget to put something in the washing, it's your own fault. You just have to make do.'

'Sometimes you really need something, I expect. It

wouldn't matter if you needed to wash something, Emma.'

'Oh no, it's not for me.' Emma stopped rolling the edge of her top between her thumbs and fingers. 'I was just wondering.'

Jess picked up the basket of clean washing. 'I tell you what. Do you think you could persuade Kate to come downstairs? There's something I'd like to show you both.'

Emma met her look, shrugged slightly. 'I don't know. I don't think so.'

'Why don't you have a go? Could you bring the peg bag?' She set off up the garden, the basket under her arm. When they reached the kitchen, Jess said, 'See if you can find Kate and come downstairs to the utility room.'

'I'll try,' said Emma.

Jess put the clean pile of clothes on the kitchen table, and took the basket down the stone steps. It was cooler down there and she shook herself in the chill. Silly to feel jittery at the possibility of an encounter with Kate.

She deposited the basket on the painted red floor beside the washing machine, and erected one of the drying racks. Then she prayed.

'What is it that's so important it can't wait?' she could hear Kate demand of her sister, as they thundered down the stairs.

Jess took a deep breath, unclenched her fingers. 'Girls. Just wanted to show you something.'

Kate's frown descended down her face like a shutter.

'Won't take a moment,' Jess ploughed on. 'There's a rapid wash on this machine—only fifteen minutes—so if you have anything you need to wash quickly, it's very useful. Especially anything you've forgotten.'

'What do you need to do?' said Emma, not quite looking at Jess.

'You turn the dial, here. Then the time comes up. You can change the spin speed, so if you were doing a towel or bedding, say, you could set it to the faster spin, like this. If I was doing gym kit or something like that, I'd leave it on the slower speed. There's some spray too, which I'll leave beside the washing liquid, if you've got any marks you want to come out. The rack's there for hanging stuff and anything you needed to dry overnight could be put in the airing cupboard in the big bathroom. It's warm in there beside the hot water tank.' *They get it. Stop talking.*

Emma glanced at her sister. 'We'll go and get—'

'Yeah. Thanks.' Kate shoved her with a sharp elbow, took the stairs two at a time.

Two words, one of thanks.

Emma gave Jess a small self-conscious smile. 'Thank you.'

SAM

'All peaceful?' Sam shut the bedroom door, kicked off his shoes and pulled his shirt and t-shirt over his head in one graceful movement.

Jess laid down her book and eyed him from the comfort of the generous double bed. 'Well, it *was*.'

Sam laughed, extending his arms as if acknowledging appreciative applause. He dropped his clothes onto the chair. 'We aim to please. All quiet upstairs?'

'As far as I know, everyone's in the correct bed.'

'Tired? You came upstairs early.' He took off his watch, peeled off his socks.

'Ah. Yes. Sam.'

'Jess.' His eyes connected with hers. He stopped undressing. 'You know you can say anything, don't you? Even if you're having thoughts.'

Jess grinned. 'Thoughts?'

'Thoughts. About me. About what our bodies could do together. You know, I'm still not used to the idea that we get to sleep together every night.' He stretched out on top of the bedclothes beside her, wearing just his trousers.

'I know. But that wasn't exactly what I was thinking about. Earlier. Before an attractive man came into my bedroom and started stripping off.'

Sam nudged her arm, skin to skin. 'Am I distracting you?'

'Yes. Put a shirt on.'

He wriggled his toes. Jess was quite keen on his bare feet. An evening of foot fondling in Oxford came to mind.

'I'm about to have a shower. What were you thinking about?'

Jess turned her head and met his eyes. 'I was thinking about Kate. Both girls really. I was wondering if she's started her periods yet.'

Sam pulled his attention away from entwined feet. 'Sorry? Kate? She's…'

'She's twelve. Lots of girls have started by then.'

'She still seems so young. Pre-pubescent, rather than pubescent.'

'I know. Emma was asking me about doing some washing, and it made me wonder. I showed them how to use the quick wash on the machine. That's why I came upstairs. I wanted to leave them in peace in case they were embarrassed.'

'What were they washing?' Sam wracked his brains for any conversations with his ex-wife about his daughters' physical development, but he couldn't think of anything. He and Elizabeth didn't really talk like that. Their conversations fell into one of two topics: academic progress at school, or things the children needed, such as shoes, sports equipment, money for a school trip.

'My guess would be gym kit. And it occurred to me that maybe Kate was embarrassed and didn't want to show anyone because she'd had a bit of an accident or something. Emma was very sweet and protective.'

Sam put his arm around Jess and drew her into a side hug. 'They're very lucky. I'm very lucky.'

'Don't be silly, Sam. I may be quite wrong. But I think I'll stock up on tampons and pads, and put them in the bathroom cupboard. Just in case.'

'I can't believe I'm such a stereotype,' he said, into her shoulder.

'What are you talking about?'

'Doctor neglecting the health of his own children.'

'Don't be ridiculous. They're the picture of health. All this stuff is normal development. And usually a mother's area rather than a father's. I could be wrong…'

'Bet you're not. Thank you for taking such an interest. Making such an effort.'

'You're welcome.' She kissed him. 'You'd better get a move on if you don't want me to be asleep by the time you come back from the shower.'

Sam leapt up. 'Give me five seconds.'

ROB

A slim dark girl with startingly long eyelashes opened the outer door to the office. 'Hello? Can I help you? You're not Steve?'

'Hello,' he said, climbing the stairs and extending his hand. 'Rob Randall. Hoping to catch Anna.'

The girl shook his hand. She had very long nails. 'I'm Jade. I think she's on her way. Is she expecting you?'

'Not exactly, Jade.' He grinned. 'Can I let you into a secret?'

Her face broke into a smile. 'Er…like…you're…'

'I'm an old friend from home. From Manchester. I saw Anna again in London recently…'

'Come in,' said Jade. 'It's not yet 10 o'clock in the morning and you don't look like a thief or a mugger.'

'Absolutely not. But I do need your help. I'm hoping to take Anna away for the night. But perhaps she has a meeting with Steve?'

Jade led him into the office. 'Tea? Coffee?'

'I'm fine, thanks,' he said.

'Have a seat. Steve's meeting is with me, and I'll need to check Anna's diary.'

'Please. Go ahead. Anything that couldn't be moved?'

She peered at her computer screen and tapped a few keys, while Rob sat on a comfortable sofa. The open plan office was light and airy. Everything that could be so, was either white or a pale neutral. Here, it was restful. So much lovelier than his dingy flat.

'Er,' said Jade. 'I'm not sure. Maybe I should check with Anna.'

'Of course.' He smiled. 'Great if we could have a plan ready. If I can persuade her.'

She smiled back, her shoulders dropping. 'I don't think today's a problem, but there is something in the diary first thing tomorrow…'

'Ah. Any possibility it could…' He spread his hands, palms upwards.

'Let me see if I could move it to Friday…'

'You are an absolute star.'

While her nails clacked over the keyboard, he surveyed the room. Large windows on either side looked out over the small business estate of converted barns towards green fields.

'Sure you won't have a drink?' she offered.

Rob wiped his palms along his trousers. He'd left Earls Court before seven and had had three espressos already. 'Really. I'm fine. Although maybe some water…'

So it was that Jade was in the kitchen when Anna shouldered the door open, her arms full of bags.

'Whose is the Audi outside, then?' she said, before she came to a stop, released the bags and stared at Rob.

He stood up.

Jade appeared with two glasses of water. 'Er. Rob's perhaps?'

She handed him a glass and proffered the other to Anna, who took it and drank.

'I'm hoping you can leave things in Jade's capable hands for twenty-four hours.' He scanned her face.

'I can't just drop everything if you show up,' she said.

He chose not to point out the bags around her feet. 'Is there anything that really couldn't be moved? I can have you back here by tomorrow afternoon.'

'What are you talking about?'

'I'll just take the post over to the studio.' Jade seized a small pile of envelopes on the edge of her desk and clattered down the stairs.

Rob stepped towards Anna. 'I thought it might be easier to talk in person. And there are some very lovely hotels not too far from here, so I took the liberty of booking dinner, bed and breakfast.'

'I've just said I can't drop everything at a moment's notice.'

'I know. Jade was looking at your diary to see what might need to be moved.'

'Nothing needs to be moved—'

'Anna.'

She scowled. 'I don't need to be rescued.'

'I'm not rescuing you. In popular parlance, I'm asking you on a date. Overnight. In an extremely plush hotel.' He watched her frown at the floor. 'We don't even need to talk. You can sleep the whole time, if that would be more relaxing.'

'God, you're paternalistic. I don't want to be handled by you!'

'Oh. I thought that was exactly what you did want. In a non-paternalistic way.'

She pursed her lips. 'So you've come here to say you've changed your mind.'

'No. I keep trying to tell you. I was thinking. I never said no. And now I'm taking you up on your offer.'

She shuddered. 'Well I've had time to think too, and this is a bad idea. Let's just—'

'Anna.' He stepped in front of her, and put a hand on her shoulder. 'Look at me.'

Her eyes swerved towards his.

'Please.'

Her lips in a firm line, she looked up.

'Let's go and have lunch somewhere. Wherever you like. If you want to carry on after that, great. If not, I'll bring you back here, no harm done.'

'Don't patronize me. I can drive. In my own car.'

He dropped his hand, stepped back. 'Or you could let me. And then you could relax.'

She worried her lower lip with her front teeth.

'Yes? No? I'll leave if you'd rather…'

Jade thundered up the stairs. She swerved round the pair of them to reach her desk and tapped on the keyboard. 'Great. I've moved your 10 a.m. tomorrow to Friday, so you don't have to rush back, Anna?'

'Really,' said Anna. 'I'm going to the loo.'

Rob shrugged at Jade. 'I think I may have misjudged her enthusiasm for seeing me.'

'Oh no, she'll be fine. She's just catching up.'

When Anna came back, she spoke to Jade. 'Right. Well, I'm on my phone then.'

'Of course,' said Jade. 'Have a lovely time.'

Anna didn't look at Rob as they descended the stairs.

He unlocked his car and opened the passenger door.

She unlocked her own car. 'What would make more sense is driving to my house so I can pick up a change of clothes.'

Rob closed the door, leant against it and folded his arms. He let out a breath. 'That sounds like a plan.'

'You'll have to follow me,' said Anna.

ANNA

Anna spent most of the fifteen minute journey checking her mirror. Rob stayed a constant, safe distance behind her, and when she pulled into her drive, parked behind her and got out.

'This is a great house,' he said.

She exhaled, unclenched her jaw. 'Thank you. I like it.'

He followed her up the front steps, along the hall to a large kitchen with a back lawn and fruit trees beyond. A comfortable, book-lined sitting area faced a big window overlooking the front garden. This was her favourite room in the house.

'Do you want something to drink?'

'I'm fine. Point me in the direction of a kettle and leave me to it.'

Upstairs, she stared at her wardrobe. She was wearing ankle length trousers, a silk top, a jacket and wedge sandals. What was the appropriate clothing for this kind of assignation?

Eventually, she grabbed a pair of linen trousers, a long skirt, another top and a scarf. In the bathroom she tipped most of her toiletries into her sponge bag, grabbed a disposable razor—she had not been expecting to take her clothes off in front of anyone—and retrieved her make-up bag from the shelf.

What else? A second pair of shoes, suitable to wear for dinner.

Something to wear in bed. Oh, God. She usually wore

cotton pyjama bottoms and a t shirt. Functional and comfortable. But somehow not the thing. She felt about at the back of her drawer and eventually located a strappy black silk nightdress.

Underwear. She ignored the usual t-shirt bras and cotton knickers, and threw two sets of matching lacy underwear into her leather holdall, positioning the scarf on top.

Downstairs, Rob was stretched out in the armchair, looking out over the front garden. 'This is a great room. Very tranquil.'

'Thank you.' She stood stiffly at the kitchen table.

He unfurled himself from the chair. 'They do have a very picturesque outdoor pool, if you want to bring swimming things. It's going to be warm enough.'

'Oh no, I never…' She ran out of words. He'd already seen her in a swimming costume. Not much point in saying she didn't wear one if she could possibly help it, because they were too revealing.

'You could pack it. Just in case.' He tilted his chin, and she saw the challenge.

'Maybe.'

'Give me a tour?' he said, in the hall. 'I didn't get one last time.'

She bit her lip. The Isle of Wight. She'd felt so uncomfortable then, not wanting him in her world. Luckily he hadn't been able to get away quick enough. 'What?'

'Please?'

She showed him the dining room and the Chinese red sitting room. He admired two abstract paintings. 'This house is like you, Anna.'

For a moment their eyes met. What did that mean? And what was his flat like? Not like this, she concluded. 'I'll show you the rest some other time.'

ROB

By the time they reached the hotel, Anna seemed to have stopped holding her breath. Every time he asked her a question she had paused, waited, preparing her answer as if to give as little of herself away as possible.

But her shoulders were no longer up by her ears, and there'd even been a half smile when he told her where they were going.

Now, as they walked up the wide steps to what looked more like an exquisitely kept country house, rather than a luxury hotel, he was glad he'd made the effort to do this.

He took her hand, but she slowly pulled it away.

Their ground floor room was at the end of a modern wing, overlooking the gardens.

'Nice and quiet,' he said. 'We won't be disturbed down here.'

'It's lovely, Rob.' He watched her as she surveyed the pristine bed, put her head round the door of the bathroom, registered the impressive claw foot bath by the window.

'Oh my,' she breathed.

'And no one will hear us.'

Her eyes connected with his.

'In case you turn out to be a screamer,' he said.

'What?'

He grinned at her. 'Just preparing for all eventualities.'

'I am not a screamer,' she said.

'Not yet, baby.' He winked.

'I— Uh—' she faltered.

He flexed his fingers. Why did he feel the need to behave like some overconfident idiot around Anna? Was it because he remembered only too well his inflated self-belief when they were teenagers? He wanted to put her at ease, not make her look at him as if she didn't understand a word he said. 'We could explore if you like. There's croquet...archery... Or a swim? We've got plenty of time before dinner.'

She looked through the French windows to the bright, sunny gardens.

Rob went to stand behind her and put his hands lightly on her waist. 'Why don't I head to the pool, and you can join me if you like?'

'It will take me a few minutes—'

'Take as long as you like. No rush.' He dropped his hands and went into the bathroom to slough off his clothes and put on one of the white towelling robes. In the mirror, he mouthed, 'Calm down,' at himself. Then he slung a towel over his shoulder. He could leave her in peace, and swimming would give him a chance to pull himself into a better frame of mind. Focus. Focus on Anna. That was what it was about.

She was still gazing at the gardens.

'See you in a bit.' He padded to the door and quietly closed it behind him.

ANNA

When Anna found the walled garden that enclosed the outdoor pool, half the water was already in shadow. A couple sat on steps in the shallows. Rob, his thick dark hair slicked back from his forehead like a sleek otter, swam towards her. 'Water's fantastic.'

The essential depilation had taken longer than she expected, and made her feel even more naked and vulnerable. Before she changed her mind she dropped her towelling robe onto a lounger and stepped quickly into the pool. The water was surprisingly warm. 'Wow.'

'I know.' He trod water as she swam a prim breaststroke towards him, still trying to work out if she could get away with not getting her hair wet. Or whether she could be bothered to wash it and do something with it before dinner. She swam past him, towards the sunny end of the pool, dazzled by the reflection on the sparkling, shifting surface.

He followed her to the side, blinking droplets out of his long eyelashes. His usually smooth, straight hair was kinking into ringlets as the water dripped into the pool.

'Your eyes have a little green in them,' she said, before she engaged brain.

'That's a movie quote.' He was very close, his hands on the tiled edge, either side of her.

'Is it? Are you channelling Omar Sharif?'

'Omar Sharif?'

'You look completely different. Your hair…'

'As long as you're thinking Dr Zhivago rather than Genghis Khan.'

His lips were warm, slightly salty, and on their pressure, she opened her lips. His tongue pushed deep into her mouth and her stomach fell away. He tasted different, more Rob rather than nicotine this time. He wrapped her in his arms and kissed her until they started sinking. He felt much broader and more solid than Jon.

He pulled back. 'Probably best not to drown you.' He rolled onto his front in the water, and reached the other end of the pool with four easy freestyle strokes.

She followed with her sedate breaststroke. Then she abandoned trying to keep her hair dry and alternated lengths with backstroke and front crawl. The sky was a bright, clear blue above her, at the same time vast and close.

When they found themselves back at the sunny end of the pool together, he pulled her to him, her breasts pressed against his chest. 'Refreshing way to spend a Wednesday afternoon.'

'Surprising,' she said, as the sun was blotted out by his kiss.

When she shivered, despite his presence, he said, 'Come on, you're getting cold.' He pulled himself up onto the edge of the pool in one economical movement, retrieved her robe and held it out for her to walk into. Then he picked his up from the chair where he'd dropped it.

Anna was still shivering when they reached the room. She couldn't quite think of it as their room. Collective nouns. A minefield.

'Why not have a shower? Or a bath even? There's plenty of time.' He wore an elegant stainless steel watch he had not taken off to swim.

'I'll have a shower. Do you want…' She gestured to the bathroom.

'Go ahead. I'll see what's happening with the cricket, and then I won't need very long.'

In the shower, Anna washed her hair and counted to sixty while she waited for the conditioner to work. She concentrated on functional washing. She did not dwell on touching certain parts of her body. She felt her senses heightened, the slightest brushing of fingers against her skin setting her shivering again.

She knew she couldn't put it off any longer. She was going to have to tell him.

ROB

In the soft, flattering light of the restaurant, Rob watched Anna's face, as she described her work to him. Her hair fell in loose tendrils around her face, softer and freer than usual. She'd emerged from the bathroom, her hair wet from the shower, and dressed for dinner while he had a quick shower and dried his hair. He never felt quite Rob Randall when his hair was curly. He was someone else then. Someone he didn't know so well.

'Are you listening, Rob?' She looked directly at him. She must have done that clever 'no makeup make-up' because she looked really good.

'Of course. You're very animated when you talk about your business.' He kept his eyes firmly on hers, although the temptation to drop them to the narrow V of her silk top was almost too much. He remembered the smooth weight of her as he'd kissed her until she overbalanced when they'd walked away from the wedding reception.

'Work has always been my baby.' Her face wobbled.

He grabbed her hand. 'It's OK. It's going to be OK.'

She looked up, blinking. 'There's something I need to tell you.'

'Anything.' He willed her to look at him, but the ceiling held her attention until there was no fear of a tear escaping. 'Is this about the Isle of Wight?'

'Uh. Jon and I…we don't… It's been a very long time since…'

His face tightened at the sound of Jon's name. Concentrate.

'Are you saying you don't have sex?'

'I've probably forgotten everything. Not that I knew much in the first place. It's never— I'm not—' She stopped talking and took a deep breath. 'What I'm trying to say, very badly, is that I don't want you to be disappointed.'

'Anna. I promise. I will not be disappointed.'

She pulled her hand away, picked up her wine glass. 'Really. You don't have to be so nice.'

'I'm not. I'm looking at you. I'm remembering you in the pool. It's not going to be disappointing.'

'Sometimes your certainty is breathtaking.'

'And deeply attractive.'

She cracked a small smile. 'And intensely annoying.'

Smile at me again. 'While being irresistible.'

ANNA

Anna endeavoured to pace herself during the meal. They'd started with champagne, dry and deliciously cool on her tongue. To accompany her fish, she'd had a small glass of white, while Rob had red to go with his lamb. She'd refused pudding, wine, coffee or a digestif, having only fresh mint tea, conscious her palms were damp. She couldn't stop gazing at Rob's brown hands. He used them when he talked. Smooth, long-fingered, with thumbs that curved in what seemed a creative and sensitive way. She shuddered to imagine the touch of his palms on her bare skin.

She'd hoped that when he was in front of her she would know what to do, but she felt as gauche as she had at the age of twelve. Breasts well before most of the girls at school. Breasts that kept growing until she wore nothing but flowing tops she kept pulling away from her skin.

The temptation to flap the pale silk top away from her was strong, and had it not drawn even more attention to her chest, she would have done so.

He had valiantly focused on her face all evening and she loved him for that.

No. She did not. She appreciated him for that.

'Shall we?' He stood up, dropped his napkin on the table and took her hand.

Her mouth dried the instant his palm connected with hers. She licked her lips, smoothed her other hand along her skirt.

Somehow these casual gestures of affection had thrown her off balance. Wouldn't it be much easier if it was a physical transaction that took place between them, rather than what started to feel like the beginning of a relationship? Why was he behaving like this? He had no intention of pursuing a relationship with her, she knew that, so the sooner she managed to rein in her fantasy life the better.

He smoothed his thumb over the back of her fingers, squeezed her hand before he let go to open the door to their room. The air was cooler inside. Rob turned up the thermostat on the wall beside the bathroom door.

'Cold?' he asked.

'It'll soon warm up.' She hugged her upper arms.

'Are you OK? You've gone silent.'

Anna licked her lips again. *It's time to do something different. I chose this.* She gazed into his deep brown eyes, which momentarily dropped to her mouth.

'You can say no any time you want.' He stepped closer, shrinking the gap between them.

'I know.'

He kissed her, softly at first—a hello kiss—a suggestion of things to come.

Tentative almost, attentive and enquiring, until she fell into the kiss. Then his arms wrapped around her, pulling her firmly against his body, one hand at the back of her head as he kissed her purposefully. With certainty.

Her legs began to give way, and he pulled her onto the bed, rolling in one easy movement on top of her, his hands in her hair. This time, the weight of him felt grounding, safe, erotic, which blurred the mental separation of church and state she needed to focus on in her mind. Rob over there. All romantic feelings well away from him, over here. What overwhelmed her were the feelings of safety, an exhalation that breathed, 'home at last'. This was not good.

Just focus on the end game. A baby. But it felt as if the mountain she had to climb to reach there just became impossible.

'Anna.' Rob drew back enough to focus on her face, slumping sideways slightly, one hand on her waist. 'You're thinking.'

'No, I'm not.'

'Are you sure?'

A pause, until she looked at him and said, 'I'm sure.'

He leant over and pulled back the covers on the other side of the bed, and then made her laugh at the ease with which he rolled them, together, onto the cool sheet.

'You've done this before,' Anna said.

'Nah.'

But she felt he had, so many times. He seemed so relaxed and at ease in his body. 'Bien dans sa peau,' the perfect French description, sprang into her mind. He eased off their shoes, unzipped her skirt and slid it smoothly onto the floor.

She swallowed. The minutes were ticking by, and yet it all felt too fast.

She had asked him to be here. To do this. It wasn't as if she couldn't say no or call a halt. She just felt it would be terribly bad form to do so. He would be justifiably furious and she would be the worst sort of tease. Allumeuse. The apt French word again popped into her head.

No, she'd better get on with it. She unbuttoned his shirt, sliding her hand across his chest. This was OK. Better than OK. Just appreciate the delicious feel of skin on skin, thrill to his intake of breath.

It was when he rolled up her top and cupped her breast,

over the lace of her bra that she found it increasingly hard to pull air into her lungs. Not the time to have a panic attack.

'Anna. What is it?'

'Nothing. It's fine—'

'Sweetheart. I can feel your heartrate soaring. And while I could be flattered at the effect I have on you, I think it's something else. Are you having second thoughts?'

She bit her lip. He was being so kind she could cry. 'Uh.' She sat up. 'Just give me a minute?'

She made herself not lock the bathroom door. As she washed her hands, she stared at her reflection in the mirror. All will be well.

When she emerged, relief that Rob was sitting on the side of the bed still fully clothed, washed over her. Naked, even under a sheet, would have been too much. His brown feet and forearms, where he'd rolled up the sleeves of his shirt, the 'v' of the neckline, the way his hairline was grazed by the back of his collar, she was acutely aware of them all, most of all his hands and how his fingertips had felt on her skin. She had the simultaneous wish to be immediately naked with him, and to get away from this room as quickly as possible.

As if mindreading her stance, poised for flight, he stood up. 'Cold feet?'

She hesitated.

'Go on, say it. My ego can take it a second time. I think.'

She shrugged, palms upwards. 'I'm out of practice. I haven't done this with someone new in over ten years. I'm freaked out.'

'Well, don't feel pressured by me.' His eyes narrowed. She had the feeling he was weighing up whether or not to launch another seduction. 'We could get ready for bed?'

'Did you bring pyjamas?'

'Not really. I don't tend to wear them. But I can find a t-shirt and boxers if that would make you more comfortable. Do you have something to sleep in?'

'It would usually be a t-shirt. But I have brought a nightdress.'

'Why don't you get ready, and then I will.'

ROB

When Anna reappeared, enveloped in a white towelling robe, she had that frown of concentration on her face, the one where she looked as if she was counting something.

'Won't be long.' In the bathroom Rob washed his face and brushed his teeth. Don't lunge for her lips, he told himself. Don't fixate on her breasts. Not that he would be able to distinguish an outline, underneath the heavy fabric.

She was sitting up in bed, her phone in her hand.

'You're going to be awfully warm in that,' he said.

She struggled out of the robe, pushed it onto the floor and wriggled her way under the sheets, but not before he'd seen enough strappy black silk and cleavage to wake him right up. *I can do this.*

He climbed into the other side of the large bed, switched off his phone and turned towards Anna, bunching the pillow to make it comfortable, a hand under his head.

'It's so strange.' She turned her head to look at him.

'What is?'

'That it's you. Don't you find it odd that it's me?'

'Odd is not the first word I think of.'

She raised her eyebrows.

He countered by raising one eyebrow.

'Impressive. Is that something they teach boys when girls are otherwise occupied?'

'What's not impressive about you having the guts to say what you want, and then go for it?'

'Or not, as the case may be,' she said.

He raised his eyebrow again. 'The night is still young.' He was right, it wasn't even eleven-thirty.

She rolled onto her side, towards him, her body moving under the smooth silk in ways that appealed to him far more than expected.

Was one of the reasons he was lying in bed with Anna that she was so unlike most of the women he'd been with? He'd spent too long rolling around with taut, thin, hard-angled models, with sculpted breasts. They didn't have her curves, her assets. Well, they didn't have her natural assets.

He caught his thoughts. Sometimes he despaired over the more primitive aspects of the mind of the adult male. He clamped his free hand under the pillow with his other hand, to quell the thought of reaching out and caressing the curve of her neck to her shoulder, the slope of her breast under the taut silk.

Her face was so close to his, and when she surprised him by closing the gap and kissing his lips, he let his eyelids fall and concentrated on the sweet pressure. Minutely—no sudden movements—he withdrew his hands from underneath his pillow and drew her against him. Their limbs tangled, her legs smooth against his, arms wrapped around her.

He dedicated his attention to kissing her thoroughly, one hand in her hair, the other spread at the base of her spine, holding her against his chest. Waiting. Minutes of kissing, wanting to make a move, to feel the curve of her breast in his hand, to stretch his fingers across the smooth skin of her stomach, to nudge his thigh between her knees and leave her in no doubt as to his arousal.

And then she pulled him with her as she rolled onto

her back, the weight of him on top of her, her legs wrapped around him.

He put a hand either side of her, pushed himself back enough to focus on her face. 'Anna.'

She had one hand on his chest, warm through his t-shirt, the other rested against his cheek, her fingers caressing his ear, her gaze on the side of his face.

He waited.

'Rob.' She looked into his eyes. Finally.

'Are you sure?'

Anna nodded.

'Yes?' he said.

'Yes.'

He lunged for her mouth, his hands in her hair, his whole body pressed against hers. With great efficiency he divested them both of their garments until she lay naked in his arms, their legs finally wrapped around each other. Right at the last moment, he raised himself up on his forearms, wanting to see her face, to connect with her as he sank into her dark warmth, slowly, oh so slowly. Exquisitely.

He tried to stay still, to take in the moment, the pulse of him surging in his veins, feeling the beat of her heart beneath his chest. Captured by the taste of her, the silkiness of her smooth skin, pale against his own, feeling cradled by her, everywhere, shimmering below him, her cheeks flushed pink, her eyes bluer than ever, eyelids fluttering, strands of hair trailed across her forehead, the faintest freckles on the bridge of her nose. All this he registered, as he began to move, knowing he would not last as long as he'd like.

Then he fell into her, cradling her face, tasting her lips, kissing her deeply.

At last it felt as if she'd properly joined him. Her participation dissolved his indifference, as her diffidence melted away.

Afterwards, he made to move sideways, but her arms held him around his waist.

'Sorry, that was quicker than—'

'Rob, it's fine.'

'I must be squashing you,' he said.

'True.'

He rolled them both so they were on their sides. Even after everything, he was distracted by the way her breasts felt again his chest. Skin to skin, the contrast of pale and brown. 'You could put your feet up.'

'What?'

'Turn around and put your feet up the headboard.'

'Why?'

'Oh.' He raked a hand through his hair. 'Is it an old wives' tale that lying like that afterwards increases your chances of getting pregnant? No harm in trying.' He eased them both around the bed, moving pillows, lying beside her, while they manoeuvred their feet up the tall, linen-covered headboard.

'OK?' he asked.

She eyed him. 'You surprise me.'

'That's because you think I'm a bastard.'

'Not true.'

'Are you sure?'

'I just didn't expect you to know about things like this.' She waved at their feet.

'Would you like some water?' He rolled off the bed and ran the basin tap for cool water. When he came back, she'd pulled the sheet across herself, and he felt a momentary pang. Unlike some of the thin women he'd known, she looked so appealing, so round and sexy without her clothes on.

He handed her the glass and lay down beside her, the back of his head cushioned by his arm.

When she propped herself on an elbow, he watched as everything shifted under the sheet. Really, he could watch her move endlessly.

'How are you?' he asked.

'I'm fine. You?'

He stretched a finger to brush the hair off her forehead and behind her ear. 'I'm fine too.'

ANNA

She'd slept much quicker than she expected, when they still seemed to be speaking to each other now and then.

He'd somehow made the whole situation less embarrassing and more bearable than she anticipated. Even the aftermath had felt easier, calmer than imagined, helped enormously by his ease with his own nakedness. When they'd righted themselves and spread the covers over them, she was so comfortable and relaxed she didn't look for her nightdress, and he didn't hunt for his boxers. When she turned onto her side, away from him, she could nevertheless feel his warmth behind her, the steady quiet sound of his breathing in the silence.

That was the worst thing. The evidence of another human being. His breathing presence undid her in a way that no number of glimpses of his flat, bronzed stomach, smooth chest with just the right amount of hair, the sensations he had created as he kissed and caressed her had done.

Anna woke again when it was still dark, although there were hints of dawn beyond the curtained windows. It was very still, and she was extremely hot, her legs wrapped in the sheets. As her eyes grew accustomed to the subdued light, she looked over at Rob, who lay on his side, one hand under his cheek, the shadow of his lashes fanned across his cheek. Carefully she eased her way from the bed.

She searched for her nightdress and shrugged it on, then felt her way to the bathroom, rather than chance waking Rob by turning on a light. When she lay back down, there was no indication he was awake. Until she felt his hand on her waist.

'You got dressed,' he murmured in her ear.

'Go back to sleep.'

In the morning, she woke with a start, hot in the circle of Rob's arm, the length of him against her back, his knees tucked behind hers.

She was too hot. She couldn't catch her breath. She eased herself out of his hold and escaped to the bathroom. In the mirror she examined her reflection. To the casual glance, she looked the same as she had yesterday. But around her eyes, the skin was easier, less tension about her mouth.

Anna set about removing last night's make-up and reapplying enough to make her look as if she was not in fact wearing any, and always looked this smooth-skinned and glowing. She swallowed when she heard movement from the bedroom. Deep breath. She fiddled with her hair until she forced her face to relax.

Rob sat on the edge of the bed in his boxers. 'Morning. What do you eat for breakfast?'

'Nothing usually.'

'How did I know you were going to say that?'

'I need to get going. And I'm sure you've got somewhere you need to be?'

He stood up and looked straight at her. 'Not immediately.'

Anna turned away. His brown torso really was too much this early in the day. She found clean underwear and a fresh top to go with her linen trousers, retreated to the bathroom to dress.

She had managed to dupe herself into thinking that a

familiarity in their teens—more than twenty years ago—equated to a connection now. But the problem with going to bed with someone she really didn't know very well—and the incomplete communication and lack of transparency between them was proof of this—was that it was excruciating facing them the following morning. Not that Rob looked remotely embarrassed. Which started an unhelpful train of thought—an insistent monologue in her grandmother's voice—about how often he must find himself in this situation.

Jon. She hadn't thought about him once. In many ways, she'd relegated him to the past in her mind. She paused, one hand on the door handle and examined her reflection in the vast mirror above the sink. She looked calmer than she felt.

'So. Breakfast's on for another hour. Or would you prefer room service?' He stopped on his way to the bathroom. 'You may not want to eat anything. But I do. And I'm convinced you want a cup of coffee.'

He was quick. Maybe he didn't trust her to still be there. Had she been less of a coward, she'd have packed her bag and left. But her car was at home. Again, she berated herself for not thinking this through. She could always call a cab. Her sanity was more important than the expense. She grabbed her phone.

'You're still here,' said Rob. He wore a dark blue shirt, the collar of which was slightly damp from the back of his hair.

An image of him breaking the surface of the pool and shaking his head to get rid of the excess water in his hair, slid across her mind. 'I did contemplate leaving,' she found herself saying.

'Ah, some honesty at last.'

ROB

It had all worked out for the better, what with Anna wanting to get home. Breakfast could have become a bit too cosy for his liking, not helped by the slightly too informal waiter addressing them as if they were married. It would not have bothered him. But there was a jolt of something across Anna's face which hit him in the pit of his stomach. How could he have been so stupid as to not appreciate what she really wanted? And who could blame her? Of course she wanted the security and safety that marriage could bring. He knew it, even if she denied it. It made him feel shitty in all sorts of ways.

He had registered the previous night that the ring she usually wore on the third finger of her left hand had gone. When exactly had she removed it? He tried to remember if she was wearing it when she reached the office. Had she taken it off before or after she had understood the reason for his arrival?

So there he was, experiencing one of his least favourite feelings. Backed into a corner somehow, trying to justify his actions when he had never intended to give anyone the wrong impression and matrimony would never be on the table. Since the farce of his own short-lived marriage, he had grown to believe that a happy marriage was like a rare and exotic plant. Needing constant tending and very thin on the ground. It was unrealistic, in this post-modern age, to think that marriages could last the distance, and so many had broken down in such pain to all concerned, even those he had thought would survive.

Anyway, who wanted to be in a relationship that was just about surviving? Why did people bother to keep trying when the odds were stacked against them?

An A-list Hollywood actor—still married to only his second wife, after many years—had told Rob in an interview that the secret to a long and happy marriage was committing to keep loving your wife after you've fallen out of love with her. While that sounded logical to Rob—sensible and pragmatic, even—it had made him feel unbearably sad and more alone than ever.

He had spent most of the drive back to Anna's house trying to gauge her mood. At first she was jumpy, her right foot involuntarily pumping the floor of the passenger footwell when she thought he was driving too fast. But after a while she stopped, her breathing deepened, and she folded her hands in her lap. Then the very air in the car seemed to whisper a sigh and relax.

After that, the journey was quick. Rob recognized the route, needing very little guidance to find Anna's turning and reach her house. He switched off the engine and faced her.

'Thank you,' she said, her hand on the door handle.

'Anna.'

'It's fine. Thank you for the—'

'When? Do you want to…?'

'No. I don't know. Let's leave it.'

'If what you really want is a baby—'

'Don't Rob. It's all become too complicated—'

'Not necessarily. Don't make any decisions now. Give it time…'

She looked at him then. 'You don't have to be so nice.

What I was asking was unreasonable. It's not fair. On either of us.'

'You didn't hold a gun to my head.' He smiled. She looked so serious, frowning at him, her eyes surprisingly blue.

'I need to go to work. And I'm sure you've got places to go. People to see.'

He shrugged. 'So. I'll ring you.'

'You don't have to.'

'You already said that.'

The drive back to London was uneventful, the headache when he arrived back at his flat unusual. He was used to sleeping in different beds, to snatches of rest, to changes of time zone, but somehow twenty-four hours with Anna had upset his body clock. He had slept last night, but the lightest sleep possible, with a low-lying awareness of the room, of Anna lying beside him, throughout the night. He'd had to play Bowie very loud on the motorway to stay alert, which didn't help his pounding head.

Perversely, her reticence when he delivered her home had made him press her more than he usually did. More than he ever did.

He was not unaware that one of his skills as an interviewer was his attention. He and Sam had talked about this ability to be present, to achieve clarity of thinking, to ensure nothing was missed. They'd spoken about times during Sam's training as a doctor, when he'd spent sleep-deprived hours in A & E fighting to focus, to stay in the room.

Rob was not at quite such a front line, but there were times his senses heightened, as he tried to work out what the stranger opposite him was really wanting or not wanting to say. He had trained his scrutiny of his subject, noticing their breathing patterns—particularly if they held their breath at all—the dilation of their pupils, eye accessing cues, variations in skin tone… Their scent—perfume, toothpaste, deodorant, body odour, what they'd just eaten—gave him useful clues, as did the way they sat, and how they moved their limbs. Often it could be the restlessness of a person's feet that indicated when to press a subject for more information.

He had reached the point when he could assess within two minutes of meeting an interviewee whether or not he would glean anything new or insightful. The norm seemed to be a guarded defence, masking an acute fear of giving something away, of denting their reputation forever.

Such attention was a mixed blessing. Yes, he could write a decent interview. He had people skills. He could get them to relax, to associate saying yes with him, ask them questions that made them feel special.

The downside was that he was far more attuned to the here and now. He spent very little time thinking about the past. Wasted energy, he considered it. From a practical point of view, he focused on the future only to plan his diary. He would rarely dwell, daydream or test scenarios, wanting the searing beam of his attention at his disposal. All well and good when he was with someone, but so often, out of sight was out of mind.

He'd learnt this to his cost with his own family. He liked his parents and sister, but he'd had to make a conscious effort to ring, to check in, to remember the things they had in common, rather than the many differences between them. And there had been times, particularly in his self-absorbed twenties, when forgetting his mother's birthday had landed him in a landscape of resentful silence which he'd had to work hard to end. He knew it was the right thing to do, although it had occasionally been such an immense effort to restore relations. Was this rooted in his adoption and the tenuous links he felt with the family he'd grown up with?

His lack of attention had also been a charge levelled at him—with, he had to admit, due cause—by his ex-wife. Was his effort to make a plan to see Anna again a defence mechanism? Why did it bother him that she might feel badly towards him if he forgot about her? It wasn't something that usually registered with him, so what was different now?

Maybe it was just that they'd known each other such a long time. No. That wasn't right. They used to know each other, over twenty years ago. He'd not been paying attention when they'd met at other weddings over the years. Why had he been so struck by her at Sam's and Jess's wedding? There was something—a feeling in his stomach he couldn't quite explain—that happened when she looked at him with her clear blue eyes. A sense of knowing him, of seeing him, in a way he didn't recognise, in a way that made him fearful of what she might discover if he let her.

And yet, he didn't want to shut it down.

He wanted to be truly known. By Anna.

SAM

By the middle of June—when they'd been married just over two months—Sam began to fear that family life with five children was overwhelming Jess. In many ways, the tension with Kate and Emma has eased somewhat. A mostly silent truce had evolved. Kate had stopped being overtly rude and Emma had the courage to withstand her sister's opinion, and engage Jess in conversation. Josh and Ben seemed to knock around together fairly easily. The only issues there usually involved a shared piece of sports equipment, and they were pretty good friends. Millie could be a madam, but as long as she regularly had Em's attention, even if briefly, her nature was sunny.

To begin with, the challenge had been to encourage Jess to relax. But in the past couple of weeks, Sam wondered how she was spending her time, when he and the children were out of the house. The meals still appeared, the house was tidy, but she looked so exhausted and seemed to crave sleep so much in the evenings, he began to wonder if she spent hours of her day asleep as well.

'Tell me about your day,' he would say, in the most interested and least threatening tone he could muster.

'Oh, the usual,' she'd reply, before turning the conversation to the children.

One night he climbed into bed when her side was already cloaked in darkness, the hunch of her shoulder turned towards the wall.

'Jess? Is everything all right?' He braced himself for the

brush-off, but she rolled into his arms, fighting to pull off their nightclothes, her hands pressed against his bare chest. The fire leapt in his veins, fingers in her hair, mouth to mouth, tongues tangling.

She pressed herself against him, twisting and arching above him, straddling him, always connected by the kiss, feeling his arousal meet her wet warmth while his fingers bit into her hips, pulling her down to him as he rocked higher and higher.

Her skin was damp against his palms, her face flushed as she shuddered above him, catching his rhythm, clenching around him, and the pulse built, pounding in his ears.

'Jess,' he said, between clenched teeth, knowing he couldn't last much longer.

'Don't stop,' she breathed against his lips.

He clasped her waist, one arm around her, the other circling to the full swell of her breast, tight against his chest. Surging against one another, she bit his shoulder, with a muffled cry, before slumping on top of him.

'My God, Jess. What brought that on? Whatever it was, I'm in favour of it.'

'I love you,' she said, against his neck.

'I know. I love you. Everything's going to be OK.'

'You do know you don't have to come tomorrow, don't you?' Sam stretched his legs out under the table and topped up his glass. He had plenty of things to do, but it was Friday night. He could stop for the moment. Hopefully the children wouldn't damage each other too irrevocably.

Jess looked as if she was about to jump up and start clearing surfaces.

'Don't, darling. Not straight away.' He tipped the bottle towards her.

'I shouldn't.' She pushed her glass under it.

'Perhaps you should.' His eyes connected with hers as he poured.

'I do know I don't have to be there. But I'd like to see Stuart again.'

'He'd like that. You wouldn't have to spend any time with James and Fiona…'

'It's OK, Sam. Really. You know he regrets what happened. It was all a very long time ago.'

Sam touched her hand, curled around the stem of her glass. 'I know. Things are so very different nowadays.'

'Agreed. Which is a good thing. There's no way Kate would stand for any of that treatment.'

'Too right. Oh, and you can talk to Rob. He's coming.'

'Really? Lovely.'

'Do you have to sound so enthusiastic? I'd rather you didn't make eyes at him.'

Jess smirked. 'You are sweet. But he's an ally. Doesn't take himself too seriously.'

'Ah. That's the attraction.'

'Quite. Nothing to do with his good looks.'

Sam laughed. 'It'll be good to see him. Find out what's going on. In his life.'

'Do you really think there's something going on with Anna?'

'Maybe. He's been a bit cagey on the phone.'

'As long as he doesn't hurt her.'

'He's not the one in the long-term relationship. If anyone's going to be hurt, maybe it's him?'

'Rob Randall? Darling of social media? Anna's quite as lovely as the girls he's usually photographed with, it's just that we're all about twice their age.'

'Perhaps she's good for him. Perhaps he's growing up.'

'Do you really think that their relationship's a good thing?' said Jess.

'You'll have to ask him. Find out whether it's a relationship… Or a dalliance…'

'Dalliance. That has a Jane Austen ring to it. Although I'd go straight off him if he's messing her around.'

'Or she him. Men don't have the prerogative on mean behaviour,' said Sam.

'It's just the stakes are higher, the older you get. Especially for women. I'd hate to want a baby and not be able to have one.'

'Luckily we don't have that problem…' said Sam.

'No. Although five between us is plenty. Isn't it?' She blinked at him.

'Of course it is. They keep us busy enough.'

She didn't quite meet his look as she drained the rest of her glass. 'They do.'

He put out his hand to her, but she picked up the plates and turned away before he reached her.

JESS

Having Sam beside her was a real comfort. It was fine, of course. Her body no longer reacted in an uncontrollable, scary way of its own when James was in the room. Now she could breathe, didn't flounder as her pulse hurtled to twice its usual rate.

She knew she relaxed with Sam in a way she hadn't for many years—not when she had found herself on her own with two small children, certainly not during her marriage to Tom—and that security made the prospect of several hours in James's presence possible. Not as daunting as it had been at his wedding to Fiona, or even the last time they'd met, on New Year's Eve.

Then, when he'd found her alone in the kitchen, she'd felt physically threatened. She would not allow that to happen again. She was now a very different person to that frightened teenager who managed to fight off a drunken James in a downstairs loo.

What sort of Christian would she be if she didn't forgive him properly? Even if that meant an ongoing process of forgiving. Again and again.

In the end, there were enough people at the lunch for her not to have much close contact with James or Fiona, who made herself scarce whenever a child came too close. Or was Jess imagining that?

'You're looking decidedly pensive,' said Rob. 'And we never got to the bottom of why you have such a problem with James. What's that about?'

Jess turned to Rob. He looked bronzed and relaxed, in jeans and a blue striped shirt. 'Lovely to see you too. How are you? What's new?'

Rob kissed her cheek. 'Really. You can tell me.'

Jess raised her eyebrows. 'Yeah, right.'

Rob said nothing.

Jess folded her arms. She'd put her glass down when she'd taken Millie to the loo, and she'd have been glad to have it to hold on to right now. 'I know this game. Wait till the other person says something incriminating.'

'Incriminating?' said Rob. 'Now you're talking.'

'No. I'm really not. James and I have made peace. There's nothing to tell.'

'Peace over what?'

'That's all you're getting, Rob. What about you? How's Anna?'

Rob shifted his steady gaze away from Jess to scan the room. 'Anna?'

Jess leaned over, close to his ear. 'The Anna who caught your attention at my wedding.'

'Why, what's she said?' he asked.

Jess laughed. 'Not a lot. I thought you could fill me in.'

Rob frowned. 'About what?'

Jess shrugged. 'You tell me.'

He slugged his drink.

She waited.

'So. You and Sam talk,' he said.

'This is true.'

'Then, he told you…' Rob glanced at her sideways.

Jess uncrossed her arms, raised her hands. 'No judgement here.'

'Seriously?'

'None. I can't imagine the pain of wanting a baby and

not having one. For whatever reason. Anyway. Why would you care what I think?'

'Why wouldn't I care? It's not the sort of situation I can talk to many people about. Maybe I want the support of some of my oldest friends. Friends who know us both.'

Jess eyed him. 'Are you OK? I can't remember you being this serious.'

'About time. That's what you're thinking.'

'I'd be less worried if you looked a bit happier about it. I like the idea of you being with someone. Not alone.'

He grimaced. 'I'm hardly *with* Anna.'

'Well. No. So, it's not the most conventional situation, but...'

'But...?'

'At least she's in the right age range. You do not want someone half your age, who misses most cultural references. Too shiny and new.'

Rob laughed. 'Not like us, you mean? You look pretty shiny and new to me.'

Sam appeared. 'Break it up, you two. You're having far too much fun.'

'Rob cheers me up.' Jess smiled at Sam.

Sam eyed her. 'Do you need cheering up?'

Jess gave him a straight, open look. 'I do not.' She put a hand on his arm. 'Everything's fine here.'

Rob shrugged, palms upwards. 'I didn't touch her.'

Sam shook his head. 'Not you.'

Jess watched Rob warily. He had morphed from lazily relaxed to alert and focused.

He trained his warm brown eyes on her. 'Who?'

'It's all fine here,' she said, grateful for the anchor of Sam's arm, solid under her hand. Even more so when he put it around her waist.

Rob switched his attention to Sam. 'What were you talking to Stuart about for so long?'

'Guitar pedals, if you really want to know,' said Sam.

'About which you know so much,' said Rob.

'I can play the guitar, you know,' Sam retorted.

Jess turned to him. 'Did I know this?'

'All right. I *could* play the guitar. In the mists of time. Stuart plays in a band, hence the guitar pedals.'

'How is he?' asked Jess.

'Stuart? In good form.'

'Does he have a partner or anything?'

'He does. Although he works on a Saturday.'

'Who does?'

'His partner. He's a hair stylist. Works in a big salon in the centre of Manchester. Salva. He's Spanish.'

'I'm so glad he's not alone,' said Jess.

Rob rolled his eyes. 'There are worse things.'

'Not if you don't want to be alone,' said Jess.

'Who says I don't want to be alone? Maybe I love my unencumbered life. Maybe I relish my freedom.'

Jess contemplated him for as long as she dared. 'Nope. You're all ready to launch into full family domesticity. Look at how great you are with the kids. All of them. I don't just mean Kate.'

'Ah, Kate,' said Rob. 'Shall I have a little word?'

'Please don't. It'll only make matters worse. She'll think I've tried to turn you against her.'

'We're taking a view on which battles to fight,' said Sam.

'Perhaps she needs a jolly good slap,' said Rob.

Jess laughed in relief. 'I don't think you're allowed to voice that thought any more.'

'Why not? It might shock her into behaving better. Your restraint doesn't seem to be working.'

'No. You're wrong. Can you imagine how Elizabeth would—'

'Darling,' said Sam. 'He's winding you up.'

'Is he?'

'Of course he is. Successfully deflecting attention away from his pitiful single life.'

'Sam, I don't think you can say that either. He may have a hugely fulfilling life in which he happens to be single.'

Rob grinned. 'Don't mind me. Watching you two interact is fascinating.'

'See?' said Jess. 'He's taking notes. For settling down.'

James appeared, clapped Rob on the back. 'No floozy in tow, then?'

Jess met Rob's eyes.

'Not this weekend,' said Rob.

'Not like you,' said James. 'Usually there's a nubile blonde on your arm.'

'Did you know that 'nubile' just means 'of a marriageable age'? Although the word seems to have taken on all sorts of other implications,' said Rob.

'A blonde of marriageable age,' murmured Jess.

'Unfortunately the blondes in question are hardly nubile. They're all far too young to get married,' said James.

'Just because you waited till you were practically forty to do it,' said Rob.

'And you have yet to make a go of it,' said James. 'What's your point?'

'Suiting you, is it?' said Rob.

'Absolutely. Fiona is a great asset.'

'So she counts for your meteoric rise at the Treasury?'

'As I said. She's an asset.' James turned his attention to Sam and Jess. 'How's married life?'

'Suits us very well, thank you,' said Sam.

'Must be busy. All those children.'

'And rewarding. And fun,' said Sam.

'And exhausting.' James looked straight at Jess.

'That too,' she said lightly. She'd been standing up for too long. Her back ached, her feet hurt, and her temples were beginning to throb. How soon could they go home?

'Darling, there you are,' said Fiona. 'Are you going to say a little word?'

'I wasn't planning to…'

'Your mother would so appreciate it.' Fiona stood her ground until James smiled and turned away to follow his wife.

'That's the way to do it.' Rob spoke, close to Jess's ear.

Jess focused on Sam, who grinned. 'Whatever you say, darling.'

Several hours later, Sam slumped onto the sofa beside Jess. 'How about a break, the two of us?'

'What do you mean?' She shuffled the piles of documents and post together so that the tedious sorting would not have been entirely futile.

'You and me. Long weekend away.'

'How can we manage that? I don't have the energy to last an evening, let alone a weekend.' It was true. She was exhausted from the moment she woke up to the moment she closed her eyes. She felt so, so lucky to have met Sam again. For them to have found each other. Naively she had assumed that the amalgamation of their two households in his childhood home would be easy—that the love they felt for each other would carry them through—and yet it was stressful in ways she had not considered.

Sam leant his arm against hers. 'I rang your mother.'

'What? Why?' She'd made such an effort to appear normal. Coping. Happy, even. Was this the moment he said it wasn't working for him?

'You're doing such a good job of looking after us. I thought it was time we had a break.'

'I'm fine, Sam.' Her thumping heart eased fractionally.

'Weekend after next. I've got the Friday off. My three are at their mum's anyway, and Felicity's going to hold the fort here till Sunday.'

'When did you ring her?'

'I thought we could celebrate our three month anniversary. To be honest, I put the date in the diary with her weeks ago.'

'But I was fine then.' Jess bit her lip. 'I'm fine now.'

'Having a weekend off just gives us a chance to relax. Both of us.' He smiled at her. 'Remember all the things we like about each other.'

'I haven't forgotten how amazing you are. You know that.' Her heart thumped, her palms clammy, armpits damp.

'I do know that. Just want to show my appreciation.'

'We don't have to go away to do that—'

'Look, Jess, if you'd really rather not, I can cancel, but I like the idea of a weekend off too. Thought we could go back to the hotel in the Lake District.'

Jess cast her mind back to the elegant hotel with stunning views over Windermere, where they'd spent the start of their honeymoon, enjoying rich meals and full-bodied wines, and walking across the hills. The weather had been changeable, with showers and gusts of wind at unexpected moments. Their room had been luxuriously furnished, and after an afternoon's buffeting by the elements, they would come back to make love and have a bath, before they prepared for dinner.

'Ah. The calm before the storm,' she said.

'Exactly.'

'It's a lovely idea.' Jess gathered the papers. The sorting was meant to have cleared things off the 'to do' pile, but she didn't seem to have made a dent in it.

'But?'

She eyed him. 'We can't keep escaping every three months.'

He eyed her back. 'Why ever not?'

Ten days later, Felicity arrived in the early afternoon, in time to accompany Jess to collect the children. Once the children had been fed, bathed, read to, and were ostensibly going to sleep, they sat down at the kitchen table, where Jess started matching clean socks.

'You look awfully tired, darling,' said Felicity.

Jess shrugged. 'I am awfully tired.'

'Well, times of change are stressful.'

'People keep saying that, but I can't keep falling back on that excuse.' The words alarmed her when she spoke them aloud.

'How are you sleeping?'

'Oh, you know. I lie down, close my eyes…'

'Do you sleep? All night?'

Jess could feel her mother's perceptive attention trained on her as she rolled a pair of Millie's stripey socks together. 'Usually. It's waking up in the morning that's the hard part.'

'Have you thought of having a blood test? Maybe you're short of iron.'

'Mum. I'm married to a doctor.'

'Which means absolutely nothing. Everyone knows they often don't pay much attention to their own families.'

'You can't possibly say that about Sam.' She recalled the kindest, tenderest moment in this very kitchen, a year ago, when he had gently placed a fingertip under each eye to ascertain how red the inside of the lower lid was, as an indication of her iron levels. She'd thought about it the previous night, and found herself doing the same thing in the bathroom mirror. Looked fine to her.

'You're right. I'm sure he looks after you. I think this going away is a very good idea. I thought that when he first mentioned it.'

'When did he first mention—'

'We're none of us getting any younger, and running a household of seven people—'

'I can't keep using that as an excuse.'

'I'm sure Sam would like a few days away too.'

'Does this make you think of anything in particular?' Sam nudged her shoulder with his chin, as she lay back against him in the bubbles. The scent of lemon verbena filled her nostrils.

'Apart from our Christmas tryst?' She felt very comfortable lying in the hot water, with Sam's arms around her.

'That's what I was thinking of… I've played back that evening many times since then. Especially when you were two hundred miles away.'

She closed her eyes and lazily ran her fingers down his thighs to his knees, either side of hers. The water, soapy from the foam, slicked across his skin.

'Oh yes,' he said. 'You look particularly stupendous from this angle.' He bit her neck, just below her ear, his hands floating through the bubbles to cup her breasts, fingers circling her nipples.

Through her eyelashes, she watched his hands on her

pink skin, flushed from the heat of the water. 'I'm going to turn into a very red prune if I stay in here much longer.'

'I can take a hint.'

She levered herself up and out of the bath, found a towel, resisting the instinct to pull it tight around her body.

Sam stepped out of the bath and stood behind her as she unscrewed her pot of moisturizer, smoothed some on her face and down her neck. She met his gaze in the wide mirror above the sink.

'You do look especially voluptuous tonight, Jessica.' He placed his hands on her shoulders as the towel loosened over her breasts, falling open at just the right moment for him to slide his fingers across her collarbones, trailing down the slope of her bosom. 'Look at how beautiful and round and full you are.'

His face took on a flat, arrested expression.

'Sam? What is it?'

He took the ends of the towel, folded them across her chest, reached for a towel of his own.

'Are you all right? You look as if someone just walked over your grave, or whatever the expression is.' She turned around to face him, connect with him, rather than his reflection.

'You've been very tired,' he said. 'More tired than usual.'

'Yes.'

'Wanting to sleep. Feeling as if you had no energy.'

'Yes.'

'Sensitive skin. Sensitive breasts.'

'What are you saying?'

'When was your period?'

'Not that long ago. I'm thirty-nine Sam.'

'How many periods have you had since you arrived in Millingham? Not more than one. Contraception is not fool proof. And your actual age is not necessarily indicative of your reproductive age. Women fall pregnant well into their forties.'

'But not usually. Your fertility drops off a cliff after thirty.'

'Not always. Jess, do you think you could be pregnant?'

The urge to stick her fingers in her ears and shout, 'La, la, la, la,' was fierce. She turned back to the mirror, opened the towel, saw what she had already perceived and denied. Her breasts were sensitive, the nipples darker, slightly swollen—all signs she remembered distinctly from her pregnancies with Ben and Millie.

He stood behind her, hands at her waist.

She raised her eyes to meet his gaze.

'Don't cry. We're in this together,' he said.

She could feel her eyes brimming, looked up, willed herself not to blink.

He kissed her by her ear. 'Lean back on me.'

She rested her head against his shoulder while he grazed the side of her face with his lips. 'Did you know. Your head weighs about eight kilos.'

She laughed. It was an old joke, from their first kiss the previous summer.

'We don't need to decide anything now. I'll stand by whatever decision you make. It's very early. Anything—'

'I know, Sam. Anything could happen…' She turned in his arms, pressed against him, leaned in, kissed him hard. Closing her eyes forced the tears down her cheeks but she didn't care. For a moment there was the joy of how clever they'd been, how they'd managed to create a life together. Sam's baby. A shared pregnancy with the love of her life.

She squashed down the sense of panic, of life sliding out of control. She didn't need to choose now. They still had time.

ANNA

She was becoming accustomed to their waking up together. Usually she was too hot, despite being naked in bed with Rob. He seemed to exude heat. She habitually felt the cold, but she didn't with him. Even her feet were warm. So warm she often arranged the covers so that her toes could peep out. He'd thought it endearing. He'd even kissed them on his way back to bed last night.

The room was quiet and dark. She wondered what time it was. Heard him stir behind her. His hand swept up to her shoulder, down to her hip, rested there. Not usual. She should move. Maybe he wasn't properly awake. She let the weight and heat of his palm sink through her skin. She couldn't get over how hungry she was for his hands on her, the feel of skin on skin. His was more olive brown next to her pale skin, an almost bluish tinge on the insides of her arms.

He closed the gap between them, his chest pressing against her back, and then she felt the length of his erection against her buttocks. His hand began to stroke her hip lazily.

'Rob, it's me,' she said.

'I know, Anna. I can feel it's you.' His other hand stroked her hair.

'It's morning,' she said.

'I know,' he said.

'Really, Rob, soon it'll be time to—'

His lips nuzzled the nape of her neck, kissed her ear.

'You're still ovulating, aren't you?'

'But…' She lost her train of thought as the hand on her hip trailed upwards to clasp the fullness of her breast.

'You really do have the most fantastic breasts, Anna.' His palm pressed over her nipple, across the soft skin, his fingers gently grazing, fondling, stroking.

She was lost in the sensations he created, heat coursing through her, eager to kick the covers off them completely.

'Lift up,' he said, manoeuvring his other arm under her shoulder, to caress her other breast. Both hands were working hard now, circling and pressing, until he pinched her nipples and she nearly orgasmed.

ROB

Ah, thought Rob, as Anna arched against him. She liked that. He firmly pinched her nipples again. Finally getting somewhere.

He loved working on her body, but he sensed that however close to climaxing she might be beforehand, it somehow ebbed away, once he entered her. By that point, the wet warmth of Anna was too much for him, and however hard he tried to last, tried to focus on her, he usually reached the point of no return too quickly. Justifying to himself that this was what she wanted, as he ejaculated with force.

Afterwards she would turn away, lie with her feet up the wall, wrapped in the sheet, her hands clasped over her stomach, and the moment for stroking her, for kissing her was lost.

But this morning, his erection had been too much, she'd been too soft and warm and inviting as he studied the nape of her neck, the line of her spine, the curve of her hip. One hand dropped to her waist and he pulled her firmly against him, kissed a trail from her ear, across the silk of her cheek—she really did have the softest skin—to the side of her mouth.

She moaned as he moved his hips, so that his erection slipped between her legs. Against the warm centre of her. He trailed his hand to the underside of her breast, down the swell of her stomach, into the soft curls, pressing against her, feeling the hard length of him against the side of his hand.

She tipped the covers away, tilted her hips, rocked against the pressure of his hands, and he caught the rhythm, as her thighs clenched.

Down his fingers slipped, one easing into the dark warmth, teasing the soft lips tight around him, and he counted, counted, in order not to come. Not yet. He hunched his shoulder, rose up on his elbow to kiss her properly, his tongue mirroring the rhythm of his finger.

'Ah,' she uttered.

He loved the sounds she made when they were in bed together. The language of her arousal. 'Tell me what you want. Do you want me to…?'

'Not yet. Don't stop,' she whispered against his lips, her hips in rhythm with his, everything in perfect sync—tongues, fingers, the clenching of her thighs tightening against his palm.

He counted. Counted. Tried to think about anything but the friction of her tight skin against his erection. He would last even less time than usual at this rate…

'Ah, ah,' she gasped, as she arched against him, shuddering around his finger, one last spasm against his chest. He wrapped his arms around her, holding her tightly. She lay still for a second, but then she whispered, 'Now.'

'This won't… I won't…' he uttered.

'No matter,' she said.

He slid down behind her slightly, and she angled her hips towards him.

'So good,' he murmured against her ear.

A hand under her, lifting her leg to rest over his thigh as he found the heat of her.

'Yes, there,' she said.

'Show me.' Her surprisingly cool fingers found his hard

length and guided him in. His hand covered hers, a constant pressure against her as he began to move. So good. So good.

'So good.'

It was Anna's voice echoing the thoughts in his head. He wanted to shout out, feeling her tighten against him as he kept up the pressure of his palm.

She slipped her fingers away, cupped her hand to the back of his head, turned her face again to kiss him as they surged together, over and over, heat building and building until he could count no more, could no longer stop the force of his climax, the release, the final clenching of their slick bodies.

Her head fell back against his arm, while they panted together, catching their breath. His hand slipped to her inner thigh, feeling himself soften as she still held him inside her. Their breathing slowed. He kissed her neck, rested his forehead between her shoulder blades, trailed his hand back to her hip. Where it all started.

'Feet up?' he asked.

'Don't go,' she said, twisting around, pushing the pillows aside, shuffling her hips towards the headboard, tipping her legs up the wall. He turned with her onto his side, propping his head on one hand, no longer resisting the impulse to bend his lips to her breasts, kissing her nipples.

'Rob,' she said, but then she just looked at him.

His other hand found her hand and held it firmly as he watched the tears run silently down the sides of her face into her hairline. She closed her eyes. His thumb caressed the back of her hand.

After a long time, she opened her eyes. 'You're still here.'

He squeezed her hand. 'You know I am.' He reached out a finger to smooth the tear stains, caress her cheek.

'This isn't what you signed up for,' she whispered.

'And yet, here I am,' he said. He didn't want to break the spell. Didn't want to return to his world. His world without Anna. And he didn't want to process that thought. Just think about her perfect skin.

'Thank you for not saying anything,' she said. 'Words don't help.'

'I know.' Somehow, in the last twenty-four hours, they'd moved beyond words.

ANNA

Her challenge had become thinking about something else. Her conscious self was now so attuned to the minutest change in her body that there was no peace of mind.

She knew people at work were eyeing her warily. Jade had leapt to conclusions, having met Rob early on, and seemed to have taken on the role of his confidante. She made sure she'd at least get to wave at him, if he appeared to collect Anna. It was intensely annoying. Not that she mentioned that to either of them; it would only encourage more pally joshing.

As Anna drew closer to the next assignation, her body began to twitch in anticipation. It was pathetic. Her resentment towards Rob for how she was feeling would build inexorably until that first moment she saw him, and then it would all scatter, leaving her unclenching, a gentle warmth washing through her chest, settling in the dissolving knot of her stomach.

A lot of this upset, this heightened awareness of her own physicality, had her skipping meals. Until Olga, her designer, started questioning her. 'What did you eat?' she would demand, in her most strident tone. 'How can you survive without fuel, Anna?'

Workwise, she was just about holding it together. Much of each season's collection followed naturally from the previous one. A tweak of a collar here, a hem or a pocket there, but all the key rules of immaculate tailoring still applied.

Increasingly, Anna noticed colours or patterns she found mesmerising. The clashes of yellow and purple; red and green; blue and orange. These were Van Gogh's contrasts, a primary colour paired with the mixture of the other two primary colours. How they zinged, to Anna's eyes and yet she didn't quite have the courage to use them in any quantity. The lining she'd told Jess about months ago had stayed a lining.

Repetition and slight variations on a theme had kept her business successful. She told herself she didn't have the nerve to make what might be an expensive mistake…

Now and then, she thought to herself, 'You wouldn't be alone.' Olga, Stefan, her team would all back her. Perhaps most surprisingly, Margaret, her longest-serving member of staff—an instinctive pattern cutter without whom Anna was well aware she would not have achieved what she had—was the person who said, quietly, 'Life is short… There's less time than you think…' Just because it was Anna's name on the door didn't mean she was alone.

Alone. Well, she was. This thing—whatever it was—had been embarked upon to achieve a particular purpose. Each month, as she failed to get pregnant, the possibility of what might happen next, receded further into the distant future. It had seemed unlikely for years. A brief flaring of hope, the possibility that a different man could bring about a different outcome, had faltered as her menstrual cycle carried on regardless.

The possibility of actually becoming pregnant was now a chimera, an ethereal mist, a distant dream. What might happen beyond that point, if it was ever reached, was too unbelievable and painful to contemplate.

Instead, she lived in the here and now. Breathing out. Breathing in. For so long the structure of her existence had been dictated by the two main, six-monthly collections. She knew her place in the year because of what she was focusing on at work.

This year though, she'd lost the sense of where she belonged in her life. Untethered. Unfettered.

The vast iceberg of her longing encased everything else, including her increasing need for contact with Rob.

This wasn't meant to happen. In the old days, she'd successfully kept him at bay. But now he was even more unsuitable, she wanted to fling herself at him. For him to catch her and never let go.

Where was her self-sufficiency now, when she really needed it?

ROB

Sunday. Rob had thought that a long session pounding round the machines at the gym would make him feel better. Or tire him out. Or something. But by the time he slumped onto his sofa, if anything he felt worse than when he'd left the flat earlier.

He'd had a couple of texts from Hannah, but he hadn't sent either of the messages he'd composed. He couldn't quite find the words without feeling like a complete bastard. What they'd had had been casual. A flirtation at work that had been allowed to spill into his personal life. Plus, she was too young and shiny. Shiny hair, shiny nails, shiny skin. He hadn't realised quite how young until they'd talked about 9/11. She couldn't remember much of it—certainly not the horror he'd watched unfold throughout that whole day—as she had been at primary school.

His sister Natalie had FaceTimed him from the northern suburbs of Sydney on Saturday morning, and the conversation had depressed him. Despite it being winter there, the sunlight had poured into their brightly painted family room, covered in the detritus of life with toddlers, splashes of colour on every surface and all over the floor. His heart constricted at the mess, but the contrast with his silent, colourless flat made him moan about his pathetic living space.

'God's sake Rob. Buy some cushions then,' snapped Natalie.

'Cushions won't help,' he replied.

'Why do you care? You're hardly there.'

'I don't care. What are you up to this week?'

He'd turned the conversation and tried to stay focused on the myriad activities that made up Natalie's family life.

Later in the day, he'd walked up to Peter Jones and bought some white seersucker cotton bedlinen. Shutting down any thoughts about why he'd managed to buy bedding but not cushions.

He'd even come back and put it on the bed. A momentary feeling of peace at the clean white stripes. Not that he'd slept in there. As was becoming a habit, he'd lain on the sofa with too many whiskies late into the night, and woken up with a pounding head.

But now he looked around his walls, searching for one object of beauty. It had never seemed important to him. Why did it matter now?

He took a deep breath, sat up, reached for his phone. One o'clock. Sunday. No claims on his time. Blue sky outside. He could walk down to the gardens shared by the surrounding flats, sit on a bench. Take a book to read. He'd never bothered to get to know many of his neighbours, it felt like a mainly international, transient residence, but maybe Jean-Pierre and Ysabelle would be out there with the children. Jean-Pierre was a financier who'd come over from Paris four years before. Still talked about going back. They sometimes bumped into each other at the gym, had a beer together.

Yes. That felt like a plan. He could walk towards the King's Road if he wanted. Stop for a coffee somewhere. If he walked as far as Peter Jones this time, maybe he wouldn't be defeated by the cushions.

He grabbed wallet, keys, phone and a Graham Greene

paperback, which he slipped into the inside pocket of his linen jacket.

Despite the clear skies and the sunshine, there were very few people in the gardens. No sign of families or children, French or otherwise. Rob sat down, took out his book. Read the title. He'd meant to pick up *The Quiet American*, but he held *The End of the Affair* in his hands. Same red spine.

He sighed; flicked. *'You needn't be so scared. Love doesn't end. Just because we don't see each other…'*

He stood up, shoved it back into the pocket of his jacket. The book bumped against his heart. Peter Jones it was.

But nothing could make him buy a cushion.

The walk had done him good. He'd passed girls in short, twirling skirts and vest tops, their smooth skin caramelizing in the July sun. July. That's why the whole area felt lighter than usual, not quite so weighed down by people. They had better places to be than Earl's Court on a hot, dusty weekend.

It wasn't even three o'clock.

What the hell.

He texted Anna: *Hope you're enjoying the sunshine in your garden.*

Then he turned his phone to silent, slipped it into the back pocket of his jeans and walked towards the river. He didn't allow himself to look at his messages for a full ten minutes, by which time he'd reached Albert Bridge. Staying north of the river, he walked west. When did this part of the river become such a community of houseboats? There were plants and lines of white washing rippling in the breeze. A couple sat in the stern of their boat drinking wine.

She'd replied: *I'm in London.*

His finger hovered above her name at the top of the messages. He brought up her contact details, pressed 'audio'. Heard the phone begin to ring.

'Hi,' she said. 'Hold on.'

He heard the murmur and clatter of a restaurant. 'Where are you?'

'Sorry. Can you give me five minutes? Thanks.'

The phone disconnected. Rob scrutinized the screen. Not like Anna. She'd sounded abrupt, business-like, detached. He put his phone away and kept walking. Retrieved it to remove the silent mode.

He'd reached King's Road again by the time she phoned back.

'Rob. Sorry about that. Where are you?'

'Chelsea. You?'

'Bayswater. Heading south.'

He thought rapidly. 'Kensington Gardens?'

'Yes.'

He had the phone to call if he couldn't find her, but he sensed she'd head for the Broad Walk, dissecting the park north-south, and he saw her before she spotted him. She walked quickly, a bag across her body, a hold-all in her hand.

She smiled when she saw him, half-raised a hand, which he mirrored. Kept eye contact, biting her lip, smiling, until he stood directly in front of her. Very close. Not touching. She dropped the hold-all.

'I thought it was you,' she said. Her breathing quickened.

Her lashes fell as he closed the short distance and kissed her lips. Warm. So soft. His hands moved, one to her waist, one behind her head, pulling her tight against the length of him, his fingers slipping through her silky curls. They were slightly damp at the nape of her neck in the heat. She traced his mouth with the tip of her tongue, her arms clamped around him, and he fell into the heat of the kiss.

He pulled back when he began to feel dizzy. Heat perhaps. Or loss of blood to the head. 'What are you doing here?' he asked.

'Hello,' she said.

'Where do you have to be?'

'Nowhere.'

He fell into the kiss again.

It hadn't been quite what he expected, but when he tempted Anna with a digestif, it was Cointreau she chose.

Such a stupid drink—he couldn't even remember where the bottle had come from—and yet Anna sipped it with such nonchalant, stylish appreciation that he began to think there was no hope for him.

He finally had to face what he was well aware he'd ignored for weeks. He'd fallen hard and fast, so far he couldn't find a foothold, let alone negotiate an escape route.

They'd taken the bus back to Earl's Court, detoured to his local deli for bread, sundried tomatoes, olives, Italian cured meats, and then to his flat, bathed in late afternoon sunlight.

Now the room glowed by candlelight, soft music played, and the remnants of their meal spread across the table. They'd started with one chilled glass of champagne, followed by a good bottle of Bordeaux, and then a digestif.

She smiled across the table. 'Rob. You've been turned to stone.'

Stone was not quite the right word, although his erection pressed painfully against his jeans. He eased back in the chair, thankful for the wooden table between them.

She wore a pale satin shirt that moulded her full breasts as she rested her head in her hand, loose blond ringlets of hair whispering across her fingers. Her lips parted in the beginning of another smile. 'Rob?'

'Not stone. How's your drink?'

'I never drink Cointreau, but tonight it's perfect.'

'I know.' He despaired. He was meant to be a man of words, but anything resembling witty repartee had vanished. He could only speak in single syllables.

'You're drinking whisky.'

'Yes. I know.' He frowned. She was beautiful. A sure thing. Making love to Anna—for months now it had properly been making love—had happened before and if he didn't fuck it up, it would happen again.

Just enjoy it, urged his ego. *It never lasts, you'll soon be bored, so enjoy it.*

His role as stud was not to be dwelt upon. She was smiling at him. Right here. In the room. Now was not the time to take stock of the situation, nor analyse his—or her—motives, feelings or emotions.

When she smiled with her eyes, he reached across the table and grasped her hand.

'What's got into you tonight?' she said. 'It's not like you to run out of things to say. I'm expecting you to regale me with fun facts about goats or how a zip works.'

Rob let go of her hand, stood up and shook himself. 'A change of mood.' They'd been listening to George Michael, Annie Lennox, the mellower repertoire of David Sanborn, Jackson Browne.

He picked up his phone, which lay face down on a shelf

in his wall of books. 'Shuffle. Then we dance.'

'Oh no, Rob, I can't.'

The voices of Elton John and Kiki Dee filled the room. There was not much floor space between the dining table, sofa and coffee table, but he shook his head at her, grabbed her hand and wouldn't let go. 'Don't go breaking my heart.' He sang along in a clear voice.

She laughed. 'You're not serious.'

'I'm always serious. Dance with me.' He pulled her up into a ballroom hold, one arm round her waist, turning her on the sixpence of a dance floor.

'I haven't heard this song in the longest time.'

'Bet you know all the words,' he said, his lips by her ear.

'Not really.' But she let him propel her in his arms and they crooned the chorus.

'What'll Shuffle bring us next?' he said, Anna's cheek comfortably against his shoulder. The first bars of 'Sarah Smile' by Hall & Oates filled the air. He closed his eyes and breathed in her complex scent, which suggested spice, flowers, a hint of musk.

He echoed the words of the song. 'Yes…stay…until tomorrow.'

He felt his breathing deepen, sensed Anna's breath slow too, completely aware of everywhere they touched, one hand curved around his shoulder, resting on his upper back, one clasped in his, now comfortably close to their bodies, their feet moving in a coordinated rhythm, tracing a slow circle. The music washed over them, as he brought her closer, his thigh moving between hers, their hips meeting. She felt soft and precious in his arms, her curls against the fabric of his shirt. She stirred and the sensation of her body along the length of his—her breasts, the heat of her legs—was intensely arousing.

The moment was broken by the next song: 'Rock the Casbah' by The Clash.

'That's my cue.' She freed herself, returned to the table, picked up her glass and didn't look at him.

Just as well. Gave him a moment to retrieve the heavy whisky tumbler, sit down and breathe.

But the atmosphere between them had morphed into something else. He put his free hand over hers, never taking his gaze from her face. 'You're beautiful tonight.'

'Don't,' she said, trying to take her hand away, but he stood, not letting go, gently pulling her up, leaning into her. He kissed the corner of her mouth, across her cheek to her jaw, to the pulse on her neck, the edge of her shirt, her collarbone. She arched against him, her arms around his neck.

His lips grazed her cleavage and she clung to him while his hands found her waist, slipped under the silk, up her ribs, to cup her breasts in his hands.

He'd never thought of himself as having any particular preferences. He genuinely considered himself to be a person who liked everything about women: their scent, their faces, their bodies, their legs. Shiny nails and laddered tights, voluminous bags full of scuffed paperbacks and sharpened lipsticks. He liked it all, especially their company. The way they ordered food, contemplated it, weighed what arrived against the imagined picture of what it would be like; the moue of disappointment or the giggle of delight.

So there had always been an expectation of enjoyment in Anna's company. That first walk across the common to Lake Court had captured his attention, not because of the tears so much as the weight of her in his arms. The memory had preyed upon him. Maybe that arrested night on the Isle of

Wight had veered off track so abruptly because she sensed his enthusiasm had somehow taken over. Had scared her. Had transported her back to another time.

He'd held himself in check since then, and his powers of attention had served him well. Sex was no longer a gratifying recreation purely for his own amusement. Going to bed with Anna became a task to perform to the utmost of his ability. It was all about her.

And yet tonight, he couldn't quite bring her into focus. His own emotions—his own sensations—threatened to flood him. The sensation of her breasts in his hands felt exquisite. There was no impatience. Yes, he wanted to be naked with her, to make love to her, and yet that was only part of it. No desperation to reach that goal because he was already aroused, thrilled, content to stroke and kiss her. The journey *was* the goal, somehow.

'Rob,' she said. 'You don't have to...'

He'd gone beyond taking offence at her insults; he knew they were her own method of defending her emotions.

'I know,' he said, kissing back along her jaw, finding the corner of her mouth again. 'Come this way.'

He led her from the living room to his bedroom. High-ceilinged, a nothing colour, it contained a low bed with small cabinets on either side, and fitted cupboards along one wall. An armchair squatted in front of the shadowed window. 'Sit down here.'

He switched on the side lights on either side of the fresh white linen-covered bed. Inordinately grateful he'd had the foresight to buy new bedding.

Then he came back, stood in front of the chair and unbuttoned her shirt to the waist. He removed her shoes from below the long skirt she wore.

'I may not even be ovulating,' she said.

Their eyes connected. 'But you might be,' he replied, kneeling before her, nudging her knees apart, reaching inside the silk of the shirt, parting the fabric, caressing the smooth, silky fabric of her bra.

He watched her parted lips as he stroked her breasts through the thin material, the sharper intake of breath as his fingers teased aside the edge of the bra, pulling it down, freeing her breast into the palm of his hand, first one, then the other. She leaned back into the chair, settling her hips, knees parted, the full fabric of the skirt grazing the floor, as it bunched between them.

'Lift your arms?' he asked, not expecting her to take any notice, but she did, raising them and hooking her hands over the back of the chair. He appreciated the curves of her breasts, lifted by the motion of her arms, and he slipped the satin under the soft contours of her breasts, pushed together by the bra. He touched the tips of her large, rosy nipples, his eyes on hers, watching her face. His fingers stroked from her collar bones, down to the tips of her breasts, a hand caressing each, lightly, teasingly, until his palms pressed against the fullness and she pushed back.

He stroked down to the waistband of her skirt, a hand along each thigh to her knees, now far apart. He gently moved the material upwards, bringing the hem from the floor, past her ankles, shins, back over her knees, her thighs. He smiled. 'Matching knickers.'

'We aim to please.'

'Lift up.' He tugged the fabric gently along the smooth surface of her legs, knees brought closer together as the silk and lace slid to her feet, was pushed aside on the floor.

His hands on her knees again, a solid weight, which he leant on to push himself to his feet. 'Don't go anywhere.'

He reached for a plump pillow from the bed.

'Lift up?' he said again, and slipped the pillow behind her on the armchair, bringing her hips forward on the seat. The movement had caused her skirt to slip back down to her knees, which was in itself arousing, allowing him to reveal again her pale thighs, inching higher and higher, gentle fingers on her smooth skin. He concentrated on the sounds she made: the sharp gasps, the sighs, the soft groans from the back of her throat, leaning towards her, kissing her full on the mouth, at last his tongue hard in her mouth, hers coming to meet it. His hand in her hair, the feeling of her naked breasts against his chest.

A sudden impatience for skin on skin: he drew back far enough to pull his shirt over his head in a single movement, closing the gap between them, hard chest against the soft swell of her breasts. A hand to her taut nipple, his lips on hers, trailing down her neck, pulling one nipple, then the other, into the heat of his mouth to circle his tongue around them, feeling the contours, the tips, his ears full of the sounds she made.

He pressed his hips between hers, his hands pulling her against him, wandering over the fullness of her backside, pressing against her inner thighs.

'What shall we do now?' he murmured.

He shoved off his jeans and boxers, saw her register his arousal through the widening of her eyes, all the while kissing her breasts. He moved a palm over each one, the fullness pressed against them. Anna's lips parted, eyes closed, her fingers in his hair.

Down he kissed, across her stomach, his fingertips pushing the skirt all the way down to a pool at her ankles, discovering the warmth and then the wetness between her legs. Rosy flesh, inviting lips he bent to kiss, his hands on her hips, anchoring her as she flexed against him, tasting her, pushing his tongue into her, feeling his own throbbing hardness.

'Oh God. Rob.' Her hands in his hair, holding his head, pressing herself to him as he built a rhythm, higher and higher. Soft moans and groans reaching the rush in his ears. Feeling her tense and shudder against him while he held her, his hands firm on her hips. So much quicker than he expected.

'Bloody hell.' He raised his head and waited until she opened her eyes.

'Sorry.'

'What for? Don't apologise, it's hugely flattering.'

An almost-smile quirked at the corner of her mouth. 'Like you need more flattery.'

Still spiky. 'Come with me.' He pulled her over to the bed, fell backwards, holding on to her. 'On top?' He'd learnt to check. There was something to do with his weight on her that made her freeze.

She didn't reply, but rolled off him, lying on her back.

'You sure?'

'Oh, for God's sake!'

'OK, OK.' He stopped when she raised her face to kiss him. So he kissed her back, sliding between her legs, rocking into her. Slick. High. Tight. A deeper rhythm. They held hands, interlocking fingers, raised above her head, against cool pillows, as they rocked, harder and hotter, their tongues thrusting and intertwining until he could hold back no longer.

'Anna.'

'I'm here.'

He slumped, head in the pillow. 'My turn to apologise.'

'Shift your weight and I'll think about it.'

ANNA

She'd managed to keep her emotions in check until he'd taken her into his bedroom.

The flat was weird. She couldn't believe he'd lived here for several years. There was so little of his personality anywhere. There was a card on the fridge that said, *'I am the sole witness to my home coming'* but when she asked him about it, he'd laughed it off, said Sebastian had sent it to him when they were both newly divorced.

There was a densely packed wall of books—biographies, politics and novels—classics and twentieth century writers: Waugh, Somerset-Maughan, Hemingway, Stephen King, Iain Banks. They told her a little more than the wall plastered with post-it notes and articles, which seemed to be entirely about work and revealed very little of Rob himself.

His bedroom even less so. No pictures on the walls. Very little on the bedside cabinets. The bed itself covered in white linen. And the armchair.

She had never been made love to with quite so much deliberation. Her own history was unexciting—few partners, unadventurous sex—so for her, his attention as he undressed and caressed her had been unexpectedly tender and deeply arousing. Quite different to most of the more business-like sex they'd had at the hotel.

She had always felt her breasts were too big, the nipples too pink, too large, and although she had a proportionately narrow waist, she also had substantial hips. Her body felt unfashionable; not androgynous enough, particularly in the fashion world. She had started her clothing business for women with curves, although as her clientele expanded, she now designed with two shapes in mind, the rounded and the slender, with women from both camps equally loyal.

When Rob parted her shirt, when she felt his hands on her, when she watched him survey her body, she began to consider herself differently. His desire was unspoken, but she knew she could trigger it by turning a certain way, brushing against him, even leaning in so that her curls grazed his cheek.

When they were alone, she was learning a new confidence that allowed him to work on arousing her in a way she had not imagined. The armchair was a case in point. With Jon, she had felt the need to concentrate, to imagine, to fantasise, in order to become sexually aroused. But with Rob, the sensations he caused as he trailed his fingers down the fullness of her breasts to the tips of her nipples was so exquisite that it was impossible to keep any other thoughts in her head. All she could do was lose herself in his touch.

But what undid her was the realization that she was lying in pristine cotton sheets. So pristine they were probably new. *He's done that for you,* her ego whispered. A thought it was difficult to dislodge.

'New sheets?' she asked casually.

'Ha. You would not have approved of my other ones.'

'So you had this planned?'

He rolled onto his side, to look at her. 'Not planned. Hoped.'

Much later, Anna was jerked out of the depths of sleep by Rob bolting awake.

'Uh,' he panted, moving to sit upright, his outline visible

in the faint glow of street lights behind the bedroom blinds.

'What is it?' she said.

'I always think I've forgotten something.'

'Something important?' She shifted up the pillows, trying to see his expression.

'A condom. I guess it's strange to be doing the complete opposite of what I've been doing for so many years.'

'You didn't forget this time.'

'I know. I know when I'm awake.'

'Have you had this dream before?'

He shrugged. 'Maybe once.'

'Are you having second thoughts?'

'What? No. Nothing like that. It's just a different reality.'

'Are you sure? You're not under any obligation, Rob.'

'Shut up and move over.' He lay down again facing Anna, who turned so that he could curl himself around her. Within minutes he was asleep, his light breath on the back of her neck, the weight of his palm on her hip.

She felt comfortable and relaxed but sleep didn't come.

The strange sensations that her arms were empty was like almost catching something from the corner of her eye. Always there, unfathomable, out of reach. It was as if, as she had turned thirty-five, the ticking clock's alarm went off, and try as she might, she couldn't stop it. Sometimes it sounded louder than others, but it was the backing track to her consciousness now.

She had begun to feel desperate enough to contemplate —in her imagination—scenarios that made no sense to her. Conversations with stressed mothers, offering to unburden them of one of their children. Kidnapping and bribery. The murky world of illegal adoption. And yet. What she wanted was her own baby in her arms.

She and Rob didn't talk about it any more. He knew

more than any other person had ever known about her menstrual cycle. In a way his detachment made it easier. He was matter-of-fact. Didn't fuss or question her, which, in this circumstance, was for the better.

May, June, July had all passed, each remarkable for the monthly night of sex they'd had, but still she bled. Anna's plan had been for the sex to be functional, focused, purposeful, and yet right from the beginning, he'd muddied her thoughts by holding her hand, smiling at her, making her laugh with his latest ridiculous facts. Which had made it so hard to keep a clean separation between her heart, and what they were doing.

It was only when she lay down with him beside her—another breathing human touching her—that the incessant ringing of the fertility alarm faded into the background. With the weight of Rob's wrist on her hip, she was anchored to him, they were tethered, she didn't feel quite so alone. And when they were together—at least, when they were in bed—her arms were not empty, and the ache faded into the background.

She tried not to think these thoughts too often. She had been with Jon for such a long time—more than a dozen years—and become accustomed to their lack of physical intimacy. Even in the beginning, he had not been an intensely passionate man.

But her body's response to Rob had taken her entirely by surprise. She had never felt so aroused by a male body. Now that she'd learnt the feel of him, his preferences (not difficult, he pretty much liked it all), his trigger points (many and various: looks, touch, the caress of her curls), she thought about sex and the physical side of relationships in a new way.

No. Not relationships. She and Rob had an arrangement. A temporary arrangement. She repeated to herself. Often.

JESS

It was rather wonderful to be nudged awake by the warm golden presence of Sam behind her, wrapping his arms around her and hugging her tight.

'I'm going to miss you,' he murmured against her ear. 'Two whole days. One whole night.'

She turned to face him, pressed herself against his firm chest, felt the throb of his erection against her increasingly taut stomach. 'Me too.'

'How much?' He smiled and kissed her, running a hand along her leg, putting her knee over his thigh. 'Good morning.'

She laughed. 'Are you just pleased to see me?'

He nuzzled her neck. 'Always. How many clothes are you still wearing?'

She glanced at the door.

'It's still early. But I'll lock it.' He slipped out of bed and padded to the door with its discreet new lock.

'That was a very good idea.'

'Essential I would say,' he said, grinning over his shoulder. His neck and arms were bronzed from the sun, and when he turned around, his eyes were so dark they were practically black.

He climbed back onto the bed, lifted the covers as if he were unwrapping a gift, sending desire coursing through her body. 'You're still dressed. Let me help you.'

Together, they eased off her nightdress.

He caressed her sensitive, full breasts with cool, gentle

fingers. 'Fantastic.'

She felt warm just from the way he looked at her.

'What would you like?'

'You. Now.' She reached for him.

'Like this?' He nudged a knee between hers, a hot hand stroking up her thigh, parting her legs. 'Jess?'

'Yes.' She shuddered against his touch.

'You are very beautiful first thing in the morning.' His fingers reached the top of her thighs, caressing the softest skin of her inner thigh, gently, gently finding pink lips, parting, stroking. He leaned towards her, kissing her shoulder, her face, easing his weight on top of her, positioning himself at her very centre. 'Now?'

'Yes.'

'Watch.' He inched into her wet, dark, warmth, pressing her knees apart. 'Jess,' he breathed, against her mouth.

'Yes.' She wrapped herself around him, hooking her feet behind his calves as their hips rocked.

He cradled her face, kissed her over and over until he arched into her and she hugged him tight.

He panted in her ear, brushed the tendrils of hair from her cheek, kissed her neck. 'Are you well, my darling?'

'Very well.'

'But you didn't…?'

'But it felt so good. It always feels so good…'

'Anything I can do to help?' He ran his hand down to her hip, stroked her bottom.

'Really. All fine. I'd better get up. Lots to do before Caroline collects me.'

'You said.' He leant up on an elbow. 'Sure?'

She kissed him. 'Sure.'

In the bathroom, Jess turned on the shower and peeled off her nightdress again. Already her breasts were bigger, her nipples dark and full.

She stared at her reflection in the mirror over the sink, pulled the hairband off her wrist and around the short ponytail she made with her hands.

'Very well. All fine,' she whispered, flicking away the tears on her cheeks with the pads of her fingers.

She stared so long that her image in the mirror stopped making sense to her. She nodded. 'It's going to be fine. Really.' All she had to do was get through breakfast. She didn't fancy food at all, but she knew from experience it would be wise to at least force down some toast.

At least her nausea didn't spill over into actual vomiting, and it tended to ebb away throughout the day. Yet again, she gave thanks that Caroline was going to drive. She just didn't have the energy.

Was it really only seven weeks? That meant only another thirty-three—give or take—to go.

And there was still time. If she had the guts.

ANNA

Anna spotted Ruth and Stella arriving at the hotel while she was still lurking in the furthest reaches of the car park. Ruth swept her smart black Mercedes into a space close to the imposing Victorian building entrance just as a car reversed out. Her smart dark clothes and black bags contrasted with Stella's riot of colours: a bright green scarf, a roomy red bag, a flowery holdall.

Anna watched them ascend the steps to the open double doors of the hotel. Then she opened her door and eased herself out of the car. The drive had been relatively clear and uneventful, and yet she felt fatigued and headachy. She took a few deep breaths, retrieved her bags and followed the others towards reception.

She just needed coffee. More water.

She still had not worked out what she would or wouldn't say to her oldest friends. Could she survive the next twenty-four hours by not revealing the most confusing relationship she'd ever had? No. An *arrangement*. Yet again, the sense that she'd started something she could not control, spread through her. She tried to think when she'd last felt so out of control. University, probably.

She knew Rob was a player. Not to be relied upon. Not like Jon. Maybe that was the attraction.

Not attraction. She almost stamped her foot. What kind of Pandora's box had she opened, and would she ever be able to close it again? It had become a tough mental task to control her thoughts. Time and again she'd been caught out by the almost visceral sensation of his hand at the nape of her neck, the glorious touch of his palms covering her breasts, even the weight of him. Suppressing that stamped upon, repressed, hidden memory of long ago which intruded into her conscious mind. Just out of sight. Lurking.

She rolled her shoulders, climbed the steps and walked through the main entrance. Ruth and Stella had set up court on one of the enormous sofas in the Great Hall.

'Anna!' shrieked Stella, enveloping her in a fragrant hug. Ruth's was brief and firm.

'So lovely to see you both. Looking so well.'

Ruth looked tense about the eyes.

Stella in contrast was almost bouncing on her heels. 'Love that top, Anna.'

'Not sleeping?' Ruth raised an eyebrow at Anna. 'You look exhausted.'

'Thank you very much.' Anna sank into the overstuffed cushions beside Stella.

'Tea, darlin'?' Stella indicated the cups and saucers, teapot and plate of shortbread. 'Oh the joy of a cup of tea without a toddler clinging round my legs.'

'Coffee, actually, if that's OK?' said Anna.

Ruth's perceptive gaze swept over her. 'Of course it is. It's a hotel.'

'Caroline! Jess!' Stella actually clapped her hands.

Anna stood up, hid herself for a moment on Jess's and then Caroline's shoulder as they hugged.

'The five of us. Together at last,' said Stella.

'Not since your wedding, Jess,' said Anna.

'You can't imagine how I've longed to see you all,' said Jess. 'How were your journeys? How's London? How's Bath?'

Glowing, Jess was, thought Anna, picturing her own

grey image when she flipped down the visor in the car to peer in the mirror before she steeled herself to get out.

Ruth commandeered a waitress, ordered coffee, mint tea for Jess. When it was brought by a lanky young man with brown hands, Anna averted her eyes, focusing on Jess's chatter, on the general catching up.

She fielded enquiries with, 'Yes, all fine. Work's going well…'

Jess in particular was asking questions but not necessarily waiting for the answers, and Caroline and Stella interrupted each other as they talked. Conversation in dollops. It was only Ruth who kept silent, observing. She looked serious in black, worked high up in HR at one of the big banks, but today she gave off the air of a sartorially elegant spook. Anna had the sense that, iceberg-like, she only ever revealed a tenth of what she was thinking.

Their eyes met across the chatter. Anna sipped her coffee, put her cup back on the low table. It was truly awful: bitter and dry in her mouth. She reached for her water bottle, tried to swig away the taste.

During a brief pause, Ruth said, 'Time to check in. I'm going for a swim.'

Behind the rather grand Victorian façade, much of the ground floor of the hotel had a distinctly Jacobean feel, particularly the Great Hall, with its colossal fireplace. At the back of the building, joined by a chilly glass walkway, was an extensive gym, spa and pool.

As they stretched out on loungers beside the pool, Anna felt as if she were on a film set, the elaborate murals and ceiling details not quite real and permanent. It seemed that the slightest knock could cause something to fall and reveal insubstantial plasterboard underneath. But the towelling robes and slippers, the puffy towels and wooden slatted seating seemed substantial enough.

Ruth ploughed up and down the azure pool in an economical front crawl, Stella doing a sleek backstroke.

Caroline lay back on the lounger next to Anna, and Jess perched at the bottom, swathed in towelling, her arms crossed in front of her, wriggling her coral painted toes.

'Did you go to any of the University 150th Anniversary celebrations, Anna?' said Caroline. 'Philip said he was going to contact you about it, see if you could meet up, but something came up at the last minute and he didn't make it.'

Anna focused on her toes, grateful to have squeezed in a wax and a pedicure. That would hopefully last past this weekend, certainly as far as her monthly assignation on Wednesday night. However, the deep maroon nail polish had not been a good choice. She'd wanted something different, something she wouldn't usually choose, but her toenails looked too dark, too out of place against her skin.

She glanced briefly in Caroline's direction. 'I did consider going, but in the end it clashed with a work thing.' Well. It was work. They worked bloody hard. Well, Rob did. He could be surprisingly dedicated to giving her pleasure.

'Philip was very disappointed not to go. He's always had a bit of a soft spot for you.'

Anna swung her feet over the side of the lounger, away from Caroline, away from Jess. 'He's never had a soft spot for me.'

'Oh well,' said Caroline. 'It might have been fun to go back, see who you recognise, meet up with people from your time there…'

'All those sweaty undergraduates. No doubt doing fascinating jobs now.'

Caroline laughed. 'Thanks very much. Philip's not that sweaty and at least he does something intellectually stimulating.'

'Don't you worry about all those pretty history undergraduates he lectures, though?' said Jess. 'I don't know what I'd do if Sam fell in love with one of his patients.'

Anna turned towards Jess. 'You don't really think that, do you? He hardly looks at another woman while you're in the room.'

Jess hunched over, her folded arms on her knees. 'What about when I'm not in the room?'

Caroline shook her head. 'Philip wouldn't risk it. More for his academic reputation than because of me and the girls, I suspect, but he'd never have an affair. He's a decent man.'

Anna stood up as Ruth said, 'Come on you lazy buggers. Work off some of those biscuits.'

'How about a sauna? Jess?' said Anna.

'Swim for me. Then maybe a quick dip in the jacuzzi,' said Jess.

Caroline peeled off her bathrobe. 'I'll come for a sauna if you like, Anna. Ruth?'

'I'm going to try the steam room.' Ruth walked out of the pool, grabbed a towel, rubbed her hair. Her eyes fell on Caroline's arm. 'What the hell is that?'

Caroline put her hand over a long bruise on her upper arm. 'I walked into the door, would you believe?'

'Yeah, right,' said Ruth. She tossed the towel on the nearest lounger and headed for the steam room.

'What was that about?' said Anna, trying not to contemplate how painful that bruise looked.

Caroline looked close to tears. 'Ruth works very hard. And I think they've been trying for another baby. Jack is three now…'

Anna stumbled, putting out a hand to steady herself against the tiled wall.

'Are you OK?' said Caroline.

'Fine,' said Anna. *Not fine*. Suffocating under her need, her want, her secret desire.

They'd lingered at the pool, alternating between swimming, the jacuzzi and the steam room, until the shadows lengthened, then taken their wrinkly-skinned selves up to their rooms to change for dinner. When they'd started these overnight get-togethers a couple of years previously, they decided to maximise chatting time by sharing rooms, and now had a rhythm. Anna and Ruth, Stella and Jess, with Caroline—who admitted to being a very light sleeper—having her own domain.

Anna's bed was strewn with the detritus of getting ready. She'd brought three dresses and now peered, in her stockinged feet, into the badly lit mirror over the dressing table to apply her make-up.

Ruth stretched her legs out on her bed, still in her bathrobe. 'Who brought the champagne? I could really do with a glass.'

'Caroline said she brought a bottle, and Jess has some crisps. I don't think the bottle I put in the minibar is very cold yet.' Her heart lurched as her phone—on silent mode—lit up. Rob. Again. She turned it over.

Ruth tapped at her own phone. 'What time's dinner?'

'Caroline did tell me. Eight-thirty, I think. I've finished in the bathroom, if you want to use it.'

Ruth tossed her phone onto the bed beside her. 'Pass me a beer, would you? Are there any nuts?'

JESS

Jess had encountered a little difficulty zipping up her slim navy trousers. Luckily it was a spacious bathroom, and she had managed to lie on the floor to inch the zip up over her already firm stomach, without having to engage Stella in misleading explanations. When she'd tried them on three days ago, they had not been this tight.

With any luck, there would be at least a couple of months of a more impressive bosom than usual, before she turned into a whale. Her breasts were already burgeoning and sensitive, as Sam had spotted just that morning. She felt them tightening against her bra, stared at her reflection above the washbasin, could see the outline of her erect nipples through the lavender blue silk top. Ridiculous to be this turned on when she was miles away from him. It felt like a base, animalistic Pavlovian response sometimes.

She gathered her make-up bag and hairbrush, hung up her towels, and opened the bathroom door. 'I'm so glad everyone wanted to meet up again. Aren't you?'

Stella smoothed a patterned dress down her legs, stepped into coordinated heels. They were beautiful; designer; exclusive. 'It's fun to see everyone. We've started a tradition, I guess.'

'We've known each other so long that we can be completely honest about what's really going on in our lives. The opportunity to properly catch up—'

'I suppose so.' Stella picked up her straighteners, parted a section of her thick, blond hair. 'If we are honest.

What about Ruth? She seems so distant.'

'Does she?' Jess was reminded of an illuminating conversation with Anna, on holiday in Devon the year before, when she'd been made painfully aware of her own self-absorption. At the expense of others. Somehow, the pregnancy was drawing her into herself again. She must pay attention to what was happening in front of her.

Stella ran her fingers through the smooth curtain of hair. 'Distant, bordering on rude. She must use this tone of voice on her many employees.'

'Maybe she's tired. Big job. Long drive? I know I'm going to sleep well, and I didn't even do the driving. I seem to have got out of the habit. Sam does most of the driving—'

There was a loud knock.

Jess opened the door to Caroline and Anna, both wielding bottles of champagne. 'Come in, I'm finishing my make-up.'

'Ruth's still getting ready,' said Anna.

They admired each other's outfits. Jess was pleased Caroline also wore trousers, with a dark red top. Her mouth dried, as she remembered occasions when her ex-husband Tom had cruelly withheld information, or misled her, so she turned up wearing quite the wrong thing.

That was a long time ago. Pathetic to experience such vivid anxiety still.

'This is not really cold enough yet. Shall I put it in your fridge?' Anna proffered the bottle to Stella, while Jess fumbled for eyeliner, mascara.

'This should be cold enough,' said Caroline, as there was a rap on the door.

Ruth strode into the room, head to toe in black, her hair still damp.

'Shall we make do with tumblers?' said Caroline.

'No. Why should we?' Ruth leaned across Jess, still rummaging through her make-up bag, and dialled room service on the phone on the dressing table. 'Hello? Yes, I'd like five champagne flutes—no, just the glasses—and a bowl in room…'

'214,' said Jess.

'214. Immediately. Please.' She put the phone down. 'I'll need a couple of quid.'

'Oh. OK.' Jess cast around for her bag, but Caroline had already opened her purse and passed some coins to Ruth.

Really, the way they all fell into their historic roles again was remarkable, thought Jess. Her fear of finding herself at the edge of the group—excluded, the belief that four was a much easier number than five—kept creeping up on her. Enough. She was a married mother of nearly three. She could choose not to do what she'd always done.

But a part of her was impressed at the ease with which Ruth commanded the situation, seamlessly tipping the waiter when he brought their glasses, twisting open the bottle of champagne. Jess had managed to get to the ripe age of thirty-nine without ever opening a champagne bottle. Maybe it really was time to do something different.

She found the large bag of designer crisps and shook some into the bowl, while Stella handed round the glasses.

They exchanged gifts. Jess had brought little pots of autumn bulbs. From Caroline, tea-towels that read, "I had a really nice dream about Daniel Craig last night"; delicate bracelets in her own design from Stella; stunning Missoni scarves from Ruth; small leather bags from Anna: cerise for Jess and Stella, navy for Caroline, purple for Ruth.

'What a fabulous selection,' breathed Jess, stroking her brightly patterned scarf. Sam would approve, and there was even a shade of blue to match her silk top.

'Are we setting a precedent? Presents every year?' said Anna.

'Oh yes, let's,' said Caroline. 'Something to look forward to.'

'A toast,' said Jess. 'To our oldest and dearest friends.'

'Old friends,' said Ruth.

'Old friends,' the others echoed.

ANNA

The five of them sat at a round table in the middle of the spacious dining room. Soft pools of light spread across the room, reflected in plain mirrors along the walls. Again she had the idea that somehow the décor was a facade. The Victorian panelling appeared authentic, but the mirrors and lights looked better suited to a domestic setting. They were quite the wrong scale for the dimensions of the space.

She sat back after the starters. They'd chosen the tasting menu, which had taken the business of trying to choose out of their hands. The food was fine. A bit fussy, overwhelmingly brown, but some mouthfuls had been delightful.

The conversation so far had focused on homelife, news of the various children, which Anna allowed to wash over her, concentrating on breathing steadily.

Until Caroline turned to her. 'What about you, Anna? How are things with Jon?'

She felt her hand shake, put both hands in her lap, laced her fingers. 'Oh, not much to report.'

'How's the house?' asked Stella.

'I was never going to persuade him to move to Bath. I've been in that house nearly four years, and I'm so tired of being alone.' She'd said it now. It was out there.

'I know just what you mean,' said Jess. 'What are you going to do? Is there anyone else? Sam's got several gorgeous friends. Wouldn't it be tremendous to find you someone to whisk you off your feet? Oh, we could arrange—'

'Anna?' said Caroline.

Anna picked up her glass and took a sip, despite not wanting it at all. It was something to focus on. 'Yes?'

'Have you met someone else? You have, haven't you?' said Stella. 'Not someone at the wedding?'

Anna felt the scrutiny of all four sets of eyes.

She swallowed. 'Nothing. Nothing's happened,' she said, at the same time as Jess said, 'Really? A friend of Sam's? How fantastic. Who is he?'

'There's nothing to tell.' The words felt like ash in her mouth.

'Lying doesn't suit you, Anna,' said Ruth. 'You've had several calls you've chosen not to take, on your mobile.'

Anna frowned. 'How did you— how do you—'

'A name. That's all you're being asked for,' said Ruth.

'Go on, love, you know you want to.' Jess laid a hand on her arm.

Anna met Caroline's eyes. Unfiltered, at the mercy of her emotions, she feared blurting out his name. It might have been possible to say something to strangers, but she couldn't manage to say anything to her oldest friends.

She took another sip of wine. It was worse, if anything. Where was the next course? Not that she was hungry. At all. 'I told you. It's nothing.'

'What would you like it to be?' said Caroline.

Anna felt as if a chasm opened up in her mind's eye. She'd stamped down on all the thoughts that had escaped into her conscious mind so many times. Shored up a reality where there was no possibility of any kind of future in which Rob featured. But it was as if this frail construction crumbled on Caroline's words, and the pictures she'd banished to the furthest reaches of her subconscious now presented her with a huge, colourful alternative universe. Where things were the same, and yet not the same. Where she and Rob had a baby. Together.

'I take it we're not talking about Jon. Someone unsuitable then?' said Jess.

Anna clenched the stem of her glass.

'Don't tell us then.' Ruth drained her glass, reached for the bottle, topped up Stella's and Caroline's empty glasses.

Anna searched for the right words. She couldn't bring herself to tell them that she'd finished her relationship with Jon. Months ago. Before the Isle of Wight. She couldn't tell anyone. It would bring her new reality in which she'd very firmly put all her eggs in one basket into startling focus.

'Please don't have an affair.' Stella's eyes were very bright. 'They only end in tears.'

JESS

There was a lull after the main course. They'd had a vegetable velouté, scallops, cod on a bed of lentils, beef with pommes allumettes and the finest green beans. The waistband of her trousers was almost unbearably tight, not only from the food. She didn't fancy more than the tiniest sips of wine, but she'd been drinking glass after glass of water.

'It's the one thing we don't really talk about,' said Ruth.

Jess tried to focus, to still the internal dialogue. 'What is?'

'Sex of course,' said Ruth. 'We're all far too middle-class.'

'Maybe we *do* talk about it,' said Stella. 'Just not to each other.'

'Perhaps,' said Ruth.

'Maybe it's painful when we don't understand what phase we're in,' said Stella.

'What do you mean?' said Caroline.

'You know. The power of attraction. Sex as recreation. When you can't get enough. Then the rut. When it's all the same. Then procreation.' She laughed. 'Then nothing. Or something.'

'Some marriages keep the magic going,' said Jess. 'Don't they?'

'I have no idea,' said Caroline. 'You tell us.'

'I haven't even been married for six months. Ask me in six years.'

'But it's different, even now? Better than with Tom?' asked Stella.

'Everything's better than with Tom. But that was not hard.' Jess shivered, pulled her mind away from the early years of her first marriage. When Tom's caring concern for her had morphed at lightning speed into absolute control.

'How is it with the kids?' asked Ruth.

'I think we're very lucky. For stepfamilies, we all get on terribly well. I mean, Kate has her moments, but I must remember what it's like for her. To be twelve and suddenly have your father re-marry. The others have a great time together. We all do really.'

'That's nice,' said Stella.

'Sam just wants to make me happy.'

'Yes,' said Caroline.

'As we're talking about sex.' Jess blushed, bathed in sweat. 'He does want to have a lot. Which of course is fine. Lovely, really. We're still newly-weds. It's just that I'm so tired. All the time.' A wave of heat. Tears trickled from the corners of her eyes.

Caroline put a hand on her arm.

'I'm pregnant. Can't face it. Not at my age.' She knew she was saying absolutely the wrong thing but she couldn't stop.

'Oh, Jess.' Caroline squeezed her arm.

'I don't know if I can go through with it. Sam will stand by me, whatever I decide. But it's my body. I mean, I can decide, can't I?'

'Yes, you can,' said Caroline.

Jess hunched over, not wanting to meet anyone's eyes, knowing they were exchanging looks. 'Would tip me right over the edge. I'll have to get rid of…'

'You've still got plenty of time to make a decision, haven't you?' said Stella.

'I feel as if time's accelerating,' said Jess. 'I'm on a bullet train and I can't get off.'

'It'll be ok,' said Caroline.
Jess sat back up.
Ruth and Anna were silent and motionless.

ANNA

Anna concentrated hard on the food. She'd abandoned her wine entirely. After a fairly tart sorbet, they were greeted with large platters dotted with chocolate confections. Ruth ordered Armagnac.

'Maybe it's because we're approaching forty. Feeling as if half our lives have already been lived,' said Stella.

'You've all done something with your lives. You're married. You have children. There will be people to succeed you,' said Anna. How dare Jess be pregnant! She was already surrounded by kids and was pretending she didn't want another. Tonight the usual restraints had been loosened. Once she'd seen into the abyss, there was nothing to stop her sliding in.

'Have you always felt like this?' asked Caroline.

'No. I've never felt that maternal, not when you were all having babies and complaining about your lack of sleep. But then I had the feeling that I'd forgotten something really important. Eventually I worked it out. My arms are empty.'

'So you'd like to…' Jess bit her lip. 'You want a baby. And I want an abortion.'

'No. You don't,' said Ruth.

'Chocolate.' Jess stuffed some more into her mouth. 'It's the only answer.'

'But what would I do?' Anna didn't seem to be able to stop talking. 'I never got pregnant with Jon. Not that we had much of a sex life…'

'Different phases,' said Stella.

'I just can't bear the idea that this is it. You're born, you live, you die. Surely there's something more?'

'And you think procreation's the answer? I pity the poor baby.' Ruth swirled her Armagnac, took a sip.

'I think you're right, Ruth. Abortion's not the answer, Jess.' Caroline twisted a dark curl round and round her finger. 'I got pregnant. Three years ago now. The girls were five and eight. But Philip didn't want another. He felt he'd done his time at the coalface, and he didn't want to go back. He persuaded me to have the abortion.'

Anna went cold, hearing her friend's words. She clutched her hands, pleating her fingers first one way, then the other.

'I can't imagine Philip doing that,' Jess exclaimed. 'Surely you made the decision together?'

'No.' Caroline's tone was uncharacteristically firm. 'He's not the man you think he is.'

'Philip? We've known him for nearly twenty years. He was at Uni with Anna. Surely he's the man we think he is,' said Jess.

Anna felt Jess's eyes on her. She released her wringing hands, balanced her wrists on the edge of the table. Unravelled an inch further. 'No. He's not.'

'What do you mean?' said Jess. 'How can you just say—'

'What do you know?' Ruth interrupted, Anna in her sights.

Anna tried to catch her breath, to clamp her lips together. She hadn't spoken Rob's name. Now was not the time to speak of Philip.

She couldn't look at Caroline. 'I didn't really know Philip until third year. I was living in a student flat in Camden. We'd been for a drink. He and I ended up chatting in my kitchen. Until after the last tube had gone. Persuaded me to let him kip on the floor in my room.'

'No,' said Jess.

'Quiet,' said Ruth.

'We chatted. He went to the bathroom so I could change into my pyjamas. Went to sleep.' It was OK to speak the truth. She concentrated on her fingers; smoothed the nail of one thumb with the pad of the other.

'I couldn't understand what was happening when I woke up. He was on top of me. Already having sex. He was strong and heavy. Nothing I could do.' Even now, she had a visceral memory of his weight on her, his thighs between her legs, the endless friction as he thrust into her. The dry pain that spread through her body. Eyes tightly shut.

'Oh my God, Anna.' Stella put her hand to her mouth. 'He raped you.'

'You never said,' Jess whispered.

'No. It's easier to keep silent. Until it can't be kept in any longer.' She couldn't look at Caroline. An icy fear flooded through her. What had she done? To one of her longest-standing, kindest friends? Just because she was unhappy and jealous—yes, jealous of these friends and their families—that didn't mean she could stamp all over Caroline in this way.

Ruth sat back, looking almost as if she'd expected some such revelation from Anna.

'I can't believe it,' said Stella.

Anna made herself look at Caroline. 'I felt responsible. You met him through me.'

Caroline put her crushed napkin down on the table. She stood up and walked away.

'Anna, how could you keep this a secret for so many

years, and decide to talk about it now?' said Stella.

'Don't,' said Ruth. 'Not now.'

It felt as if walking into the Ladies to face Caroline was one of the hardest things Anna had ever done. She couldn't even blame her blurting out this hard nugget of longheld information on too much drink. The wine had tasted sour and bitter in her mouth; she'd barely drunk a glass. So, why had she so uncaringly decided to spill the beans? Was this the only opportunity she'd ever had to tell Caroline the truth?

No. In those early years, shame had kept her silent. Shame at her own stupidity. And the longer she chose not to say anything, the more difficult it became.

At the time, Philip seemed not to have noticed what had taken place between them. He had left, no words spoken, and nothing was ever alluded to again. Their social circles occasionally overlapped. At an informal catch-up with a bunch of university friends a couple of years after graduating, he'd arrived in the pub, greeted Anna, met Caroline. And much too quickly—too quickly to say anything—they'd become a couple, got engaged, married, pregnant.

Anna had thought she could erase what had happened, and sometimes she thought she had. Like a bad dream. But like a nightmare, it would resurface at odd moments. Funnily enough, not with Jon. His physicality was so unlike Philip's. He made love to her tentatively, almost as if most of his attention was elsewhere.

With Rob it had been completely different. That first night on the Isle of Wight, as they kissed on the sofa, he'd expertly put himself there. His thighs between her legs. Broad, solid, so much stronger physically than she was, and her body had erupted in visceral fear. Escaping upstairs had been cowardly, but there hadn't been another solution.

Since then, she'd pushed down what had happened, every time it threatened to surface. But as her emotions became tangled up in whatever she and Rob were doing, that bleak episode from her past seemed to have been caught up and reactivated by muscle memory.

Stuck, until compelled to speak the truth, the only way to puncture the power of the memory. And yet, as she stood here, having lived with this episode for the best part of twenty years, the worst feeling was that somehow she'd inflicted it on Caroline in front of the others, in order to have solidarity, company. Preferable to being alone and having to face up to it honestly. She was never going to confront Philip. For many years the marriage had seemed to be a success. They had two beautiful daughters. Which took Anna back to the visceral, green sensations of subsuming jealousy. Not fair. Was that was why she was dumping this on Caroline, now?

Anna stood in the centre of the spacious room, a wall of cubicles reflected in the mirrors above the bank of washbasins opposite. Someone was retching behind the one locked door.

'Caroline?' Her voice sounded thin in the high-ceilinged room. She tucked her hands across her body, under her armpits. God, her breasts ached. Her reflection looked rosy and fresh above the basin, but that was just the lighting. Nothing could disguise the bleak look in her eyes.

Eventually the toilet flushed and Caroline emerged from the cubicle. Swollen-eyed, she wiped her mouth with some loo paper, stepped past Anna to a basin. Met her eyes only in the mirror. 'You knew that about him and you kept it secret. Was there never even one opportunity to tell me what happened?'

'I'm so sorry. was so ashamed of what happened. It made no sense. I couldn't reconcile what he'd done with the rest of his behaviour, which was so normal. I began to think I'd imagined the whole thing—'

'I've spent fifteen years of marriage thinking that my husband…his childhood had damaged him, but not irrevocably… I had to make allowances, to understand… I thought I was married to a man who was flawed, but essentially decent. How could you not have told me?'

'I didn't know how. I didn't want to make it into a big thing.' Even to herself, the words sounded absurd.

'But it *is* a big thing.' She turned on the tap, held her hands under the water.

Anna scrabbled for words. 'Things have changed. The whole concept of consent has altered. Even if rape still happens—and I know there are men who still think it's OK to behave like that—it's completely frowned upon now. It was very different eighteen years ago. The whole 'Me Too' movement has changed the conversation.'

Caroline twisted the tap back again, shook her hands. 'Is that why you felt the need to tell me now? Because of 'Me Too'?'

Anna swallowed and waited until Caroline met her eyes in the mirror. 'I'm—I can't believe I said it in front of the others. I didn't mean to.' She put her hands over her stomach. 'I ache. No, not about the past. About wanting a baby. About having left it too late. My arms are empty.'

'You want to shock me with this revelation because I have kids?'

'I'm trying to explain my appalling behaviour, Caroline.

You—you and…Philip. You have seemed happy…'

'Which justifies you not saying anything until now?'

'Over the years, I've thought about it in different ways. My decisions. Allowing him to stay the night. I was naïve to say the least. We'd been drinking. I can see that he could have thought we'd been flirting. That an invitation to sleep on my floor was more than that…' She took a conscious breath. 'I felt culpable. Ashamed. As if it had been my own fault. That I'd not understood the rules. Afterwards, I didn't trust my memories. For a long time I didn't think about it at all.'

Caroline leant on the basin, staring at her reflection in the mirror.

'You got on with life in a way I've always found impressive,' Anna continued. 'I vacillate and go over and over things, whereas you and he… you got together and got on with it. The whole thing. The first of us to marry, to have children, to build a family. I thought you were happy and I didn't want to get in the way of that.'

'So, why now?'

'I think I've left behind the usual social niceties. It feels as if I'm unravelling somehow. I've stopped being able to suppress it.'

Caroline reached for a small square towel and wrung her hands dry. 'Because of wanting a baby?'

'It's such a primitive, ungovernable desire. It feels animalistic. Basic. I look at parents, at children, and I want to scream. But I really didn't mean to lash out at you.' She turned and gazed at Caroline. 'Are things ok at home?'

Caroline gave a hollow laugh. 'Now you ask. How's life with that man? The one who's behaviour you forgot to mention?'

Anna glanced at Caroline's upper arm, but she couldn't

formulate the words to ask. It seemed more and more unkind, what she'd done, and she didn't know how to make it better.

'How are the girls?'

'Would you rather I hadn't asked you to be Rebecca's Godmother?'

'What? No. Of course not.'

'I thought you chose not to have children. Focusing on your business.'

'For a long time, I did. Look, I really didn't say it to drive a wedge between you...and him.... That's your business. Life has gone on all these years, without it needing to have any impact.'

Caroline stared. 'Yeah. Naïve. You think this is going to have no impact on my marriage? Seriously?' With that, she threw the hand towel into the bin and swung out of the room.

Anna ran the tap, holding the backs of her hands under the water as it got hotter and hotter. Some part of her had thought she'd feel relief at finally being honest with Caroline, but all she'd done was dump subjective, unhelpful history on her, in an attempt to deflect the aching pain she lived with: regret over how her life might have progressed.

JESS

Jess, Ruth and Stella sprawled on vast sofas around the imposing fire in the Great Hall. A tray of mint tea and petit fours perched on the low table in front of them.

'I hope they're ok,' Jess said. 'Should we go and find them…?'

'Absolutely not,' said Ruth. 'Give them space.'

At that, Caroline appeared in the doorway by reception. For a moment it looked as if she would turn away, but then, slowly, she wound her way through the groups of armchairs and low tables to reach them.

'Come and sit down,' said Jess, drawing her feet up to make space for her. Anna followed a minute or two behind, and slumped into the space beside Ruth. Neither of them spoke, but Jess hoped that was because they'd managed to talk in the Ladies.

'You've always seemed content, Caroline,' Stella said.

'We have been. Most of the time.'

Ruth sat up, elbows on her knees. 'Yeah. Right. Would you like to tell us how you actually got that whopping bruise?'

'I don't believe it,' said Stella. 'You said it was an accident, Caroline.'

Caroline ran the tip of her tongue over her dry lips. 'Yes. That's what I said.'

'Would you like to expand on that?' said Ruth.

Caroline regarded her. 'I don't know. Is there anything *you'd* like to expand on?'

Ruth compressed her lips into a thin line. 'Where's the waiter? I need a whisky.'

Despite her fatigue, Jess found it impossible to fall asleep. She would have liked to have talked to Caroline and Anna individually. She remembered Caroline's non-judgemental, soothing presence, when she'd told her about James's assault. She had managed to fight him off, but of course she'd been wide awake. She shuddered to think of the horror of what had happened to Anna, which sounded both inconceivable and absolutely believable. Statistically, Jess supposed that most other female friends of their age would have similar stories among them. If not rape or assault, then misogyny, prejudice and put-downs. How she'd wanted to hug Anna, to declare solidarity in some small way, to reassure her she was not alone.

She listened to Ruth breathing. She was going to be even more exhausted than usual if she couldn't sleep. And she couldn't wait to get back to Sam. Somehow these concentrated periods of twenty-four hours together were never as relaxing and easy as she optimistically anticipated they would be. There were too many undercurrents, secrets, varying degrees of intimacy within the group. And yet, she treasured these times together, however unsettling they might prove.

Quietly, so as not to disturb Ruth, Jess left the room to join the others at breakfast. Anna and Stella had tucked into the buffet and their table was covered in fruit, yogurt, pastries, toast and plates of hot food. Caroline arrived soon after Jess. She looked better, but as Jess scrutinized her, she realised that could be due to the assiduous use of blusher and concealer.

By the time Ruth sauntered in and ordered coffee, Jess was feeling jittery, striving to fill the lengthening silences. Ruth's mood did not seem to have improved overnight. If anything, it had deteriorated even further.

'It's been so good to pick up where we left off, and really talk about the things that matter to us…' Jess said. It wasn't *good*. That was completely the wrong word. Ruth's glare transported her back more than twenty years. The constant fear of saying the wrong thing.

'Sometimes I don't know what planet you're on,' said Ruth. 'We are not the intimate friends you insist on thinking we are. We used to know each other, a long time ago, for a relatively short period of our lives. What do we really have in common? Except for the fact we all went to the same school?'

Caroline sighed. 'You may not choose to tell us about what's going on in your life. But whatever you think, we're not entirely stupid. We know something terrible must have happened.'

Ruth glared at her. 'For fuck's sake. Why don't you show any anger? Why don't you rail against Anna for not telling you before what a shit Philip was? Why don't you go home and throw him out?'

Jess raised the glass of fresh orange juice to her lips. The taste, on top of the strong coffee, was an unpleasant combination, but her mouth was so dry.

Caroline leant towards Ruth. 'Is that what this is about? Andy doesn't strike me as the unfaithful type. In fact, quite the opposite. But nothing surprises me any more.'

Jess shook her head. 'Andy wouldn't do anything like that—'

'Shut up.' Ruth poured more coffee, took a sip. 'No. It's not Andy. But, as we've already established, our lives have nothing to do with each other any more. Why would I tell you what's going on?'

'Because…' Caroline sat back. 'Because, despite the fact that we don't see each other all that often, like it or not, there is a bond. A long time ago, at a crucial time of our lives, we were exceptionally important to each other. And you can deny it all you want. But perhaps you still believe a fraction of that, otherwise you wouldn't be here.'

'Perhaps I just wanted to get away from the domestic scene,' said Ruth.

'I'm sure we all had several reasons, including wanting to see each other,' said Stella.

'Maybe.' Ruth helped herself to toast, butter, marmalade. She focused on Jess. 'What are you going to say to Sam?'

'Well, I'm not going to betray confidences, if that's what you mean,' said Jess.

Ruth smiled. A smile that looked incongruous on her face; a smile that didn't seem to get much use. 'What are you going to say about the baby?'

Jess bit her lip. 'I don't know. I don't think I've got the strength to go through with it. But I'm not sure I've got the guts to have an abortion.'

'Think very carefully before you decide on an abortion,' said Ruth.

'What do you mean?' said Stella.

Ruth laid down the knife she was wielding to spread butter on the toast. 'I should be twenty-one weeks pregnant. At thirteen weeks I had a scan. All normal. At sixteen weeks I miscarried. A daughter. She was perfect. No reason. No reason that makes any sense.'

Jess scanned the group of women around the table. Saw how Anna met Ruth's gaze. Nodded.

'We went to some friends for lunch. I couldn't get

warm, even though it was a sunny day. My hands and feet were chilled and even cupping a hot mug of tea didn't seem to help. When we got home, I went to bed. Much to Andy and Jack's annoyance. They're forever saying they don't see enough of me. Andy thought I was just trying to wriggle out of organizing supper.' She sat back, her face a mask. 'I managed to fall asleep, but when I woke up I knew something was really wrong. Cramps. Bleeding. Nothing I could do.'

Caroline stretched out a hand. 'Oh, Ruth.'

'What a thing to go through.' Anna shivered. Becoming pregnant and it ending in miscarriage was a scenario she didn't contemplate. Her speculations always stopped at confirmation of the pregnancy.

Jess swallowed. 'How dreadful. We've been talking about our own problems, and you're having to deal with…'

'Yes. Well.' Ruth picked up her knife, scraped butter onto her toast. The noise rang out in the silence.

Anna laid her cutlery down on the side of her almost full plate. 'I didn't mean to say what I did. I've become someone I don't recognise…I'm sorry.'

'Bit late to feel remorse,' said Ruth.

Anna turned to Caroline. 'What are you going to do?'

Caroline shrugged; shook her head.

The journey home defied the expected pattern of whizzing past quicker than the journey there. Maybe Jess felt the silences more acutely because she was fighting sleep. Having slept so badly, she struggled to keep her eyes open in the comfort of the moving car.

'Not too tired?' Jess asked.

'You've asked me that already, Jess. I'm fine,' Caroline answered. 'Are you tired?'

'Slept terribly. I'm no good at sleeping somewhere new.'

'I surprised myself by managing to sleep. There's something peaceful about being on your own. And there were enough hotel sounds to stop me from feeling lonely.'

Jess glanced at her. 'Do you feel lonely at home?'

'Sometimes.'

'I'm sorry I didn't notice.'

'There's no reason why you should have.'

'Isn't there? Don't you think the nastier aspects of my controlling ex-husband might have made me more sensitive to the difficulties in other people's marriages?'

'I don't think it works like that. And I know I've done my best to keep it hidden.'

'When I came back for the school reunion last summer, I thought Philip was just not very keen on company.'

'He's not very keen on company.'

'He likes his girls, though?'

'Yes. He's a caring father. It's just me he doesn't like.'

'Oh, I'm sure that's not… Sorry. I don't know why that's my default setting.'

'I hope our daughters aren't such people pleasers. I hope they go for what they want, and get it.'

Jess considered her daughter Millie, her step-daughters Kate and Emma, and Caroline's girls Rebecca and Catriona. Spirited. Determined. *Long may it last.* 'I sometimes think I'd have done better on my own. But then I wouldn't have the joy of Ben and Millie.'

'Yes. Exactly.'

'What are you going to do?'

Caroline checked her mirrors, pulled out to overtake a lorry. 'Carry on. Be there for the girls. I don't know about Philip.'

'You know you can ring me anytime. Anytime.'

'Thank you. You too.'

'I had all sorts of pangs about leaving London after so many years, especially leaving friends behind, but it's lovely having you just down the road.'

Caroline glanced away from the road, met her eyes. 'You too,' she repeated.

'Strange how these times together, the five of us, can be a bit challenging and stressful during. And yet, afterwards, I feel nothing but love towards you all. We are significant to each other. However Ruth might refute that.'

'She doesn't mean it. She told us something very private and painful. You only do that with your closest friends.'

'Even when it's a bombshell?' Jess eyed Caroline, who kept her eyes on the road.

'I think Anna's in uncharted territory. No filters. No capacity to see much beyond her all-consuming ache for a baby.'

'Still. What she said. In front of us—'

Caroline glanced in her direction briefly. 'I did wonder if you knew. If you and she had ever talked about…'

'No. And whatever took place eighteen years ago, things are very different now, aren't they? Philip's always been…well, he's…he's a good father, isn't he?'

'He is.'

Later, when Jess arrived home and retreated from the noise downstairs to unpack her bag, she thought about how she'd uttered aloud the option of terminating the pregnancy. Until that point, that was something she had not done.

Ruth was right. It was not a possibility for her.

Already she dreaded the road ahead, feared the fatigue, the shadow of depression.

And yet. There was a growing life inside her, created with Sam. That jolt of joy shot through her.

He'd be a much more hands on father than Tom ever was. She'd be surrounded by willing helpers. Hopefully.

They could make this work.

ANNA

Anna felt limp with fatigue by the time she pulled into her driveway, but pleased she'd made an effort to source that timer. The table lamp in the sitting area in the kitchen threw warm, sunny light into the gathering dusk.

Such a strange sequence of events. She still couldn't believe she'd basically launched a missile into Caroline's marriage. Her own pain combined with the various confessions and revelations had kept her on edge most of their twenty-four hours together. Stella had been the only one to emerge relatively unscathed, it seemed, although there had been a throwaway remark about affairs, when she had turned pink. Or was that just Anna's imagination?

Despite Ruth's crushing language, Anna knew these friends were special, that these relationships meant something. It was true that they didn't see that much of each other, but there was a deeper degree of understanding, a shared history, a shorthand to their experiences together, and she couldn't bear to have fatally wounded her friendship with Caroline. She had thought that unburdening herself about what had happened nearly twenty years ago might provide relief and clarity, but dread lodged in the pit of her stomach.

She'd submerged Philip's assault—even in her mind she couldn't call it anything else under layers of guilt. Guilt towards her younger self, for allowing such a situation, for not waking up while she could still have stopped him, for not screaming out, for not going to the police, or telling the truth, all of which was subsumed under the guilt she now felt towards Caroline. By the time she and Philip met, Anna's memories of that night had been suppressed hard, long enough for her to doubt her own veracity as witness, as victim. Had she said anything —to anyone—she would have had to face herself and her loss of autonomy, relive the physical helplessness of being trapped under him. Pinioned by his weight, his size, his strength.

Was that why the men she'd been attracted to after that, the man she'd spent more than a decade with, were so different physically? Had it felt safer with Jon because, although relatively tall, he was slight compared to Philip? Had she chosen him because he didn't display any macho tendencies and had a relatively low sex drive? Or was that just with her? Would he ignite with passion with Saskia? Who knew, maybe he already had?

When Rob had kissed her, on that unexpected walk during Jess and Sam's wedding reception, she'd experienced for herself how it felt to be held in the arms of someone whose strength definitely exceeded her own. Had she thought of Philip then? He'd been at the church with Caroline and the girls, but only Caroline had been present at the reception.

Perhaps it was a latent comparison that only surfaced when she and Rob were rolling around on the sofa in the house on the Isle of Wight. She frowned. That could have quite legitimately put him off, and yet he'd had the patience to try again.

Did she feel the need to tell him about Philip?

Much of the time, she convinced herself she didn't, not really. It had happened such a long time ago.

But at other times, she knew that she owed him an explanation, that being honest about what had happened, was crucial. She and Jess had spoken about the need for honesty, about Jess's conviction that Sam should know about the sexual assault she'd suffered at the hands of James. An ongoing relationship with Rob—in whatever form—would be more authentic if she told him what had happened. If she trusted her memories and told it from her point of view.

In the last few months, she'd grown accustomed to Rob's size and physique. Apart from the physical reminder of the attack—when she set it aside—there was something undeniably attractive about a man substantial and strong enough to make her own weight and how she felt about her size dwindle into insignificance. She was well aware of how much Rob's evident pleasure had made her revise her own feelings of guilt about her body. Beside him she didn't feel quite such a heffalump.

The compartments in her mind crumbled a bit more. Not that they'd been that sturdy in the first place. Had she really wanted this arrangement—or whatever it was—to remain uninvolving and purely transactional, she would not have chosen Rob. There was too much shared history, too many mutual friends, too many connections. He had seen it more clearly than she had. He was the one who had taken five days to consider her proposition.

Whereas she'd taken one look at him at the wedding, sized him up, and decided he was the genetic material she required. Maybe it really was as base, as biological a need as she feared. The selfish gene.

Not that it had ever been just about biology. Oh, she'd tried. Done her best to keep things casual. Not clung. Not fallen. Not needed. But a line had been crossed. Months ago. Text conversations that were no longer about imparting information: rendezvous, dates, locations. They tipped at some point—somewhere between months one and two—into something much more domestic, with chats about food, a film, an article. A long riff on goats, of all things, and their rectangular pupils, which gave them excellent peripheral vision for spotting predators or navigating uneven terrain. The best part of an afternoon on the subject of zips, with Rob providing essential facts about invention, patent and Zipper Day on 29 April each year, rendering her lyrical about the secret weapon of a beautiful hidden zip. She'd tried hard not to initiate these virtual conversations, but she'd been unable to resist replying.

And then she'd responded to that Sunday text, when she'd sat in a restaurant with old work colleagues, wondering where he was, what he was doing, and with whom. The intense thrill of his message. Knowing it would be so much kinder to her mental health not to respond, or to pretend she was at home. Already aware that the blurring line—hotel sex on one side, a developing connection on the other—would be rubbed out if she agreed to meet him on his own turf.

Maybe it was the novelty of spending the afternoon together, going back to his flat, discovering more about him, that had been so intoxicating. Not to mention the sublime heights of pleasure he'd taken her to on that armchair. She blushed to think of that. Couldn't quite look at—much less sit in—the chair in the window of her kitchen, without that heightened sense of awareness.

The flat itself had been a puzzle. It seemed to reflect so little of Rob's personality. Apart from the wall of books, everything else had felt so temporary. Almost as if he'd found himself there, in his late thirties, not quite believing it was where he lived. She knew he travelled for work, but to think his base was so functional, so impersonal, was heart-wrenching.

He didn't seem to have one object of beauty. No pictures. A couple of photos of his sister and family stuck on the fridge. But who was she to judge? She'd spent ten years of her life creating a home, filling it with beautiful objects, with pictures and furniture, but she lived as much alone as he did.

She didn't know why it felt so much worse tonight, as she sat outside her house. Sunday night. Fatigue and hunger didn't help. Perhaps it was all brought into sharper focus, the choices she'd made, because Jess, Caroline, Ruth and Stella were all going home to husbands and children. Their two days together had shattered some of her illusions about the bliss of family life. She needed to remember the complexities of marital relationships, the challenges of bringing up children, of family dynamics, and allow herself to think that her misery was not unique. But there was still a stubborn, self-pitying part of her that clocked that she had nothing to return to except a lit lamp on an automatic timer.

She pulled the key out of the ignition, opened the car door. *Keep on keeping on.*

Two more days. She only had to hold out till Wednesday.

She put her head in her hands.

ROB

Apart from the aberration, when she'd come to his flat in London in July, they stuck to the now familiar monthly routine. He would collect Anna on a Wednesday afternoon, before driving to the hotel. After check in, they would go for a swim. They'd retire to their room—usually the same one each time, with a view over the gardens—to change for dinner, scrupulously polite about taking turns to use the bathroom. A glass of champagne. Dinner at eight. Back in the room for serious sex by ten o'clock.

Usually face-to-face conversation covered safe topics. Work. Theatre trips. Newspaper articles. Films. Holiday dreams. Families occasionally.

But tonight, Rob reached across and took her hand. 'Are you OK? You look tired.'

Anna pulled her hand away to pick up her untouched wine glass. 'Of course. I'm fine.'

'How's Jon?'

'Fine.'

'What do you tell him about these monthly trips?'

'Nothing.'

'Suppose he had to get hold of you urgently, and couldn't?'

'He wouldn't. He never has.'

'I don't understand you. You don't strike me as the sort of person who can live a double life.'

'It's not a double life,' she said, wiping her palms on the napkin by her plate.

'Yes, it is. How do you…when you think about it, how do you…?'

'If you want to stop, you just have to say so,' she said, pleating her hands.

'I don't want to stop.'

The words hung between them, while the silence grew.

Rob eyed her while she wove her fingers back and forth. 'How was your weekend with the girls?'

She jerked her head up. 'Did I tell you about that?'

'You did.'

'I must remember. That you remember things.'

'How was it?'

'Full of revelations,' she said, without thinking. She held up her palm. 'Nothing to see here.'

'What do you mean?'

'Private revelations. Ordinary secrets. No story here.'

'Is that what you think? That all I do is search for an angle?' He held her gaze. 'But it was good to see them?'

'Yes.' She bit her lip, raised her glass, but didn't seem to make any inroads on actually drinking its contents, set it down again.

Eventually he sighed. 'I'll see you back at the room. There's something I've remembered. I won't be long.'

ANNA

Anna put away her clothes and smoothed the pillows. She trembled as she fiddled with the straps of her nightdress. Ten minutes. The door opened.

'Sorry about that,' said Rob. He flung his jacket over the chair, kicked off his shoes and sat on the bed beside her, legs stretched out in front of him. 'Come here.'

His lips were soft against hers, caressing her mouth. He stroked her cheek with one finger. His tenderness made her want to cry. She clung to him, not letting go, even as she teased his clothes off.

Afterwards she lay in his arms for a long time. She didn't even bother to put a dressing gown on any more. Not after that first time, when he'd coaxed it from her. He nuzzled her shoulder, and held her breasts, one in each palm, his thumbs tracing lazy circles as they drifted towards sleep.

When she woke up, he was propped on one elbow gazing at her. She turned to face him.

'Are you having periods?' he asked her.

'Well not right now. You know that. This is the middle of the cycle.'

'So when was your last one? The beginning of the month?'

'I'm— well—'

'Were you planning to tell me you were pregnant?'

'I don't know that I am.' She sat up, not bothering to cover herself.

'Does Jon know? Have you told him?'

'No. Of course not.'

'What do you mean, of course not?'

Anna slid her feet to the floor.

Rob grabbed her arm. 'We need to talk about this.'

'I don't even know if I'm pregnant.'

'Well, that can soon be rectified.' Rob leant out of bed and pulled a paper bag out of his jacket pocket, which he dropped into her lap.

'Why do you have one of those? Do not tell me you asked at reception and they just happened to have one?' Anna stared at the blue and white box, instantly recognisable because she'd walked past shelves of them in several chemist's over the past few weeks. But she'd never had the confidence to actually buy one. In this limbo, she might be pregnant. She was petrified that doing the test would confirm she was not.

'Call it a sixth sense.' He held up his hands. 'I'm sorry... I bought it...left it in the glove compartment.'

'Rain Man,' she muttered.

'I've been called that before.'

She met his look.

He shrugged. 'Sam.'

'He knows you well.'

ROB

Rob was not in the mood to travel to Manchester, far less by train. He wanted to be somewhere other than in London in his depressing flat, that was for sure. But he didn't want to be heading north.

Anna had stopped responding. Even in the beginning she'd kept him waiting, sometimes overnight. But she did reply eventually. Now there was nothing.

He had to make himself be patient. Not a comfortable state. He'd promised his editor flexibility over a particular interview he was doing, and when it was moved from London to Manchester, refusing to go was not an option. With his parents away, he could play the dutiful son, visit the house and check all was OK. When he'd mentioned this half thought, they'd been very enthusiastic about the idea. Backing out would have been fraught.

So, here he sat, on the Manchester train, working through his research for the interview, his emails, his planner, until his phone buzzed.

His heart thudded, as he turned it over.

A message from Sam: *James in town too, so we'll both see you at the Italian tonight.*

Rob thumped the phone down on the table. He had no patience, felt as taut as an overstretched elastic band, liable to snap any second. Seeing James held no interest, and he didn't want to be the object of his scrutiny. Or Sam's for that matter. But at least Sam was relaxed company. There was always an agenda with James, and however hard Rob tried, his journalistic antennae would not dial down around public figures, whether they were old friends of his or not.

There was something that hadn't felt right about James. For a long time.

He rarely bothered to analyse it, but occasionally he had a physical feeling in the pit of his stomach that alerted him to someone lying. Conversely, he had a sense of congruence, of peace, when they told the truth. Now and then, he was presented with an interviewee who had no interest in deviating from a very thoroughly prepared script, but most people could be drawn out, flattered, cajoled into revealing something.

When he thought about the conversations he'd had with James—both before and after he was elected to Parliament—there was nothing he could pinpoint, but there was a fractional hesitation when asked about certain topics. Stuart and his head injury. And something to do with Jess? They niggled.

Then there had been that weird evening when he and Pete had seen James and the Chancellor of the Exchequer, with those four young men. Something had definitely been off, that night, at odds with how James liked to talk about a stable society, with a united family unit at its core. He had unfashionable opinions about the importance of fathers, and was known to quote statistics about Finland.

'All well and good,' Rob had said to Sam. 'Yes, they have a very stable, well-functioning society with low divorce rates and an excellent state school system. But there are only about seven of them.'

Sam had laughed. 'Not seven, surely?'

'You know what I mean. It's a small, broadly homogenous country. It's an unrealistic comparison.'

Rob's current monitoring of the newspaper headlines

confirmed that James was proving very popular with the right wing of his party. His wedding, in his old Oxford college the previous autumn, just after his by-election victory, had caught the media's attention. He was good-looking enough to fuel tabloid interest, and adept at producing a catchy soundbite. His wife Fiona's standing in public relations had done him no harm at all.

Sure, there were things to admire in James. He'd spent the past ten years or more cultivating the great and good in the party. Starting at Oxford, where he'd managed to infiltrate the Old Etonian set, despite his public school education taking place in Manchester. It was paying off. He was widely hailed as number two at the Treasury. But to Rob, it all felt like a performance. Having had various conversations over the years on economics, he suspected that James's views were far more centrist and egalitarian. Yet politically, it suited him to court those far to the right of him.

Having progressed this far, it made sense for James to want his reputation, his past, to remain unblemished.

Rob sighed. Maybe there was nothing to find.

Still. It was useful to turn this over in his mind. It pushed the ever-present, lurking presence of Anna out of his conscious mind for a second or two.

He was determined to find at least some time with Sam before getting to the restaurant, so after the interview, he took the tram to Millingham from the centre of town and walked up the hill to the house on Woodham Road. He dropped his bag at his parents' house, conveniently on the way.

Jess greeted him with a kiss. 'Rob. How delightful. You look well.'

'You too.'

A moment when they eyed each other, as if verifying what had been said.

'Everything OK? You're not joining us for dinner?' Rob said.

'Oh no,' she said, perhaps too quickly. 'Houseful of children. Plus, I'm shattered.'

Rob had already registered the shadows under her eyes, but her skin looked clear, her hair full and shiny. Married life, this time around, seemed to suit her.

Sam thundered down the stairs and gave Rob a hug. 'You look peaky. What have you been up to?'

He felt the searing attention of two sets of eyes. 'Nothing special. What?'

An exchanged look.

'Time for a beer? Or a glass of wine?' Sam led the way down the hall to the kitchen.

The three of them sat at the table, the boys with beers, Jess with a mint tea.

'I should go and see what sort of carnage is taking place upstairs,' she said.

'In a minute,' said Sam.

'Not keen to see James, then?' Rob asked Jess.

'What? No. It's a boys' night.' Jess kept her eyes on her cup of tea.

'Jess can't wait for us to leave so she can crash out in peace.' Sam smiled at his wife.

The tender look pierced Rob. What was wrong with him? He'd vowed for years that marital bliss would not suit him. But sitting here, in this comfortable kitchen, the focus of the house, filled with the presence of children, he felt more alone than the fateful Sunday in July. Before he'd texted Anna and she'd answered.

That was his BC/AD moment. Before that, he had it all under control. After, chaos.

He pulled his mind back into the room. Something was going on, but it was slipping out of sight.

Jess smiled at him. 'It's true, I can't wait to get rid of you.'

Rob drank his beer, rather than study the soft gesture of Sam squeezing her hand.

James was already seated, when they arrived at the Italian restaurant. Years ago it had been French, but for a long time now it had been a weekend staple of Rob's parents, and Sam and family also came here. Traditional Italian food—antipasti, pasta, pizzas, typical meat and fish main courses—were prepared by the older generation Italian owners and served by their children.

James sat over a platter of olives, salami and bruschettas, swigging a large glass of Chianti. 'Join me before I gobble the lot.' He stood up to hug Rob. They hadn't seen each other since they'd all been together in July, for James's mother's birthday.

When he sat down, Rob observed a quick, almost touch-free hug between Sam and James. Usual if they'd seen each other recently, perhaps?

'What brings you to Manchester?' said James.

Rob exhaled. He needed a drink. 'Work mainly. You?'

'My mother. Mainly.'

Sam waved at the waiter, who took orders for drinks and food.

Rob opted for another beer. He wanted to stay clear-headed, and it would be trickier with red wine.

'How's Fiona?' asked Sam.

'Marvellous. She looks after me terrifically well.'

'And the house in Witney?'

'That too. Married life agrees with me. How about you, Sam?' James looked straight at Rob as he said those words.

Rob felt his skin prickle, the hairs on the back of his neck bristle. He usually felt much more in control.

'Yeah. Jess is great. It can be tiring of course. House is full all the time.'

'Ah yes. All those children?'

James directed all his questions at Sam, but fixed his gaze on Rob. Why did it feel as if he was being interviewed? He was much less keen on being the other end of the questions. And he did not want to talk about children.

'Planning to make your move at the Treasury then, in time for the autumn statement?' Rob asked.

'Party conference to get through before that.'

'Rallying your troops, surely.' Rob steered the discussion through politics, jobs, work, until they reached the end of the main course. He felt better for a tasty seafood risotto, and he'd made sure his water consumption kept pace with the beer.

As he sat back in his chair, Sam said, 'How's Stuart? Have you seen him?'

James blinked, focusing on Sam. 'Yeah. Fine.'

'What's your brother doing now?' said Rob.

James's gaze flickered towards him fleetingly. 'He's working. Which is good.'

'He was always cleverer than the rest of us, wasn't he?' Rob asked.

'Oh, I don't know about that. Not much point in having intelligence if you struggle to combine it with living in the world.'

Rob leaned forward. '*Does* he struggle with living in the world?'

'No. He's fine.'

'Does it go back to the head injury?' Rob stopped. He'd been wanting to ask the direct question for years. Still, he was not convinced by the wisdom of his timing. If he'd wanted any sort of revelation, it would have been better if it had just been the two of them.

A minute flinching towards Sam and back. 'What are you talking about?'

'The head injury? Falling from the tree?'

'When he was just a kid? Of course not.'

'No?' Rob let the question hang. Not for the first time, he doubted his own judgements. He needed to ring Anna. He'd keep ringing her until she answered him. Convince her they could…it would work out…there was a life in which…

'No.' James finished the last of his glass of red. With Rob and Sam on the beer, he'd drunk the whole bottle on his own.

'He's still with Salvatore?' said Rob.

James jerked his head up. 'How did you know—'

'As brothers, I don't think of you being very similar. And yet you both had Spanish boyfriends. Didn't you? Raoul was—'

'Raoul was a close friend and that was a very long time ago.'

'I see. Well, don't worry. There's a whole public school cohort in the Cabinet with very close same sex friendships—'

James sat forward, planting his large hands on the table between them. 'This is nobody's business—'

'Had you stayed in the City,' said Rob. 'When you became a Member of Parliament you lost that anonymity.

There are sections of the press who consider your private life anything but.'

'You're part of that—'

'I'm not. But don't be naïve.'

James turned to Sam. 'You're quiet.'

'I can't get a word in.' He laughed.

Neither Rob nor James joined in.

'So, married life is just the two of you?' said Sam. 'No plans for the patter of tiny feet?'

'Absolutely not.' James grinned—or positively leered—at Rob. 'Like to fuck Fiona from behind. Not too often. Keep her tight as a boy.'

Before Rob gathered his thoughts, Sam said, 'What the hell? Fiona would be disgusted to hear you talk like that.'

'So you'd like to think. My wife is very broadminded.'

'She'd have to be,' said Rob.

James stared him down. 'There's a lot to be said for marriage, Rob. Look at Sam and me. You still hanging around infants, or are you going to grow up?'

'We're not talking about me,' said Rob.

'We are now. Sam, what do you know? Have you met Hannah?'

Sam raised an eyebrow at Rob. 'Who?'

'She's young, and lithe, and top-heavy,' said James.

'What?' said Sam, as Rob said, 'Don't encourage him.'

'Curvaceous,' said James, motioning large breasts with his hands. 'Additionally enhanced, I'd say. The rest of her figure does not suggest big tits.'

'You're unbelievable. She's a colleague.' *Sam, please don't mention Anna. Not to James.*

'Yeah, right. She'll want kids of course. So, if you're not interested in fatherhood, step away quickly.'

Sam looked at Rob. 'I think he *is* interested in fatherhood.'

'Really,' said James. 'We'll see. Nature or nurture. What will out—'

'Fuck. Off.' Rob balled his hands into fists. It didn't matter what James thought, what he said, and yet he so badly wanted to hit him. Hard. How could he speak that way? *About his wife?*

'Yeah. That language will go down well when you're bringing your kids up. If you stay the course and don't fuck off, before then.'

Sam held up his hands. 'OK, children. Time for the bill.'

They settled up and waited for James's taxi. Getting up from the table, putting on jackets, shaking hands with the waiter who'd looked after them, papered over the absence of any physical contact between the three of them. Having seen James into the cab, Rob and Sam walked back up the hill.

'Not like you to react to him like that, Rob. You're the man who keeps his cool.'

'Yeah. I never want to set eyes on him again.'

'You're not the only one.'

'Was he always such an offensive idiot? Or is it more recent?'

'Don't fall out with him entirely. You never know. He might be a very useful Rob Randall interview candidate, one of these days.'

'How I managed not to deck him, I'll never know.'

'But you did manage. Your mother would be so proud.'

Later that night, Rob pondered that phrase, 'Your mother would be so proud.' It seemed fraught with too many meanings and connotations. His mum would have been appalled by the downward trajectory of the conversation tonight. And Sam was right, at least it hadn't degenerated to the physical.

It still didn't seem quite possible that James had said what he said about Fiona. He wrote it down in shorthand in his Moleskine notebook, along with the date, the place, the occasion. Wanted to pick up the phone and talk to Anna, to make things normal again. But things were not normal. As far as he knew, she continued to be pregnant. She was carrying his baby. His entirely bachelor, unfettered life, had gone up in flames.

How would life ever be normal again?

ANNA

She felt as if she'd spent the whole week on edge. All silences were freighted with meaning. The presence of Rob—just out of her field of vision, glimpsed from the corner of her eye—had disappeared entirely.

He'd been there for months, the one person who had stepped up. And how he'd stepped up.

They had shared one glorious moment once they'd registered the clear blue line. She'd seen a jolt of something, of what must have been joy, pass across his face, knowing it was mirrored in her own.

But it was quickly replaced by a befuddlement about what happened next. They'd eyed each other nervously, as if checking that the other person was still there.

There was far too much to say.

Or nothing at all.

Her head hurt. She couldn't breathe. She'd taken her clothes into the spacious bathroom to dress, and this time she locked the door. She looked exactly the same in the mirror. Or completely different. She couldn't decide.

Managed to talk him out of breakfast. Couldn't face it. The thought of food, of coffee, brought on strong nausea she controlled only by sheer force of will. Had a sudden important work deadline she needed to rush back for.

He drove her home to collect her car. She'd jumped out of the passenger seat, grabbed her bag from the back seat.

He hadn't stopped her.

When she came downstairs from dumping her stuff,

finding her laptop, he'd reversed out of the driveway. She'd opened the front door. Nothing. Not even the sound of the Audi fading into the distance.

Since then, he'd sent her a few texts. She'd failed to respond. She just didn't know what to say. 'Thanks? For getting me pregnant?'

This was unchartered territory. A land she'd never allowed herself to contemplate properly. She had not a clue how to proceed.

But it was what she had wanted for such a long time. Wasn't it?

It was becoming harder and harder to relax. She jumped at the slightest sound. More than once, Jade had remarked at how jittery she was. Despite ignoring Rob's texts, she was perversely annoyed that he didn't ring, or just turn up. Force her hand, somehow. So when she turned her phone over, sitting alone in the armchair at the end of her kitchen, she felt as if her heart did actually sink, when Jess's name came up. They hadn't spoken since their girls' weekend together.

'Everything ok?'

'I was going to ask you the same thing,' said Jess. 'See how you are.'

'Fine.' It was Anna's automatic response, and she wanted a normality between them. Felt fragile and fractured and as if any kind words from Jess would dissolve all that resolve and she'd start sobbing.

'I wanted to...well...to say, I know a bit of what you went through.'

'What do you mean?'

'I was thinking about the *Brideshead Revisited* party.'

Anna's heart thudded uncomfortably. 'It was a long

time before you spoke about it. About James's assault.'

'Actually, it was Caroline I told,' said Jess.

'Did it feel better? To have told someone?'

'It made it seem real again. True. As if I hadn't made it up, and as if it mattered. As if I mattered.'

'Did you feel relief?'

'I think it was more validation. That I was believed. That I hadn't gone mad. Do you feel relief?'

'No. Regret. I still can't believe I did that.' She'd wanted to pick up the phone to Caroline, but she felt so awkward. Somehow she still hadn't.

'Did you ever want to talk about it before?' asked Jess. 'What made it come out the other weekend?'

'I wish I knew. I think when you don't feel in control, it's easier to lash out at others.'

'And you don't feel in control?'

Anna hesitated. 'Have you spoken to Caroline?'

'We've texted. Have you?'

'Do you think they...will she stay?'

'I think marriages don't just stop. Particularly not when children are involved.'

'But the attack? Can he be forgiven?'

'Yes, he can be forgiven. But it involves remorse and redemption. And forgiveness doesn't mean condoning the behaviour. It's particularly shocking because it's so unlike Philip. He seems so hesitant, so outward focused, so deferential, in a way,' said Jess.

Anna didn't want to think about that. It was confusing. 'What about James? You went to his wedding. Have you forgiven him?'

Jess sighed. 'Well, that would involve remorse and redemption, and I've seen very little of either so far.'

'So, we try to make sense of the world, while they're

both in it carrying on as if nothing happened. No consequences for them, while we are left to feel more and more out of control.'

'Is everything OK with Jon?' asked Jess. 'You hardly mentioned him.'

'I met…' Anna stared at her hands. 'It's Rob.'

'Rob. Rob Randall? Have you fallen in love with him?'

She jerked her head up, eyes wide, and gazed around her kitchen. Forced herself to bite back the words, 'No, of course not.'

She took a breath. 'I don't know.'

The days crawled by, underpinned by a stifling nausea. Anna's mind yo-yo'd between a settled, 'This is it. I got what I wanted. You've served your purpose,' and a heart-in-mouth precipice over which she projected the birth of a family unit. A mother and father working it out together. Two people who'd started up in a less than conventional manner. Who'd perhaps concluded settled family life was not for them, but late on had glimpsed a new and unexpected future, and rather than retreating, were contemplating a different path...

Her instinct as far as Rob was concerned had not been so very wrong. He'd accepted her challenge all those months ago. He'd even lived with the limited information she'd provided.

He hadn't pried about Jon. He'd been patient; constant; kind.

His messages reflected that.

She was convinced now that he had a right to know what had happened, however much she might think it would disturb the tentative balance between them. Previously she'd dismissed his frankly puppyish enthusiasm. For life, for food, for new experiences, for knowledge. Definitely for sex. So many things made him smile. He told her the latest ridiculous facts to catch a second of her suppressed smile—that's what he'd said.

Increasingly, his attitude seemed to be all that was missing in her somewhat joyless life. Creating a beautiful home, and spending her work life striving to make perfect garments no longer fulfilled her as it had. But assigning all her resentful disappointment to her inability to conceive—maybe that had been wrong. Had she conflated two areas of dissatisfaction and would the pregnancy fail to address the other void?

Her phone buzzed again. She glanced at the screen and turned it face down. When she hadn't responded, Rob had started texting, '*Bueller*?' It was a reference to the 1980s film *Ferris Bueller's Day Off* which never failed to make her smile.

The least she could do was let him know she was still here. Breathing in and out. Trying to make sense of it all.

She reached out and picked up her phone.

Acknowledgements

Thank you to the many friends, family and colleagues who have encouraged my writing. Thank you Julia Boggio and Flora Dunn, very supportive fellow writers. A big thank you to my mother Ann Ford, who has always encouraged my writing, and has become a book marketer extraordinaire since *Like Me* was published. Many thanks to Lucy Hemmings and Kara Holdsworth. Special mentions for Christine Lipton, Charlie Walton, Gaby McWhinnie, Liz Burrell, Tash McDonald, Charlotte Billett, Anna Culwick, Celia Richardson and Rachael Craig. Thank you to Paula Tindale-Paul, Kathy Wemyss, Brie Doyle, Victoria Rawls, Debs Koby, Jude Beazley, Lucy Hartopp and Alex Vanotti. Your ongoing support means a lot.

Thank you Ed and Lou Davies for your amazing promotion of the book at Mission Possible, the St Michael's church charity fundraising event, and the generosity of Lize Strydom and Russell Johnstone, who successfully bid to name characters in this and future books. Anna's neighbours Elena and Hein Campbell are named for Lize's parents and family, and appear in this and the next book. Russell's mother Lisbeth lends her name to a doctor in the next book.

Thank you to various experts in their field, who were patient enough to answer my questions, including Eric Koby, Martin Lipton, Robin Swithinbank and James Paget.

Thank you Marta Michalowska, Labeja Kodua Okullu, Laurence Kershook, Anne Phipps and the alumnae of The Novel Studio, 2018-19. Thank you Ursula Hirschkorn, Tanzila Rashid and Jo Estrin, the first readers of excerpts of

Me Too. I really appreciated your thoughtful, enthusiastic advice.

Thank you Emily Pedder of www.thebookedit.co.uk for a fantastically helpful edit. Your feedback made it a much better book.

Thank you Simon Avery of nicegraphicdesign.co.uk and Gillian Healey of left-bridge.co.uk for a great book cover design. Thank you Caroline Goldsmith of goldsmithpublishingconsultancy.com for making the manuscript print ready, and Philippa Makepeace of studiomakepeace@gmail.com for my website. I could not have done it without your kind expertise.

Thank you once again to the friends of my youth, especially Sarah Pickstone, Bronwen Roberts, Jane Scrivner, Kathryn Skelton and Sophie White. Please forgive my purloining various aspects of our lives together, and using them to create fiction.

For the launch of *Like Me* I also made contact with old friends David Moreton (who wins the prize for surprise guest), David James, Simon Hicks, Andrew Murray, Rebecca Weetman and Angus Loughran. Thank you so much for coming.

Finally, thank you Aidan, Christian and Imogen. I am so grateful for your endless love and support in so many ways.

The Millingham Series: Book Three

YOU TOO

Anna has finally got what she longed for.

After years of focusing on her career—ignoring the quiet, insistent need for a child—a chance encounter with Rob led to an arrangement that changed everything.

Now she's pregnant.

But nothing about what comes next is simple. This was never meant to be a relationship, let alone a future. And as her pregnancy becomes more difficult, Anna retreats—unsure how to face Rob, or the feelings she can no longer ignore.

Because wanting a baby was one thing. Letting someone in is something else entirely.

Rob always knew their arrangement had limits. He didn't expect Anna would quickly become the one person he can't walk away from. Watching her pull back, determined to do this alone, is no longer something he can accept.

But building a life together means breaking through the walls Anna has spent years putting up—and risking more than either of them ever agreed to.

Now, both must decide what they're willing to fight for. This time, it's not just their hearts at stake, but the family they never planned to become.

...and if you missed the first story:

The Millingham Series: Book One

LIKE ME

When exhausted single mum Jess returns to Manchester for her twenty-year school reunion, she's hoping for nothing more than a well-deserved break from reality. What she's not expecting is to bump into her secret teenage crush, hot single dad Sam, or to remember quite how much they have in common.

But they live so far apart, their kids aren't always easy, and there are events in their shared past it's best not to revisit. Surely the idea of a future together is just a crazy dream in their messy, adult lives?

Though when Sam invites Jess to accompany him to a mutual friend's high-profile wedding, the years they spent apart once again melt away. What will it take for them to be together? Can they use their second chance to finally get it right?

About Katharine Light

Katharine Light was born in Glasgow and lived there until her family moved to Manchester when she was ten. While in her teens, she began writing stories for her younger sister. These mostly centred around a naïve heroine and a 1980s pop star (some would say the hero was modelled on John Taylor of Duran Duran).

She did a degree in psychology at University College London, and after a year travelling, worked in corporate film production for several years, before taking a break to raise her children.

For many years she wrote mainly during the holidays, around her busy work for a local church.

Her first novel *Like Me*, published in 2023, was shortlisted for The Selfies Book Awards 2024. Her short story *My arms are empty* which is based on an episode from *Me Too* recently won the City University competition City Writes.

Katharine lives in London with her husband. She loves singing, walking, painting, looking at art, and going to the theatre.

Author photograph by Alex Vanotti

Sign up to Katharine's author newsletter at:

www.katharinelight.com

Follow updates on Instagram / Threads:

katharinelightwrites1

Facebook: Katharinelightwrites

X: @katelightwrites

If you have a moment, please leave a review on Goodreads, Amazon, or a Facebook reading group, it's very much appreciated—thank you!

Printed in Dunstable, United Kingdom

83438658R00214